The critics adore Miranda Jarrett

Starlight
A *Romantic Times* "Top Pick"

"The quick pace, touch of magic, and absolutely endearing characters bring readers that warm glow and wonderful feeling so special about a romance. Miranda Jarrett continues to reign as a queen of historical romance."

—*Romantic Times*

"Delightful. . . . The story line is fun and filled with nonstop action, as expected from a Miranda Jarrett novel."

—Harriet Klausner, *Klausner's Bookshelf*

"Beautiful and mysterious . . . *Starlight* is bursting with excitement . . . very romantic and fast-paced."

—*Rendezvous*

Star Bright
A *Romantic Times* "Top Pick"

"As the companion to *Starlight*, *Star Bright* twinkles just as brightly with shining humor, poignancy, and magical charm that enchants. Ms. Jarrett's ability to always draw the reader into a fast-paced tale peopled with likable and realistic characters and a thrilling plot is a crowning achievement, and *Star Bright* delivers what readers expect from this romance luminary."

—*Romantic Times*

"Another winner. . . . an entertaining Georgian romance . . . filled with twisting intrigue and loaded with engaging characters."

—Harriet Klausner, *Klausner's Bookshelf*

Sunrise

"Enchanting. . . . Loved this, Miranda!"
—*The Philadelphia Inquirer*

"Poignant, endearing, tender, and charming."
—Patricia Gaffney, *New York Times*
bestselling author of *The Saving Graces*

"Jarrett . . . draws her protagonists vividly and with charm."
—*Publishers Weekly*

Moonlight

"Five stars! . . . Fast-paced and delightful!"
—Amazon.com

"What a touching, heartfelt story! . . . Every detail will keep you wanting more. Beautifully written."
—*Rendezvous*

Wishing
**A *Romantic Times* "Top Pick" and a
"Pick of the Month" for January 1999
by Barnesandnoble.com**

"Readers are sure to find themselves swept off their feet by this utterly enchanting and imaginative romance by the mistress of the seafaring love story. Delightfully charming and fun, yet poignant, exciting, and romantic, this is Miranda Jarrett at her finest!"
—*Romantic Times*

"Sheer pleasure."
—*Rendezvous*

Cranberry Point
Named Amazon.com's #1 Best New Romance Paperback and a "Pick of the Month" by Barnesandnoble.com

"A vivid and exciting portrait of colonial America. A memorable tale of trust and love, of healing and passion, and most of all the magic of romance."

—Romantic Times

"[A] passionate love story rich in history and characterization. . . . This is an award-winning saga from a sensational author." *—Rendezvous*

"Everything Jarrett does is magic."

—Affaire de Coeur

"A delightful book, well-crafted and vividly written. I'm enchanted."

—Linda Lael Miller, *New York Times* bestselling author of *My Lady Beloved*

The Captain's Bride

"As always, Ms. Jarrett takes the high seas by storm, creating one of her liveliest heroines and a hero to be her match."

—Romantic Times

"Fabulous...loaded with action and high-seas adventure."
—Affaire de Coeur

"Deliciously entertaining . . . a swift, rollicking romance . . . with a richly textured understanding of the seafaring life."

—Mary Jo Putney, *New York Times* bestselling author of *The China Bride*

Books by Miranda Jarrett

The Captain's Bride
Cranberry Point
Wishing
Moonlight
Sunrise
Starlight
Star Bright
The Very Daring Duchess

Published by Pocket Books

Miranda Jarrett

The Very Daring Duchess

SONNET BOOKS

New York   London   Toronto   Sydney   Singapore

An *Original* Publication of POCKET BOOKS

A Sonnet Book published by
POCKET BOOKS, a division of Simon & Schuster, Inc.
1230 Avenue of the Americas, New York, NY 10020

ISBN: 0-7434-1792-5

First Sonnet Books printing September 2001

10 9 8 7 6 5 4 3 2 1

SONNET BOOKS and colophon are trademarks of Simon & Schuster, Inc.

For information regarding special discounts for bulk purchases, please contact Simon & Schuster Special Sales at 1-800-456-6798 or business@simonandschuster.com

Cover art by Alan Ayers

Printed in the U.S.A.

For Susan of the South
(relatively speaking, anyway).
A first-rate friend, art historian,
and commiserator.
This one *had* to be for you,
didn't it?

Prologue

"*B*ad news always comes in hired chaises," said Edward Lord Ramsden glumly as he peered through the boxwood to the drive where the plain black chaise was waiting, there before the front steps. Tomorrow was his tenth birthday, and sure as blazes here was wretched luck to spoil it. "I don't like this, Will. I don't like it at all."

"Maybe it's only a tradesman," suggested William, Viscount Carew and Edward's best friend in all the world, crouching beside him here where they wouldn't be seen by the footmen or the grooms. Before them lay the sprawling expanse of Winterworth, the country seat of the Dukes of Harborough. Winterworth was Edward's home, too, seeing as it was his considerable misfortune to have been born the present duke's fourth and final son. "Maybe it's the tailor bringing down new shirts for you from London."

"Tailors don't come in chaises, you ninny, and never to the front door." His mood darkening by the moment, Edward shifted the horehound drop in his mouth from one cheek to the other, working it against his teeth. There were often things he had to explain to William, who was still nine, and would be for another fifty-six days. "Physicians come in hired chaises. Solicitors, too, and tutors, and dancing-masters. No one you wish to see."

"I know, Ned!" exclaimed William, thumping his elbow into Edward's arm. "I'll wager it's some special surprise for your birthday!"

"Not bloody hell likely," said Edward, borrowing one of his older brother's more wicked expressions to convey his own gloomy certainty. "Maybe in your family, sure, but not mine. Think on it, Will. What's the only real reason that chaise would be here? Who'd anyone come to see? Who's likely already here?"

"His Grace your father." William let out a low whistle of commiseration. "Did you know he was coming back today?"

"I never know," said Edward, already beginning to pluck the twigs and leaves from his hair. "Likely he's only on his way somewhere else, anyway, and won't stay beyond tonight. But best I go in now, before he raises hell and I get double the thrashing."

"Stinking luck," said William solemnly. "Before your birthday and everything."

Edward nodded, grateful that he wouldn't have to say any more about his father to his friend. As quickly as he could, he brushed the worst of the dry grass from his jacket and breeches, straightened his waistcoat, and tugged the stickers from his stockings, trying to undo all the damage that building a fortress in the elm tree behind William's house had wrought upon his clothes.

"Good enough?" he asked, standing before William with his arms outstretched. He hoped he'd be able to run up the back stairs to his room to wash and change, but his father had waylaid him in the kitchen before, and it was better to be prepared for the worst. Some manner of the worst was already inevitable, since Edward hadn't seen his father since the last reports had come down from school. It was not going to be a pleasing encounter.

"You'll do." William sniffed, wiping his nose on the cuff of his coat. "Come back to Charlesfield as early as you can tomorrow, Ned. We can finish the palings on the fortress, and Mother said she'd have Cook bake you a special cake for tea. That orange and cocoa one you like best."

"Mates forever, then," said Edward, tapping his fist twice against Will's in the secret signal they'd invented. "I'll be there tomorrow whenever I can get away."

"Mates forever," said Will, his grin lopsided with missing and half-grown teeth. "And don't be late."

Silently Edward nodded, not letting himself think too long about either the orange and cocoa cake or the celebration that William's mother and his sisters would doubtless lavish upon him in honor of his birthday. That would come tomorrow, his reward for surviving today.

He pushed through a break in the boxwood, and hopped and ran his way down the hill toward the back door to the kitchen. In the courtyard, the road dust was being scrubbed from the Duke's green traveling coach, while the grooms were still walking the four matched gray horses to cool them from the road. Clearly his father hadn't been here much longer than whoever had arrived in the hired chaise. His heart thumping, Edward raced through the kitchen and past the bustling servants into the hall, determined to reach the stairs before he was noticed.

He didn't succeed.

"Ah, here's the little snot now!" brayed his brother St. John, his mouth half-filled with a cream biscuit he'd filched from a tea tray. St. John was the third brother, seventeen, tall and gangly in his still-new regimentals, and a perpetually terrifying force in Edward's world. "Obey your elders, snot, and come here directly."

"You're supposed to be in Bath," said Edward sullenly, considering whether or not he was fast enough to dart past St. John and escape. "You're supposed to be there stationed with your regiment, not here."

"I *was*, but I'm not now, am I? Father was lonely, and so he's taking me to London with him for a fortnight of whoring and gambling. Of course Colonel Hodges obliged when Father asked." St. John looked scornfully down at Edward, licking the cream from his thumb. "Not that he'd do anything like that for *you*, you disgusting little worm."

Edward's hands tightened into fists of helpless frustration at his sides, hidden beneath the skirts of his coat where St. John wouldn't see them. There was never any point in fighting St. John, who had on his side size, strength, and years of experience in the refined torture of his younger brother. Like contentious cockerels, there had always been a pecking order among the four Ramsden brothers, encouraged by their father, and Edward's place was perpetually and painfully at the bottom of the roost.

"I hope some London whore gives you the pox, St. John," he muttered now, his bitterness overcoming wisdom. "I hope you get the pox, and your eyes fall out and your ugly nose rots clear off your face."

Instantly St. John grabbed him by the back of his neck, bunching Edward's coat and queue tightly into his fist, worrying him back and forth like a terrier.

"I should pound you senseless for that, snot," he said imperiously. "Maybe I will still, once Father's done with you. Come now, he's waiting for you in the front drawing room."

"I—I'll beat you yet, St. John!" gasped Edward helplessly as his brother dragged and shoved him across the marble floor. "Someday I—I'll win, and—and you'll lose!"

"Oh, yes, and someday buggerly little snots like you shall fly, too, upon the toe of my boot." St. John opened the door to the drawing room and shoved Edward stumbling inside ahead of him. "I found him at last, Father, though he didn't come willingly, as you can see for yourself."

"Where the devil were you, Edward?" demanded His Grace. "Am I so wrong to expect a genteel welcome from my own son? For God's sake, stop quaking like some blasted girl and greet me properly!"

Struggling to make his features impassive, Edward forced himself to lift his gaze to his father's angry face.

The Duke was still considered by the fashionable world to be a most handsome gentleman, but to Edward he was a red-faced, furious deity in a white powdered wig and stiff brocade coat, a distant London-god that could never be pleased, and one who swept in and out of Edward's life at will to dispense terrifying justice.

"Good day, Father," he said, his voice turning to a wretched squeak as he bowed over his leg the way he'd been taught. "I pray your journey here was a pleasant one."

"Bah, and what pleasure am I to find in your disappointments, Edward?" said the Duke sharply, rocking back and forth on his polished heels. "Your schoolmasters have little good to say of your performances, sir, and less of your behavior. I had no hopes of a scholar, not with your dull wits, but I did expect your actions to suit your station as my son. Do you comprehend that much, Edward?"

"Yes, Father." Shortly before the end of the term, Edward and three other boys had crept out one morning before dawn to raid a local baker's stock of blackberry pies set out to cool. They had, alas, been apprehended, their undeniable guilt stained purple around their mouths. "It shall not happen again, Father."

"It most certainly won't," said the Duke grimly. "Since you have demonstrated so little regard for education, you may consider yours complete. I've made other plans for you, sir."

"Yes, Father." A faint hope fluttered through Edward's breast. When his brothers had been asked to leave school—and for far more serious offenses than pie-stealing, too, offenses involving strong drink and tavern wenches—their lives had improved wonderfully. George and Frederick had both been sent on extended tours of the Continent, while St. John had been bought a commission in a fashionable regiment. Edward stole a quick glance at St. John, at his fancy bespoke uniform glittering with brass buttons and fancy lace and a gilt dress sword at his hip: a thrillingly great improvement indeed over parsing Latin in a stuffy classroom. "Thank you, Father."

The Duke grunted, and flicked his hand with the gold rings impatiently toward a short, stout man that Edward had neglected to notice. So this must be the visitor in the hired chaise, a man with a ruddy, weather-beaten face who wore his own unpowdered hair, not a gentleman. His uniform was dark blue, fading to a shabby gray at the cuffs and color, and though golden epaulets sat on his shoulders and a small sword hung from his waist, this uniform had none of the glittering appeal of St. John's.

"Edward, this is Captain Crane, of His Majesty's ship *Andromache*," said the Duke curtly. "Captain Crane, my son Lord Edward, as sullen and stubborn a boy as ever you shall meet. I give him to you, Captain, and if you can find some good in him, then you shall have succeeded where those damned costly catamite schoolmasters have failed."

"The navy, Father?" croaked Edward with horror. The navy was neither dashing nor alluring, and it most certainly wasn't St. John's jolly regiment in Bath. It was months, years, away at sea, hard work and bad food and constant peril, or so he'd heard from a boy at school whose brother was a lieutenant. "You are sending me to sea, Father?"

"He seems a good-sized lad, Your Grace," said Captain Crane, his eyes frankly appraising Edward as if he were a horse at the fair. "Strong, too, from the look of him. How old did you say he was, Your Grace?"

"Nine," said the Duke. "I am glad you find him agreeable, Captain, for I vow he is the runt of my own litter. You see one of my other sons here, sir, strong as a young bull."

"I'm nearly ten, Father," protested William. "Tomorrow is my birthday, and then I shall be ten."

Abruptly the Duke wheeled around to face him. "Don't you think I know that, Edward?" he demanded, practically spitting the words into Edward's face. "Don't you think I shall always remember that day of your birth, to the hour, to the minute?"

"Father, I didn't—"

"Silence, Edward." The Duke turned back toward Captain Crane, his back pointedly squared against Edward. "It is an old loss, Captain, but one that grieves me still. Against all the wisest medical counsel, my wife Her Grace did insist upon another child. A daughter for herself, she said. That was what she wished, though I swore three sons was family enough. But instead she died birthing this ungrateful little wretch, the fourth son that neither of us wanted, and one that robbed me forever of my wife."

Ignored and belittled, Edward refused to cry. He'd heard this all before, over and over, so many times he could have recited the story in unison with his father.

All that mattered to Father was what his birth had taken away, the mother Edward hadn't had the chance to know or love; whatever he'd brought to this life in himself would never be enough to replace her. He knew that. How could he not? But it still hurt to hear the unhappy truth explained yet again, it *hurt,* worse than anything he'd ever felt.

But he was almost ten, and he would not cry.

"I am sorry for your grief, Your Grace," said the Captain, clearing his throat to hide his discomfort. "But the good Lord believes that every child is a blessing to his parents, and certainly every man-child is a boon to His Majesty's service. I shall see that Lord Edward is well treated in the midshipman's berth, Your Grace, and that he is—"

"Treat him same as you would any other boy," ordered the Duke with a dismissive wave. "Grant him no favors, no levity, for he deserves none. From this day forward, I have washed my hands of him."

The Captain cleared his throat again, coming to stand before Edward with his legs slightly spread and his hands clasped behind him, as if this drawing room were his quarterdeck.

He would not cry. . . .

"Your father has arranged a glorious future for you, Lord Edward," said the Captain, his bluff, broad face showing more kindness now than his own father's ever had. "You will come on board the *Andromache* with me, lad, and this night we shall make you a midshipman in His Majesty's navy."

"Tonight, sir?" asked Edward, fighting his panic as his world disintegrated around him. He couldn't leave without saying good-bye to Will, or explaining why he'd have to finish their fortress in the elm tree alone. He'd want to say farewell to Will's mother and father and sisters, too, and thank Lady Bonnington specifically for remembering his birthday with the kind of cake he liked best. "Must it be tonight, sir? Another day, please, sir, and I'll—"

"Tonight, Lord Edward," said the Captain firmly. "Your first lesson as a midshipman is that the morning tide waits for no man, not even an admiral. Your trunk is already being packed, and we shall clear off for the *Andromache* as soon as it is ready."

"But, sir, I—"

"Your second lesson, Lord Edward, is that I am your captain and your master," interrupted Captain Crane sternly, "and if you ever dare question me in this fashion again, it is my duty to make you regret it until the day you die. Is that understood, Lord Edward?"

Of course Edward could understand that. Hadn't he already spent his entire loveless life regretting the day he'd been born?

" 'Aye, aye, sir' is the response I expect from you, Lord Edward," continued Captain Crane. "That is how you must agree in the navy: aye, aye. Is that understood, Lord Edward?"

"Aye, aye, sir," repeated Edward in a miserable croak. "Aye, aye, sir."

He agreed and he understood, but finally he could bear no more, and to his father's everlasting disgust and scorn, Edward bowed his head, and wept.

1

Naples
The Kingdom of Two Sicilies
November 1798

*H*eedless of the lurching progress of the hired cart, Captain Lord Edward Ramsden absently traced the gold lacing on the sleeve of his dress uniform coat and thought of all he'd survived since the first of August. For that he could thank Fate, and damn her, too. Even here in Naples, he felt the chilly memory deep in his bones, where not even the bright afternoon sun could warm it away. He'd seen too much blood spilled, heard the screams of too many dying men, for it to be otherwise. His body might have escaped unwounded, but his soul was nearly broken.

He frowned, once again struggling to put the memories behind him, his fingers still tracing the intricate gold braid. He'd already seen to the repairs the *Centaur* had needed after the battle, completed his reports, and visited the wounded among his crew in the hospital on shore, called upon the ambassador and his wife, and composed letters by the score to be sent back to London. He'd always been thorough that way, taking care of the things he could control in a life so full of uncertainty and risk.

But it still wasn't such a bad showing, even for a fourth son, and gradually Edward's frown relaxed. At thirty he was a captain and commander of a ship of the line in His Majesty's Navy, the youngest of Admiral Horatio Nelson's self-styled "Band of Brothers"; he'd just helped win one of the greatest victories of this war against the French; he was, God forgive him for being honest, even a hero.

Perhaps he *was* entitled to a small respite, even a bit of out-and-out idle amusement. Considering the dismal way this war was going on land, they could all be ordered back to sea and to battle with tomorrow's tide. Not even Admiral Nelson was devoting every waking hour thinking of ways to confound the French.

All of which was why Edward sat riding in this shabby hired carriage behind a pair of white Neapolitan mules, listening to his old friend Lieutenant Henry Pye babble on about their plans for the rest of the day.

"You can go wherever you please in Naples, Edward," Henry was intoning with a ponderous, wine-induced solemnity. Their midday meal at a water-front taverna had been lengthy, the local marsala splashing freely and often into their glasses. "If your heart's set on gawking at one more broken-down pagan temple, then go. I'll not stop you. Myself, I'm bound for Signora Francesca's most illustrious *studio d'artista,* and if you've half a drop of red blood left in you, you'll come with me."

"Shall I now," said Edward mildly. He'd known Henry since they'd both been midshipmen in the old *Andromache*, far too long to take his slander seriously when it was just the two of them, and besides, the tavern's rich, plummy wine had worked its magic on him as well. "So is that what they call a whorehouse in this benighted city? A *studio d'artista?* I should watch my purse if I were you, Henry. Artistry like that sounds costly."

"Bordellos," said Henry with excruciating patience. "That's what the brothels are called. Bordellos. I've only told you that at least a thousand times, Edward. Not that you care. No whore's fine enough for your tastes, anyway."

"None that I've met, no," agreed Edward. He'd always preferred females who could hold his interest in conversation as well as in bed, a discernment that marked him as a curiosity among his friends. He'd no patience with the tawdry, mercenary women that preyed upon sailors in every port—the common ones here in Naples had shown their gratitude to the English by giving at least a third of his crew the pox while stealing the purses of the rest—nor had he any interest himself in privately entertaining the more expensive doxies, the greedy local actresses and opera singers, in his cabin the way other captains did. "Consider it a favor that I've left all the more harlots for you."

"But I say, Edward, Signora Francesca's not some common harlot," insisted Henry. "She's a whole other breed of wickedness."

"There are degrees in Naples?"

"Hell, yes," said Henry righteously. "Signora Francesca's establishment is a family concern, you know, inherited from her late lamented father. I wonder that your brothers never told you of it."

Edward's smile grew guarded, the way it always did when his brothers were mentioned. Younger sons, even the younger sons of dukes, were generally regarded as a burden to their families and a trial to genteel society. As the fourth son of the Duke of Harborough, Edward had understood this truth from the distant time he'd been a tiny boy, barely breeched. There would always be three others between him and the endless bounty and good fortune of being a peer of the realm in the greatest country in Christendom, that most obviously being England in the reign of His Majesty King George III.

It wasn't fair, of course. Edward knew that. Little in life was. Instead of a grand tour across the continent with a tutor and servants, Edward had been sent alone to sea on his tenth birthday, a newly minted, broken-hearted midshipman in His Majesty's Navy. He'd never seen his father again, and he'd never returned home to Winterworth Hall, either. There'd been no reason to, especially not after his father died and George had inherited the title, nor did Edward see reason for explaining any of this now to Henry, the much-loved only son of a baker from Birmingham.

"My brothers and I have never had the pleasure of discussing Naples," he said instead, "let alone something as sordid as this particular young woman."

"But that's the best of it, Edward, leastways for

someone as particular as you!" exclaimed Henry, his round, ruddy face glowing with excitement. "The signora's not sordid at all. She's a great beauty, *and* she's half English."

"One glass of wine, Henry, and they're all beauties to you," said Edward, relieved to be able to shift the conversation away from his family. "Half a bottle, and this woman would be Venus herself."

"I am quite in earnest, Edward, even if you choose to mock me," said Henry, scowling. "The lady *is* beautiful, in a Latin sort of way. Everyone says so. Even you must remark it. But that's not the reason for calling on her. One goes to Signora Francesca's to view the paintings."

Edward raised his brows with amusement. "Since when did you become such a connoisseur, eh? Must we search your cabin for plundered Titians or Guidos before we sail again?"

"Not paintings like *that,*" said Henry, leaning forward and lowering his voice in eager confidence. "You wouldn't want these paintings hanging in the parlor at home. Not at all! Signora Francesca's paintings are more what you'd have about for, ah, entertainment. For gentlemen. You know, for amusement."

"Henry, I don't see—"

"Edward, they're lewd," said Henry bluntly. "The paintings, I mean. Like *Fanny Hill* and Aretino, only in the antique style."

"The signora traffics in wicked pictures?" asked Edward incredulously. Now *this* sounded diverting indeed. "Your fair young goddess?"

"There you go again, Edward, twisting my words

about to make me sound like a damned fool," said Henry with a wounded sniff. "The lewd ones aren't the only ones she has. They say she has more polite pictures, too, along with heaps of other old rubbish for sale, for the Neapolitan ladies who visit her studio. And Lady Hamilton, of course. They say the signora's a special favorite of her ladyship."

Edward made no comment beyond a discouraging shake of his head. Lady Hamilton was an uneasy subject for English officers in Naples, what with their very married admiral so openly enamoured of the equally married wife of the English consul.

But what could this young signora with the peculiar mixture of goods in her studio have to attract a worldly woman like Lady Hamilton? Was the girl herself that clever, that witty, or simply so beautiful that her company would be irresistible to women as well as men? But if that were so, then how could such a winsome creature maintain a business on her own?

Edward frowned again, thinking. He liked reason and logical explanations, and he'd always been fascinated by the puzzles people made of their lives, trying to decipher why and how they chose the paths they did. From Henry's telling alone, this beautiful half-English signora with the obscene pictures was offering more questions than answers, and that was enough to intrigue Edward mightily.

Or at least mightily enough for an afternoon's diversion. Aye, that was what he needed more than anything else, a simple entertainment to help him forget, if only for an hour or two. What more, really, could he want?

The cart lurched to a halt, the driver grinning and sweeping his whip to the right to indicate they'd reached their destination in this crowded, close-packed street. The house was typically Neapolitan, narrow and three stories high, the stucco painted a pale candy-pink with carved, curling flourishes over the door and square windows like swirls of white icing.

In the slanting sunlight, striped curtains fluttered at the open sashes, and even though it was November, lush red flowers still spilled cheerfully from the window boxes. The homely smell of frying onions and fish mingled with the salty, damp air from the sea, and the street echoed with sounds of stray dogs barking and vendors shouting and children shrieking and women gossiping in the accelerated southern Italian that Edward couldn't begin to understand. It was all unabashedly domestic, and not at all the place one would expect to visit to view lewd pictures.

That is, one might not expect it, but Henry certainly did. In a single enthusiastic leap, he'd hurled himself from the cart to the street with the same eagerness that he'd use for boarding an enemy ship, and with another two strides he was up the steps and pounding on the door's heavy iron knocker.

"Subtlety, Henry, subtlety," cautioned Edward as he paid the driver and followed his friend up the steps. "We're here to view the signora's wares, not make a prize of her house."

But the elderly manservant who opened the door to them more than matched Henry's cheerful enthusiasm, his grin wide to make up for his haphazard

English as he took their names, then showed them up
the staircase to a large parlor that ran the width of
the back of the house.

"D'you think this is the signora's studio, eh?"
asked Henry hopefully as soon as the maidservant
left them alone.

"It's not exactly her kitchen, is it?" With unabashed curiosity, Edward gazed around the cluttered, high-ceilinged room, so different from the
cramped but tidy spaces between decks where he
lived himself.

The yellow walls were covered with paintings of
every sort—martyred saints, landscapes and sunsets,
still lifes of decaying fruit, maudlin little girls clutching kittens—except, of course, the subjects that
Henry was so eager to see. Pale marble statues in familiar classical poses were arranged around the room
like unwelcome guests, staring bleakly through blind
white eyes at additional disembodied fragments—an
orator's hand, a goddess's sandaled foot, a headless
satyr propped in one corner. Black and red painted
antique vases were displayed on a green-draped
table along with small mosaic medallions and twisted
chunks of volcanic rock from nearby Vesuvius. The
fragrance of the scarlet flowers at the open windows
hung heavily in the warm, sun-filled room.

Cautiously Henry leaned over one of the black-
figured vases, keeping his hands clasped tightly behind him like a small boy warned not to touch.

"I say, these aren't exactly wicked," he said, clearly
disappointed. "How's a fellow to be interested in a
jumble of old pots like this?"

"Perhaps the signora keeps the wicked ones for private viewing," suggested Edward dryly. Although he couldn't claim a true collector's eye, most of the signora's paintings struck him as second-rate at best to out-and-out forgeries at their most obvious worst. Privately he was beginning to doubt that her more lurid wares even existed; it wouldn't be the first time that English gentlemen had exaggerated what they'd seen or done abroad. "For only her most special customers."

"By Jove, then I hope she approves of us," said Henry, anxiously smoothing the front of his dark blue uniform coat. "There, Edward, can you see the spot from the sauce last night?"

"For God's sake, Henry, you look more than well enough. The girl's a wretched shopkeeper, not the queen." Edward sighed, and shook his head over his friend's uncertainty, as if this woman's opinion actually *mattered*.

Not that he'd never worried like this himself. When he'd been younger, much younger, on leave in London, he and Will—now the Earl of Bonnington—had spent any number of hours in any number of elegant parlors, waiting for some young lady or another to deign to show herself. Strange how they'd all blurred together in his memory, those blue-blooded Georgianas and Charlottes with golden hair and angelic smiles, and when he and Will would reminisce about those long-ago girls now, they couldn't begin to sort one from another.

But while Will had been boundlessly full of charm, a great favorite with the ladies of every age, Edward in his awkward, lovesick youth had found those well-bred girls perpetually, achingly unattainable. They still were, really. No matter how many Frenchmen he'd managed to dispatch, even the greatest heroics always paled beside the prospect of a title and the fortune that went with it.

"Ah, *buon giorno,* good day, good day, my most gallant and deserving of dear gentlemen-heroes!" exclaimed a breathy, feminine voice behind him, followed by some garbled, gulping reply from Henry.

Roused from his memories of the young ladies in London, Edward smiled wryly, thinking of how not one of them would dare greet strange gentlemen with such scandalously warm enthusiasm or with such a lilting, singsong accent, either. He was smiling still as he turned, yet as soon as he did, those sweet-faced young ladies in white muslin were instantly banished by the sight of the signora before him.

She was younger than Edward had expected, no more than twenty-five, her figure round and lush, and if the quality of her paintings had been exaggerated, then the promises of her beauty most certainly had not. Her skin was golden, burnished with rich rose, her eyes as dark and fathomless as midnight, and as full of sensual promise. Her hair was black as well, glossy and gleaming, and parted in the center.

And her dress—Jesus, he'd never seen a female dressed in such a fashion, a mixture of Turkish fantasy and fancy-dress costume that somehow managed to be alluring and enchanting and completely her own. Her gown was peacock-blue satin looped up over a yellow-striped petticoat, the sleeves trimmed with brown fur cuffs and the bodice cut low over a sheer linen shift embroidered with scarlet silk. She'd wrapped another length of striped silk into a turban and pinned it into place on the back of her head with a black plume and a garnet brooch, and from her ears she wore large swinging gold hoops strung with single pearls.

Everything about her seemed to shimmer and glow as she walked, emphasizing the curves of her body and the warmth of her smile, and it took every bit of Edward's well-practiced reserve not to gawk outright. It didn't matter that the paintings and sculpture in her studio were trumped-up trash; *she* was the one true work of art, and a most rare—and likely most costly—one at that.

"Lieutenant Pye, is it not?" she was saying breathlessly as she curtseyed before poor dithering Henry, granting him a stupefying view of her bosom in the process. "How honored—most genuinely honored!— I am to have you grace my little studio! For what your brave navy has done to save this kingdom, to fight back those evil French and their hideous republic—why, whatever you wish, dear Lieutenant Pye, whatever you crave, is yours, yours!"

It was humbug and nonsense, every last pretty word. Edward could see that at once. She didn't have the slightest intention of giving away one broken-down saint. She wouldn't have to, either, because Henry was already reaching for his purse, so besotted that he'd gladly give her double whatever she tried to refuse. The more she fluttered and blushed and praised his gallantry, the more Henry would be willing to pay, and it wouldn't be until later, when he'd found himself in the street with some bastardized portrait of Aphrodite and an empty pocket to show for it, that he might—*might*—begin to realize what had happened to him.

Not, of course, that Edward had any intention of letting that happen. That was part of the reason he'd agreed to come with Henry in the first place, to keep him from mischief. This girl might be the most enchanting female ever put on this earth to bedevil honest men, but he'd extricated Henry from worse disasters in the name of friendship and for the good of the service.

"Good day, ma'am," he began, purposefully keeping his voice stern and his bow as perfunctory as possible. "I am Captain Lord Edward Ramsden. Your servant, ma'am."

"Oh, my lord captain, I am the one who must serve *you!*" She smiled brilliantly and tipped her head to one side as she spread her satin skirts and dropped him a curtsey, flattering him with the same charm that had worked so well with Henry. "An English lord in my humble little home! How my dear, late Papa would have loved to live for such a great day!"

"Indeed," answered Edward with another cursory bow. "And how proud, too, he would have been to see his daughter engaged in so thriving an establishment."

She flushed, his meaning all too plain, and Edward almost regretted the pointedness his words. No respectable Englishwoman would wish her home referred to in such a way, no matter if it were true.

But still she held her ground. "Indeed he would," she answered, her ear-bobs swinging against her cheeks. "Though Papa passed most of his life here in Naples, he never forgot his English home, or put aside his loyalty to his English sovereign."

With a graceful sweep of her hand she gestured toward an engraving of King George and his Queen Charlotte. Cynically Edward wondered how long the British king and queen had actually hung there—since Lady Hamilton's first visit, perhaps, or only after the English fleet had sailed into Naples to refit earlier this autumn?

"If dear Papa could but see me here now," she continued, somehow contriving to bring the brightness of genuine tears to her eyes, "in conversation with a gentleman who is next to royalty himself, the son of an English duke!"

"Only a fourth son, ma'am," said Edward, wondering if she kept a copy of the peerage in another chamber for assessing her customers. "A powerfully long step from royalty. Far better you should honor how I serve His Majesty as a captain in his navy."

She nodded in silent agreement. But there was a new interest in her eyes as she appraised him again, an expression that, in an odd way, put Edward more on his guard than before. He didn't trust cleverness in a woman, especially when it came coupled with beauty. At least now he could understand Lady Hamilton's affection for her: they were much of a piece, two low-born, quick-witted women who weren't above using coquetry and a pretty face to get what they wished.

"Here now, signora, here," asked Henry importantly, clutching a small stone Cupid in his arms. "I'd wager my sister in Brighton would fancy such a gewgaw in her garden, there among the hollyhocks. What's he cost, eh?"

"This little fellow?" she asked, fondly running her fingertip along the statue's nose, and not-quite-accidentally brushing her plump, bare forearm over Henry's hand. "He's very old, you know, very ancient, at least from the time of the Caesars. But would your sister welcome the mischief such a statue would bring with him? Cupid is Venus's little son, you know, and given to making us mortals fall into love most inconveniently."

She smiled coyly, and Henry grinned back, as ripe and simple a moon-calf as Edward had ever seen.

"Give me that infernal thing, Henry," he ordered sharply, wresting the Cupid from his friend's arms. "Before you hand over your gold, use your eyes instead of your—well, use your eyes, damn it. This statue is no more from ancient Rome than you are yourself. Mark how these stains in the marble look like someone's spilled tea on it, trying to make it seem old. And here, see how clean these chisel-nicks are in the stone. Wouldn't you think they'd have worn down a bit in, oh, the last thousand years or so?"

Henry scowled down at the fat-cheeked Cupid, then up at Edward. "What are you truly saying, Edward?" he demanded petulantly. "That I'm a right royal jackass? That I haven't your high-born eyes for art? That the signora here is lying?"

Edward sighed with exasperation, and awkwardly shifted the offending Cupid to his other arm, where its stone wing wouldn't poke him. "What I'm saying is that perhaps you're, ah, confused. Aye, confused. And so's the signora."

The signora smiled with surpassing sweetness, turning her face upward to Edward as if fair begging to be kissed in the most innocently cunning way imaginable.

"An English ship captain who is also a connoisseur, a scholar," she purred. *"Che miracolo,* how I do marvel at your great gifts, my lord!"

"I make no such claims, ma'am," he said as brusquely as he could, wishing she would keep to English. It was taxing enough to concentrate on the nodding plume of her turban instead of the myriad of temptations offered lower down on her person. "But I do know I've seen this exact same statue in the garden of the British ambassador's palazzo last week. What are the odds of there being two such here in Naples, eh?"

"Oh, my lord!" she gasped, her hand arching over her breasts with an undeniable emphasis. "To think that a great scholar such as the ambassador has been taken in by a counterfeit!"

"Damnation, that's not what I'm saying at all!" exclaimed Edward with mushrooming frustration. "What I'm saying, ma'am, what I'm *trying* to say, is that—"

"Is that this Cupid and the one in the ambassador's garden are both the work of the same master carver." She laughed merrily, and Edward had the uncomfortable feeling that, for the first time since she'd entered the room, her smile was genuine.

What had happened to his logic, his reasonable explanation? What had happened to his *control* of this situation?

"Signora Francesca," he said as sternly as he could. "You misconstrue my words, ma'am."

"Oh, I rather think not." Gently she took the statue from him, cradling it in her arms as if it were a real baby with its stone eyes turned adoringly up toward her. "I beg you to remember that you are in Naples, my lord, and that here anything—anything!—is possible."

Edward frowned, the sort of black-thunder frown that would have set his crew scurrying to obey.

"Perhaps," he answered, more of a growl, "that is why your King Ferdinando has gotten himself into such an infernal kettle of hot water. If his majesty had relied more on sound judgment and less upon wishful possibilities, then *perhaps* you Neapolitans, ma'am, would not be relying so heavily upon us English to rescue you from the coals now."

"*Perhaps* that might be true, my lord," she said, openly mimicking him. "But you see, since I am an English lady as well as a Neapolitan one, a tidy half of each through my parents, then I can claim both wishfulness and judgment, whichever serves me the better. A wise woman must always weigh and consider her options, my lord."

Righteousness welled up inside Edward. Francesca Robin was most certainly *not* English, nor by anyone's lights could she be considered a lady. Options, indeed. As soon as Napoleon's army appeared, likely she'd recall a grandfather who'd stormed the Bastille and change her name to Françoise. If this was the sort of twin-faced deceit he and his men were offering their lives to defend, then he'd just as soon open the city's gates to the French himself and be done with it.

"Your dubious patriotism, ma'am," he began, "is not what I wish to—"

"Hold now, Edward, and leave off the poor lady," interrupted Henry gallantly. "I came here to see the pictures, not listen to you insult her."

Instantly Edward swung around to face Henry. For the sake of friendship, he would overlook the difference in their ranks when the two of them were alone together, but not before this wretched girl, and not for her sake, either.

"You forget yourself, Lieutenant," he said curtly, and at once Henry straightened to attention.

"Aye, aye, sir," he said, his shoulders back and his eyes forward, the camaraderie that they'd shared earlier with the wine shattered to bits. "I forgot myself, sir."

Silently Edward cursed himself for squabbling with Henry. A chit of a girl, three bottles of wine, and two men who should know better: could there be a worse combination?

"We've tarried here long enough, Lieutenant Pye," he said gruffly. "High time we returned to the ship."

"Pray tarry a moment longer, *per favore,* lieutenant," said the young woman softly, settling the Cupid into Henry's arms. "You would not wish to leave without this."

Edward's frown deepened. Damnation, did the girl have no shame at all? "I do not believe we shall be making any purchases today, ma'am."

"But *I* am making a gift of the Cupid to the lieutenant, my lord captain," she murmured sweetly. "Because the lieutenant fancied it, my lord, I'm offering it to him in return for his service to our little kingdom."

Somehow she was managing to make her expression as meek as the women who gathered each morning on the steps of the cathedral before mass, her head bowed and her eyes full of worshipful thanks. A low actress's trick, Edward told himself sternly, but that still didn't keep him from feeling like an overbearing, ungrateful ass.

Blast her for doing this to him!

"Lieutenant Pye doesn't want the statue," he said, his voice more defensive than he could have wished. "He came here to see your infernal pictures."

Her eyes widened with disingenuous surprise. She was as bright and ever-changing as quicksilver, this girl, and as damned elusive, too. "My pictures, my lord? But my pictures are all around us!"

"The special ones, signora," he said impatiently. "The paintings that you've shown to the other English gentlemen."

"Ahhh," she said, nodding. "My *father's* paintings. His series entitled the *Oculus Amorandi.*"

"Eh?" asked Henry, mystified. "The eye what?"

"The *Eye on Loving,*" said Edward. "Rather like the eye of a peeping Tom at the window, I would wager."

"But done in the most scholarly and correct manner after the discovery of a brothel in Pompeii," she said promptly. "Done directly from the wall paintings that portray the most scandalous diversions of the pagan ancients."

"Aye, aye, *those* paintings," said Henry eagerly. "The wicked ones."

But the signora only sighed, spreading her hands and shrugging with dramatic Neapolitan resignation. "Alas, alas, dearest sirs, I cannot show them to you, no matter how much I wished it."

Edward allowed himself the slightest of smiles. So the pictures truly didn't exist, the way he'd always suspected. Perhaps Signora Francesca wasn't so very hard to pin down after all.

"No, signora?" he asked lightly. "And pray, why ever not?"

She turned the shrug into a graceful half-turn, her skirts *shushing* so distractingly around her ankles that Edward nearly forgot what he'd asked in the first place.

"These are such unsettled times, my lord," she explained, "uneasy times that make the hair prickle on the back of a dog's neck. The censors from the royal court have visited me—oh, such unpleasant men! and forbidden me to display—"

"Censors?" interrupted Edward incredulously. While the Neapolitan court was one of the last to survive Napoleon's Republican army, it was also one of the most louche, corruptly Bourbon to the center of its licentious heart. "If there is one ruler in all Europe that keeps no censors for decency, it must be your King Ferdinando. They say the man has so many bastards by so many mistresses he's lost count himself!"

She shrugged again, the golden afternoon sunlight sliding over the skin of her shoulders, not at all scandalized that he'd speak so freely before her.

"I will acknowledge that His Majesty is the most fortunate parent of fourteen children with Queen Maria Carolina," she said coyly. "As for the others— ah, my lord, you must remember that this is a very different place than your London. Who knows what may happen here tomorrow, the next day, or the next?"

"Meaning that if Lieutenant Pye and I were to return here upon another day, you would produce your father's old *Oculus* for our amusement?"

"Who can say for certain, my lord?" the girl answered, her words as insubstantial as a sigh. "But if you return to honor me again on another pretty afternoon, perhaps, perhaps, I will be able to grant what you . . . *wish.*"

She smiled then, that same charming, clever, conspirator's smile that Edward had found at once so unsettling and so beguiling. It didn't matter that Henry was standing there beside him with the wretched Cupid still clutched in his arms. The air in the studio felt close and velvety soft, the scent from the scarlet flowers heady with the temptation that seemed an inescapable part of Naples, and as natural to this girl as breathing itself.

She was challenging him, teasing him, daring him, and Edward would wager fifty guineas that it wasn't just a hackneyed old statue at stake, either. He recognized the signs well enough: The aristocratic mamas and daughters in London might disdain him, but he'd be a golden prize to a saucy little adventuress like this one. If he accepted the signora's challenge and whatever she was offering with that smile, he'd be soundly congratulated for his good fortune by every one of his friends and fellow officers. Not one man in his acquaintance would fault him.

Not one, that is, except himself.

He'd come here this afternoon for diversion, that was all, and to keep hapless Henry from mischief. He no more sought a mistress than he wanted to buy her ancient rubbish. If he encouraged her, he'd be the same as any other common sailor frolicking with his harlot. The only difference would be the cost.

He straightened his shoulders, shaking off the final mazy effects of the wine, and motioned to the manservant hovering by the doorway for his hat. The last thing he needed to complicate his life was a woman, especially one who was this charming, this clever, this seductively beautiful.

And no matter what she claimed, she wasn't English. She most decidedly wasn't a lady, either.

"Remember, my lord," she said, still teasing him with her smile. "In Naples, anything is possible."

"Perhaps for you, signora, because you were born here," he said curtly as he took his hat, "but not for an Englishman like me. Good day, ma'am."

And then, being a gentleman of his word, he promptly left.

2

The arm was wrong, completely wrong, bent oddly backward as if there were an extra joint at the shoulder, and so distorted that if the arm's owner chose to unbend it, surely her fingers would drag upon the marble floor like an ape's.

Francesca scowled at the drawing, adding another stroke of dark-red chalk to try to fix that awful arm. It wasn't like her to be this unfocused with an important patron sitting before her, or to let herself be so distracted from her work by the memory of a single botched sale three days before.

No, she must be honest with herself. It wasn't the lost sale—though considering the sorry state of her finances, she'd been an impulsive fool to give away the Cupid to the freckle-faced English lieutenant— that was plaguing her now, but the gentleman that had made her do it. She'd known from the moment she'd seen Captain Lord Edward Ramsden's broad-shouldered back that he'd be trouble for her. Stiff and unyielding, the kind of man who refused to be cosseted or charmed into doing anything against his will.

God knows he'd come by his arrogance honestly. From what she'd been able to learn, he'd been born to wealth and position as a nobleman's son, and those blessings had been coupled with the kind of handsome, emotionless face the English prized in men, weather-beaten, thin-lipped, blue-eyed, and cold as a winter day. Being the captain of one of those huge navy ships in the bay was the final touch, making him a floating dictator and a hero as well.

But instead of being awed or intimidated by the magnificence of Captain Lord Edward Ramsden, Francesca had seen it as a challenge, a chilly wall to be taken apart stone by stone. She'd made light of his rank, and instead lavished her brightest smiles upon his lowly lieutenant. He'd tried to question the authenticity of her wares, and she'd turned his words against him. He'd come to see Papa's infamous *Oculus,* and so, perversely, she'd held back showing him the paintings with a trumped-up story about censors. She'd shamelessly teased him, coaxed him, out-and-out taunted him, and accomplished nothing beyond humiliating herself with a thoroughness she'd never sunken to with any other man.

And, with the mocking way her fortunes had gone this year, she'd failed, miserably, horribly, absolutely. He'd ridiculed her studio, mocked her wares and her talent, and worst of all, he'd rejected her wit and her charm and her smiles. He'd rejected *her*.

In the three days since he'd walked from her studio, she'd hated herself for tossing aside her pride, she'd hated him for tempting her to do it, and, most painfully, she'd hated *caring*. Time was only making the memory worse, and with a sigh of frustration she rubbed her chamois rag over the charcoal sketch and swept the awkwardly drawn arm away forever.

"You are not happy with the drawing, little Robin?" asked her ladyship with concern, sliding her gaze awkwardly toward Francesca without breaking her pose. "You are not pleased?"

"Uno momento, per favore," said Francesca, hurriedly fixing the drawing as best she could. If her ladyship had seen the hopeless incompetence of that dislocated arm, then she'd never pose for Francesca again. Emma, Lady Hamilton was a famous beauty who had been painted and drawn by the very best artists of the day, and she did have certain expectations. Besides, as the English ambassador's wife, she had a right to be shown with arms that matched, no matter how ill-tempered Francesca herself might be on this late afternoon.

"We are not inspired today, are we, my dear little Robin?" asked her ladyship with a sigh of her own as she pulled aside the shawl she'd draped over her head for the pose. "What a wretched sort of goddess I must look to you like this!"

"Oh, no, my lady," said Francesca quickly. "If the picture doesn't come well, it's my fault, not yours."

"Don't be so wicked noble, dear Robin," said her ladyship with a philosophical sigh as she plucked a jam-filled biscuit from the tray beside the chair where she'd been portraying Demeter, complete with a small sheaf of wheat in her lap. " 'Tis *my* fault, and I know it, and has been ever since Sir William and I returned from the villa at Posillipo. I vow that here in Naples, here in this house, I cannot seem to make anything but a muddle of my thoughts."

Francesca nodded solemnly, the one answer she'd dare make. Only Lady Hamilton could fault this grand house for making her feel out of sorts. The Palazzo Sessa was the most elegant home in Naples short of the king's, with every comfort and convenience imaginable for the extravagant entertainments that both her ladyship and her husband so enjoyed. Each chamber was a testimony to the ambassador's renowned taste, as well as to the doting affection he lavished on his much-younger wife. Here in the music room, he'd not only supplied a harp, pianoforte, and harpsichord for her amusement, with down-filled cushions to make the chairs more comfortable, but also lined the wall opposite the windows with looking glasses so that his Emma would always have the splendid view of the bay wherever she turned.

And so, of course, that Sir William could in turn admire Emma. While he'd come to appreciate her quick wit and sweet nature, it had been Emma's great beauty that had attracted him most, and still made her the prize of his collection of rare and beautiful objects. That his wife was the illiterate daughter of a Cheshire blacksmith hadn't fazed him any more than that she'd first come to Naples as the cast-off nineteen-year-old mistress of Sir William's own nephew. She was thirty-three now, her thick chestnut hair not quite as gleaming, her famous figure coarsening, but at sixty-eight Sir William admired her still, and loved her all the more.

And while Francesca, like the rest of Naples, realized that Admiral Nelson was far more distracting to Emma than any mere palazzo could be, she was also wise enough to keep pretending for the sake of her commissions. Francesca's trade was already suffering on account of the wars. She could hardly afford to become over-nice about whispers and scandal, too. Besides, what better way to put her own foolish behavior with Captain Lord Edward Ramsden into perspective than to consider the much greater disaster that Lady Hamilton was courting with her own energetic hero of the Nile?

"It is my muse, not yours, that has eluded me today, my lady," she said diplomatically, carefully settling her chalks in their box and dusting her hands together on the chamois. "Besides, the light is already fading. Another afternoon, and I'm sure I'll succeed in capturing the likeness."

"Oh, fiddle, let me be the judge." Lady Hamilton rose and came to stand over Francesca's shoulder, trailing her shawl and biscuit crumbs along the marble floor after her. "You've given me no body to speak of—hah, what license is that!—but my face is rather nice. What was that word Sir William told me the other day—*pensive*, that was it. My eyes look *pensive*, wouldn't you say?"

To Francesca, her ladyship expression had looked simply bored, which was part of the reason the drawing had been such a struggle. "Demeter would be pensive, wouldn't she? Isn't she the one whose daughter was carried off to Hades?"

"Truly?" asked her ladyship with fascinated dismay as she swiped a glistening blob of red jam from the corner of her mouth. "How horrid. I do not think I would have chosen to portray Demeter if I knew that. I wished to make a gift of the picture, you see."

"Then say it's Penelope instead, my lady," suggested Francesca swiftly, propping the picture up against a vase on the table to display it to better advantage. Of course the gift must be for Admiral Nelson, not Sir William, and Francesca thrived on being able to make such quick and accurate conclusions about their patrons. "Beautiful Penelope waiting for her brave, heroic Odysseus to return. A truly tragic and poignant scene, my lady, and most fitting as a gift."

"Oh, my, yes!" exclaimed Lady Hamilton with satisfied delight. She leaned forward, sweeping her finger in an oval around the drawing's face. "Penelope I shall be, and most clever of you to describe it so, little Robin. Have it set up in a simple gold frame, like so, with perhaps a bit of a wreath to give it a Roman air. Such a pretty conceit! I wonder that you don't go to London, little Robin. Your gifts would make you the fashion at once, and you'd make your fortune in no time at all."

"*Grazie,* my lady," said Francesca, smiling demurely, as was expected. Her father had described London as a cold, crowded place that smothered artists, full of grim, serious people like Captain Lord Ramsden, and gray, sooty buildings, and as unlike the cheerful, sunny disorder of Naples as any place could be. The only part he'd missed had been his brother

John. The sicker Papa had become, the more he'd spoken of John, and not having the chance to see him again before he died had been one of Papa's few regrets. "I am quite content here in Napoli."

"But you see, that is exactly what I mean!" cried her ladyship with her usual enthusiasm for arranging others' lives. "You would be a great exotic for them there. You say your sweet *grazie, grazie,* and the gentlemen will come running to nibble from your very palm. You have beauty and charm, and you draw and paint like an angel. Oh, yes, how they would love you in London!"

Francesca's smile grew more forced. She had no difficulty charming young English gentlemen into purchases when she knew they were only visiting Naples, soon to leave for the next city on their tour. It was a game to her, bartering back and forth with an edge of meaningless flirtation. The extravagant, exotic fashion in which she dressed to receive them, the way she smiled and laughed and flattered them—it was all simply part of the pretty experience she was selling to them along with a painting or vase, a story to tell and embellish for the envious friends at home. None of it meant more than that to Francesca. All that mattered was how much of their foreign money they managed to leave behind.

But everything would be much more complicated if she were to try her same coaxing coquetry in London, the home of so many of those same touring young gentlemen and a place where gossip was practically shouted from the chimney pots. And if she behaved as foolishly with even one of those young

gentlemen as she had with Captain Lord Ramsden—
oh, it didn't bear considering.

"I've no wish to leave Napoli, my lady," she said
more firmly. She slid her chalks into her leather
workbag and began untying the front of the rough
linen smock she wore to protect her gown. "It's my
home, and always has been."

"Then let me be frank." Lady Hamilton settled on
the edge of the chair next to Francesca, and took
both her hands in her own. "In this embassy, I hear
many things, my dear, and all of them say that you
would be wise to leave Naples while you still can.
You don't want to be here when the French take the
city, or worse, when your own Neapolitan mob takes
the king."

"But that cannot be!" cried Francesca, unconsciously squeezing the older woman's hands. "Everyone says our army has routed the French to the
north, that soon they shall reclaim Rome!"

"Then everyone is wrong, little Robin," said her
ladyship sadly. "King Ferdinand's army did win one
battle, yes, but they are no match for Napoleon and
never were. It will be the talk of Naples soon enough,
and it's already bubbling like a vile brew through the
back alleys and markets. Sir William and the admiral
both fear the French will be here before the new
year, and you, with your English father and your pictures of kings and queens—you must be gone before
they do."

Her ladyship had no reason to lie to her, or even
to exaggerate, yet at the same time Francesca could
not imagine that affairs could possibly be as bad as

Lady Hamilton was describing. She might be half-English, but she was also half Neapolitan, and she couldn't believe her country, with its fine army, was in such peril. Lady Hamilton would naturally present the pessimistic English view, that *their* navy and *their* army were the only ones fit to protect the world against the republican madmen, just as she must certainly wish to live in London.

"You must have suspected this would happen, my dear," continued her ladyship gently. "Hasn't your trade fallen off? No one wishes to journey here for pleasure now. Sir William and I have had fewer guests this year than I can ever recall, and those were mainly fleeing from the armies in the north."

"But my lady—"

"All I ask is that you consider it, my dear," said her ladyship. "Advice is all Sir William and I can offer to you, you know, for you are not exactly an English-woman or our responsibility. No. But a small convoy of merchant ships will be leaving for Portsmouth with an English escort next week. You could yourself easily find passage with one of them."

"But what you are asking, my lady! To abandon my home, my studio, all my belongings for the sake of a rumor!"

Lady Hamilton sighed, and shook her head. "I would not wish it known through the city, and especially not at the palace, but in those same ships, Sir William is sending the choicest articles of his private collection."

"I do not—"

"Hush, and listen. There will be room in the hold

for your best things as well. Not the rubbish you keep in your front rooms for show, but the good pieces that your father collected, the real ones. Let those be sent to safety. As insurance, if you will, in the event that you must flee later yourself. Then you could make your own way in London without—what is it, Rudolpho?"

The footman in the sky-blue Hamilton livery bowed. "A gentleman for the admiral, *mia signora.* Another officer."

"Another officer?" Lady Hamilton sighed irritably as she rose, flicking her white muslin skirts impatiently to one side. "Another officer, another officer. Will they never leave the poor, dear man alone to rest?"

The footman bowed again. "He says his business is most urgent, *mia signora.*"

"It always is, isn't it?" She sighed again, this time with resignation, as she briskly folded the blue shawl over her arm. "Ah, well, I cannot turn him away, no matter how much I might wish to."

"Then it's well that we are done for this day, my lady," said Francesca as she hurried to gather her belongings together. "I'll deliver the framed drawing myself on—"

"No, no, do not desert me just yet!" ordered her ladyship with a regal wave of her plump white hand. "You shall stay and help me amuse this fellow until Sir William and the admiral return. Certain of these officers can be quite prickly toward me, you know, so you must help me divert him. Rudolpho, what name did this urgent officer give?"

Rudolpho bowed one last time as he backed through the doorway. "Captain Lord Edward Ramsden, *mia signora.*"

"Captain Ramsden!" Francesca gasped with dismay. What dreadful trick had luck played upon her now? "That is, my lady, I am, ah, surprised that the captain would, ah, be here instead of with his ship."

"You are already acquainted with the gentleman, little Robin?" asked her ladyship, arching one brow coyly as she turned back toward Francesca. Gentlemen—*all* gentlemen, even the ones who weren't particularly gentlemanly, either—were of great interest to Lady Hamilton, as she in turn was to them. "Then you must know he is one of the admiral's most trusted captains, and with every reason in the world to come call upon his leader here."

Miserably Francesca nodded. She must be honest now, for the truth was sure to come out regardless. Lady Hamilton lived her own life so completely without secrets and in the public eye that she expected the same openness from everyone else, and would not be satisfied until it was.

"Captain Ramsden and I are not exactly acquainted, my lady," she said, still hedging, "that is, he once visited my studio, but that is all."

"Did he?" Her ladyship's smile widened. "I have found Captain Ramsden to be a most charming and handsome gentleman, and far, far more intelligent than most sailors. I don't wonder that the Admiral depends upon him. A great credit to the service and his country, don't you agree?"

"Yes, my lady," answered Francesca carefully.

"Though because he is a military man, I did find his manner more, ah, more rigidly formal than I am accustomed to."

"More *rigid,* you say?" asked her ladyship wickedly, her meaning unmistakable. "Was he that way before or after you showed him those brothel paintings of yours?"

"I never showed them to him at all, my lady," admitted Francesca, and for the first time in memory she realized she was blushing about the *Oculus.* "He didn't—that is, the time did not seem right."

"Oh, fiddle, to men the time is always right for lewd amusements," declared her ladyship with a droll chuckle. "I'd rather thought that was the entire reason for having those wicked pictures in the first place. The Temple of Priapus, the Grandissimo Bordello near the water, the beautiful Signora Robin and her papa's *Oculus Amorandi*—that's what those callow little pups come traipsing clear from Hampshire and Somerset to see in Naples, not to take tea with Sir William and me."

"It wasn't like that, my lady," said Francesca quickly, though she wasn't quite sure exactly what it had been like instead. "I'd never want—"

"Ahh, Captain Lord Ramsden!" exclaimed Lady Hamilton, relishing every syllable of his titles as she swept forward to welcome him, her arms outstretched and the slightly buck-toothed smile that still could dazzle. "How honored we are to see you at Palazzo Sessa again!"

And then he was in the room with them, his curt bow reflected over and over and over in the mirrors that lined the walls everywhere that Francesca looked. He was tall and he was handsome, just as Lady Hamilton said, and precisely how the English would contrive a captain, lord, and hero to be.

His uniform was exactly the right blend of sober blue wool and glittering gold lace and epaulettes, his waistcoat and breeches so immaculately white that she wondered with amusement if his ship kept a laundry maid on board. Certainly he sailed with some sort of barber, for his jaw gleamed with closely shaved perfection, and his sun-streaked hair, cropped fashionably short around his face but still long behind in best sea-going style, had been plaited into unfrizzled submission and wrapped with black silk.

Oh, yes, he was handsome, handsome, but that wasn't what struck Francesca the most. Unlike her own life, with its constantly shifting layers of deception and display that placed her on the edges of respectable society, this man's existence was as ordered and regular as a life could be. Just from those flawlessly polished brass buttons on his coat and his ramrod straight posture, she knew he would be certain of his convictions, decisive and without regrets or second thoughts. He'd demonstrated that soon enough when he'd challenged her about the stone Cupid on behalf of his friend.

But black or white, right or wrong, a worthless fake or a priceless masterwork: What an uncompromising way to see the world! He would be the perfect ruthless warrior because he'd never hesitate, and he'd be so sure of himself that others would be, too, his loyalty and his honor would be unquestionable.

She couldn't conceive of a man more different from herself, as different as London was from Naples.

And she wanted no part of either.

"Sir William and the admiral are not here at present," her ladyship was explaining as Captain Ramsden bowed over her extended hand, "but I expect them back within the quarter hour. Please, please, be seated, my lord, and I pray you might make do with our female company until then. You are already acquainted with Miss Robin, are you not?"

He straightened gracefully, and turned toward Francesca as instructed, though she'd suspected he'd noticed her as soon as he'd entered the room. She doubted those icy blue eyes overlooked anything. Now he let his gaze find hers and held the link a moment too long before, at last, came the smile of breeding and good manners and precious little else.

"Signora Robin, good day," he said, taking her fingers lightly in his own, the same way he had with Lady Hamilton's. "I am pleased to see you looking so well."

She glanced at him sharply, hunting for the sarcasm that surely must lie behind his words. She wasn't looking well, at least not the way he would consider it. The fingers he now held were grimy with smudges of red and black chalk, her once-neat hair had begun to loosen and come wispily unpinned through the afternoon's frustrations, and the shapeless smock she still wore to protect her gown could hardly be attractive to a gentleman like this. Over and over she could see herself reflected in the mirrors like this, and it wasn't a picture that pleased her.

"My lord captain is looking well, too," she said as she tugged her hand free of his. As quickly as she could, she pulled off the utilitarian smock and tossed it over the chair. Though the gown she wore beneath was a simpler version—pale green lawn embroidered with roses—of the flamboyant costume she usually wore for receiving visitors to her studio, it was clean and stylish, and more the equal to that blindingly perfect uniform. "But then I should fancy every officer would look as well when calling upon his admiral and his ambassador."

"It's more a matter of being shipshape, Signora Robin, than looking well." He clasped his hands behind his back with that same show of tidiness, his legs slightly spread as if commanding from his quarterdeck instead of standing in the middle of Lady Hamilton's music room. "At sea there is no allowance for clutter or disorder. Everything must always be ready and at hand, for there is never a moment to spare between life or drowning, victory or defeat."

"Bene," murmured Francesca, not above a bit of sarcasm herself if it would ruffle all that tidy perfection. "Life or death, victory or defeat! What a grave parcel of responsibility to lay upon your poor unbesmirched waistcoat!"

He didn't smile—in a perverse way she would have been disappointed if he had—but the throat-clearing growl he made instead was telling enough.

"My waistcoat, Signora Robin, is incidental," he said sternly. "What I meant is that every item and person on a ship serves a single purpose, dedicated to the furtherment and efficiency of the whole."

"But if that is true, then you cannot deny that your waistcoat is an item on board your ship," she countered, tipping her head to one side, "and therefore its purpose, too, must be that same furtherment and efficiency. Otherwise over the side it should go, my lord captain, and into the ocean, and leave you to your furthering in your shirtsleeves. That is what most seamen do, isn't it? Toiling most efficiently beneath the sun in no more than trousers and a neckerchief?"

Lady Hamilton laughed heartily, and poked her finger into the captain's arm. "Ooh, we ladies should all enjoy that, wouldn't we, my lord? Every one of the king's officers dressed in scarce more than the uniform God gave them?"

But again the captain didn't laugh, his expression if anything more serious than before. "If one takes away all the signs of rank that come with uniforms, my lady," he argued, "then one might as well be a Godless French republican, and declare all men equal regardless of merit or accomplishment."

"Because they are naked, my lord?" asked Francesca, unable to resist. "I should rather think men in a natural state are far less equal than when they are clothed."

He frowned, his brows pulling sharply together. "Signora Robin, I do not think—"

"Oh, stop calling her that, Captain Ramsden," ordered Lady Hamilton cheerfully. "She's no more a signora than I am. Her father was as English as John Bull, and so you must address her as miss. *Miss* Robin. If she were a true Italian, then she'd be Signora Pettirosso—that's what robins are named here, you know—which is far too great a mouthful for any lady as young and fair as my dear little Robin. *Miss* Robin: try it now, my lord, just to oblige me."

"Miss Robin, then," he said with a slight bow toward Francesca. "Your servant, Miss Robin."

A servant who wished to throttle her, decided Francesca as she nodded in return. What was it about the man that made her behave so *badly?*

"Quite properly done, my lord captain," said her ladyship, her chuckle rich with earthy indulgence. "Though I should say she's bettered you and gotten your worm, the way any good little Robin should."

Francesca smiled, though she felt her cheeks warm. His worm, indeed: She'd never intended matters to slip to *that* level, any more than she wished to be reminded of her English blood and surname. But then she should have known better than to let herself be tempted into this sort of ribaldry with her ladyship, who was infinitely more worldly and experienced at it.

And was she really that eager to humiliate herself like this before Captain Ramsden again?

"We were speaking of waistcoats, my lady," she began more tentatively, "and not of—"

"I know *exactly* what we were discussing, little Robin," interrupted her ladyship again with a wink, "and I know what his lord captain wished—oh, fiddle, what is it now, Rudolpho?"

There was a hurried, whispered conference between the footman and Lady Hamilton. To avoid meeting the captain's gaze again, Francesca briskly folded her smock and stuffed it into her workbag with her chalks. It was time she left, anyway. On this short winter day, the sun had nearly set, a bright red circle sliding into the bay beyond the balcony, and it was not wise for her to walk home alone after dark or to squander her hard-earned money to hire a chair or cart.

"My lord captain, my dear little Robin, you both must excuse me," said her ladyship with an over-wrought sigh. "It seems there is an intemperate dispute below stairs between the cook and a footmen involving knives and a cleaver that I must attend to at once. Amuse yourselves, you two, and I shall return as soon as I can."

"But your ladyship, I must leave myself!" protested Francesca. "That is, I have waited upon your hospitality long enough, and I should return to my own home before nightfall."

"Of course you can stay," said her ladyship impatiently. "I wish you to, Miss Robin, and that should be reason enough. I'll send you home in my own chair later, if that is what worries you. Now pray, keep company with this poor gentleman while I make peace in the kitchen."

"Yes, my lady," murmured Francesca unhappily, dropping a perfunctory curtsey as her ladyship swept from the room.

Behind her Captain Ramsden self-consciously cleared his throat. "Do not feel yourself under any obligation to 'amuse' me, Miss Robin. I came to this house on navy business, not to be entertained in a social manner."

She turned quickly, the light lawn of her skirts

swirling around her legs. "Then we are in the same kettle, my lord captain. I, too, came here for business, not for amusement. It is only Lady Hamilton who chooses to confuse the two."

"Doesn't she always do so?" Captain Ramsden smiled, a wry sort of smile that Francesca already associated with him. "Lady Hamilton is well-known to be a woman incapable of separating her pleasure from business."

"Lady Hamilton possesses the rare ability to find pleasure and delight in everything, my lord captain," said Francesca. She'd liked that smile of his when they'd first met; it had promised the same kind of droll, dry wit with which she herself viewed the world, if only he'd dare set it free. "It is a most pleasing trait, and one that has endeared her to many."

But the captain's expression darkened. "Her ladyship would do better to find her pleasure with her own husband, and not be as concerned with endearing herself to quite so many others."

"If you were referring to Admiral Nelson—"

"I was not," he said curtly. "I'd be a damned fool if I did, wouldn't I?"

She shrugged. " 'Tis not so grave as all that. You would only be commenting upon an arrangement that is already so commonly known as to be unremarkable."

"For you ladies here in Naples, perhaps it is," he said, his shoulders shifting as if balancing the weight of his disapproval. "Here scandal means nothing, with ladies taking lovers as openly as—"

"Not I," she interrupted with blithe honesty. "My

heart is my own, and always has been. That is my choice. A true artist cannot give her love away to a man, or risk losing the soul of her talent with it."

He paused, openly skeptical. "As you say, Miss Robin."

"As I do say, and as I believe, whether you do or not." Like every other man, he'd believe what he wished about her; she'd no control over that. "But tell me, *per favore*. Does my lord captain have a faithful, loving lady wife of his own waiting at home in England?"

"No, Miss Robin," he said. "I most certainly do not."

"No lady wife?" she asked wickedly, the temptation to devilment too much to resist. "Or none who is faithful?"

"No lady wife in England or anywhere else," he said firmly, "faithful, loving, or otherwise."

"*Bene, bene.*" She sighed dramatically. "That is most wise of you, my lord captain. A roving sailor is so very seldom at home to offer the comforts that a wife—"

"Exactly, Miss Robin," said the captain, and there again, where Francesca would never have expected it, came that wry, dry smile. "Just like you, I have chosen to keep my heart to myself. Now this drawing of Lady Hamilton here—is this something you've brought for her to purchase?"

"Oh, no, I drew it myself," she said, still puzzling over his response. She'd been teasing him about being a cuckold. How could he smile over *that?* "This afternoon. I've portrayed her as Penelope, awaiting the return of the brave Odysseus."

"Penelope?" he repeated, amused in spite of himself. "I'll not say a word to that, not one blessed word. But the drawing is most fine."

"Grazie, my lord," murmured Francesca. The room was filled with the rosy beams of the setting sun, bounced back countless times by the mirrors, and the warmth of the light seemed to warm him, too, burnishing his hair to dull gold, glinting off the polished buttons and braid of his uniform, softening the harsh lines the sun and wind had carved into his face. "It's only a sketch, done in haste to capture the passing mood of a moment."

"But most handsomely done." He nodded, then to Francesca's dismay he began to look through the other drawings in the portfolio on the table, quickly done chalk or ink pictures of Neapolitan mothers with their children that she'd brought at Lady Hamilton's request. "Are these yours, too?"

"Yes, but they're not meant for showing," she said, hurrying to his side to try to shift the portfolio and the pictures away from him. "Lady Hamilton has a taste for such subjects drawn from life, and so I bring them to oblige her. But they're not finished works, of no interest to a gentleman like yourself."

"But they are," he said softly, putting his hand on the edge of the portfolio to stop her. He had large hands, strong, brown hands more fit for a laborer than a gentleman, dusted on the backs with fine golden hairs and crisscrossed with old scars. "Yet you have no child of your own?"

"No." She leaned forward, trying to reach around him to close the portfolio. As hastily sketched as these drawings were, they seemed somehow too personal, too private to share with a stranger. The tenderness and love she'd captured between the mothers and their children in the market, or sitting on the sunlit steps of San Domenicho Maggiore, or playing on the sand near the water—all revealed too much of her own longings and emotions to be so coldly displayed and perhaps mocked. "Please, my lord, they are not for show or for sale."

"They should be." He turned the sheets, smiling at the next drawing that showed a fat-cheeked little girl gleefully chasing a goose with her chubby arms outstretched, and her mother in turn chasing her. "Surely your own mother must have run after you like this as well, yes?"

"I have no memory of my mother," she said quickly. "She was gone when I was still a babe. Now, please, *per favore*—"

"My mother died young, too," he said, his voice carefully impassive as he turned another page. "A great loss."

But *her* mother hadn't died. One morning she'd simply left Francesca's father and their baby daughter and run off to Marostica with a goldsmith, and she'd never come back. That would have been scandal enough for the righteous Captain Lord Ramdsen, even without the rest of the sorry story: that Francesca's mother had been one of her father's models, and that despite Francesca's birth, they'd never quite bothered to marry.

Oh, yes, she kept her heart to herself, and how many reasons she'd learned for doing so!

Swiftly Francesca ducked beneath his arm and slid the portfolio across the table away from him, shuffling the sheets back inside as she closed the boards together.

"I must go, my lord," she said, trying to concentrate on tying the portfolio's ties together as her fingers inexplicably shook. *"Mi scusi,* but I must go now."

"You've nothing to be ashamed of, Miss Robin," he said gallantly, misreading her decision. "Those drawings are far better than anything for sale in your studio."

"I am not ashamed, my lord captain," she said, slinging her workbag over her arm and clutching the portfolio in both arms over her chest. "This is Naples, my lord, not London. Here we do not waste our worries over shames or scandals, nor do I—"

But she broke off at the sound of the voices on the stairs. Lady Hamilton's laughter announced her return, her cheeks flushed with pleasure as she entered the room between the two most famous Englishmen in Naples. On one side was her husband Sir William Hamilton, his shoulders rounded with age and habitual scholarship, his half-smile as courtly as his impeccably powdered wig. On her ladyship's other side was Admiral Lord Nelson, a slight, hollow-eyed man whose wounds and scars—the empty sleeve that marked the amputated arm, the shade slanting over the half-blind eye, the fierce, raw scar on his forehead from the September battle at Aboukir Bay—still couldn't diminish the commanding vibrancy of his personality or his attention to Lady Hamilton.

Oh, there was no shame in Naples, thought Francesca wretchedly as she mumbled her farewells and excuses to Lord Nelson and the Hamiltons, no shame anywhere. But she fled without saying good-bye to Captain Ramsden, running down the palazzo's marble steps with her portfolio still clutched tight in both arms and her heart pounding in her chest. It wasn't until she was halfway home, alone in the dark of her ladyship's private chaise, that she realized she'd left her shawl behind, and with a forlorn sigh she leaned back against the soft leather squabs and closed her eyes.

Her head ached abominably, the throbbing punctuated by the horses' hooves clopping on the cobblestones. The murderous French army and the icy gray sanctuary of London, the tall captain's large hands so carefully holding her drawings and his chilly scorn as he'd judged her, Lady Hamilton smiling between her lover and her husband and the red sun sliding into the golden bay, all jumbled together in her aching head. As soon as she was home she'd ask Nanetta to make up one of her sleeping powders, and then to bed she'd go. Yes, yes: A good night's sleep and a fresh dawn would cure everything.

Everything but the odd little ache in her heart, that heart that she swore she'd keep for herself.

The chaise stopped before her house, and the door opened. Slowly she stepped outside, unaccustomed to the attention of one footman in sky-blue velvet livery steadying her hand, another holding a lantern to light her path.

But the illusion of luxury was short-lived. Even

before she'd alighted, the door to her house flew open, and Nanetta, her housemaid and cook, flew sobbing down the steps to clutch at Francesca's skirts.

"Praise the Mother of God, at last you return! While you were gone, Mistress Francesca—such a shock, such a violation, I can hardly speak of it!"

Francesca caught at the old woman's arm, dragging her back to her feet. "What happened, Nanetta? Tell me!"

"Thieves, signora, in the studio!" cried Nanetta, shaking her head as she wiped at her face with her apron. "And oh, mistress, what the black-hearted devils have stolen from you!"

3

~

"*Y*ou are most fortunate, Signora Robin," said the constable as he tapped his gloved finger to the empty nail where, until last night, had hung a portrait of King Ferdinando. "Your losses do not seem to me to be nearly as severe as you described."

"Not severe, Signor Albani!" exclaimed Francesca. "How can you look at this—this *disaster* and say my losses are not severe?"

Indignantly she swept her hand through the air to encompass the sorry state of her studio. She had ordered Nanetta not to clean until the constable came, and in the watery morning light the gaps among the pictures on the wall seemed sadly conspicuous. But at least the thieves had cared enough about those pictures to carry them off. A dozen or so others had been mutilated instead, the canvases slashed to jagged tatters that drooped forlornly from the frames, and all complete losses, beyond repair. Pottery vases had been smashed against the wall or on the floor, two chairs broken into sticks, and cinders from the grate tossed onto the wreckage. It was the wantonness of the destruction that angered—and frightened—Francesca the most, and when she looked at the ruined paintings she could almost feel the willful slash of the knife, an attack upon herself as much as upon the pictures.

But Signor Albani did not agree. "And I say again, signora, that you are fortunate your losses are so slight." He bowed slightly, his yellow-toothed smile anything but reassuring. "A beautiful young woman such as yourself, living alone—"

"I do not live here alone, signor," she said haughtily, drawing herself straighter against the constable's insinuation. "I have two trusted servants who live here with me, and have served in this household for many years. And if you mean to imply that this attack is somehow my fault, simply because I do not rely upon the protection of a husband to—"

"I imply nothing, lovely signora." He smiled again, trying to soothe her, holding his black-gloved hands upward. "I would never mean to show you any such grave disrespect."

"Why didn't Signor Mazzetta come himself?" she asked pointedly, referring to the older, more senior constable. "He has always come to my summons before. *He* perfectly understands my situation."

"Ah, poor Signor Mazzetta." The constable sighed, and shook his head. "His health is not what it once was, you know, and at last he was persuaded to retire to the country in the care of his daughters. For his own good, you understand."

"And you are his replacement?" Signor Mazzetta

had been the model Neapolitan public servant, cheerfully corrupt and too lazy to be more than competent, who'd always treated Francesca like one more daughter.

"Times change, signora, and so must we." The new constable bowed with a flourish. "I am your servant, in all things."

To Francesca, his insinuating manner carried the sour charm of a professional litigator, as did the affectation of his all-black clothes and black wig, and she suspected there'd be none of his predecessor's cheerful incompetence, either.

"Then how do you propose to catch these villains, signore?" she asked sharply. "How will you protect my house so that this will not happen again?"

The black-gloved hands now became part of his shrug. "Perhaps it is not so much what *I* can do, Signora Robin, as what *you* shall do to protect yourself. If the door to the street had been locked—"

"I was not at home," she said defensively, feeling more like the thief than the victim. "It is not my custom to have the doors locked until I have returned for the night."

Another shrug, this one with just a hint of scorn. "Then your servants must learn to be more attentive to your property, signora. For them not to hear these men enter your house and this studio, to be deaf to this destruction despite the loyalty you say they owe you—this perplexes me, signora."

It had perplexed Francesca, too, though she'd never admit it to the constable. "Nanetta and Bartolomeo were in the kitchen, away from the front stairs and door. Besides, they are not young, and their hearing is not what it once was. If you had seen their terror last night when I returned, signor, you would not question them now about these thieves."

The constable turned back toward the wall, idly tracing his thumb along the place where one of the pictures had hung. "True, they may be loyal to you, signora. But what are their feelings toward his majesty, eh? Are your servants good subjects of the king, or do they look to the lure of the north, to the republican promises of the French?"

"Nanetta and Bartolomeo?" She couldn't fathom such a possibility. The two servants were more like aged relatives, too busy grumbling and quarrelling with each other to consider such traitorous politics. "I do not think they could even tell you a single republican promise, let alone be lured by it."

He glanced over his shoulder at her, his upper lip drawn tight over his teeth. "Then what of your own beliefs, signora? You are widely known to welcome all manner of foreigners, even Frenchmen, here to your studio."

"But such touring gentlemen have always been patrons of the artists in this country," she protested, "and without their gold guineas or louis d'or, we would likely perish!"

He was watching her closely. "You are most independent for a lady, signora. Perhaps liberty, brotherhood, and equality hold attractions for you as well, or at least long enough for you to buy favor with the ruffians in the street."

Francesca gasped, shocked by such an accusation.

Personal infidelities might not matter for much in Naples, but political intrigue, informers, and spies most certainly did. If this man persisted, she could easily find herself accused, tried, and buried forever in some dark little prison cell. "I summoned you here because of a theft, Signor Albani, not to be interrogated as a traitor!"

"Calm yourself, dear signora," he said, his voice silky soft. "It is simply my task to consider all possibilities, to ask all questions. I would be derelict in my duties as constable if I did not."

Her hands were damp, her heart racing with panic, things that she prayed the constable wouldn't notice and see as signs as guilt. "But I do not see how—"

"Consider the nature of the pictures that were, by your own reckoning, stolen or defaced," he answered easily. "All portraits, signora, all of royalty and aristocrats from Naples and other places—kings and queens and grand dukes."

"That is what sells to my titled visitors, signor," declared Francesca swiftly. "And surely there could be no greater sign of my own devotion to the crown!"

"As you say, signora, what doubt could be left?" He turned back toward her, gently rubbing his black-gloved hands together. "I shall do what I can to recover the lost paintings, though I must tell you I have little hope. And I advise you to begin locking your doors, and your lower windows, too. With so many foreign sailors in our city, a lady must show caution."

"I shall do that, signor." With a desultory sigh, Francesca looked past him to the shambles of her studio. She'd suspected herself there'd be little chance for finding either the paintings or the thieves, but hearing the constable say it turned her suspicion into cold fact. "If there is nothing further for you here, then I'll call Nanetta to show you out."

"Thank you, lovely signora, but I can find my own way." He bowed and turned, then turned back as if he'd forgotten something. "Your neighbors told me you returned last night in the English Lady Hamilton's chair. But then, you are often a visitor to Palazzo Sessa, yes?"

Francesca frowned, wishing her neighbors were not quite so willing to discuss her habits with the constable. "At Lady Hamilton's express invitation, yes. She has been a kind patroness to me. But I do not see how—"

"A great kindness, yes, and what better way to recognize your own Englishness, eh, signora, or should I say *Miss* Robin?" He smiled, this time showing all his teeth along with his dislike for all things English. "But while you are most clever to promote such connections with the ambassador and his wife, I must caution you not to align yourself too closely with them, or risk the consequences when they leave you behind."

"Lady Hamilton has offered me her patronage because of what I offer in return to her, not because of where my father was born," said Francesca quickly, even as she remembered her ladyship's warning. "Besides, the English will not soon leave Naples. Admiral Nelson needs our harbor to supply his ships and sailors. Everyone knows that. And what would become of Naples were the English to leave us?"

"Exactly so, my dear signora," said the constable, his smile now gone. "What *would* become of Naples without the English lion to guard our gates? Alone, could we survive this General Napoleon and his French demons?"

"But the English will *not* leave," insisted Francesca, her heart still racing and her hands knotted into tight fists at her sides. Did this man have spies in the English ambassador's own villa, to echo so precisely her conversation with Lady Hamilton? "King Ferdinando would not permit it!"

"Times change, signora," repeated the constable, lightly smoothing the sleeve of his coat. "Just as His Majesty must consider what would become of us without the English, a lady alone like you must be wary as well. If you are not careful to keep your head, you may well lose it. Good day, signora."

She watched him go without offering any farewell, nor did he linger to receive one. For a long minute she didn't move, simply standing in the center of the broken pottery and slashed paintings. What kind of warning could such destruction be?

She'd always considered being able to speak both English and Italian a benefit, but not now. Now it seemed as if she was too English to be considered a true Neapolitan by her neighbors, yet too Neapolitan to be accepted by the English. And if the French ever did come, the way everyone seemed to fear, then what would *they* make of her?

She felt more alone than she'd ever dreamed, more lonely than she'd ever admit. With a shaky little sigh, she shook her head and pushed the sleeves of her gown high to her elbows, and began to decide which paintings she would send to London.

If ever there were a fool's errand, thought Edward glumly, then this was it, conceived and executed wholly by himself, the greatest fool in Naples at present, which, considering the dim-witted populace of Naples, was no mean accomplishment.

Yet he'd come this far, and now he'd see the foolishness through. A fool he might be, but he didn't quit. Wryly he looked down at the dark red shawl folded over his arm, the long fringes clinging to his sleeve and the rich color of the fine wool glowing in the half-light of the staircase. The shawl's owner glowed like that, too, bright in any shadow, and he resisted the temptation to brush his fingers over the soft cloth again. Last night when he'd gallantly offered to return the shawl to Francesca Robin after she'd left it behind at the ambassador's palazzo, he'd no idea how sensuously evocative a mere strip of cloth could be.

It wasn't just the softness of the wool that reminded him of her skin, or the color that made him think of how her skin turned golden by candlelight. It had been the scent that had clung to the shawl, *her* scent, spicy and exotic, so filling the closed chaise on his ride back to the inn that he'd thrown open the window to the chilly night air rather than let his senses be overwhelmed.

Velvety skin, pale gold and scented with orange-blossoms and jasmine, a laugh so deep and full of husky promises, a full red mouth made for kissing, made for teasing, made for a man to savor . . .

Oh, aye, he was a fool, all right, letting himself dwell so indulgently on this scrap of fabric, as if he'd nothing more worthwhile to occupy his thoughts. He grumbled wordlessly and shook his head as he headed up the stairs. The door had been open, and though he'd knocked, no servant had appeared to let him in. He remembered the way to the signora's studio, though, and even if she weren't within—and it would likely be best if she weren't—then he'd place the shawl where she'd find it, and leave.

Simple, direct, and uncomplicated, the way he liked to conduct his life. The way he *did* conduct it, when he wasn't letting himself be beguiled by some infernal Neapolitan chit.

So why, then, was his heart racing with inappropriate anticipation?

"Signora Robin?" he called heartily at the door of the studio, not wanting to seem furtive or to frighten her. "Signora Robin! Are you within, miss?"

She was, turning gracefully to meet his gaze before sinking into a curtsey. "My lord captain," she murmured. *"Buon giorno."*

But though the words might have been the same ones she'd used to greet him and Henry Pye, nothing else was. The cheerful clutter of her studio had been scattered in a whirlwind of destruction, her expression of forlorn determination at odds both with her curtsey and her welcome. This time she wore a coarse linen apron instead of a silk gown, no jewelry beyond small gold hoops in her ears, her dark hair bound in a tight braid beneath a peasant-woman's kerchief.

"What has happened here?" he demanded, aghast. "Who did this?"

"Who, indeed?" Wearily she glanced around the room, as if seeing it for the first time. "The best answer the constable could offer was to say it was someone who didn't care for me."

She gave a sad small laugh, and held up a painting that had been slashed, a portrait of some elegant lady whose painted throat had been jaggedly cut. "He told me I should be grateful they hadn't done this to me instead, as if that were any sort of solace."

"But that is reprehensible!" exclaimed Edward, outraged. "For your property to be vandalized like this and you to be insulted—"

"These are troubled times, my lord," she said, carefully setting the ruined painting down on a bench. "That is what the constable told me, and what I must accept."

"But that is not the point," he began, then paused. What exactly *was* his point? That she'd been robbed, and received no satisfaction from those appointed to help her? Or was it more selfish—that she wasn't the gaudy, flirtatious creature he'd come half-hoping to see again, but a real, more genuine woman facing serious difficulty?

"Troubled times, my lord," she said wistfully, as if comforting him instead. "Dangerous times, too, even for poor artists like me."

"I can have a crew of men here in an hour, signora," he volunteered firmly, more of an order than an offer. "If they can make the *Centaur*'s deck spotless four hours after a battle, think of how swiftly they'll put things to rights for you here."

"And doubtless more tidy than they've ever been before, eh? Ah, to make me as shipshape as that waistcoat of yours!" For the first time her smile seemed to carry a share of her old merriness as she wagged her finger at him, a sly version of every nagging fisherman's wife. "Am I so disreputable that you would rather set your poor men to women's work than leave it to my unworthy hands?"

"I intended to offer you assistance, signora," he said stiffly. "I meant no insult to your, ah, housewifery skills."

She curtsied broadly, spreading the skirts of her white apron as wide as a sail. *"Ah, mi dispiace, mio egregio signore, mi dispiace!"*

He hated it when she spoke in Italian like this. His grasp of the language was slight at best, his vocabulary heavily weighted toward navigation and shipyards, and he had a constant, secret fear that every Neapolitan was mocking him without him understanding a single, singsong word of the insult.

"Look here, now, signora," he said, trying to sound stern rather than merely exasperated. "I'm not about to carry on a conversation when I cannot tell what in blazes you're saying."

"Ah." She stood upright, and let her skirts drop to her sides. "I said I was a wicked untidy wench, and then I said I was sorry, my dear sir, very sorry. And I am, too. It's only that certain Italian words are much more, ah, expressive than English. I often don't even realize that I've chosen one over the other, you know."

"You should," he said, wishing her explanation

didn't make quite so much sense. "Here I was simply trying to make you a useful offer of assistance, and you go babbling off saying the devil knows what."

"But the devil *would* know," she countered gleefully, "for at least in your proper English world, Signor Lucifer must surely be a gentleman of Naples, yes?"

He stared at her as coolly as he could, his irritation simmering just short of out-and-out anger. It had been years since anyone had dared treat him with this kind of disrespect, and he didn't like it.

He bowed curtly. "It seems we have nothing more to say, signora," he said, determined to leave before she once again twisted his own words back against him. "I shall therefore wish you good day."

Good day, and good riddance, he told himself sternly as he turned toward the door. The chit was a trial, with no place or use in his life.

"No, no, my lord captain, please, wait!"

Francesca's hand on the crook of his arm stopped him at once. He was no more accustomed to a lady's touch than he was to having his words misinterpreted, especially when the lady's little fingers were spreading along his sleeve and stroking and, well, *caressing* his arm with unusual familiarity. With her standing this close, her scent was there to beguile him again, to fill his head with the same wrongful, lustful imaginings that had haunted him last night as he'd held her shawl in the chaise.

He frowned down at her hand, not quite knowing what else to do. To pull free would seem unnecessarily violent, but to ask her to release him would sound ridiculous, as if he were the protesting maiden in some third-rate Drury Lane play.

And how heartily he wished he were back at sea, where life was so much less complicated!

"I apologize, my lord," she said swiftly, as if she feared he'd leave before she'd finished. "Again I must, and again! Your offer was most kind, *ver-aménte*, the true mark of a generous spirit, and how very much I should like to accept!"

"Then why the devil don't you?" he asked gruffly, still frowning down at that little hand instead of meeting her gaze. Her hand was not a lady's hand but an artist's, the fingertips callused from holding a brush and stained beneath one nail with drawing ink. "My men have little enough to do while we sit idle in the harbor, and this is far too much for you to do alone."

"But I am not alone, you see," she said disingenuously, holding the moment long enough that he, too, held his breath, as if he might honestly care who shared this house with her.

And blast it all, as long as she was keeping her hand on his sleeve, he *did.*

"I keep two servants," she continued at last, "and they shall continue helping me as soon as they return from the well with more water for scrubbing this floor."

"Then they shouldn't have left the door unlatched when they went, signora," he warned, remembering how easily he'd entered himself.

"They—they did?" she asked, faltering for only a second. "But that is no concern to you, my lord captain. What must matter between *us* is your offer. For me to accept such a kindness now would be as grievous to you as it would to me."

"Why?" he demanded. "I thought there wasn't any scandal in Naples."

"Not scandal," she said sadly. "Politics, and spies everywhere. If you were an ordinary English gentleman, then I could take you as my lover without scandal, for no one would think anything of it. But because you are an English officer, a gentleman with great power and position, I cannot let your men help me because of politics. Oh, I know, it is ludicrous, but that is what would happen, and there's no help for it, either."

She patted his arm, more consolation than seduction. But it still didn't erase how casually she'd mentioned being his lover, and only a lifetime of the navy's discipline kept his expression impassive. He'd never stayed on shore long enough to keep any woman as his mistress, nor had the idea ever held much attraction for him. Such arrangements had always struck him as too commercial, anyway, the kind of coldhearted couplings that his older brothers favored.

But that wasn't what Francesca Robin had said, was it? She'd said nothing of the rent to be paid for this house, or the clothes and jewels she desired, or the carriage she needed to impress her friends—all the things that mistresses notoriously expected their gentlemen to provide. No: The word she'd used had been "lover," and she'd made it clear the choosing would be done by her, for pleasure, not for profit.

I could take you as my lover ...

"Why, you've returned my shawl," she said, drawing it free from where he'd looped it over his arm. She flung it over her shoulders, arms stretched wide like red wings, and, heedless of how incongruous such a luxurious piece looked with the rough apron and kerchief. "How careless of me to leave it behind last night, but how very thoughtful of you to bring it back."

"I'm glad to be of service, signora," he said, pleased that she was pleased, but wishing her hand were still upon his arm, connecting them. "I, ah, know how ladies like to keep their things about them."

"Just as *I* know how gentlemen don't like to be kept from their endeavors by the carelessness of ladies," she said, smiling as she stroked the fringe of her shawl. "I am grateful, my lord captain, most grateful, that you have taken your time on my humble errand. *Grazie, grazie, egregio signore!*"

"You're most welcome, signora." He knew that *grazie* meant "thank you," and the rest she'd said after that meant "dear sir." He liked the sound of dear sir, even in Italian, and especially from her. " 'Twas no trouble at all, I assure you."

"Ah, how well you play the gallant, my lord!" She sighed, and curtseyed, twirling the end of the shawl around her wrist. "But I cannot keep you from your duties any longer. How could my poor conscience endure it?"

She was right, of course. He did have a hundred matters pressing. Even sitting in a safe harbor, the

Centaur and her crew demanded his attention. Any day, and with no notice, the orders could come that would send them back to sea or to battle. He had to be ready, and standing here mooning over a pretty young woman in a red shawl was hardly productive.

He should go; he *must* go. And yet something stronger inside him urged him to stay, to linger just a little longer in the glow of her company.

"The paintings that were stolen," he said, purposefully moving past her to study the wall. "It won't take you long to redo them, will you? At least as I recall, nothing here was near the quality of those drawings you showed me last night."

From the corner of his eye he saw her scurry to stand beside him, though this time she kept her hands inside the shawl and not on him. "They must be replaced, not redone. They weren't by my hand, you know."

He glanced down at her skeptically. "But not by the great masters you'd like me to believe, either."

"Well, no," she admitted. "I won't claim otherwise, not with you. But the artists who did paint them live in Rome, and since the French invaded, it's been impossible to send anything in or out of the city. I've been waiting for an eternity to be paid by a dealer there for three paintings of my own. Good-sized canvases, too, that I know perfectly well he's sold. War is quite bothersome to people in my trade, you know, and I rather wish the people in *your* trade would be done with it."

"Aye, signora, so would I." So she thought war was "bothersome." Like most Neapolitans, she'd clearly no experience with the awful reality and destruction of war, and he'd pray she never did. "But why don't you sell your own paintings here?"

"Oh, it is not the custom," she answered glibly. "Besides, my specialities are lady-portraits in the style of Raphael, and no buyer would expect to find a true Raphael in Naples. But in Rome, an Englishman can be persuaded that an elderly *marchesa* in embarrassed circumstances has been forced to part with a family treasure, and *che miracolo!* Everyone is satisfied."

"Including the Englishman who's been cheated?" he asked incredulously.

"It is not a cheat, my lord," she said firmly. "It is a business. The Englishman has bought a beautiful painting that will make him proud and give him pleasure, and will make him the envy of his friends at home. He might even feel doubly pleased that he coaxed the painting from that poor old *marchesa* for such a pittance. So I ask you, my lord captain, where is the cheat in that, the *mistificazione?*"

"But what of the truth?" he demanded righteously. "What of honesty?"

"And what of making an honest living?" she retorted. "My paintings will not fade away or grow less beautiful with time, any more than the Englishman's pride in it will lessen. Surely the exchange is a fair one, my lord."

Edward frowned, clasping and unclasping his hands behind his back while he considered. Truth had always meant a great deal to him, and he'd never had much patience with anyone who juggled right against wrong. But Francesca Robin was being far more logical than he'd expected any woman to be, and grudgingly he could see how her argument made a certain sense.

"But if the gentleman truly treasures his painting," he countered, "he would also be devastated to learn it is false."

"Then do not tell him," she said with a shrug that slipped the shawl from her shoulders. "Why destroy his contentment with your smug little truth? Poor dear Raphael died when he was but thirty-seven. He could never have painted a tenth of the paintings you English lords crave."

"Thirty-seven?" He hadn't known that. One more gentlemanly bit of knowledge, he supposed sourly, that he'd missed learning when he was packed off to sea from the schoolroom.

"It is, however, entirely possible that this English gentleman's treasure *is* a true work of Raphael's genius." She sighed, but with the sly hint of a smile. "Or my father's. Or even mine. Who can tell for sure, eh?"

"Then show me," he commanded. "If your work is so damned fine, then show it to me."

Her eyes widened warily, and she drew back a step. "Alas, my lord captain, that is something I do not do," she demurred uneasily. "It is not my practice to display my own work."

"Why the devil not?" He didn't know why it suddenly mattered so much that he see the paintings. Was it only because he wanted to confront this careless deceit regarding her art, or because he wanted to regain that intimacy, that private glimpse into her true feelings, he'd experienced last night when he'd seen her drawings at the ambassador's palazzo?

She took another step away, wrapping the shawl more tightly around her body. "The only two canvases I have here are unfinished, and not fit to be viewed. But if you wish, my lord, I could show you the paintings in the *Oculus* instead. Praise the saints, the thieves didn't touch them."

"The *Oculus?*" He knew he'd heard the word somewhere, but couldn't quite place it.

Francesca nodded vigorously, clearly eager to distract him. "The *Oculus Amorandi,* my lord! The paintings you and your lieutenant first came to me to see—the paintings that are among the most celebrated in all the Two Sicilies! The crowning works of my father's illustrious life!"

"I want to see your paintings, not his." Why didn't she want him to, anyway? "Unless you're ashamed of them. Unless they're not as good as you claim they are."

Instantly her chin flew up, determination incarnate. "No, my lord captain. They're *better.*"

"Then you'll show them to me?"

"Naturalmente." She turned on her heel, briskly beckoning him to follow. As he did, he allowed himself a small smile of triumph that she wouldn't see. Whatever made her leery of showing her work couldn't hold a candle to her pride in those same paintings. Women weren't generally so combative, so quick to accept a challenge, but then she'd made a point of being different from other women, and to his own wry amusement, he realized he liked her all the more for doing so.

She led him up a winding back stairway with ancient steps so narrow only half his feet would fit on each one. At the top she pushed open a heavy panelled door and swept inside, holding her arms outstretched as she stood grandly in the center of the small room.

And the room *was* small, little more than an attic closet tucked up under the house's flat roof with the rough-hewn crossbeams visible overhead, pale light from the north filling the space through three uncurtained windows.

Clearly this was a private sanctuary, without the calculated effect of the studio gallery below. If Edward had judged the studio to be cluttered, then he never could have envisioned all that was packed within this magpie's space: rolls of canvas and bundles of wooden stretchers, ancient velvet costumes that mice had nibbled at, bizarre seashells and twisted bits of coral, curling sketches and dog-eared prints pinned haphazardly into the plaster, pots of paint and oil and pigment and jars of ink and boxes bristling with brushes and goose-quills and colored chalks.

But all of this Edward noticed later. What captured his gaze in that first minute and held it fast was the painting propped on the easel. It was a small picture, the sort that a lady or gentleman would keep for personal enjoyment and reflection in a bedchamber or closet, and it obviously wasn't completed—the landscape in the background was barely roughed in, and the larger figure of a woman still oddly suspended, almost floating, against it. Yet her expression as she watched over her infant son, reaching out for a white dove on the grass at her feet, held the same vibrant joy that he'd seen in Francesca's drawings of the young peasant women with their children.

Now Edward would never claim a conissieur's eye, and he couldn't say how the finished painting would be judged by expert critics. He didn't have much experience with love, either, especially not the kind that fair radiated from Francesca's painting, but he knew enough to recognize it when he saw it, and admire it, and, deep down in the most shadowed corner of his heart, to crave it with the desperation of that long-ago motherless boy banished from his home.

And when he smiled in turn at the mother's smile and the little boy reaching for the bird, he could forget the agonizing screams of the men who'd died around him at Aboukir Bay, forget the white-hot fire of the burning French flagship before it had exploded so close to the *Centaur*, forget the dismembered, blasted bodies bobbing in the sea around them, a thousand men dead in a single fiery instant.

He wasn't conscious of how this was happening, or why; it simply *was*. Through the rare gifts of Francesca's talent, he could briefly forget all that was evil and violent in the world and concentrate instead on what was right.

Which, for this moment, included Francesca Robin herself.

"It's not finished, of course," she was saying now, defensively misreading his silence. "I've had to put it aside while I finished another Raphael. But this painting's still nothing to be shamed of, my lord captain, and I'm not."

He looked at her swiftly. "Then why the devil do you lie and hide yourself behind another, eh? Why don't you paint only these, and sign your own name?"

"Oh, *naturalmente!*" she exclaimed, not bothering to hide her bitterness. "How very easy it all must seem to a fine gentleman like you, graced with birth and power! For a *man*, everything is so simple, so easy!"

"What in blazes does that have to do with it?" he argued. "If you're proud of what you do—and God knows you should be, with a gift like this—then that should be reason enough for not wasting your talent on forgeries."

"Perhaps my *reason* is I like to eat," she said, her scorn withering, "and have wood for my fire, and keep this house as my own. I must live by my wits and my talent, my lord; I have nothing else. But how much do you think a rich Englishman would pay for this painting signed by Francesca Robin? A mere *woman* of most humble ancestry, who has studied with no great master, served no apprenticeship, belongs to no grand academy?"

Impatiently he glanced back toward the magical painting, refusing to accept her explanation. "You said yourself, signora, that the pleasure of a picture is the same regardless of the artist. So why cheapen yourself with deceit?"

"*Perdizione!*" Furiously she sliced her hand through the air as if to cut through his protests. "Why must you be so thick-skulled? I have no other support beyond what I can earn for myself, and I can earn far more for a painting signed by Raphael than for one by myself. I have no *choice,* my lord. That drawing I made for Lady Hamilton last night—she is most generous, but she will pay me only a single *zecchíno* for it, and most of that will go for the frame. Yet I can at the least expect three hundred times that sum for one of my Raphaels, maybe more. If that is deceit, then I am rotten with it, gladly and gratefully."

"Don't talk like that about yourself," he said sharply. "You don't deserve it."

"Why not, when by your definition the only truth in my life *is* a lie?" She laughed bitterly, flicking her skirts back away from him. "But then you are an English gentleman, and you always tell only the truth, my lord captain, don't you?"

He bowed slightly, wondering how she'd managed to make the truth sound as grim as death. "I endeavor to be truthful, aye. My honor as an officer in His Majesty's navy demands it."

"Aye, aye, so very English," she said, and though she defiantly raised her chin again, he thought he heard another, more vulnerable note beneath the tartness. "Truthful you are, and truthful you must be. So tell me, then, my dear, truthful, lord captain, tell me what no one else will. Will you and all the other honorable English officers soon sail away from Naples and leave us to the French?"

Instantly he felt his face freeze into the blank mask of a senior officer, caculated to reveal nothing. "Why do you ask, signora?"

She swallowed hard, and laughed, quick and nervous. "Why? Is it so very wrong to ask what my future may bring?"

"Because that is not all of what you ask, ma'am," he said softly. "And because of who I am, I couldn't give you the answer, even if I knew it."

"My lord captain is the master of one of the greatest English ships of the line, and a confidant of the admiral himself. If you do not know whether I should be preparing my neck for the arrival of monsieur guillotine, why, then, I—"

"Signora, you make me speak plain," he interrupted, trying not to think of her and the Frenchmen's gruesome executioner. "I am an officer of the crown, for my king and my country, and there are confidences and knowledge that I have sworn not to share with anyone, especially here in Naples."

She flushed, suddenly understanding. "When I said that this city was full of spies, I did not include myself."

He sighed, wishing things hadn't come to this. "They say the guillotine is not much used any longer, especially by Napoleon's men, and not here in Italy."

"Mi scusi! However did I overlook my good fortune?" She made a little gasping sound, a sad attempt at a laugh to accompany an even sadder jest. "To be a lone woman, waiting for the arrival of an enemy army! Oh, yes, they shall let me keep my head, and in grateful return they can claim whatever other part of my person or possessions they please!"

Unhappily he sighed again, at a loss for how to comfort her. As a Neapolitan, she wasn't his responsibility, and for the security of his own men, ship, and country, he could not let himself become entangled in her personal affairs. It was his duty to always decide for the good of the majority, and not concern himself with individuals. When the long-expected orders finally arrived from the admirality offices in London and the goodwill and survival of King Ferdinando was no longer deemed important to England in this war, then the navy ships would sail from this harbor, and the French would swiftly conquer this last, most southern kingdom in Italy.

Unfortunate, yes, even tragic, but also somehow inevitable. Edward was an experienced commander of high rank, and he understood the unfairness of war. The English navy could hardly be everywhere in the Mediterranean, could they?

But inevitable, too, was the danger to Francesca Robin. The jackals that filled the French army were rewarded with wholesale permission by their generals to murder, rape, and plunder wherever they conquered. Frenchmen who'd murdered their own king and queen without a qualm wouldn't think twice about sparing the home—or the body—of this lovely young woman who had proudly displayed portraits of royalty.

She knew it, and so did Edward, and to his shock the knowledge made him want to take her into his arms and hold her and keep her from the harm that was swirling around her. All too vividly he could imagine how she'd be to hold, warm and trusting against his chest, her golden skin like velvet and her scent enticing and womanly. For once he'd know exactly the right things to say to make her feel safe and to comfort her. The image was so vivid and soft and warm and so shamefully wrong that he could barely meet her eye.

"You should plan to leave Naples for a short while, signora," he suggested instead, fighting to forget how much he still wanted her in his arms. "Surely you've a friend or relation you could visit elsewhere, on Sicily, say. I want you to keep yourself safe and from harm, lass, until affairs here are, ah, more settled, a month or two."

"Affairs will only grow worse, not better. Don't dissemble, *per favore*," She was staring down at her hands, her fingers clasped so tightly together that the knuckles had paled. "You are quite abominable at it, and besides, such a blatant lie is scarcely worth the stain upon your much-vaunted honor."

"But damnation, I do care what becomes of you!"

"Go," she whispered. "Just—just go."

She was right, and if he'd any pride left he'd leave at once. In miserable desperation he stole one final glance at the painting on the easel, as if he'd find inspiration there for what to say or do next.

"I'll give you three hundred gold *zecchíni* for the picture, signora," he said. He could have this part of her, if nothing else. "Signed by your own hand, mind?"

With her lips pressed in a tight, grim line, she flipped the painting around and away from his sight, then with a flurry of skirts went to pause by the doorway. "The picture is not for sale, my lord."

"Why the devil not?" he demanded, hating the

way she was dismissing him. "Because your country is not the same as mine?"

"No, my lord captain," she said, her voice dropping off into a fierce whisper as she stood in the doorway. "Because I have no country, and you do. Because you have a future, and I have—I have my fate. *Buon giorno,* my lord, and farewell. Farewell!"

4

For the last time Francesca traced her fingertip along the proud arch of the painted horse's neck, then carefully wrapped a strip of lamb's wool around the narrow neck of the black and red vase. The vase had miraculously survived, unchipped, uncracked, for two centuries, and now all she could do was to pray and trust to cedar shavings that it would remain intact a few months more, through storms and war on the long voyage to England.

I want you to keep yourself safe and from harm, lass, until affairs here are more settled . . . that was what Edward Ramsden had said, wasn't it, breaking his precious, honorable silence to say so? And the way he'd said it, as if he actually cared what became of her, the way no one else did. She'd remember that; she'd remember him.

Damnation, I do care . . .

If only it were as easy as he'd made it sound, as easy as wrapping herself in lamb's wool. . . .

"Sainted Mother of God, how the old master would weep to see you do this!" muttered Nanetta, loud enough for Francesca to hear but still soft enough that she could pretend to be speaking only to herself. "Sending off his treasures to this London, the one place on this earth he hated the most—ah, ah, how he must be weeping in his grave!"

With an exasperated sigh, Francesca placed the now-swaddled vase into its packing crate, and sat back on her heels to confront Nanetta, perched across from her like a cross-tempered crow in her rusty black gown. True, Nanetta had served her father and now her since before Francesca herself had been born, and as a worthy old woman who must have seen at least sixty summers, Nanetta was also entitled to certain allowances.

But this morning Francesca's patience was stretched as taut as her nerves. She had been packing without stopping since late yesterday afternoon, feverishly working to meet the English merchant captain's sailing date. Preparing each piece for the voyage was far more than merely wrapping or boxing, for every vase, or painting, or bronze had a story, a memory that she'd shared with her father. It was almost as if she were losing him all over again, parting with his favorite belongings, no matter how much she knew she'd no real choice left to her.

"My father is not weeping, Nanetta," she said crossly, "not in his grave or heaven or anywhere else, and I'll thank you not to pretend that he is."

Nanetta's toothless jaw set more stubbornly. "The master would weep if he could. You selling all his fine things like this, before his body is even cold!"

"I am not selling all his things." Wearily Francesca rubbed her temples with her fingertips, trying to remember exactly what Lady Hamilton had advised her to say to slow the rumors that the English would soon be abandoning Naples. "I am sending them to London now to have them appraised, so I might know their value."

"You would let a filthy Englander set his own price so he might rob your pocket?" She made a disgusted noise deep in her throat. "Be meek and take whatever the bastards offer! Ah, that the old master—"

"That is quite enough, Nanetta," interrupted Francesca sharply. "You forget that my father was himself English."

"I remember him better than the daughter who would sell his treasures to thieves for a dozen *zecchíni!*"

"If I sell any of my father's collection, it will be for a fair price, and only because I must," said Francesca firmly, striving to convince herself as much as the old servant. "You're not blind, Nanetta, though you pretend to be. Do you see my studio full of patrons, the way it once was? When was the last time I called you to light the lanterns to show the *Oculus* to some young gentleman on his tour?"

"If times are hard, mistress, then it is the bastard Englanders who are to blame." Nanetta turned her head toward the window and the harbor with the English ships and contemptuously flicked her fingers beneath her chin. "The Englanders, and our own whoremonger of a king. If you want times to be better, then the people of Naples should speak, and throw open the gates to the French, and to freedom."

"Nanetta, hush!" gasped Francesca, appalled, rising swiftly to her feet. Nanetta had always been temperamental, but she'd never dared speak as strongly as this to Francesca, and about such dangerous ideas. "That's treason! If anyone hears you—"

"Let them," said Nanetta with a cackle. "I'm old enough to see the truth, and speak it, too."

But for Francesca, the truth was taking a new and ugly turn. "The paintings that were destroyed here last week, the paintings of King Louis and the others. So help me, Nanetta, if that was your doing—"

Nanetta gasped with indignation. "I, mistress? I? Ah, ah, what your father would say to hear you accuse poor Nanetta like that?"

"What else am I supposed to think when you say such wicked things?"

"Not wicked things, mistress, but the truth. The truth!" Nanetta's dark eyes glittered ominously. "You'll see soon enough. When the Englanders leave, the king and his fat queen will follow the same path to the guillotine as her Austrian sister. You are the blind one, mistress, the one with the bad English blood!"

"Stop this, Nanetta!" ordered Francesca, seizing the older woman by the shoulders. "You will not say such things, not in this house and not—oh, perdition, there's someone below at the door! Go, now, answer it, and bring whoever it is here to the studio directly. Go, go, do as I say at once!"

She let Nanetta go, and the servant touched her

forehead and bowed. But the new boldness in her expression unsettled Francesca, and when Nanetta left to answer the door, Francesca pressed her hands over her mouth, struggling to calm herself and push back her fears. All she was trying to do was survive, and yet everything was changing too fast for her, like sand sliding from beneath her feet.

It wasn't as if she'd no experience being on her own. Papa had died slowly from the disease in his lungs, painfully, but he'd taught her the workings of the studio and explained his network of fellow artists, dealers, and forgers. Since then, and before this war, she'd done well for herself, in some ways better than when Papa had been alive. She'd always been clever and brave and strong and resourceful.

I want you to keep yourself safe. . . .

"Emma, Lady Hamilton, mistress," announced Nanetta. "To see you, signora."

Instantly Francesca composed herself as best she could, sinking into a graceful curtsey of welcome. She couldn't afford to let her own troubles show. Instead she must be sure to demonstrate how aware she was of this honor, the way her ladyship expected.

"What a snug nest you keep, my dear little Robin!" exclaimed her ladyship, letting her gaze wander around the studio with unfeigned interest. She was dressed for the cool December afternoon in a close-fitting, high-waisted pale blue jacket with a diamond brooch on one lapel, a white fur muff, and one of her favorite blue velvet hats with a tall crown and white plume, all designed to emphasise the color of her famous eyes. "Why have I not come to visit you here before, I wonder?"

"What matters is that you honor me now, my lady," answered Francesca, glancing sternly toward her maidservant to make her obey, at least this once. "Nanetta, biscuits and a pot of chocolate for her ladyship."

"But this cannot be the same chamber where the vandals ravished your work, is it?" murmured her ladyship as she walked toward the wall with the paintings. "Such a dreadful, cowardly crime! One would never believe such a thing would happen to a lady here in Naples."

"Nothing of real value was lost, my lady," said Francesca, belatedly remembering to untie her apron and whisk it from sight behind a carved panel of Bacchus. Twice now she'd been caught looking more like a peasant's wife than the artistic sultana that she'd wished to appear to be, and the last time, with Edward Ramsden, had—but no, she couldn't think of that now.

"A bit of sweeping, my lady," she said hurriedly, reaching out to straighten one of the paintings, "and a bit of rearranging, and everything's set back to rights."

"And so it is," said her ladyship cheerfully, the white plume in her hat bobbing over one eye. "Though now I do not wonder that you've forgotten to bring me my drawing."

Francesca gasped, her cheeks hot with embarrassment. "Oh, my lady, *mi scusi,* I am so very sorry! However could I have forgotten? To be sure, it is with the framer—and such a cunning frame, my lady, you will be most pleased by—"

"Hush, hush, little Robin, it matters not," said Lady Hamilton, chuckling as she squeezed Francesca's hand. "You've far more important things to consider. Which is truly why I've come to you, to wish you well upon your journey."

"My journey?" Francesca drew herself straighter, trying to keep her smile in place. "I am sorry to disagree, my lady, but I'm not leaving Naples."

Lady Hamilton frowned. "But clearly you are packing, and I heard from Captain Peters himself that you'd come to call upon him to make arrangements."

"I did make arrangements with Captain Peters, yes," said Francesca, swallowing her frustration as she slipped her hands free of her ladyship's. "He agreed to carry my belongings to London in his hold, but he'd no place between his decks for me to sail as well."

"No place!" exclaimed her ladyship indignantly. "Why, I told Captain Peters of your need! I was most specific, too, on account of how the ambassador and I could do nothing for you ourselves. *Most* specific."

Francesca flushed again, this time with mingled resentment and shame. "Perhaps you were too specific, my lady. Captain Peters told me that on account of the distressing news from the north, he'd granted all his cabin space to true English passengers, and he'd no room to spare for anyone who wasn't."

Her ladyship gasped, one hand arched over the spray of diamonds in disbelief. "But he has no right to turn you away like that!"

"He says he has every right, my lady," answered

Francesca. Her conversation with Captain Peters in his cabin had been thoroughly humiliating, with him using far worse language than she'd repeat now. Only her pride had managed to see her through it, though if she'd begged and groveled, he might have found a space for her after all. "He said he'd leave it to Admiral Nelson and the rest of the navy to rescue the Italian rascals, for he'd not risk his own soul to do it himself."

Now it was Lady Hamilton who blushed, mortified. "I cannot believe he'd dare say that to you, to refuse you passage because of your being Neapolitan!"

"Half Neapolitan," said Francesca softly, "and half English. *Che miracolo!*"

A miracle, and one that Francesca noted her ladyship wasn't about to address, either.

"For Captain Peters to speak of the dear Admiral in such a way, especially when he is trying so very hard to do the proper thing, is vastly unfair and unkind," she said indignantly. "He and Sir William and I have been toiling day and night—day *and* night!—to make certain that everyone at court will be properly sheltered, and that is not to mention all the English who've been foolish enough to be caught here. It is not right for Captain Peters to speak so, and not fair in the least!"

Already Francesca knew what wasn't fair or right, and yet she couldn't help herself from making certain. "But Captain Peters was correct to say that the English navy will grant passage to King Ferdinando and his people?"

"Well, yes. Yes," said her ladyship, frowning a bit as she smoothed the plume on her hat. "If it becomes necessary, the navy will accommodate their royal majesties and all their nobles, even though the Admiral grumbles that it will be a righteous tight fit on board. But we'd hardly leave them behind to be slaughtered by the French, would we? Not that we wish it to be known, of course, on account of the common people panicking and expecting to be rescued, too."

"Of course," echoed Francesca, her voice turning brittle. "How dare we common people have such expectations, eh?"

To keep yourself safe, lass . . .

"Oh, my dear little Robin, I didn't mean you!" cried her ladyship contritely. "That is, you're not at all common, but now you understand why I am so cross with Captain Peters."

"Thank you, my lady," said Francesca, holding her head high, "but I shall manage. Surely in this harbor there must be some shipmaster who will not scorn me or my passage-fare. Or perhaps I shall stay after all, and simply add portraits of this General Napoleon to my wall, yes?"

"Forgive me, Miss Robin, please," said her ladyship, reaching out to rest her hand on Francesca's arm.

But Francesca pulled away. She would be strong, she would be brave, and she would do it on her own, the way she always did. She *would* be strong. She must depend only on herself, and forget the help that would not come from others.

"There is nothing to forgive, my lady. I am doing exactly as you suggested, sending my belongings to my uncle in London for safekeeping. Though we have never met, I believe he should make a better caretaker for Papa's things than the French."

"My dearest little Robin, I beg you—"

"That is a most unusual brooch you are wearing, my lady," said Francesca, willing the tremor from her voice just as she was trying to will the conversation to fresh topics. *"Bellissima!* A gift from the ambassador, no doubt?"

Absently her ladyship shook her head as she fingered the diamond pin. "Rather a gift from the queen. It belonged to her sister first, you know, sad little Marie Antoinette, which makes it doubly dear to me now."

"Her Majesty gave that to you?" asked Francesca, startled. It *was* a handsome piece, worth at least a queen's ransom, a swirl like a feather with the largest stones set *en tremblant,* dangling on wires to catch the light, and any other day Francesca would have admired it honestly. But now she saw the brooch only as a symbol of Queen Maria Carolina's farewell, and how few days Francesca herself might have left to make plans.

"A small token, yes, a sort of keepsake," said her ladyship vaguely, clearly thinking as she looked past Francesca to the half-packed crates on the floor. "Just as the brooch was first given to her from her sister. Are you sending your papa's wicked paintings to London, too?"

"The *Oculus Amorandi?"* She certainly hadn't expected her ladyship to ask after that. "They were my father's most famous paintings. I'd never risk losing them, though God only knows what Londoners will make of such pictures."

Her ladyship smiled. "They will make the same of them in London as they do here in Naples. Come, show them to me, little Robin, and let me judge for myself. It might well be my last chance."

"Are you certain, my lady?" asked Francesca doubtfully. No other lady, let alone the wife of the English ambassador, had ever asked to view the *Oculus,* and while she wasn't shy around the paintings herself, she did wonder what her ladyship's reaction would be. "The paintings were not prepared to please a lady's refined taste."

"And there'd be plenty who'd say I'm no lady," said her ladyship, laughing. "Now pray show me this lewd marvel before I perish of curiosity."

Resigned, Francesca ushered the other woman from the studio and across the hall. It wouldn't be *her* fault if her ladyship was shocked, and besides, since everything else in her life seemed so topsy-turvy, why not this as well?

The paintings were kept in a small windowless room—Papa had always told visitors that this was to preserve the "delicate historical condition" of the paintings—and shown by the light of the lanterns along the wall that Francesca now lit. That the darkened room had also served to increase the anticipation of viewing the paintings and to enhance their forbidden quality were things Papa had explained only to her, chuckling gleefully as he'd described how the flickering lantern light could make impressionable young gentlemen swear they'd seen the painted figures move.

"The *Oculus Amorandi* is a most rare and important work, after the antique, my lady," began Francesca solemnly, reciting the same introduction she'd spoken countless times before. There were sixteen small paintings in gold frames to explain in detail, all the better to allow the visitor the proper time for unabashed viewing. "By special arrangement, my late father was permitted to attend the excavations of the lost city of Pompeii. He made these paintings after the murals of the most notorious brothel of the ancient world, murals that were regarded as so inciting, shocking, so depraved, that they were ordered destroyed for the sake of—"

"That's completely untrue," interrupted her ladyship cheerfully, bending close to inspect the first painting. "Nothing like this ever existed in Pompeii, let alone was destroyed, for Sir William would have told me."

"My lady!" exclaimed Francesca, stunned. Not only was Lady Hamilton the first lady to view the paintings, she was also the first person, male or female, to question their authenticity. Of course knowing she was *right* was entirely incidental. "If you asked to view the *Oculus* only to mock the paintings—"

"Oh, hush, little Robin," scolded her ladyship as she settled on the viewing bench, "and stop defending your father's gift for cleverness. Considering how he must have invented these pictures out of his own head, he made a most amusing job of it."

"You are certainly entitled to your opinion, my lady, but if others began to doubt the verisimilitude of—"

"Oh, my dear, don't protest upon my account," said her ladyship with the same good-natured cheerfulness. "Long, long ago, when I was still a green lass fresh from the country without any gentleman-friends, I posed as the Goddess Hygeia at Dr. Graham's Temple of Aesculapius in London, dressed only in a scrap or two of white linen while gentlemen gawked and told themselves they were being 'educated.' What you have here is no better nor worse, though I will grant that with these pictures in your possession to keep you in sixpence and shillings, you need never fear starving in London. These, and the best of your father's collection. Englishmen will gawk at anything novel, as long as they can tell themselves it's edifying."

"Yes, my lady," said Francesca faintly, striving to digest all that her ladyship had confided. If she could support herself in London by showing paintings, then she could stop the forgeries and concentrate on her own work, a glorious, glorious possibility. "That is, I trust you are right, my lady."

"Oh, I am, I am," said her ladyship shrewdly, glancing at her shoulder back at Francesca. "And what did dear Captain Ramsden make of these pictures when you showed them to him?"

Francesca blushed, something she thought she'd never do around the *Oculus*. "Captain Lord Ramsden did not wish to see them, my lady. I offered, but he declined."

"How very surprising!" He ladyship twisted her mouth in wry disbelief. "He is a sea-going man, and in my experience they are the most amorous and randy creatures alive. I thought surely he'd seen your pictures when he offered to return your shawl. Perhaps he was even hoping for the two of you to enact some of these pretty little scenes between yourselves."

Automatically Francesca's gaze shot back to the paintings, to the gods and goddesses who'd been enthusiastically frolicking together as long as she could remember. She'd always found their antics not so much arousing as peculiar and foolish, especially the gleeful smiles in spite of the peculiar postures.

For Francesca, there'd been no girlish fantasies of love, no romantic pining after the boys she saw in the market or the arrogant young foreigners who came to the studio. How could it be otherwise, with such pictures at home to keep from romanticising the facts? When Papa had made her swear to dedicate herself to her painting instead of to a husband or lover, it had been the easiest promise in the world to make.

So why, then, when she looked back at the familiar paintings, did she think of Edward Ramsden?

He bore absolutely no resemblance to the licentious ancient revelers. Not in his looks, of course—he was as broad-shouldered and golden-haired as any god from Olympus—but in his manner. He was too steadfast, too orderly.

But maybe that same difference *was* the reason. He hadn't swept into her studio spouting aristocratic demands, and he'd even seemed almost ashamed to be a duke's son. He'd been amazingly immune to her customary manner with male visitors to her studio, the automatic teasing, cajoling flirtation that had convinced a great many men to buy a great many third-rate paintings. He'd barely been able to meet her eye, let alone ogle her like all the other men, and he'd been so overly courteous and formal that he'd made her wary and wonder what he was hiding behind such a straitlaced facade.

But all that had changed when he'd glimpsed her drawings at the ambassador's villa. It wasn't just that he'd seen pictures that she'd made for her own enjoyment. He'd responded to them with such open pleasure and understanding that she'd been left stammering and flustered. His interest had been as personal, as intimate, as creating the pictures themselves had been for her, and it had made a bewildering bond between them that she'd never sensed nor sought with any other man. The feeling had only grown when he'd come to return her shawl, his concern for her welfare achingly genuine, and when he'd chosen to see her own paintings over the lewd showiness of the *Oculus*.

He'd chosen her as she truly was, alone with her paints beneath the roof, instead of the flirtatious braggadocio of her very public persona. In turn he'd let her see beneath the gold lace and brass buttons, and glimpse the heart that beat inside that righteously formal exterior. And, oh, what that had done to her!

Now when she looked at the writhing figures of

the *Oculus*, her imagination leaped to the same shocking idea that Lady Hamilton proposed. She imagined herself lying naked beneath Edward, her legs curled around his waist and her back arched and her head tossed back in ecstasy as he rode her as fiercely as any of the ancient lovers. Her heart began to race and her body grow warm and heavy with desire as the wicked, tempting images of the *Oculus* mingled with the reality of Edward's body joined to hers, of feeling him driving deep within her in a way she'd never considered, never imagined, never wanted with any other man.

To lose herself in him like that, to desire a man with that intensity—no wonder it frightened her near to death.

"There will be no scenes of any sort between me and Captain Ramsden, my lady," she said almost curtly as she forced herself to look away, thankful that the muted light would hide the lust that must show now on her face. "It is not meant to be."

"Because of the war?" prodded her ladyship gently. "Because he is an English lord? Because of a thousand other little protests you could make, all of them meaningless?"

"My lady, the French could be here any day!"

"And Vesuvius could wake and bury us all beneath hot ash while we sleep tonight, and we'd be just as dead." Her ladyship sighed, and shook her head. "If you lead your life looking for sorrow, then trouble will most certainly find you first."

"But to conceive of an intrigue between me and Captain Ramsden—"

"You're a virgin, little Robin, aren't you?" asked the older woman softly. "Here, in Naples, despite so much temptation and pleasure, you're still a virgin."

"By choice, my lady," said Francesca defensively, striving for the conviction that she'd never questioned in herself, or at least not before now. *"My* choice. Why should I wish to grant my life and my art to a man to ruin?"

But her ladyship only smiled sadly, lightly tapping the diamond plume on her lapel. "So you've never been in love, either? Oh, my dear, whatever your reason or excuse, pray don't close yourself away from all the joys of love!"

"From this?" Scornfully Francesca swept her hand through the air, encompassing the sixteen different paintings of the *Oculus* with sixteen writhing couples. "Why should I be eager to give myself over to *this?"*

"Base couplings like these are not the same as love, little Robin," said her ladyship. "Any beasts can do this, or at least inventive beasts. Love, the truest love, comes from the union of two souls, two hearts, and not just their bodies. Sometimes a lifetime can pass before that special one appears, but when he does—ah, you'll risk all to be with him. Look at me. I know what I am. I'm no longer young, nor beautiful, and I'm wed to a man who treasures me above all others, and yet my heart was not complete until Horatio Nelson sailed into my life."

The wonder and joy in the older woman's smile had nothing to do with age or beauty, but only the little one-armed admiral that had captured her heart.

Francesca remembered the glances the two had exchanged, how even in a room with others they hadn't needed words to share their feelings.

So this was love, and against her will she thought of how Edward Ramsden's stern lord-captain's face had gentled when he'd studied her painting, how that gentleness had remained when he'd shifted his gaze to her, how she'd felt the warmth of it curl like smoke though her body.

But what would happen when this love Lady Hamilton so cherished was gone? Even in Naples, the scandal of what she and the admiral were doing was carving the first cracks into his career and her reputation. Sir William's diplomatic career was in shambles, and he'd become a figure of mockery, every caricaturist showing him with cuckold's horns. The admiral fared scarce better, his triumphs at sea tainted with public outrage and sympathy for his wronged wife at home in England. Disgrace hovered upon the horizon, and if—no, *when*—the two lovers returned to London, the scandal could ruin them both with an efficiency that would make Napoleon envious. They'd lose their fortunes, their homes, their spouses, their friends, their careers, and for what?

For *love*. But to Francesca, this sort of grand love that her ladyship had found was no more appealing, no more tempting, than the kind that her father had painted in the *Oculus*.

And no matter how Edward Ramsden smiled at her, she wanted none of it.

"You don't believe me, do you, little Robin?" With a sigh, Lady Hamilton rose. Briefly she looked up at the ceiling, blinking hard as if to stop tears before they came, then smiled at Francesca again. "Perhaps it's something that can't be taught. Perhaps it's something you must learn for yourself. All I can do is pray that you do."

"Yes, my lady," answered Francesca dutifully.

" 'My lady, my lady', as if I were born any better than you!" To Francesca's surprise, her ladyship leaned forward and kissed her on each cheek, the diamond plume sharp where it grazed against her shoulder. "Take care, my dear. You have a good head, and a better heart, and I know wherever you land, you will thrive."

Confused by such a gesture, Francesca twisted away, unconsciously touching her cheek where her ladyship had kissed it. Only one other had showed any such concern for her, only one other in all Naples since Papa had died.

To keep yourself safe and from harm, lass, until affairs here are more settled . . .

"I don't know where Nanetta can be with the biscuits, my lady," she said in a rush. "She has been so willful today, that I cannot promise that she hasn't forgotten entirely. *Mi scusi,* my lady, and I'll go fetch them myself."

She didn't know why her eyes were blurred with tears as she hurried down the back stairs to the kitchen, her skirts bunched in her hands. She'd never been a weeper, or given to tears to get her own way—except, of course, when it meant a sale, though that was entirely different. Perhaps it was being with her ladyship, who cried all the time as a way of drawing attention to her eyes, or maybe it was simply because she was so tired from packing and worry about her future.

Yes, that must be it, reason enough for anyone, and swiftly she wiped her eyes with her sleeve, gulping away the last of her tears before she pushed open the door to the kitchen. She needed to be stern with Nanetta for forgetting to bring the chocolate and biscuits, not weak and sniveling with self-pity.

"Nanetta," she said as she pushed open the door to the kitchen. "Nanetta, why haven't you—*ohh!*"

A feral young man with a scraggly beard and hollowed eyes, Nanetta's nephew Carlo Brigatti, was sitting not at the table, but crouching on a low stool in the chimney corner with his back pressed against the warm bricks: A young man long reputed to be a half-mad troublemaker, and whose enlistment in the army had brought nothing but rejoicing in their neighborhood. He clutched the porcelain chocolate cup in one dirty hand and a half-eaten biscuit in the other, the same chocolate and biscuit that had been intended for Lady Hamilton.

"Carlo, you must leave at once," said Francesca sharply, her heart pounding. At least with Nanetta here in the kitchen, too, Carlo should behave himself. "You have no place in this house, nor are you welcome. Why aren't you with your regiment? Why are you skulking here like a coward, instead of fighting the French?"

"Carlo is no coward, signora!" said Nanetta defensively, hovering beside him with her hands tucked in her apron. "He fought bravely, as a hero!"

Carlo spat into the fire, emptied the cup, and flicked his dirty fingers beneath his chin in scornful disrespect.

"I am no coward, Signora Robin," he growled. "But that whoreson King Ferdinando—that is your coward, sitting here on his fat ass while we die to defend his miserable throne!"

"Carlo, no!" said Nanetta anxiously. "You swore you wouldn't say such thing about the king, not in the signora's house!"

"Bugger them all, I say," muttered Carlos. "They care nothing for us. What loyalty do we owe them? Kill them all, and be done with it."

"The army's losses have left Carlo feeling very low, signora," said Nanetta, bobbing and bowing like a nervous black bird. "A sin, it is, a mortal sin! Deserted by their officers, forced to leave their wounded behind, scattered to make their way back home to Naples as best they can! How can you fault his passion in the face of such trials?"

"Because his passion is treason, Nanetta," said Francesca as firmly as she could. Her position in Naples was precarious enough without harboring a half-mad deserter like Carlo. "I want him gone now, or else I shall call the constable to take him back to the army."

Carlos jerked to his feet, his eyes wild, and smashed the porcelain cup on the bricks at his feet. "Ten days, Signora Robin. That is all the time my friends must wait. Ten days before the French will be here, and we will welcome them, sharpening our blades for Ferdinando's throat. I would kill him my-

self! I would kill the whole royal dunghill of a family
with my own hands!"

"Hush, hush, Carlo!" warned Nanetta with a hiss,
her gnarled hands on her nephew's shoulders as she
shoved him back down on his seat upon the stool.
"You hold your filthy tongue before a lady like Signora Robin! You will spoil everything if you talk to
her that way!"

But everything already *was* spoiled, and Francesca
knew it. With a certainty heavy as lead, she also knew
now that Carlo had been the one who'd vandalized
her studio, Carlo and his fellow deserters, and the
one who'd filled Nanetta's head with so much venom
and hatred, and that even if she told Signor Albani, it
would be virtually impossible to arrest a man as well-
known and dangerous as Carlo Brigatti with the city
in such turmoil already. Oh, yes, everything was
spoiled, and what could she alone possibly do?

"You *will* go, Carlo, and never come back!" With
trembling hands Francesca grabbed the tray with the
chocolate pot and biscuit plate from the table, holding them high before her in the doorway. "This is my
house, my home, and I will not see it defiled by your
treasonous gossip! Nanetta, see that he leaves, and
that he does not return. Then you will attend directly
to me and the packing."

She didn't wait to see if they'd obey, terrified that
they wouldn't. Instead she fled back up the stairs
with the tray in her hands, her heart pounding and
her stomach sick with dread and fear.

*How many more like Carlo were there in Naples
already? How many more would join him when the*

*English ships left, and the French came in their place?
How much—how little—would her life be worth?*

"Forgive me for taking so long, my lady," she said as she rushed back into the studio. "A problem in the kitchen, no more."

But the studio was empty, and when Francesca looked from the window into the street, Lady Hamilton's elegant chaise was gone as well. With a dry little sob, she dropped the tray down on the sill, a clatter of silver and china.

Gone, gone. And so now, without a doubt and by whatever means, must she go, too.

The admiral paced back and forth as he spoke, unable to keep still in spite of the grayish pallor that betrayed the strain these last weeks had placed on his always-precarious health. He was dressed splendidly, in his best dress uniform, as were Edward and the other officers gathered here in Lady Hamilton's music room one last time before they went from the embassy to the palace for the evening's ceremonies. Tonight, just one day shy of Christmas Eve itself, the emissary of the Sultan of Turkey was going to present the admiral with the Award of Triumph in honor of his victory over the French at the Nile, with a great celebration and ball to follow.

And tonight, in the middle of that same celebration, the admiral and his little fleet would carry King Ferdinando and his family from Naples, away to Sicily and safety.

Edward leaned forward on his chair, concentrating on the details of the escape. The admiral often made last-minute adjustments and refinements to his orders, and in an action as complicated as this one with so many lives at stake, any small misstep or error could be disastrous.

"Any questions, then?" asked the admiral curtly, though he didn't pause for any to be asked, let alone answered. "Thank you, gentlemen. I have every confidence in our success this night, and may God smile upon England, and us."

With a deep-voiced growl of agreement, Edward and the others rose, eager to be off. After the long autumn of inactivity, Edward relished the excitement and challenge of the night ahead. His crew was fair bristling with anticipation, and even the *Centaur* herself seemed to be tugging impatiently at her moorings. He was glad to be going off to sea again, albeit for such a short voyage and with so many demanding passengers on board, and he was doubly glad to be leaving Naples behind.

He glanced out the windows of the music room, out across the bay. The wind had been rising since daybreak, scattering the haze that always hung over the broken peak of Vesuvius and ruffling the water with whitecaps. They'd be in for a rough night of it, even in the bay. Strange to realize that he'd never see this now-familiar view again, and stranger still to know how little he'd miss it.

But then he'd never see Francesca Robin again, either, and that—that was a loss he'd regret a great deal more than he'd confess even to himself. He frowned, trying one more time to put the girl with the rich, evocative laugh and dancing dark eyes from his thoughts.

He tried, and he failed, just as he'd failed every other time since he'd seen her four days before. If she'd been merely beautiful, he could have done it. But instead there'd been something more to her, something less rational, that he couldn't begin to explain. Each time he'd seen her he'd felt an odd kind of connection that pulled at him as surely as the moon and the tide. The harder she'd tried to convince him that she was able to look after herself, the more some damned fool part of him wanted to rush in and do it for her. Over and over again he'd reminded himself that she wasn't his responsibility, yet over and over again he'd remembered how she'd tried to be so blustery and brave speaking of the French, and instead had only looked small and forlorn and very, very frightened. Muddled into the same mess were those pictures she'd made of mothers and children, he knew it, turning him maudlin and sentimental in a way he hadn't been since he'd been a boy himself.

Pictures: What in blazes had come over him, anyway? He tapped his fingers on the hilt of his dress sword for luck, and as a reminder, too. The navy was what mattered, his honor and his duty toward his country. The sooner he put out to sea again and left Naples and Francesca Robin and her pictures behind, the better.

"Hell of a fuss to rescue a lot of blithering dagos, even if they do wear crowns," the officer beside him was saying. "But if her ladyship wants it, we obey, hey-ho, don't we?"

Her ladyship was standing beside the admiral as

she turned to say a word or two to a footman. The footman left, then returned, and with him, to Edward's shock, was Francesca Robin.

In obvious haste, she hadn't bothered to leave off her yellow gloves or her cloak, bright green and lined with fur. Her cheeks were rosy, her hair beneath her cap and hood a bit disheveled from the wind, and in her arms she carried a flat, square package, obviously a framed picture wrapped in rough cloth. At once conversation stopped, not only for security's sake, but also, as Edward knew all too well, because Francesca Robin was beautiful enough to have that effect upon men when she entered any room, blast her.

"My dear Lord Admiral," said Lady Hamilton warmly, even now the gracious ambassador's wife. "May I present Miss Francesca Robin, one of my most favorite friends here in Naples?"

"Honored, miss," said the admiral curtly. Even when he wasn't as preoccupied as he was now, he'd never been one for the ladies—except, of course, for Lady Hamilton.

Francesca smiled anyway, enough to melt more ordinary hearts outright. " 'Tis I who am honored, My Lord Admiral, and grateful, too, for all you have done for Naples."

"Oh, little Robin, you've brought my picture after all, haven't you?" said her ladyship with obvious regret. "You needn't have, you know. That's why I sent your fee to you yesterday."

"Which is exactly why I've brought you the picture, my lady," said Francesca proudly, beginning to peel back the covering. "It's only fair you receive what you've paid for."

"But you see, my dear, I won't be needing it now," said her ladyship gently. "If you feel you can sell it elsewhere, why, then, please—"

"You're leaving, aren't you?" asked Francesca suddenly, the windswept color draining from her cheeks as she set the picture on the floor against the wall. She glanced rapidly around the room, now understanding the reason for so many British officers gathered here together at the embassy. "All of you, yes? Tonight?"

Edward had never seen a room go so quiet, or so still, with Francesca fluttering miserably in her bright green cloak the only spot of real color or life. All the bravery, all the fear that he'd remembered seeing in her before now reappeared, though this time magnified to an intensity that nearly made Edward look away to avoid seeing her pain. To the men in this room, their orders were simply orders. To her they were the same as a sentence of death.

"Pray don't ask me such a question, little Robin," said her ladyship unhappily. "You know I cannot answer it, not the way you wish."

"Then I shall ask another question, my lady," said Francesca with a catch in her voice, "and of the admiral instead."

With her skirts crushing gracefully around her, she dropped to her knees before the admiral, her head bowed and her hands pressed tightly together before her in a way that made Edward long to rush forward and raise her up. No Englishwoman would ever do anything so patently dramatic, and it only served to accentuate her foreignness, differences that the admiral would never understand.

"I am a proud woman, my lord admiral," she began, "but I will bow my head and do whatever you command if I could but have a place on one of your—"

"Come, come, and stand, miss," said the admiral sharply. "There's no reason for you to grovel before me, especially for something that's not in my power to give."

Still on her knees, Francesca gazed up at him, bewildered, beseeching. "But surely as admiral, you of all others have the power to choose who will sail in your ships!" she cried, the panic and fear rising in her voice. "My father was an Englishman, born in London itself, and—"

"You are Neapolitan, miss," said the admiral, unconvinced. "I regret your misfortune, miss, but I cannot change it. I have my orders. If you had an English husband, then that would be another story, but otherwise you must—"

"I'll marry her, my lord," said Edward. "I'll marry her now."

5

Francesca must have misheard. There could, quite simply, be no other explanation for it. Edward Ramsden was a gentleman, no, an *English* gentleman and a lord and a captain in their navy, and unless he'd lost his wits entirely, he'd never, ever make such an offer to such a woman as herself.

But if she'd misheard, then Lady Hamilton had misheard in precisely the same way.

"Oh, Captain Ramsden!" she cried, clapping her hands together. "That is the most gloriously gallant offer I have ever, ever heard in my life!"

"It is the most preposterous wickedness and nothing better," declared the admiral, who was widely known to have not one whit of gallantry in his entire body. "What's come over you, Ramsden? Think of your family—think of your country! Why in blazes would you want to bind yourself in the eyes of God to a dark foreign chit like this?"

"Forgive me, sir," said Edward more forcefully, though his expression stayed so fixed that Francesca couldn't tell what he thought, "but my reasons are, ah, must be my own, and I stand by my offer to the lady. That is, if Miss Robin will have me."

Still on her knees, Francesca saw the startled faces around her begin to melt into a blur as she felt herself sway, almost as if she were literally being blown about by fate. She'd hoped and prayed for a means to escape, a miracle to rescue her when every other way seemed closed, but she'd never imagined the miracle to take quite this form.

The admiral snorted with disgust. " '*If* she'll have you!' Of course the little baggage will! You're offering her the world, Ramsden—the world!"

"I am *not* a baggage, my lord," said Francesca hotly. It was one thing to be, well, startled by such an unexpected proposal, but she was not about to stay here meekly on her knees and be insulted, and swiftly she scrambled back to her feet. If Edward was so determined to propose marriage to her, then he should be the one on his knees, not her.

"I am *not* a baggage," she said again for more emphasis. "I am an artist and an honest dealer of antiquities and art of this city, and there is not one person in all of the Two Sicilies who can truthfully bear witness against me otherwise."

Contemptuously the little admiral studied her, squinting with his good eye. "Next you'll be saying that Ramsden here should be honored to have you accept him."

"He should," she answered promptly, holding her head high as a queen's. "Especially since I've no intention of accepting him."

"The devil you won't!" Edward seized her arm and turned her to face him. He was a large man, and while his grip on her arm wasn't hard enough to hurt her, it was certainly sufficient to demonstrate his unhappiness with her. Yet what surprised her, and what held her more surely than his hand was the desperation she saw in his blue eyes, desperation that seemed to mirror her own.

But what could a man like Edward Ramsden possibly know of desperation? With all his power and privilege—with all his self-righteous *Englishness*—what could he know of the choices facing her?

"I won't," she answered rebelliously, shaking free of his hand. "I can't, and neither the devil in hell nor the angels in heaven will make me say otherwise."

The admiral snorted, and glanced pointedly at the tall porcelain clock behind him. "You have five minutes to sort this out between you, Ramsden, before we must be under way. If you convince her to be your wife, then she may come with us, but not otherwise. Though for my part, the chit is showing far more sense than you."

"Five minutes, sir." Edward took her arm again, leading Francesca away from the others to the window where they'd have at least some small semblance of privacy. The last time they'd met in this room, the setting sun had made everything warm and rosy, but now, in this harsh gray light of winter, his handsome face was grim and sorrowful and etched with lines she'd never noticed before. Was he already regretting his rash offer to her? Was that what was making his expression the very antithesis of an optimistic bridegroom?

Which, of course, he'd absolutely no right to be.

"I won't deny that this is very gallant of you, my lord," she began, "but it's entirely preposterous, as you know perfectly well."

"I don't know it," he countered sharply. "Else I never would have asked you in the first place."

She hadn't expected that, and against all logic she felt her heart flutter. Deep down she knew she'd have to accept him, for the alternative was far, far worse than even an end to her treasured independence. But she wanted to make him understand how difficult such an arrangement was going to be for them both. *He* might be fancying himself as a story-book hero, but there was absolutely no way she could afford to tumble into that same romantic delusion, and sternly she ordered her heart to stop that insipid fluttering.

"But this *is* preposterous," she insisted. "You are who you are, and I am who I am. *Naturalmente,* yes? And while you might find me passably attractive, you also consider me fast and frivolous and not entirely honest. Even that wretched admiral of yours called me a 'dark little chit.' I am too bold and far, far too Neapolitan to ever be the good English lady-wife to a duke's son like you, and—"

"Do you know what will happen to you if you remain here?" he interrupted, his voice rough with urgency. "Do you know how Napoleon's army treats the women of their enemies?"

She stiffened, her fear and panic returning. "I have heard the stories, yes. That is why I spoke to the admiral as I did. I can guess all too well what would become of me."

"I don't believe you can, Francesca, not by half,"

he said, using her Christian name for the first time, surprising her by lingering over the syllables the way an Italian would and not making it harsh and sharp and English. "But I've seen for myself the French at their worst, lass, seen it with my own eyes, and I'd not wish that fate on any woman."

His eyes narrowed just a fraction. "You told the admiral that you'd do anything for your passage, didn't you?"

Now her anxieties took a new twist, spurred by the cold determination in his voice. "But to bind myself to you forever, a man I scarcely know, to abandon who and what I am for you—*che impossibile!*"

"Evidently so," he said, clipping the words sharp with bitterness. "It is your decision, Miss Robin, but I must conclude that marrying me is not preferable to torture, rape, and death. I regret having caused you such distress by my daring to think otherwise."

"That's not fair," she said swiftly. "That's not my reason, and you know it!"

"Ah, one more assumption that I am supposed to somehow intuitively *know.*"

"But you do know this," she said, struggling to find the right words to convince him. "I told you before I'd never had a lover, ever, or even a sweetheart, and now the notion of suddenly taking you as my husband—ah, ah, it is so much for my poor head to consider!"

"Then perhaps, Miss Robin," he said, beginning to turn away, "your poor head should consider how much longer it wishes to remain attached to your poor shoulders. Good day, miss."

"Oh, please, don't go yet, I beg you!" she cried

frantically, catching at his sleeve as she remembered how Carlo and his knife could be waiting for her in her studio even now. "Could we only pretend to be married, for the sake of the admiral?"

He frowned. "You heard him. You won't be permitted aboard any vessel in the English fleet unless you're wed to an Englishman. He won't countenance anything less, and neither will I."

Of course he wouldn't, not when rules and orders meant so much to him. "Then—then if I marry you today, could we agree to allow time to know each other better?" she pleaded. "To see if it can possibly suit?"

Now his frown seemed more from disbelief than displeasure. "You wish me to court my own wife?"

"No, no!" she said hurriedly. "I wish us to have a way, a means, to separate if we find we are not an agreeable match. I am not the woman you'd ordinarily choose, Edward. I wish you to see my faults, before you must have me to keep."

"No one is perfect, Francesca," he said with a hint of irritation. "I can accept that. I myself have no fortune to offer you beyond what I earn in the navy, no home on land for you to grace, no family to welcome you. I am often at sea for months at a time, and the odds would certainly favor your being my widow for much longer than you will be my wife. I could even be shipped home to you a broken-down cripple worse off than the admiral, for you to tend and pity for the rest of my days. I am, in short, no prize myself."

"Then might we agree not to, ah, consummate our union until we are sure, so that we can more easily obtain an annulment if we do not please?"

"You would refuse me?" he asked sharply. "You would not be my wife in every way?"

Francesca nodded, her palms sweating inside her gloves. This is what came of being raised in the same house as the *Oculus,* for she could barely look at Edward now without feeling the first flush of desire for him, the swift tease of passion curling through her body, from the tips of her breasts to the secret, wanton place between her legs. She wanted him, yes, she wanted him in a way that no proper English lady would ever want her husband. But once they were wed, the law would let this man she scarcely knew command her every thought and action, and oh, saints in heaven, she wasn't ready for that.

"I would refuse you, yes, so you in turn could refuse me," she said as evenly as she could. She needed to make it clear to him that there was a far greater likelihood that she'd leave than stay, that she wouldn't let herself be governed by desire. "If we agree to separate, then I will never ask for a single shilling of recompense from you. I will simply vanish away from your life as if I'd never entered it. So refusal, yes, but also no regrets, no blame."

He didn't answer at first, clearly unhappy with such a suggestion.

"If that is what you wish," he said finally, making it perfectly clear that it wasn't what he'd choose. "Very well. But I'll warn you, Francesca. I'm a man of my word, and I don't take it back."

"Ramsden," called the admiral. "You have one minute more."

Edward rubbed his finger along the side of his

neck and sighed impatiently. "You've set your terms, Francesca, and I've agreed to them. So what's it to be, lass? Yes, or no?"

"One more question, Edward," she said, finally daring to ask what had been plaguing her from the beginning. "Why?"

"Why." He glanced downward, away from her gaze, to the well-polished toes of his shoes. "Damnation, I do not know. I hadn't planned to venture such an offer, you know, not to you or any other woman. Good sailors do not make good husbands. You haven't far to look for proof of that. But when I saw you kneeling there, begging for your own life, why, I couldn't leave you behind when we sailed. This was the only way I could make sure I didn't. The words came out on their own, and here we are."

"And here we are, *càro mio,*" she repeated, her voice turning wistful. "Here we are."

She couldn't explain exactly where "here" might be, and she still didn't want to be anyone's wife, let alone the wife of an English aristocrat. But Edward Ramsden had told her the truth, unadorned and unvarnished, something few men bothered to do, and she appreciated his bare honesty more than a thousand flowery promises that meant nothing. He'd been that way from the beginning, when he'd first challenged the authenticity of the carved Cupid, and he wouldn't change now, or likely ever. He was a man of his word, just as he'd claimed. He could have followed his admiral and dismissed her to her fate, yet instead he had chosen to save her the only sure way he could.

Francesca had never known anyone like that. Certainly not Papa, and not herself, either, not when she was already planning how soon she might escape him and follow her father's collection to London. She was *trying* to be honest about it, leastways as much as she could, but his was the genuine truth, and enough to make her feel genuine remorse as well. It wasn't simply that she and Edward Ramsden wouldn't suit one another. He didn't *deserve* to be burdened with a woman like her, so adept at slipping and sliding her way around the same truth and honor that he held so dear.

But as he'd said, here they were.

And where they went next was entirely her decision.

"Dear little Robin," said her ladyship gently, coming to rest her hand on Francesca's shoulder. "Both the admiral and Sir William are waiting, and we cannot tarry any longer. If there's anything I might do to help you make your—"

"Yes," said Francesca, the slightest breath of a word to carry so much weight. "Yes."

"Yes, meaning I might help you?" asked her ladyship, perplexed. "Pray tell me how, my dear."

But Edward understood, taking Francesca's hand in his own. "She has," he said gruffly, "done me the honor of accepting me."

He raised her hand and kissed the back of it, the heat of his fingers searing through the yellow kid of her gloves. He was strong, this convenient bridegroom of hers, and for all his honesty and breeding, he was accustomed to having his own way, his every order instantly obeyed by a crew of nearly seven hundred men. His golden head bowed low before her while his gaze held hers as fast as his fingers held her hand, marks of possession by a man whose life could well have been every bit as ruthless and violent as the enemy he'd sworn to save her from.

Until he smiled again, over her arched hand, a smile filled with almost boyish wonder and amazement and intended entirely for her. She doubted he realized how much that smile revealed, or could guess how it was making her poor, beleaguered heart flip and flop in her chest. Yet what a hopeless fool she was, to read so much into a man's smile!

"Oh, little Robin, I am so very happy for you!" cried her ladyship, bending to kiss Francesca on both cheeks. "This is the most perfect solution imaginable! My blessings and good wishes to you both, and all the joy in the world."

"Thank you, my lady," answered Francesca faintly. Though she'd never been shy around men, simply standing beside Edward now was making her feel as skittish and uncertain as any country girl. "If we are in such a hurry, then I should go home and gather my things."

"No time for that, miss," said the admiral sharply. By now the other officers had already left, and he and Lady Hamilton were the only ones left in the room, standing waiting in their cloaks for the carriage to the Turkish Embassy. "Ramsden, I shall excuse you from coming with us to the embassy tonight so that you might return directly to the *Centaur*, on the condition that you summon your chaplain to marry you directly."

"But I can't leave like this!" protested Francesca, thinking of everything she was leaving behind with her home. "I'll have no other clothes beyond what I'm wearing!"

"Nor shall I, little Robin," said her ladyship as she sadly glanced around her mirrored music room for what could be the final time. "We must simply all vanish from Naples. If we are seen making preparations of any sort, then the rumors will begin and the people will panic, and make it quite impossible for the king and queen to flee."

Francesca remembered Carlo's threats against the royal family, and shivered as she thought of all the bitter, desperate men like him scattered throughout the city, waiting for their chance. The English were wise not to take any risks.

"Farewell, little bride," said her ladyship, her eyes too bright with tears as she gave Francesca's forehead one last, hurried kiss before she joined the admiral at the door. "When we meet again you'll be a wife, and a lady, too. How I hope you find love with your gallant captain!"

Francesca nodded, all the response she could make. How could Lady Hamilton expect her to find love in a marriage like this one, born of war, haste, and necessity? Love would scarcely flourish after such a barren beginning, and as Francesca watched her ladyship and the admiral walk slowly down the stairs, she wasn't sure she wanted any part of it, anyway. In a world as torn apart as theirs, love seemed to Francesca to be at best a perilous emotion, and one that could only end in disaster and heartbreak.

"I'll make it up to you, lass," said Edward, offering his arm to lead her down the stairs after the others. "The *Centaur* isn't exactly a grand house in Grosvenor Square, but I'll see that you have everything you want."

"*Grazie,* Edward," she said softly, and slipped her hand into the crook of his arm. She *would* be brave; she must. Far better to forget what she'd lost and instead look forward to what she'd gained, and resolutely she forced herself to smile up at the tall man at her side. He, at least, deserved that much from her. "You are most kind to me, Edward, most generous."

He concentrated on guiding her down the stairs, making a wordless, grumbling sound in his throat to hide his discomfiture. How odd, she thought, that he didn't enjoy the compliment, especially when she'd meant it.

"You're my responsibility now," he said finally, "and I mean to look after you."

"But you've already saved my life, *càro mio,*" she said, curling her fingers into his sleeve and leaning against him ever so slightly. She was perfectly capable of walking down the stairs unassisted, but she knew how gentlemen preferred to believe women couldn't. "And you've offered me your name as well. Isn't that enough for one day's work?"

"Not when it's for you, no," he said solemnly. "Here's the footman Lady Hamilton said would show us through the cellars."

The footman bowed, and lead them through a doorway to a servant's stairway, the steps narrow and twisting and made of rough stone instead of the polished white marble of the front staircase. The footman held a lantern high to light their way, and now Francesca welcomed the support of Edward's arm as they began down a long, shadowy tunnel of a hallway. She didn't like dark places, particularly dark places under the earth that harbored mice and rats and spiders, and this hall, she decided with dismal certainty, was sure to be full of all three.

The stucco walls curved into a crude arch overhead, so low that Edward had to bend his shoulders to keep from striking his head, and so narrow that Francesca had to pull her skirts close to keep the fabric from snagging on the rough, dirty plaster. Although they passed several padlocked doors, there was nothing else to light their way beyond the lantern that the footman carried, the bouncing, uneven light making every cobweb and crack in the wall seem full of potential menace.

"I don't like this, Edward," she whispered uneasily, clinging to his arm. "Why are we here, anyway? I thought we were going to your ship."

"We are," he said evenly, giving her hand a slight, awkward pat. "We're simply bound on another course, that's all."

She looked up at him in the flickering light, understanding more from what he wasn't saying than what he was. "You won't tell me anything beyond that?"

He shrugged, clearly hedging, and quickened his steps. "You'll see for yourself soon enough."

"Because I am Neapolitan," she said moodily, as much to herself as to him. "You'll marry me, but you won't trust me enough to tell me where we are going."

He stopped abruptly, blocking the tunnel as he turned to face her, the lantern's light's fanning reducing him to a tall, black silhouette looming before her.

"What devil makes you say such things, Francesca?" he demanded, his anger as palpable as it was unexpected. "That's not true, not a word of it, and I won't listen to you say it. I don't care if your mother was born in Naples or on the blasted moon."

"Because *you* were born the son of an English duke!"

"Oh, aye, and a fat lot of good that's done me, hasn't it?" he said bitterly. "Listen to me, Francesca. What or where I was born doesn't signify, not to me and not to you, any more than who or what your parents were does to me. None of it's worth a tinker's dam, mind? What matters is what we *are,* what we've made of ourselves and our lives."

"Then why won't you tell me where exactly we're going?" she demanded unhappily. "Aren't you afraid I'll run off and *tell* someone?"

"Not willingly, no," he said sharply, pulling her along after him. "But if by some hell-bent misfortune we're captured or separated before we reach the *Centaur,* the less you know, the less value you'll have to our enemies, and the better the chance will be that they'll let you go without killing you. Now *come.*"

He didn't give her time to apologize, and Francesca didn't try. She felt like a great enough fool already without giving him the satisfaction of having her admit it. He'd promised to look after her, and he was doing exactly that, after a fashion, though she still didn't understand why he stubbornly hadn't explained his reasons for secrecy from the beginning.

But it could hardly be her fault for assuming what she had. Every other English man and woman seemed to believe that being English was next to being immortal, or at least a good deal better than being a lowly, insignificant Neapolitan, and being an English aristocrat was like an extra layer of gold leaf. How was she to know that Edward so obviously prided himself on believing otherwise?

The footman set the lantern down on the dirt floor, unlocked the last door, and shoved it open with his shoulder. A rush of chilly, damp air swept in, smelling heavily of the sea.

"Take care, signor," he warned as he held back a curtain of overhanging vines for them. "The harbor is home to many vagrants and footpads."

"And at least half of them are English, eh?" said Edward dryly, pressing a coin into the man's waiting palm. "Well, no matter. Here, a happy Christmas to you and your family, and promise me you'll drink a dram for old King Ferdinando instead of Napoleon. There's the *Centaur*'s boat, Francesca, in the middle of the others, exactly where it should be."

Francesca stepped forward, her shoes sinking slightly into the sand. Happy Christmas, indeed: With everything else, she'd completely forgotten that tomorrow would be Christmas Eve. The wind was sharp, colder on the water than in town, stinging at her cheeks and tugging at her cloak. Because of the clouds, there was no moon, but when she looked to where Edward was pointing, she could just make out the dark outline of four waiting longboats pulled up onto the sand beside a jetty of large stones. The boats had no lanterns, but she still could see the heads and shoulders of the men crouched low over their oars.

"You said you hadn't planned this," she said slowly, "and Admiral Nelson has only just excused you from going to the embassy with the others. So why are they here waiting for us now?"

"Because we're not the only ones they'll meet tonight," he said evenly, and this time Francesca didn't question his vagueness. "Here now, draw up your hood so your face is hidden if anyone's spying from above."

She did as he'd asked, then automatically turned to look back over her shoulder, up the steep hillside overlooking the bay. The ambassador's villa was as brilliantly lit as if he, too, were hosting another grand reception of his own, candlelight streaming from the tall windows into the gloomy evening. No one would guess that soon Sir William, Lady Hamilton, and God knew how many others would be hurrying through the same tunnel that she and Edward had just traveled, and just as eager to flee Naples.

"Ahoy, *Centaur!*" called Edward softly.

"Ahoy, Cap'n Ramsden," came the muted reply. The men in the middle boat shifted with eagerness, and two clambered over the side to run across the beach toward them.

"This should be Lieutenant Pye," said Edward. "You'll recall him from—"

"You have a gun," she said, suddenly noticing the pistol that had appeared in his hand. Gentlemen wore swords, both for defense and for show, and she was accustomed to that. But pistols were only for highwaymen, duelists, and soldiers, and the sight of this one now resting so familiarly in his hand, the long barrel gleaming dully, chilled her blood more than the wind. Belatedly she realized he must have been carrying it with him all evening, hidden beneath the long tails of his coat.

"Of course I have a gun, Francesca," he said with unexpected patience, holding it out for her to see. "In fact I have two of them. The other's still hooked on my belt. This *is* Naples, lass, and as even Sir William's footman noted, the town is filled with vagrants and thieves. Wise to be careful."

"Papa lived in Naples for thirty years, and he never kept a gun," she protested. "He said pistols were only good for taking another man's life."

"And so they are," agreed Edward deliberately. "We're in the middle of a war, lass, and my duty is to help win that war however I can. Like it or not, pistols and long guns and swords and a great deal else are part of my life. Surely you've realized by now that you're not marrying a shepherd."

"Naturalmente," she said faintly, and pulled her cloak more tightly around her shoulders. "I should never make a mistake like that, should I?"

But she could hear the excitement in his voice, the anticipation of whatever action might lie before them, and she wondered if he even heard her reply. They were already in his world, that was clear enough, and hers had ceased to matter or even exist. As soon as they'd left the tunnel and come outdoors,

Edward had seemed to radiate confidence and assurance, his gestures growing bolder and more forceful, his gold-laced coat swinging around him and his hair tossing in the breeze. Now he was indisputably the captain, the master in charge of this completely masculine world, a man that all others would obey without question.

All others, that is, excluding her. But she *would* find her place among all those weapons and obedient men; she always had before.

"Good evening, sir," said the lieutenant, puffing a bit as he touched the front of his hat, and Francesca recognized him as the round-faced recipient of the carved stone Cupid. "We weren't expecting you quite so soon."

"I—we—had a change of plans, Mr. Pye," announced Edward. "Instead of attending the ball at the Turkish Embassy, I'll take the *Centaur*'s boat back to the ship directly."

"Aye, aye, captain," said the lieutenant, trying very hard not to peer at Francesca for a glimpse of her face, hidden inside her hood. "Directly it is, sir. And, ah, is this the first of our, ah, royal passengers?"

"Oh, pah, but I am far, *far* more important than mere royalty, Mr. Pye," said Francesca with as winning a smile as she could muster, shaking her hood back from her face and thrusting out her gloved hand to the startled lieutenant. "*Per favore,* you do remember me, I'm sure. I am Francesca Robin, and I have agreed to marry your captain this very night."

Like any man who had spent nearly twenty years sailing about the world wherever his country sent him, Edward had learned to express his displeasure with great fluency, and in numerous colorful languages as well. But as he listened to Francesca blithely turn his delicate military maneuver into an extension of her own studio, he found himself completely—*completely*—without words.

"I expect we shall be seeing a great deal of one another, Lieutenant," she was saying now to the equally dumbstruck Henry Pye. "Considering how a sailing ship is like a little island to itself, I should rather think it next to impossible to avoid seeing you once we are properly on our way. And once we have rescued the poor king and queen from—"

"Damnation, Francesca, enough!" sputtered Edward. "You cannot go about saying whatever you please like this!"

She spun to face him, her eyes genuinely mystified. "And why not, pray? I was only—"

"Come." He thrust the pistol back into his belt and took her by the arm, leading her a half-dozen steps farther down the beach and out of Henry's hearing. "Listen to me, Francesca. This isn't your own little house any longer, where you could do whatever you pleased. You have to behave differently now, and with more decorum. You must be more, ah, reticent and considerate in what you say."

"Non capisco," she muttered darkly, though he suspected she understood perfectly well enough. "Because you expect your wife to be reticent and decorous? Because Mrs. Edward Ramsden is permitted no thoughts or words of her own?"

"Because by marrying me, you will become another of the *Centaur*'s people," he explained, striving to keep his temper even as she was losing hers. "As the *Centaur*'s captain, I expect you to behave in a fashion that is neither dishonorable nor hazardous to the ship."

She didn't answer at first, which he took for a good sign.

He was, alas, sadly mistaken.

"Bene, bene," she said tartly. "This is rather like your infamous waistcoat all over again, isn't it? The waistcoat that determined whether your entire fleet would prosper, or sink? Ah, ah! Everything English is so very fraught with meaning and significance!"

"There are most excellent reasons for what I ask of you, Francesca. I am not saying you are wrong, but rather that you are merely, ah, ignorant of the ways we do things in the navy."

"But you *are* saying that I must have no opinions other than your own in a fashion that is completely counter to my nature," she said sharply, but with a little squeaking tremor that hinted perilously at imminent tears. *"O maledizione! Non me ne importànte!"*

"In English, Francesca, in English," he snapped. "If you are going to curse at me, pray, at least have the decency to use words I can understand."

"So now I am not only forbidden to speak without your permission, or to whomever I please, about whatever I please, but I cannot even choose my own *words!*" The tears were there now, no mistake, her voice breaking like a wave. "In short, my fine Captain Lord Ramsden, I am to have no *pleasing* of my own whatsoever, am I?"

Edward frowned, his mood black as the sky overhead. What had become of her witty, teasing nature, or the gentleness he'd glimpsed in her drawings, or even the vulnerability that had drawn him into his gallant, impulsive, and thoroughly insane offer in the first place?

For God's sake, what had he done to make her *cry?*

He'd admit that he had little experience with women on an everyday basis, and none at all with a woman confronting the sort of personal upheaval that was now facing Francesca. But he'd never imagined she'd behave like this with him, not at all, and he took a deep breath and slowly exhaled before he trusted himself to answer.

He did not wish to become mired in a full-fledged quarrel with her here on the beach in full sight of his crewmen, nor was there time to squander on such folly. But he couldn't let her continue like this without risking out-and-out disaster, both for the success of the evening's mission and for themselves as husband and wife.

Husband and wife: What devil had claimed his senses for him to believe in such a half-witted notion, anyway?

"Miss Robin," he said firmly. "Francesca. We will discuss all of this further when we are alone, and when, of course, you will be permitted to speak. I would not wish otherwise for my wife. However, for the sake of your safety, you now must do as I ask, and do it without comment or objection."

"Your wife, oh, yes, yes, your *wife.*" She bowed her head and her shoulders sagged, her whole body seeming to surrender forlornly before his order. "All I want, Edward, is to be myself, the way I always have before. But I don't belong anywhere now, do I? What do I have left to show of my life?"

"Blast, Francesca, you have me!"

"Do I?" Her face was a pale, troubled oval turned up toward him. "Do I really?"

"Aye, you do," he answered with more conviction than he'd realized he'd felt. "You have me, and as for your place, yours is now beside me in the sternsheets of that boat."

She glanced back over her shoulder as if seeing the boat for the first time, then turned again toward him, hugging her arms around herself beneath her cloak.

"Oh, Edward," she cried wistfully. "What am I to say? *O, per favore,* what am I to do?"

That much he could answer. "You are to climb into that boat directly, else I shall carry you there and put you onto the bench myself."

"You would?" She made an oddly endearing sound, a gulp of an anxious giggle. "I have but this one pair of shoes with me, you understand. They are already quite filled with sand, and I—I cannot afford next to soak them in the sea as well."

He had an instant, vivid image of her feet in the bright silk slippers that Neapolitan women favored, delicate shoes with high curving heels and flirtatious ribbon bows on the toes. She would wear shoes like that, with the thinnest white stockings that would be as good as transparent if she got them wet in the seawater. He thought of pulling them off for her himself, of resting her little foot on his knee and lifting her skirt to untie her garter and sliding his hand along the curve of her ankle, higher, along her calf, above her knee to the soft, warm skin of her thigh, higher, and higher still. . . .

"If those shoes are your only pair," he said, his voice strained, "then we can't get them wet, can we?"

He looped his arm behind her knees and swept her from the sand. Though she gasped with surprise, she instinctively linked her arms around his shoulders to steady herself.

"This—this shall suffice, Edward," she said breathlessly, holding herself very still in his arms. "To help me into the boat, I mean."

"And to keep your feet dry," he said, though his overeager imagination had already moved far beyond the thought of her little slippers.

He had never carried a grown woman before, and though she wasn't particularly heavy in his arms, he hadn't realized how *familiar* a position this could be. He had obviously touched her before in small, social ways—offering her his arm, adjusting her cloak—but holding her in his arms intimately pressed her breasts against his arm and her hips and bottom against his chest. He could hardly ignore how insubstantial her stays and petticoats must be beneath her gown, or how, as a result, he was acutely aware of holding so much soft, yielding, fragrant female flesh so close to himself.

No, not simply female flesh, but Francesca's, the woman he had promised to marry, but not to bed.

Damn, damn, *damn*.

6

$\mathscr{F}$t was, thought Edward grimly, bound to be the next wonder of the entire fleet, and endless entertainment for them all, too. Admiral Nelson's indiscretion with Lady Hamilton would be relegated to old tittle-tattle, and instead the gossip would be focussed on how exactly Captain Lord Ramsden, who'd always forbidden loose women on his ship, had gone and married one.

"Handsomely now, and mind you keep your petticoats clean," he cautioned as he lifted Francesca over the side and into the boat. Awkwardly she settled herself on the bench, tucking her feet up to keep those infernal slippers of hers out of the muck in the bottom of the boat.

"*Bene*," she announced with resignation. "I am ready, Edward."

"Indeed," replied Edward briskly, all he could think to say. He swung himself into the boat, and when he came to sit beside her on the bench, she didn't shift away from him as he'd expected, but let her hip and leg remain touching his. Granted, there was no real room for them to keep apart on the narrow bench even if she'd wished it, but feeling that soft female hip pressing gently against him was enough to raise his overeager imagination to a simmer again.

"Proceed, Mr. Pye," he said, praying his voice sounded sufficiently world-weary and captainly. "And make haste about it. As Miss Robin has observed, we are ready."

He smiled at her, striving once again to be gallant, but she didn't answer, instead pointedly looking away from him and back at the city they were leaving.

In well-practiced unison, the men dipped the blades of the oars into the water and pulled, and the boat jumped to life, racing out away from the shore. Edward felt Francesca tense beside him at the unfamiliar motion, and saw how she clutched the side of the boat beneath her cloak, clearly trying to hide her uneasiness from him and the others. Ever since he'd become an officer, he'd been accustomed to living with the constant scrutiny and attention of his men, but she must be painfully aware of the two rows of men at their oars, unabashedly watching for any stray morsel to report back to their messmates.

"I'll be glad when this night is done," he said, as much to himself as to her as he gazed up at the shifting clouds in the night sky. "It's our luck that after a week of fair weather, we'll sail into foul. But you needn't worry, lass. The *Centaur*'s as steady a ship as there is in a rough sea."

"Indeed," she murmured, pulling her hood forward to shield her face from the spray, and from him.

"Indeed, aye," he persevered. "I promise you'll be as comfortable there as any lady ever was at sea."

"Which is to say far less comfortable than any lady on the land," she answered, still looking away from him. *"Naturalmente,* if women were meant to live upon the water, then nature would have supplied us with fins and scales and gills."

He tapped his fingertips against the side of his knee. "You're still angry, aren't you?"

"Not angry, no." At last she turned toward him, her hood limp with sea spray and flopping forlornly over her face and her hair plastered in damp tendrils to her forehead. By the light of the signal lantern in the boat's prow, he could see the faint glisten of tears on her cheeks. "Just—just frightened."

He hadn't expected that, not from her, and instantly he reached for her chilly little hand in the yellow glove.

"You've nothing to be afraid of," he said gruffly. "I told you I'd look after you, didn't I?"

She hesitated before she nodded, her fingers curling more tightly into his. "You've told me so, yes. But you see, Edward, I've never had to trust—"

"Damnation, Francesca, I'm not like my brothers!" he said harshly, then broke off, aghast at his own words. What had made him speak of his brothers *now?* None of them would have landed himself in a situation such as this, for none of his brothers cared a damn for anyone other than himself. Why the devil had they surfaced so abruptly here, making her stare as if he'd lost what few wits he still could claim?

"My brothers are not trustworthy men with

ladies," he said finally. "That is, my brothers and I have little in common."

"Then it is most fortunate that I find myself dependent upon you," she said, smiling wistfully, "and not them."

He nodded, determined not to reveal any more of his family than he inadvertently had. With luck, she'd never have to meet them, anyway. "You have my word, Francesca. I cannot offer you more than that."

"I know," she said softly, and now when her fingers tightened around his, he had the distinct impression that she was comforting him and not the other way around. "What more could I wish, *mio coraggioso inglése leone?*"

He frowned at the unknown words. "In English, lass, in English."

"Very well, my most brave English lion," she translated, smiling through her tears. "Because you *are* brave, and never know any of my sorry sorts of fears, I will be brave, too."

"An English lion?" He rather liked that, though he liked rather more that she'd added the possessive, making him her particular English lion. "Well, then, we shall have to dub you the English lioness in turn, won't we?"

She lowered her chin to look at him sideways beneath the sooty fringe of her lashes, skeptical and winsome at the same time as she fought her tears.

"Then you must not provoke me, Edward," she said with that same little broken gulp that had touched him so before, "else I shall turn fierce as any true lioness, and unleash my savage jungle nature upon you."

An open boat in a rising sea in late December was farther from the depths of a lion's jungle than any place Edward could imagine, and yet as soon as she'd spoken he felt a rush of heat race through his body that was worthy of any African sun.

His savage lioness, indeed. No proper English lady would dare even think of herself like that, let alone say so to a gentleman, and yet the more Edward considered the possibilities of what Francesca had said, the warmer he became. How the devil could she speak like that to him one moment, then vow to keep chaste the next?

It was a trial, this impulsive gallantry of his, a damnable trial. He'd always heard that the women who lived in southern climates like Naples were more passionate, but he'd never given it much serious thought before this. Now he could think of nothing else, no matter how he'd sworn to the contrary.

And somewhere in the middle of it, he decided, he must learn how to say "lioness" in Italian.

"That is your ship ahead of us, Edward?" she asked tentatively, as the boat's coxswain hailed the ship's watch. "We are almost there?"

"Aye, that's my *Centaur*," he answered as proudly as any doting parent might over a favorite child. "The finest, fairest seventy-four in the entire fleet, and I won't hear anyone say otherwise."

"*Sànto cièlo,*" she said uneasily, inching closer to him as she stared up at the enormous dark shadow of the ship before them. "It looks a great deal larger from here in the water than it did from the beach."

He smiled. "As well she should, lass. A fighting ship of the line is like a floating fortress, a bit of King George's England wherever she goes."

The *Centaur* was such a pleasing and familiar sight to him that it took considerable effort to try to imagine it afresh through Francesca's eyes. To be sure, by dark she did look more formidable, her sleek painted sides curving upward from the water like a glistening dark wall thirty feet high. The sails were still furled, the spars and masts like leafless trees rising into the night sky. The only light came from the lanterns at the stern and over the binnacle, and from the wardroom's windows and from Edward's own cabin, the silhouettes of the men on watch faintly visible along the rail.

At least in this ostensibly friendly port, the most obvious signs of the *Centaur*'s bellicose nature were hidden, with the double rows of gun ports closed. Considering Francesca's earlier response to a single measly pistol, this was likely for the best; Edward wasn't sure she'd have agreed to come aboard if she'd had to pass the muzzles of thirty-seven long guns on the starboard side alone. He'd leave it for her to discover later that even he shared his cabin with a pair of great guns, housed and lashed in their red-painted carriages to the deck until they were needed for battle.

"True, the *Centaur*'s a fighting ship," he continued, "but she's also home to six-hundred and fifty-seven men and boys. And now, with you, to one lady as well."

"Six-hundred and fifty-seven men and boys," she echoed faintly. "And me."

"You will do fine," he said confidently. The closer they came to the ship, the more easily he could picture her on board with him, a graceful new addition to his life. "You'll become the queen of us all in no time."

Deftly the oarsmen maneuvered the boat alongside the ship, tipping their oars up in the air as the coxswain used the boat hook to pull them closer. The sea had grown more choppy, the blowing spray heavier, and the rising swells were lifting the boat up and dropping it down, then smacking it hard back and forth against the ship's side.

"However do you expect me to do this, Edward?" asked Francesca with despair as she stared up at the shallow notches carved into the ship's side for footholds. "I am no monkey, you know, to scurry and scramble from branch to branch! I cannot, I can *not!* Oh, Edward, if you can teach me to be brave, then do it now, for I am in the worst need of whatever courage you might have to spare!"

"I would never expect you to climb the side like a man," he said, scandalized that she'd even think such a notion even as his imagination supplied the wicked image of her climbing up the narrow footholds with her skirts fluttering high over her knees. "You'll go in the bos'n's chair, same as we've already arranged for the other ladies to follow this night."

As if on cue, the chair was swung down from the deck: Half trapeze, half-sling, a contraption designed to preserve the dignity of ladies while they were hauled from a boat up to the deck. One of the sailors shipped his oar and reached out to steady the chair for her.

"You see, Francesca, it's as safe as can be," said Edward, wishing the sailor's smile wasn't so openly worshipful. "You sit, you're lashed in tight, then up you go, easy and convenient. The Queen of Naples herself won't have any better."

Tentatively she touched the seat, muttering darkly to herself in Italian that for once Edward was thankful he couldn't understand.

"So I am not to be a monkey, but a parrot, sitting on my little perch." Her face beneath the drooping, damp hood was both miserable and determined. "You will go first, Edward? You promise you will be waiting there for me?"

"If that is what you wish, then aye, I will," he said gravely. He touched the front of his hat to her with a quick smile, and as the swell lifted the boat he seized the hanging rope guideline and climbed up the side to wait for her.

So Edward *was* a monkey, thought Francesca glumly as she watched him clamber to the deck and a shrill welcome of pipes, moving as easily and with as little thought as she climbed into her own bed. It wasn't enough that the wetter and more sodden with seawater he became, the happier he was. Now he'd leaped from a pitching boat to climb the slippery side of his wretched ship simply because she'd asked it, ignoring the obvious danger just to be obliging to *her*.

"Beggin' pardon, miss," said the sailor steadying the bos'n's chair, "but we can't wait no longer. Orders, miss, orders. You must go, miss, else come back t'shore with us."

She hugged herself beneath her cloak, staring at the narrow seat. To dangle so high in the chilly wind, with only black, icy water below—poor, plump Queen Maria Carolina, if this awaited her, too!

"Beggin' pardon, miss," said the sailor again, more insistently. "But Lord Cap'n's waiting, miss."

She took a deep breath, almost a sigh, then turned around in the rocking boat and let herself be tied into the chair, clutching at the sidelines for dear life.

"There now, miss, all steady an' safe," promised the sailor. "You'll fly up to th' deck like a proper Christmas angel, you will."

She nodded, which he interpreted as saying she was ready, and suddenly she was being hauled up into the air, the wind whipping past her face and her hood blowing back and her feet dangling as awkwardly as a puppet's. But instead of being terrified, she felt oddly exhilarated, as if she truly *were* flying, and when she gasped, it was with delight, not fear.

With the sky and sea blurring together in the darkness, all she could focus on were the lights of Naples, tiny fairy-bright pinpricks of candlelight in countless windows, the houses and churches and even the snubbed-off cone of Vesuvius reduced to indistinct shadows. Perhaps this was how she was meant to leave Naples, with this last, magical sight to remember instead of the ugliness and hatred that had haunted her this past fortnight, a memory to hold tight against the uncertainties of London.

"Handsomely now with the lady, handsomely!"

barked Edward as two sailors lowered her carefully to the deck, bringing her back to earth as well. "You are unharmed, lass?"

"Oh, Edward, of course I'm perfectly fine," she said breathlessly, twisting around to look back at the shore. "And I would not have missed this sight for all the riches in the world! *Bellissimo, bellessimo,* like a million stars! Have you ever, ever seen anything so lovely as this night?"

Absently he followed her gaze back to the shore for a moment before concern made him look back at her, rubbing her hands to warm them.

"What I'm seeing is those clouds and the foul weather they'll bring and the wind with it," he said, all practical, unromantic common sense. "If the harbor grows much rougher, your Neapolitan gentry will want to take their chances against the French instead of in an open boat."

"Permit me to welcome you to the *Centaur,* Your Grace," said another lieutenant, bowing elegantly low over his leg beside Edward. "We are honored to be your sanctuary in your time of trouble."

Edward snorted with exasperation. "Mr. Osborne. This is not the Contessa di San Pietro. She and her party are still ashore. This is Miss Robin, a most special personal guest of mine. Francesca, Mr. Osborne, my second lieutenant."

"Buona sera, Mr. Osborne," said Francesca, shoving back her wet hood so he'd see her smile, striving to be as agreeable as possible. "I am most honored to make your acquaintance, sir."

"Your—your servant, Miss Robin," stammered

Mr. Osborne, his practiced polish deserting him. "That is, ma'am, I—we—are still honored by your—"

"Mr. Osborne," interupted Edward testily. "Has Mr. Burdumy been summoned to my quarters?"

"Aye, aye, sir," answered Mr. Osborne. "He is, sir."

"Thank you, Mr. Osborne," said Edward. "Francesca, this way, if you please."

Edward took her by the arm, guiding her along the long deck and past more men trying appallingly hard to go about their duties and gawk at her at the same time. If the ship had seemed large from the water, it now seemed enormous, this deck as broad and clear as any avenue on land, albeit an avenue lined with cannons. He'd told her the *Centaur* was like a floating fortress and those huge guns were the proof, just as they were more proof of how vastly different his life was from hers.

No, from what hers *had* been. Once she married him, his life would become hers, cannons and all.

"Here now, mind your steps on the companionway," he said as he shepherded her down a steep flight of steps, lit only by a small brass lantern swinging back and forth on its gimbal mounting. "They're a hazard until you learn your way."

But the steps were not what was worrying her now. "I didn't tell him, Edward," she said urgently. "Your Mr. Osborne, I mean. I did exactly as you wished, and said nothing at all to him about marrying you."

"Better you should have," he said moodily. "Better the whole infernal fleet knows, so all their tongues can start clacking at once."

Abruptly she stopped on the bottom step. "First you scold me for telling Mr. Pye we are to wed," she protested, "and now you are saying you wish the entire fleet already knew of it, and I am confused, Edward, *most* confused!"

"And why the devil is that, Francesca?" he demanded, turning back toward her, their faces nearly level where she stood on the step. "Why should you be confused by any of this? The admiral was right. You saw Osborne, didn't you? All you did was smile at him and say some sort of meaningless pleasantry, and he was besotted and useless. Pye was, too, and I'll wager every last man on this ship will behave the same."

"But that is scarcely *my* fault!" she cried indignantly. "I am no strumpet, Edward, no trollop bent on seducing every man I meet! Just now you said yourself that all I'd done was smile!"

"Jesus, Francesca, that was enough—more than enough! Why else do you think you could sell so much rubbish to so many men? How in blazes am I going to keep any order at all among my officers and men with you about?"

She drew back, her mouth pinched tight. "Then you'd do better to put me in chains deep in your hold, where I'll cause no more mischief."

He groaned, and shook his head. "I am not blaming you, lass. Far from it. It's me that's the jealous ass, unable to see how the other men look at you, and it's—it's—oh, hell, why can't I explain it better? It's simply how you *are*, and I would never wish you otherwise."

He'd taken her hand again, and slowly, with great care, he began to work the yellow glove down her wrist and over her fingers.

"*Per favore*, Edward, whatever are—"

"Quiet now," he said in a rough whisper. "You mind your captain, eh?"

She did, surprised but fascinated, too, by how carefully his large hands moved along hers, focussing all his attention on removing her glove. When the damp leather clung to her chilly skin, he gently eased one finger free at a time, his own fingers warm and sure around hers.

"You wished me to admire the stars, or the candle-light, or whatever other infernal sight you'd spied on shore," he said as he tugged carefully at the leather, "yet all I could see was you. Only you, Francesca."

"No one has ever said such a thing to me," she whispered uncertainly. "Not and meant it."

He smiled, still concentrating on the glove. "Then we are even. I've never said such a thing to anyone, either. And I wouldn't have said it now if I hadn't meant it."

"But you don't know me," she protested weakly. "You don't know me at all."

"I know enough," he said, turning her hand in his so her wrist turned up. "I'll learn the rest."

He raised her hand and grazed his lips over the sensitive place on her upturned wrist, there where her blood raced straight to her heart, and she caught her breath with astonishment and wonder, her wicked thoughts racing back to the wanton scenes of the *Oculus*. What he was doing to her—why had no other man thought to do such a simple thing? So simple, and yet so complicated, more than a kiss, and far, far beyond anything she might have imagined.

"Sànto cièlo," she said weakly, her knees so unsteady they felt as if they'd buckle beneath her. "You—you must not do that, Edward. You—you promised."

"If you insist upon tormenting me, Francesca, then I must do the same to you." He glanced up at her, his eyes shaded, still keeping her hand firmly in his possession. "You said we should see if we suited. How else are we to judge?"

"Through conversation," she said with quick desperation, fighting against her own weakness as much as his. "By sharing interests and confidences about our pasts, our families, and—"

"No," he said sharply, linking his fingers into hers to draw her from the step. "We shall not speak of families."

"But you promised that—"

"I know what I promised, Francesca," he said, "and I know what you promised, too. Now come. I will not keep Mr. Burdumy waiting."

He pulled her from the step, his grip so tight that she'd no choice but to follow him down the narrow companionway. He didn't look back, and if he didn't offer more explanation, she didn't ask for any, either.

What in blazes was he doing? Edward had wanted to be gallant, noble, to do the most honorable thing he could by saving her the one way he could, even making that fool's agreement to win her. But there was nothing noble or gallant about how he was treating her now. Arrogant and jealous, overbearing and unable to think beyond what his cock was ordering him to do—hell, his brothers would be proud. He couldn't recall ever feeling more ashamed, more confused, or more aroused by a single woman, a swirling, torturous purgatory of his own making from which there was no honorable escape.

He ignored the guard at his cabin, shoving open the door himself so forcibly it cracked against the bulkhead. Mr. Burdumy was already waiting, along with Lieutenant Connor and Major Harris, the two swiftly recruited witnesses, and as he entered all three stared at him with a happy expectation suitable for a wedding, but absolutely no match for his present mood.

"Proceed, Mr. Burdumy," he said curtly without looking down at Francesca beside him.

Her bare hand where he'd peeled away her glove was icy in his own, her little fingers twisting into his to seek whatever small comfort he was too damned boorish to give. He knew this hastily arranged ceremony in his day cabin would not be the wedding of any girl's dreams. There were no flowers, no silk gown, no wedding cakes or fancy iced sweets, no well-wishing friends or teary-eyed parents. Instead of joyful music, the ship's timbers and rigging were creaking and groaning uneasily with the coming weather like unwelcome guests, and the deck rocked back and forth on a queasy swell. With the deadlights in place over the sweeping stern windows to protect the glass from the rising rough weather, and the only light coming from the whale-oil lamp swinging overhead, even Edward would admit it was a gloomy excuse for a bridal bower.

"The lady's not ill, my lord captain, is she?" asked Mr. Burdumy anxiously as he peered at Francesca's face, his chubby, chilblained fingers fidgeting with his prayer book. As a navy chaplain, his duties were much more given to reading the service for the dead after a battle than performing weddings. "No maidenly qualms, I trust?"

"None," said Edward with frosty conviction. She wasn't about to change her mind now, not with so much at stake.

Unless he'd gone too far peeling back her glove like that, breathing deep of her scent as he'd kissed and nipped at her wrist, teasing and testing them both in the name of that wretched promise . . .

Uneasily the chaplain cleared his throat and pursed his lips, a sure sign of trouble. Mr. Burdumy was the single man on board who did not always respect Edward's absolute rule as captain, the only one who regarded the Archbishop of Canterbury as a higher and more worthy authority than the Admiralty.

"I am most sorry, my lord captain," he asked hesitantly. "But might I ask the young lady's name?"

"You might ask *me,* signor," said Francesca swiftly, answering before Edward could, "and I shall answer: Francesca Maria Giovanna Robin."

"Ah," said the chaplain, his gaze shifting back to Edward as if Francesca hadn't spoken. "My lord captain, might I ask if the young lady is, ahem, English?"

"She is," said Edward firmly, more than enough

answer than such a question deserved. Yet Edward knew what Burdumy was truly asking, the same question that Admiral Nelson had asked, and scores of others would as well.

It wasn't simply a matter of Francesca's English father or her Neapolitan mother, but whether she was Anglican instead of Roman Catholic, whether she was a proper virtuous woman from a proper virtuous country instead of a slatternly product of immoral Naples—whether she was, in short, worthy of the enormous honor of marrying into one of the oldest, most noble families in England. They were protecting not only Edward and the rest of the Ramsdens, but also the purity of Britain herself.

And Edward wanted none of it.

He'd spent his entire life fighting to be accepted for who he *was*, not what he'd been born, and he didn't want that same standard turned against him again now. True, he'd decided to marry Francesca on an impulse—an honorable, gallant impulse, but an impulse nonetheless—but he'd given her his word that he'd be true to her, and that, for him, was more than enough. He would marry her, and as his wife he would stand beside her as her champion against all challengers.

Finally he looked down to her standing beside him, her shoulders squared, her hood tossed back, her jaw set, a rare mixture of innocence and determination, beauty and fierce passions and courage that was every bit a match for his own: *his* wife.

"Her father *was* English, aye," he continued firmly. "Though if her heritage is of no importance to me, Mr. Burdumy, then I wonder that it is to you. I trust you are not questioning either my word or my choice?"

"Oh, dear, no, my lord captain!" said the chaplain, the starched bands on his neckcloth quivering below his chin. "I should never presume—never! Marriage is a holy sacrament, and I only wished to be assured that, for the sake of your brother His Grace, everything is as it should be."

"It is, Mr. Burdumy," said Edward. "Except for you."

Quickly the chaplain snapped open his prayer book. "You would be so good, my lord captain, as to hold the lady's hand—just so, just so."

Just so, indeed. He wondered if she realized how much her hand revealed: the ink-stained fingertips, the knuckles roughened by the cold, her palms endearingly moist from nervousness, and the same want and need roiling through him.

He scarcely heard the ceremony, his responses automatic as he listened for hers, muted but sure. None of the witnesses would be able to report any hesitation, or undue eagerness, either, though the gossips would say what they pleased. At least the admiral would be satisfied, and for now his opinion was the only one that mattered.

"The ring, my lord," prompted the chaplain. "If you please, my lord, the bride's ring?"

Oh, hell, how had he forgotten that? Swiftly he looked down at his own hand, to the ring he always wore himself. It was more of a lucky talisman to him than ornament, a gold band engraved with dolphins and anchors that he'd had cast from the first Spanish *dólar* he'd received as prize money, back when he'd been a lieutenant. Since then he'd never taken it from his hand, but now, for her, he stripped it off.

"*Sànto cièlo,* I cannot take your ring!" she whispered, scandalized, looking up to him for the first time since Burdumy had begun the service. "It wouldn't be right, Edward, not—"

"Second thoughts at the last, Francesca?" he demanded, keeping his voice low so the others wouldn't overhear. "Are you the unworthy one, or am I?"

"Neither," she said fiercely, her eyes so dark they looked black, "or both. Or perhaps we simply deserve one another."

A captain and a mutineer: Oh, they deserved each other, all right. "Then you are not turning fickle?"

"Not fickle, Edward, nor cowardly, either!"

"And if I believed you were, I would never give this to you now," he said, sliding the ring on her finger and folding her hand closed to keep it from dropping off her finger. "Wear the ring, Francesca. I want the world to know that you are mine."

She gulped, a deep breath. "They already do, don't they?"

"The ones that don't will know soon enough," he answered, "and the rest don't matter. With this ring, Francesca, I thee wed. There. Another word or two from you, Mr. Burdumy, and the deed is done, is it not?"

Hurriedly the chaplain looked back down at his prayer book. "I, ahem, I now pronounce you man and wife. Those whom God hath joined, let no man put asunder."

Another word or two, yes, and the deed was most certainly done, and to his surprise Edward felt those same words settle upon him with a finality he hadn't expected. A glance at Francesca showed she felt the weight, too, her lovely, mobile face more solemn than he'd ever seen it before, her lips slightly parted. For a marriage born of purest convenience, they each were certainly taking its consequences seriously, the silence between them stretching awkwardly, painfully long. Beyond duty, necessity, and the French to the north, perhaps they genuinely *did* deserve one another after all.

"Well done, Captain, well done!" boomed Major Harris, unaware that there was any discomfort to the silence. "Best wishes to you and your bonny lady-wife!"

But Mr. Burdumy was not quite finished. "It is, my lord captain," he said primly, "at this time customary for the groom to kiss his bride."

Blast, Edward *knew* that, without having some whey-faced cleric tell him so, and he barely bit back the retort that would have told Burdumy so. Instead he reached out to slip his hand into the rich silk of Francesca's hair and turned her face and her mouth up toward his and before she could stop him, he was kissing her, and it wasn't the dutiful, done-for-show kiss Burdumy suggested, either.

But then her lips were more yielding than he'd expected, too, lush and velvety and warm with a different promise altogether from the ones they'd just made. He circled his arm around her waist to draw her closer, gently crushing the softness of breasts against his chest.

He kissed her long and hard, her startled hands pressed flat against his chest in wordless bewilderment. He liked that, for it meant he was the first man to draw this response from her, the first to kiss her with such urgency. He could taste her surprise in the way she fluttered beneath him, yet he could also tell the exact moment when that surprise gave way to eagerness and to pleasure all her own, when her lips began to respond to his, when the resistance in her body lessened and her hands curled round his back, and when, most of all, he realized he'd forgotten everything and everyone else except the woman in his arms.

Finally he broke away, his heart thundering and his blood racing as if he'd rowed the longboat from the shore himself. With this kiss he'd meant to demonstrate to her exactly who was the captain, but damnation, now he wasn't nearly as sure himself.

Not that she'd any clearer sense of what had happened between them, either. Her expression was so confused she seemed almost dazed, her eyes heavy-lidded and her lips still parted and wet from his, her hair mussed and her cheeks flushed and all so thoroughly, infinitely desirable he nearly groaned aloud.

"Edward, *mio inglése leone*," she whispered, her voice ragged, daring, as she reached up to touch her fingertips lightly to her lips. "Who would have guessed my English lion would roar with such passion?"

"Nor you, lass," he said hoarsely, covering her fingers with his own. "Perhaps we shall suit after all, eh?"

"My lord captain," sputtered the forgotten chaplain, his jowls trembling with righteousness as he tucked his prayer book beneath his arm. "When I asked you, my lord, to seal your sacred troth with a kiss, I did not realize I'd be witnessing such a—a—"

"Thank you, Mr. Burdumy," said Edward, unwilling for even a moment to look away from Francesca, from her mouth, red, ripe, waiting, temptation incarnate. "Harris, Connor, you, too. Now go. *Go.*"

The cabin door opened, closed, to mark that they were alone, and Edward reached for her again.

"We shouldn't, Edward," said Francesca, still whispering in the hushed, heady voice of lovers as his arm slipped inside her green cloak and around her waist. "You—you promised."

"So did you," he countered. He could hear the change in her breathing, the little catches of urgency that mirrored his own. "But that's not what you want, is it?"

"You tempt me, Edward," she whispered again, confessing even as she rested her hands on his shoulders, "and you shouldn't. *We* shouldn't."

"Why, sweetheart?" Beneath her gown he could feel that she wore no stays, no whalebone or buckram to mask her shape, and he spread his fingers to caress as much of the lush, rounded curves of her hips and bottom.

"Because," she murmured, no answer at all. "I— I'm not ready, that is all."

"I'll promise not to come into your body, Francesca," he said, feeling her move restlessly against the hard proof of his arousal. Perhaps her skittishness was because she feared childbirth; many women did, and he'd only to recall his own mother's death to understand why. "I can see to it that you don't get with child."

She started visibly. "That's not the only reason."

"Then there are other ways we can pleasure one another, sweetheart, other—"

"I know," she breathed, her eyes already closed as she reached up to kiss him. "I *know.*"

For an instant his mind wrestled with that—how the devil had she learned that knowledge, anyway, and with whom?—until he remembered the *Oculus,* and her being Neapolitan instead of English, and then he stopped thinking altogether as she kissed him, her mouth hot and open to him and her clever little tongue finding his just as his hand discovered her breast, her nipple already a hard little pebble of excitement through the silk of her gown.

"Captain Lord Ramsden, sir?" came the man's shout from the other side of the door. "My lord, sir, are you within, sir?"

She flew away from him, her eyes wide, frantically tucking in stray hairpins and smoothing her gown to make herself presentable. For the first time since he'd become an officer, Edward realized he had forgotten his orders, his duty, even that constant, hovering nightmare-memory of Aboukir Bay, and Francesca was the reason. If he'd needed any more proof that he hadn't married her from gallantry alone, then here it was, and he swore long and savagely at himself and the cruelty of ill timing.

"Who the devil is there?" he roared. "Enter, man, enter!"

"Turner, sir," said the hapless midshipman who now opened cabin's door. "Mr. Osborne sends his compliments, sir, and word that the first boat with the Neapolitan gentry's alongside."

"The damned whoreson Neapolitan gentry," he muttered furiously. Of course they were here; that had been the whole blasted *point* of this evening's exercises, hadn't it? "My compliments to Mr. Osborne, Mr. Turner, and tell him I shall join him on the deck directly."

The young man nodded and fled, relieved at no longer having to see neither the obvious bulge in the front of his captain's trousers nor the disarray of his captain's new wife. At another time Edward might have laughed, but not now. Now his temper was so black, so frustrated, that he doubted he'd ever bloody well laugh again.

"I'm sorry, *càro mio*," she said softly, more regret than apology, and sorrowful enough that he nearly began swearing again.

"So am I, sweetheart," he said, not trusting himself to touch her the way he wanted to. He could swear every promise in the world, and to his remorse he knew she'd make him forget them all. "You asked me to wait, and I couldn't begin to—"

"Oh, Edward, hush," she said, her beautiful, tempting mouth twisting so he was afraid she'd begin to weep. "It's not that you kissed me, or that I kissed you. I'm sorry that I'm not the wife a fine English gentleman like you should have."

"That's not true, Francesca," he said sharply, "and I never want to hear you say it again, mind? I married you because I wanted to. Because I wanted *you.*"

"Sànto cièlo." She tried to smile, hugging her arms to herself. "What is it that you English say? You are *daft.*"

"Aye, perhaps I am." He tried to smile, too, and failed just as miserably. Tonight he'd sleep apart from her in the day cabin, the only way he'd have any chance of keeping his promise to her to wait until she was ready. The decision had to come from her, else he'd never forgive himself. "I'll return as soon as I can, but now I must go welcome these infernal people on board."

She swallowed hard, and gave her head a brisk little shake. "Then I shall come with you."

"No, lass," he said firmly, though it pleased him that she'd want his company so badly. "You'll be much better off here in my cabin, out of the blow."

"La, do you really think me such a selfish coward as that?" Resolutely she began to fasten the clasp on her cloak. "You need my help, *caro.*"

He frowned, his mind already halfway to all the problems he'd find waiting on the deck. "If you wish to be truly useful, you'll stay here where I'll know you'll be safe."

"Parla italiano?" she asked. "Do you?"

She was asking if he spoke Italian, and that simple question taxed the limit of his knowledge of the language—which, of course, Francesca knew perfectly well. His frown deepened, and he began to realize how troublesome that vow of obedience was going to be for a woman like Francesca, and, for that matter, for him as well.

"King Ferdinando's court does not pride itself on its learning," she continued, mistaking his silence for encouragement, "and the only accomplishments that are prized at the Palazzo Reale are those involving hunting, drinking, or whoring."

"Then it's no different from every other wretched court in the world," he said, thinking of how his two oldest brothers were such particular favorites of the Prince of Wales for their expertise in exactly these same areas.

"Doubtless so," she said evenly, coming closer. "I will be astounded, *mio càro*, if a single lady or gentleman among these noble passengers knows more than a dozen words of English. How will you address them, eh? How will you tell them where to go or what to do, or warn them against tumbling over the side and into the sea?"

Edward drew in his breath in a long, sorrowful whistle. She was right, blast it. She was being as logical as she was lovely, and she was *right*.

Ever since the admiral had decided to help the king and his court to flee, Edward had been worrying over this very point. He'd suffered through other similar evacuations, and seen how quickly the discipline and morale of good ships disintegrated beneath a jabbering onslaught of refugees, servants, and baggage, foreign arrogance and endless misunderstandings. Everything and everyone that was rational and functional would be English, and everyone that was shrieking with terror and imploring the heavens and cursing the English devils would be Neapolitan. Having a trustworthy interpreter on board the *Centaur* could be invaluable for them all.

But to have the interpreter be his new wife—he wasn't nearly as certain about that.

"This will be a delicate diplomatic situation, Francesca," he began. "The *Centaur* represents King George, and any misspoken word could have grave political repercussions."

She wrinkled her nose and cocked one brow, as if catching a whiff of some noisome odor. "La, la, not *repercussions!* Oh, Edward, please don't be so pompous, not alone with me."

"I am not being pompous," he said stubbornly. "I am considering the best interests of my ship, my crew, and my country."

"Why not take the burden of all the rest of Christendom upon your broad shoulders, too, just to be sure you will be made a saint?" The deck was pitching and rocking with the rising wind, and when she swayed into him, she stayed there, resting against his chest in a most distracting fashion. "Whoever your grand passengers are, they most certainly will be cold and wet and frightened. You *will* need me, Edward, and they will, too. Recall how I have earned my living, and then tell me again how I know nothing of diplomacy."

He grumbled wordlessly, and wished she'd temper this habit of hers of being so damnably astute about him. He could perhaps make more of an argument if she weren't leaning against him like this so her musky, womanly scent clouded his wits, but she was, and he couldn't.

"Besides, *càro*," she said softly, "I do want to be with you."

Hell, how could he possibly leave her behind after a confession like that? Already he could hear a babble of voices and confusion on the deck overhead, and with a sigh of resignation, he held out his arm to lead her from the cabin and up the steps. "You must be sure to express every word as I say it, without adding any other meanings. You must be mindful that you represent only the best interests of England, and not Naples."

She nodded, her smile unexpectedly wistful. "You've given me so much, Edward, and all I've done is take. I'd be most selfish if I didn't help you in return while we are together."

While we are together: Francesca couldn't make it any more clear than that, could she? Yet from the confident way Edward smiled back at her, she realized miserably he didn't understand, and didn't want to, either.

Oh, dear God, what was she to do? She'd agreed to marry him because she'd had no other way to save herself, a decision inspired by desperation and cold, hard reason, and one she planned to unmake as soon as she reached London. In London, she would find her uncle, show her father's artworks and antiquities, and never paint another forgery again. She'd make an honest new start of her life, and finally honor her promise to Papa to keep clear of men and love for the sake of her art.

But her reason hadn't counted on her heart, that seat of all foolishness. Even as she'd stood at Edward's side before the chaplain, she'd believed that she could make her vows and promises without intending to keep them. For her, truth had always had a certain convenient flexibility to it, and she hadn't expected that to be otherwise now.

And yet, with Edward, it had. She couldn't tell whether the words themselves had humbled her, or whether it had been the honorable conviction of the tall, solemn man as he'd pledged himself to her that had spurred her wayward conscience. Edward deserved more than the habitual mask of casual, meaningless flirtation that had served her so well in her trade. She cared for him too much for that, and she couldn't deny it any longer, not even to herself. She still didn't believe in the folly of love, but friendship, respect, loyalty, affection—with Edward these all seemed possible for the first time in her life.

And desire. Oh, yes, Edward was teaching her that, too, and just the memory of that kiss made her cheeks flush and her blood smolder. How could she be so deliciously weak with him, and not care a fig for the consequences? Why had he been the one to remember that this sort of play could lead to a babe in her belly, and the end to every one of her dreams as an artist? But one kiss, and Edward had made her feel things she'd never dreamed, and made her long for more than she'd realized existed. One kiss from him, and her body began to comprehend the wanton scenes in the *Oculus* in a way that her head never had. One kiss, and she forgot London, forgot her painting and her treasured independence, forgot everything but the man holding her, stroking her, kissing her, loving her.

The man that, God forgive her, she'd wed only with the intention of abandoning.

7

A night, a day, and another night.

That was how much time passed before the storm finally blew itself out. A night, a day, and another night in which Edward had allowed himself to come below here to his cabin only for a gulped mug of cold coffee and a leg of chicken eaten without the bother of a plate, a change of wet clothes for dry ones that would, as soon as he returned to the deck, become soaked as well. He'd snatched sleep when he could, tumbling exhausted into his cot for an hour at the most before another call to all hands would rouse him to join the others to fight the driving sheets of wind and spray and seas that ran high as church spires. Unlike most captains of his rank and experience, he believed in sharing his men's battles and sufferings as much as their victories, and this rare winter storm in the warm waters of the Tyrrhenian Sea was no exception.

No exception, that is, beyond that it meant he'd spent his wedding night on the quarterdeck with the rain streaming down his back, while his bride—well, he wasn't precisely sure where Francesca had spent their wedding night. He hadn't seen her since that first day, when she'd gone to help settle the Neapolitans in their quarters, and though he'd heard his men and officers call the new Lady Edward a saint—a veritable angel of sweetness and noble compassion—he would have infinitely preferred to have seen her himself, and have a bit of that sweetness lavished on him.

As soon as the wind had settled this morning, he'd sent word around the ship for her to join him in his cabin, and his weary feet quickened down the steps as he thought of her waiting there for him now. But when he entered, his day cabin was empty, except for his manservant.

"I thought I'd sent for my wife, Peart," grumbled Edward as he let the servant peel away his wet coat. "I expected her to be waiting."

"Her Ladyship is here, my lord captain," said Peart, a taciturn Irishman on the best of days. "She waits within your sleeping cabin."

His sleeping cabin: now that *was* an improvement, if an unexpected one, and a score of provocative possibilities instantly made him forget his weariness. How could it not? That kiss they'd shared had seared into his memory and burned there still, fresh and hot. Perhaps it had done that for her, too, enough that she was ready to be his wife in more than name alone after all.

Aye, aye, that would be best, and the one sure way he could have both his honor and Francesca, the only way he could still prove himself to be better than his wastrel brothers. . . .

"Thank you, Peart," he said, pulling his damp shirt over his head and using it to wipe his face before he tossed it back. He combed his fingers haphazardly through his hair to smooth it back from his forehead, and in two long strides he'd crossed the deck to the other cabin's door. She might be waiting for him, but by God, he wouldn't make her wait a moment longer, and without bothering to knock, he eagerly pushed the door open.

And there she was, sound asleep, but not how or where or even when he'd expected to find her. She lay curled in one of the leather armchairs instead of his cot, her head pillowed on her arm and her feet propped on the carriage of the great gun with one of his dark blue undress-coats draped around her legs—doubtless arranged by the ever-vigilant Peart.

Her cheeks were pale, her eyes ringed with gray shadows of weariness, and she'd tied a grimy sailcloth apron over her gown and a red sailor's handkerchief around her hair. Only the gold hoops in her ears were as he remembered, those and his ring on her finger, the back wrapped with thread to keep it from sliding from her finger.

It was curiously intimate, having her here alone with him in a place he'd never shared with anyone else, and for several minutes he simply watched her sleep, her lips parted and the swell of her breasts gently rising and falling beneath her bodice. He never slept so soundly himself. He'd seen and survived too much for that. But finding her here brought him a rare sense of peace after the howling chaos of the storm, and, marveling, he realized that this, too, was part of being wed.

What filled her dreams, he wondered, *what made her rest so complete? Was it the past or the future, the world she'd left behind, or the heady possibilities of the unknown?*

And would she ever come to dream of him?

She sighed in her sleep and shifted in the chair, just enough that the coat slipped from her legs to the deck. Instantly he bent to retrieve it, tucking it around her legs to keep out the chill.

And with a start, she woke.

"Who is there?" she asked groggily, pushing herself more upright in the chair. "Ah, *mio càro,* it's you."

"It had better be," he said, "considering this is my cabin."

"Your own dear cabin," she mused in a sleepy singsong, clearly only half awake. "My lion's private little lair."

"After a fashion, aye." He'd missed hearing her little pet names for him, an endearing liberty he'd never granted to anyone else. "How are you, lass?"

"Perfectly well, *grazie.*" She patted the coat over her lap, and let her gaze slip lower. "But if I'd known you were so terribly short of clothing, Edward, I would never have gone borrowing."

Belatedly he realized that in his eagerness to see her, he hadn't bothered to put on a dry shirt or stockings, and now stood before her in nothing more than a pair of still-damp breeches hanging precariously low upon his hips. He wasn't shy about his body—he was a well-made man, strong and lean, and besides, life in the navy had a way of destroying whatever modesty a gentleman might have—and he didn't move to cover himself now.

"I didn't want to keep you waiting," he said evenly, though that only explained the most honorable of his expectations. "If I'd stopped to let Peart dress me properly, you'd be waiting still."

She smiled and yawned, her eyes heavy-lidded, amused, and not at all shocked, and he thought of how pleasurable it would be to find her sleepy face in the morning on the pillow beside his.

"Then I shall be flattered," she said. "Few husbands would be so assiduous, especially on such a chilly morn. But is this how you hope to woo me, my lord, astounding me with your male beauty?"

He smiled wryly, chagrined that his interest had been so transparent. " 'Tis a pity I'm not a rare Indian peacock, ma'am, for I fear my poor male beauty must always pale before yours."

"That's more poppycock than peacock, I'd say," she scoffed. "Considering how bedraggled and sorry I must seem, with nary an unbroken plume to my name or my head."

"Bedraggled plumes that were most honorably won," he countered, turning serious. "I've heard all you've done for that sorrowful lot of passengers we're carrying, and not just by translating what I say, either."

She shrugged. "I did what needed doing, Captain Ramsden, that was all, and it kept me too busy to be either frightened or seasick, like everyone else."

"Don't be so modest, lass," he said firmly. He'd never expected this side of her, not from the giddy creature he'd first met in her studio, and he wanted to give her the credit she deserved. "You did far more than that. Fetching them drink from the galley, settling squabbles, nursing the ill, sorting out belongings—you've eased their fears with your kindness, even if they don't know enough to thank you for it."

"They can't," she said with resignation. "They're nobles, helpless as babes."

"Helpless as fools from Bedlam," he growled with disgust. "Do you know why we were so late to sail? His Majesty King Ferdinando refused to leave until his precious pack of hunting dogs were brought aboard the *Vanguard!* Seventy blasted dogs were his greatest concern, with Napoleon hot upon his heels!"

Francesca shook her head and clucked her tongue to commiserate. "I warned you, Edward. They've been raised to believe the world will always oblige them, and it usually does."

"And thus I was raised as well, lass," he said firmly, "yet I know enough to thank you for what you've done."

Her smile glowed with such unabashed pleasure at his compliment that he wished he could give her fifty more.

"But you are different, *càro mio*," she said softly. "You must know—oh, Edward, the children!"

"The children?" he repeated, mystified, as she threw aside her makeshift coverlet and hurried across the deck to his cot.

"Barbaruccia and Caterina," she explained in a

low whisper, carefully peeking inside the embroidered curtains of the cot. "The daughters of the Marchese d'Arienzani. Surely you remember them?"

He nodded dutifully, though he'd no memory of any children being attached to the Marchese's party, let alone these particular little girls. At the time he'd been far more concerned with getting the *Centaur* clear of the bay in the storm and keeping in sight of the rest of the ships in their convoy.

But Francesca had remembered, and as she bent over the sleeping children, he certainly could understand why his men were calling her an angel.

"Poor little creatures," crooned Francesca, reaching out to brush a wayward curl from the forehead of one of the sleeping children. "You cannot imagine how pitifully ill they both were, retching and heaving so much that all their mother could do was pray to heaven for their innocent souls. It would have broken your heart to see how they suffered, Edward."

What broke Edward's heart was seeing two recently retching little girls asleep in his cot, their golden blond heads resting on his favorite down-filled pillows, where they could very well waken and retch again.

"Surely they'd be better in their own quarters, wouldn't they?" he asked cautiously, not wishing to disturb either the children or Francesca. "With their mother and their nurse?"

"*Sànto cièlo,* but they are useless—useless!" she sniffed. "Even while she was retching herself, the marchesa was much more concerned with guarding her jewel chests from the thieving English sailors than with tending her own daughters."

Edward's expression turned black. "My men are not thieves, Francesca."

"*I* know that, Edward, and so I told the marchese and marchesa, not that they'd believe me," said Francesca. "But that is why I brought the girls here, where they wouldn't have to hear their dreadful parents wailing and cursing. And when I saw this clever swinging cradle you'd had contrived for them, why, I put them to bed directly, and we all fell fast asleep."

"Francesca, lass," he began, unable to be quite as selfless as she. "Francesca. This is not a cleverly contrived cradle for seasick brats. This is my own personal cot, where I had hoped to rest myself."

"Oooh." Her eyes widened, and she looked at the cot with new interest. Her mistake wasn't unusual. While most landsmen had heard of common sailors' net hammocks slung from the beams between decks, few had seen the counterparts for the senior officers, tucked away in their private cabins.

Edward's cot was typical, a high-sided box frame with a featherbed that was suspended from hooks in the beams overhead, designed to swing gently with the motion of the sea. Linen curtains, brightly embroidered with swirling flowers, draped down on either side like a tent to keep out the drafts, the same as they would on a landlocked bedstead. A cot also had the extra advantage of being quickly dismantled and stowed away in the hold when the ship cleared for action, and then a gun crew would come take charge of the great black gun in the corner.

Francesca ran her fingers along the edge of the cot's polished mahogany frame, a sensuous little caress that put Edward to mind of things better left unthought, especially with the girls as innocent chaperones.

"*Veraménte,* but it *is* a most curious furnishing, and a large one, too," she murmured, glancing impishly across the sleeping girls at him. Gently she gave the cot a push to set it rocking toward him. "Though you say it is for you alone, I would guess it's quite large enough for two, Edward, isn't it?"

He nearly choked at that. Damnation, this wasn't fair. How could she be as angelic as any Madonna with those two little girls one moment, then be teasing him the next as if she were the greatest coquette in the Mediterranean?

"I'm a large man, Francesca," he said as evenly as he could. "I need a large cot."

"*Naturalmente.*" She grinned wickedly, and gave the cot another gentle push. "Back and forth, back and forth. Do you never lie here at night and consider the possibilities?"

Of course he had. He was a Ramsden; he couldn't deny that, no matter how much he resolved to the contrary. And there was nothing like an exclusively male ship to make a man think more of women, and sailors from the lowest powder monkey to the admiral himself dreamed endlessly of beautiful and accommodating females of every sort and in every position.

But now he thought only of one woman, and that woman was his wife.

"How my papa would have loved such a contrivance!" she mused. "If only he'd seen this flying bedstead of yours, I do believe there would have been a sea captain and his cot among the figures in the *Oculus*, whether it was proper for ancient times or not."

And with that, Edward's beleaguered patience snapped.

"Enough," he said sharply, stepping around the cot to seize her hand. "Come."

Startled, she tried to wriggle free. " 'Come'? *Come?* You would order me about so curtly, like a wayward pet? I am not your dog, Edward!"

"No, not my dog," he said grimly as he pulled her after him, "but damnation, you are my wife."

He threw open the door to where Peart was standing, waiting in perfect impassive readiness with Edward's red kerseymere dressing gown in his hands, the way he must have been stationed for the last half hour.

"Watch over the two young ladies, Peart," he said as he snatched the offered dressing gown from the servant's hands. "If they cry, send for their nursemaid directly, and God help you if they foul my cot."

Peart bowed, unfazed. "Very well, my lord. The galley fires have been relit, my lord. Would you and her ladyship be requiring a hot breakfast?"

"We shall not," said Edward, anger clipping each word with uncharacteristic precision. "What we require is to be undisturbed."

With the dressing gown fluttering behind him like a scarlet banner, Edward stormed into the great cabin with Francesca in tow. He flipped the latch closed, making sure they would be alone, and released her hand.

"You may sit wherever you please, my lady," he said as he thrust his arms into the sleeves of his dressing gown, "or you may stand, or you may dance a jig for all I care, but we *will* talk."

"Meaning that you will talk, and I shall listen," said Francesca defensively as he began pacing back and forth before her. "Meaning that you wish me to be as meek and obedient as that pet dog."

"If that is what *you* wish, my lady," said Edward with the same razor-sharp edge to his voice, "then that is how it shall be."

Francesca backed away, her arms crossed over her chest so he wouldn't be able to see how her hands shook. She didn't sit. As long as she kept standing, then somehow she felt as if she were still his equal, his friend, his wife, and not the inferior that he suddenly seemed to wish her to be. This was the first time she'd seen Edward's great cabin, the largest and most imposing space on board the *Centaur,* designed as much to glorify all England as well as the captain who called it home.

The long sweep of windows that ran the length of the stern were covered now with the deadlights to protect the glass in the storm, but the rest was more than enough to awe her: the long mahogany table with the dozen chairs, the brass lanterns and gimbals polished to shine like gold, the bull's-eye looking glasses in gilt frames and the carved sage-green paneling that would grace the finest London gentlemen's club. She supposed by rights the great cabin now belonged to her as well—at least to Lady Edward—but instead it seemed like the purest extension of Edward Ramsden himself, a formal, chilly place with no welcome for her.

Much, it seemed, like his heart was today.

"Am I to return to addressing you as my lord captain?" she asked, her voice brittle. What had become of the warm camaraderie they'd been sharing not a quarter hour past? What had she said or done to make everything disintegrate so suddenly? "Have I become too familiar? Too common?"

She saw a tiny muscle in his jaw flicker and tense. *"Familiar* is not the word I would choose, though the ones that are more apt are not words I should ever say to my lady wife."

"Perhaps you should, and be done with it, and done with me as well," she said, desperation making her dare him in a way that she knew wasn't wise. She had scarcely slept in two nights, and her nerves and emotions were frayed close to breaking. "I warned you we wouldn't suit, Edward, yet you would not listen."

"You are still my wife," he insisted, pulling the front of his dressing gown together. "For better or for worse, Francesca. Because I gave my word, you are mine. I thought I'd made that abundantly clear by now."

Sadly she watched him whip the sash of the dressing gown around his waist, closing it over his bare chest. He was a handsome man, the muscles of his chest as well-defined as a Roman warrior's and a pleasure to see, but that was not the main reason she'd wished he'd left the dressing gown undone. Earlier he had felt comfortable enough with her not to bother with such niceties, to forget his English propriety and include her into a private life that did not always include a uniform.

"Do not do that on my account, *càro mio*," she said softly. "If you are cold, then that is one thing, but otherwise, please, do not—"

"Damnation, Francesca, this isn't supposed to be a bloody *challenge!*" he exploded, stopping his pacing to stand directly in front of her. "What more do you want from me? Wasn't my word enough? What devil has sent you into my life to torment me?"

"What devil?" she asked, incredulous. *"Maledizione,* Edward, if you believe that, then—"

"Then tell me what else I am to believe!" he demanded. "I agreed not to bed you, not to touch you, until you were ready."

"And you haven't," she said, more wistfully than she realized. "Except for that one kiss when we were wed."

"My God, that one kiss," he said with genuine anguish. "Do you know how much that one kiss has haunted me these last days? The wind howled in my ears and the rain and sea dashed in my face, yet all I could think of was that one kiss."

"Oh, Edward," she said breathlessly, reaching her hand out toward him. "How very dear and sweet—*carissimo!*—of you!"

But he lurched backward, away from her touch. "Not dear, not sweet, not how I've lusted after you. And when you describe the wicked acts in those damned paintings of your father's—"

"The *Oculus?*" she asked in disbelief. *"That* unsettles you? The *Oculus* is simply a part of my livelihood, as mundane to me as a hammer and anvil would be to a blacksmith's daughter."

"They *were* your livelihood," he said firmly. "They're not any longer, and a good thing, too. Thank God they were left behind in your studio. Now you can look to me for support, and not that pandering rubbish."

She twisted her mouth and frowned. Better he didn't know that the *Oculus* had escaped Napoleon and the mob, too, and was now bound for London.

"But my father's paintings aren't all of this, *càro mio,* are they?" she asked gently, taking a step toward him. "There in the other cabin—I thought we were doing so well together."

"Oh, aye, *too* well," he said heavily, looking down at the deck and shaking his head with despair. "You tempt me, Francesca, worse than any siren. I cannot explain it any better than that. I have vowed to you to behave like a man of honor, a gentleman, yet all I want is to ravish you like the most dissolute rakehell in London."

Francesca flushed, not from shame or embarrassment, but from confusion. Many foolish young English gentlemen on their tour had professed great love and desire for her, none of which she'd listened to with any seriousness. But Edward was different, a grown man of the world, and uneasily she wondered if there were something about herself—something she'd inherited from her own rather dissolute father, along with his straight nose, his laugh, and his talent for painting—that made men think of her this way.

"You must not claim all the fault for yourself, Edward," she suggested hesitantly. "You are a wickedly handsome man, and you—you tempt me as well."

"Not the same way," he countered moodily. "You're a passionate woman, aye, but women are different. You do not have the same base instincts that can haunt a man."

"But is that so very wrong? Surely most gentlemen must feel the same intense passions toward a woman at least once in their lives."

"No." He turned abruptly, resting his palms flat on the long table with his back toward her. "I should have told you earlier, Francesca, before we were wed. My fine, noble family is as rotten as a barrel of last year's apples. I pray you'll never be cursed to meet my brothers, drunkards and gamblers who cannot keep count of the number of whores they've paraded through their beds, same as our father was before them."

"You don't have to—"

"No, Francesca, you must hear this," he said, and took a deep breath, clearly warring with himself. "You *must.* As long as I can remember, I have striven to be different from them, to set myself apart by being more honorable, and yet here when I am truly tested, I find I'm not one damned bit better—not one!"

"Oh, Edward, don't," she cried softly. She'd listened as he'd asked, and heard far more than he'd said, and when she looked at the broad back that still wasn't strong enough to carry all his guilt and sorrows alone, her heart wept with the suffering he felt. "*Sànto cièlo,* you are the best, most honorable gentleman I have ever met!"

Before he could answer or rebuff her again, she came behind him and circled her arms around his waist, pressing her cheek to his back. She knew how much solace a touch could bring because they'd been so rare in her own motherless life. His back in the kerseymere dressing gown was warm beneath her cheek, which didn't surprise her, but holding him this way was as comforting to her as she wished it to be to him, which surprised her very much.

"You were right to keep apart from me in the beginning, lass," he said with a groan. "Haven't you been listening to anything I've said?"

"I have, *càro mio,*" she said, her fingers spreading on their own to feel the sleek, hard muscles at his waist beneath the kerseymere, feel the way he'd sucked in his breath so sharply at her touch. That surprised her, too; he was vastly different to embrace than her father had been. "And you are still the best and bravest gentleman I know."

He covered her hands with his own, lifting them from his body. "You don't know what you're doing, Francesca."

"Oh, yes, I do, Edward," she said, twisting around to face him as if taking steps in an elaborate dance, sliding between his body and the edge of the table. "I am trying to convince you that you are not nearly so bad a man as you believe."

She *was* tempting fate by tempting him like this. She wasn't so great a fool as to ignore the danger, but for now she cared more about easing his unhappiness than holding exactly to their agreement. Slowly she brought his hand to her lips and kissed it, teasing his wrist with the edge of her teeth the same way as he'd kissed hers that first night, and looked up through her lashes to see his reaction.

It was an admirable reaction, too, well worth watching. His captain's reserve dissolved and the hard, stubbled planes of his jaw—unshaven since the storm had begun—relaxed. His eyes filled with wonder and pleasure, and something darker, rougher, more excitingly male.

"Ah, lass, you've a warm nature," he said gruffly, his breath quickening as he turned his hand to cup her cheek, caressing the side of her throat with his thumb.

"Warm, and passionate, too," she said, turning her head to rub against his thumb like a little cat. "You said so yourself."

"That I did," he growled. "But I won't be burned by you, lass, even on this cold December day."

"Not burned, *leone mio*, no, no," she said, again echoing his gesture by touching her palm to his rough cheek, cradling his jaw as she threaded her fingers into his hair. "But you do need warming, *càro*. You need the merry sun of my Napoli to chase away that English chill from your soul."

She wasn't sure if she kissed him then, or if he was the one who kissed her first, but when their lips did meet it seemed the most natural, the most perfect thing in the world. This time, she wasn't startled; this time she knew what to expect, what to anticipate, what to *do*.

Eagerly she answered his kiss, slanting her lips to accommodate his. Letting him coax hers apart, she relished the exciting sensation of having his tongue play against hers, the feel and the taste of him. She'd teased him about needing to warm his proper English reserve, but there was nothing cold about how he kissed her, or the desire she felt simmering between them, the same as it had the first time he'd kissed her at their wedding.

But while she'd thought she known what to expect, she soon learned that, however passionate, that wedding kiss had been only the beginning. He had more to offer her, and much, much more for them to claim together. Emotions and weariness and denial, too, had worn away at their promise to wait to a degree that she hadn't realized until she felt his hand upon her hip, his fingers spread to caress her as he lifted her easily onto the edge of the table. She felt him tugging the front of her bodice down and his hand slipping inside her shift to the bare skin beneath. She wriggled, weakly trying to protest more because she knew she should than from any real wish for him to stop.

How could she, when what he was doing was building such a delicious tension in her body? With surprising gentleness, he'd begun by tracing little circles around her nipple with his fingertips, just enough to make her flesh tighten and ache, and when—at last, at *last!*—he found the rosy nub itself, squeezing and teasing and tormenting it between his callused thumb and forefinger until all she could do was arch beneath him and whisper sweet, urgent nonsense in

Italian into his ear, words and promises she'd never dare venture in English.

"Sweet, sweet," he murmured, feathering hot kisses along her jaw and throat, his unshaven jaw teasing rough against her skin. "Do you know how much I want you, lass? Do you know?"

"Oh, yes, *càro mio*," she whispered, her fingers pressing into the hard muscles of his shoulders beneath the soft red kerseymere. "I know because I want you more, my brave English lion, *coraggioso, coraggioso!*"

The rumbling sound he made deep in his chest could indeed have been a great cat's muted roar, or simply a sound of purely male possession, marking her as his. She wasn't sure and she didn't care, not after he shifted lower to find her breast with his mouth, his tongue flicking lightly over and around her nipple until she gasped and twisted with the unexpected sensations rippling through her. His mouth closed over her then, tugging and suckling hard enough to make her dizzy with pleasure, a pleasure great enough that she freely let him unlace the back of her gown so he could slip it over her shoulders. With an impatient twitch and a shrug, she freed her arms from the sleeves so the gown crumpled down around her waist, unabashedly bare for him and his marvelous, seductive hands and lips and tongue.

"You *are* good, Edward," she whispered fiercely, her words fragmenting into little broken moans as he caressed both her breasts. "You—are—*good.*"

"And you're mine, Francesca," he rasped, pressing

her gently back against the polished wood. "All, all mine."

He leaned into her, between her legs, and his dressing gown fell open, a scarlet tent around them, and eagerly she reached inside like a child greedy to unwrap a present. His skin was warm, sleek, over hard bands of muscle that were a delight to touch. Whorls of golden hair patterned across his chest, springy beneath her fingers, and with a purr of satisfaction she breathed deeply of his heady masculine scent, so different from her own. She kissed him again, drawing him closer against her, her breasts tight and heavy as they brushed across the hair on his chest.

She felt the chilly air on her bare legs as he pushed her skirts higher, followed by the warmth of his hands on her knee, on her thigh, high above her garters. Instinctively she shifted to accommodate him. Her body wished the same as his, completion, connection, release from all this aching, teasing torment, and some distant part of her realized she was curving her legs over his hips exactly like the disporting nymph in the fourth panel of the *Oculus* and she wanted the rest, she wanted *him* and everything that came with him, and then with a creak and a thump the cabin was filled with light. With a confused gasp she looked toward the brightness, to the now-unshuttered stern windows with two sailors gaping in at them from the stern galley, the wooden deadlights they'd just removed forgotten in their hands.

"What in blazes is that racket?" demanded Edward furiously as he stood and glared at the sailors, who in turn instantly clambered out of sight and back to the deck. He shielded Francesca as best he could, but still she scrambled backward, yanking her clothes back over her body. "What the devil do those bastards think they're doing?"

"Most likely they're following your orders, Edward," said Francesca, blushing furiously with shame. It was one thing to bare her breasts and much of the rest of her to Edward, but quite another to find herself on such flagrant display before his crew. What was it about Edward that made her so instantly, thoroughly wanton like this? How could desire make her forget all her most reliable common sense?

"My orders, hell," he said, but he didn't disagree. He still stood before the window with his back—a most rigid, frustrated, and unyielding back—to her, his shoulders heaving with frustration.

She could only guess how he felt. Her own heart was racing and her entire body felt jangled and on edge, putting her perilously close to tears. What was wrong with her, anyway? Those sailors had been the only thing that had saved her from committing a folly that would have ended her independence forever, yet here she was turning weepy over the interuption of her own ruin.

"You know, Edward," she began, wishing her voice weren't wavering. "You know we should be thanking those men for taking down the deadlights when they did, and saving us from ourselves. That's twice now, Edward, twice we've nearly—nearly—"

"You're hardly to blame, Francesca." He turned around, his face set and haggard. Instead of easing his burdens, clearly all she'd done was compound them. "Clearly I cannot be trusted to be alone with you like this."

She tried to smile, pressing her hands over her still-flushed cheeks. "Well, yes, *càro mio,* I rather am. If I'm a woman grown enough to kiss you, then I'm fully capable of accepting the responsibility for doing so."

He raked his fingers back through his hair, heedless of how mussed it had become. "You take entirely too much responsibility for a woman."

"If I didn't," she said sadly, "then I'd never have survived as long as I have on my own."

And before her waited London, she reminded herself fiercely. In London she'd draw and paint and make a grand, lasting name for herself, and forget the passing pleasure of a wanton kiss.

He grumbled wordlessly, deep in his throat. "Will you at least let me say I'm sorry?"

"I'm sorry, too, Edward," she said wistfully. "But for now, for us, it is better this way. If we'd gone on as we'd started—"

"Damnation, I'd never have forgiven myself!"

"Oh, yes, and how flattering is that to me?" She held her hand out to him, her ring—*his* ring—glinting in the pale light. "No regrets, *mio leone,* no sadness for us, yes?"

For an endless moment, he held back. "Do you know," he asked slowly, "that this wouldn't hurt so damned much if I didn't care for you?"

Oh, please, please, Edward, my fine, brave English lion, don't say such things!

"I do know," she said, and to her sorrow, she did. "Because I care for you, too."

"Then why the devil are we fighting this, Francesca?" he demanded. "Why plague us both this way?"

"Because I'm not—not ready," she whispered, tears of misery and longing once again blurring her eyes.

He sighed, and reached out to take her hand, pulling her gently toward him. "I wish to God I'd a compass or star to guide us through this, lass, for I'm feeling powerfully lost without one."

"It won't always be like this," she said through her tears, telling a truth she knew he wouldn't understand. "My poor brave lion, I won't always torment you like this."

For in London I'll be gone, and never torment you again.

"Only if we don't both go mad from wanting and waiting." He drew her back to his chest, his arms linked lightly around her waist as he kissed the back of her ear, but now they both understood with bittersweet certainty that nothing more would come of it.

Nothing, that is, but an uneasy kind of peace between them, an empathy, a shared sense that they were bound together by trust as much as attraction. He made her feel safe, and he made her feel content, wrapping her in warmth as sure as his arms were around her now.

And that was far, far more dangerous than anything they'd done upon that long mahogany table.

"Look," he said at last. "It's snowing, and us set to make La Cala and Palermo before nightfall."

"But it never snows in Palermo, Edward," she protested, glancing toward the stern windows. "Sicily's too far south for snow."

Yet it *was* snowing, fat, white flakes that swirled and danced in the wind only to disappear when they struck the dark sea.

"Not this year," he answered. "Perhaps Napoleon ordered it from the Alps to confound us. But it does look more like December at home, I'll grant you that."

England, his home, and soon to be hers: More cold, more ice and snow in one December than she'd seen in a lifetime in Naples, and with a shiver Francesca leaned closer against him. "Will there be a great deal of snow in London?"

"Possibly," he said. "But by the time I can show you London, the seasons may have turned round to summer, or summer and winter yet again."

"But I thought we were going to London after we left Palermo!"

"The *Centaur* sails where the admiralty sends her, lass, and you and I go with her. Given this war, I could be at sea another year or more, or even here in Palermo, before I'm granted leave for home."

"A year or more," she repeated, letting the awful reality of that settle around her. A year or more at sea alone with him, a year or more to wait for London and her art.

"Happy Christmas, My Lady Edward," he was saying, blissfully unaware of her thoughts. "Perhaps that's why we've snow this day, snow for Christmas. Yet I do regret I've no gift to give you."

"But you've already given me so much, haven't you?" she said wistfully. "What more could there be?"

"It's only the beginning, Francesca," he said, lifting her hand to kiss her fingers below the gold ring. "You have my word."

She looked down so he wouldn't see the tears that once again stung her eyes. Oh, yes, he'd already given her so much, and she'd no doubt he'd keep his word and give her the rest.

And she deserved none of it.

8

∾

"*This* is the first time since we've been in Palermo, *càro mio,* that the admiral has asked you to call on him in the middle of the day like this," said Francesca, her breath a frosty little cloud before her face even inside the carriage. "Perhaps he intends to send you upon a special mission of some sort."

"I doubt that very much, sweetheart," said Edward, covering her little gloved hand with his own to still its restless movement along his arm. The hired carriage was not very clean and hideously overpriced, like everything else here in Palermo, but he could hardly complain about sitting so cozily near to Francesca on the worn leather seat, her hip pressed close against his. "Rumor is that we're to stay here until Ferdinando can take back his throne in Naples, another three months or more. Besides, the admiral requested your presence, too, and he wouldn't have done that if he wished to give me new orders."

"*Sànto cièlo,* of course he could," she declared emphatically, the curling green plume on her hat nodding in agreement. "Most likely I was also invited to the villa simply because Lady Hamilton wished it. We ladies shall be packed off to amuse ourselves while the gentlemen discuss matters of state. Don't smile, Edward, you'll see soon enough that I am right."

"I am smiling, Francesca, because you make me happy," he said evenly, "not because I fault your reasoning."

She narrowed her eyes skeptically, though her own smile robbed that skepticism of any serious sting. This was what had evolved between them in this last week: A wary friendship grown from necessity and proximity, and an attraction neither could deny, but that carried a dark undercurrent of uneasy tension that both of them were trying their damnedest to ignore.

Yet while most of the other refugees that Edward had seen from Naples seemed haggard and miserable, Francesca had somehow managed to grow even more beautiful, more desirable in his eyes. Elegant, flattering new clothes had mysteriously appeared without any funding from him—most likely thanks to the machinations of Lady Hamilton—and while they weren't Francesca's former exotic striped silks and turbans, these fashionably pale gossamer woolens cut with high waists and low necklines not only accentuated her voluptuous figure, but also suited her station as the newlywed Lady Edward Ramsden. She smiled often and laughed more, and she charmed everyone she met with the same thoroughness she'd always possessed, whether in English, Italian, or French.

But as proud as Edward was of her, he was the only one who saw the little cracks in her careful facade, small missteps that she tried so hard to hide. Though she never complained, she clearly missed her work and her home, and all the small comforts and niceties that were so painfully absent on a warship. He'd seen the proof in many ways: the random, unfinished sketches he'd come across on the backs of crumpled account bills or old news sheets, the unexpected tears she barely managed to keep back, how her laugh would sometimes be too bright, or the circles of weariness beneath her eyes in the morning to prove she was sleeping as little as he.

Sleeping: what a great lie that had become! Only Edward himself (and Peart) knew the bitter truth, that each night Francesca retreated alone to his cot, while he slung a hammock in his great cabin with a latched door between them. He tried to keep as busy as he could with his duties and the familiar routine of the navy, but with Francesca on board the *Centaur,* routine was no longer quite enough. He was restless and frustrated, and ironically she was both the cause and the solution. Aye, she made him happy—what man wouldn't be happy with such a beautiful wife?— but she was also making him thoroughly miserable, as miserable as he was most likely making her.

Yet he never doubted that he was doing the right thing. Each night as he stared up at the moon's reflection off the water onto the beams overhead, trying not to imagine her lying in her shift in the next cabin, he found comfort knowing that he'd come one more day and one more step closer to winning his wife and her trust, and to proving to himself that he was a better man than his brothers.

Now he leaned forward in the carriage, trying to gauge from the buildings they were passing exactly how much farther they were from Sir William's villa. Palermo's streets were narrow and winding, closed in by dilapidated houses that had been musty in the time of returning Crusaders. There was only one inn in Palermo, and it was charging four times its usual rate for refugees to sleep six to a room on straw pallets, without fireplaces or glass panes in the windows in this unseasonably cold winter. The English ambassador was faring much better than most, having rented a vast furnished villa that was also serving as Admiral Nelson's quarters in Palermo.

"Perhaps the admiral has invited you for another reason, lass," he said lightly. "Perhaps he wishes you and Lady Hamilton to concoct some sort of grand entertainment to amuse all the bored ladies and gentlemen stranded here in Palermo."

She wrinkled her nose with disgust. "Oh, perdition! *They* do not need my help, nor Her Ladyship's, either. Even for Neapolitans, they're squandering their lives prodigiously well on their own. When I think of how His Majesty has abandoned his poor wife to go to the theater and the opera and off with his wretched hunting dogs, without the least concern for her sorrow—oh, it makes me ill!"

Two thousand refugees—Neapolitan and French royalists as well as touring English caught by the French army—had sailed from Naples in twenty merchant vessels as well as the *Centaur* and three other naval ships, yet despite the snowstorm, the only casualty had been a six-year-old boy, the youngest son of King Ferdinando and Queen Maria Carolina. While the queen was grief-stricken over the death of her little prince, refusing to leave her chambers in their Sicilian palace, the king had shown far more concern for his hunting dogs and for shooting the woodcocks that were now in season on the island, and his courtiers had scandalously followed his lead instead of his wife's.

"I always knew his majesty was a stupid man," continued Francesca, "but I didn't know he was so cruel as well. Granted, he has a great many other princes and princesses, but still, to care so little about the death of one's own child. . . ."

Her words drifted off as she stared out the carriage window, her expression full of sadness for the unmourned young prince. Her love for children wasn't benignly sentimental, or limited to the ones she'd drawn and painted. Edward had seen how she genuinely cared for all children as small, individual persons. He couldn't help wondering if the prince had been on board the *Centaur* instead of the flagship, and had been given over to Francesca's keeping like the two d'Arienzani girls, perhaps he'd be alive still.

And what if there had been a woman so loving and warm in his own life, back when he'd been a motherless boy cowering from his brothers' bullying amid the icy grandeur of Winterworth Hall? What if his family had been like his friend Will's, full of laughter and warmth, the kind of family he longed to have with Francesca?

"You would make a first-rate mother, lass," he said impulsively. "You've the perfect temperament, kind and warmhearted. I could even see it from those drawings of yours you'd made of the women with their babes in the market. Fortunate the child will be to have you bending over his cradle."

She looked at him sharply over her shoulder, her dark eyes guarded beneath the curving brim of her hat. "I have always loved children, yes, but only those of other women. That is why they are always so sweet-faced in my drawings, because I do not have to wake in the night to their crying or wash their soiled clothes."

"But surely you've desired a child of your own," he persisted, relishing the image of a laughing, plump-cheeked girl with dancing black curls, a miniature version of Francesca herself. "I thought that was something all women wanted."

"Most women do," she said defensively. "Of course I have imagined the children I could have with you. I can see them so clearly that I could draw their dear little faces here, now, if only I'd a pen."

He could imagine them, too. "A man also wishes children. Sons to follow after him, and daughters to spoil and dote upon."

"Ah, so you see that as well?" She looked down into her lap, plucking restlessly at the tip of one finger of her glove. "A handsome son to carry on your grand title, a pretty daughter for you proudly to present at court!"

"That's not all, Francesca," he insisted, wishing he knew how to explain the confused emotions swirling around him now. "Our children would mean much more than that."

"And where would that leave me, Edward?" she asked. "Am I to be that kind and warmhearted mama in your dreams, the one with the perfect temperament and endless gratitude? Dutiful, obliging Lady Edward, who is so very good with children?"

"Aye," he said, mystified that she'd even ask such a question. "Is that such a woeful fate?"

"It's not my fate, Edward," she said sadly, "but it is *your* dream, not mine. There I would be, in a rough nursemaid's apron spotted with porridge, mired on shore wiping running little noses and unclean little bottoms while my paints and brushes grow dusty and you are off having grand adventures at sea. I can see the end of all *my* dreams, *càro mio,* cast up and broken there on those English rocks. Where would I be then, eh?"

There was so much he could answer to that question. He could tell her he was rich enough to hire a score of nursemaids to do the bottom-wiping, and that he'd never expected her to wear a rough apron covered with porridge. He could assure her that she could always continue to paint and draw as much as she pleased, that such occupations were perfectly acceptable pastimes for English ladies. He could explain that he never intended to leave her alone on shore unless she wished it, that though a baby was even more unusual on board a warship than a captain's wife, it could be managed like anything else.

Or, most important of all, he could tell her how their child would be the chance to right all the wrongs they'd each suffered as children themselves, how their child would be wanted and loved by parents who loved each other.

Love: where the devil had that sprung from, anyway?

He could have told her all these things, or any of them, and through honesty redeemed himself both in her eyes as well as his own. He could have drawn them closer, and he could have taken another step toward making those children—and their marriage—real.

But instead of being honest, he was a coward. Instead of their children or his hopes for their marriage or even of love, he avoided it all and spoke of his ship.

"For now you'll be with me on board the *Centaur*," he said with a forced heartiness that sounded hollow even to his own ears. "There was a cutter came this morning, and I'd wager my eyeteeth that she's brought orders from the admiralty for us all. That's why we've been summoned at this time of day, lass. Mark my words. Within the hour we'll have our sailing orders, and be done with La Cala Bay and Palermo."

Her eyes filled, not with reproach but disappointment, and pointedly she turned once again toward the window and away from him, her fingers curled into a tight fist pressed against the glass.

"Yes, Edward," she said, so softly that he almost didn't hear her. "I suppose we shall."

"Aye, aye, we shall, we shall," he repeated, sounding like the greatest braying jackass in Palermo.

Damnation, she'd practically handed him the chance to win her, and instead he'd as much as tossed it back in her face by saying exactly, *exactly* the wrong thing. "Ah, here's the ambassador's villa now. Let's hope Her Ladyship has some hot tea or chocolate to warm you."

The carriage rumbled through the villa's gates and came to halt before the curving stone stairway. Built as a summer retreat for its titled owners, the yellow and red stone villa with its fanciful dome now looked shabby and forlorn, and on this chilly December day the writhing, life-size stone satyrs that supported the porch seemed more silly than picturesque.

Because the villa was serving as a temporary embassy and naval headquarters as well as Sir William's home, the courtyard was bustling with officers and sailors, merchants and servants, horses and dogs, stranded English gentlemen with petitions for the ambassador, French ladies come to call upon his wife, and opera singers and playwrights seeking patronage from them both.

Two footmen that Edward recognized from the Palazzo Sessa hurried forward, red-faced from the cold, one to open the door and the second with a small step stool for Francesca. Edward climbed out first, holding his hand out for Francesca. But instead of taking it, she slipped from the carriage and past him to the paving stones as if he weren't there, avoiding both his offered hand and his gaze as she smoothed the fur-lined hood of her cloak around her face.

"Do you wish me to address the driver, Edward?"

she asked, staring past his shoulder somewhere into middle space. "As I recall, his English was nearly as disreputable as your Italian."

"That is hardly necessary, Francesca," he said, irritated that she'd even make such a suggestion regardless of how practical it might be. "I shall handle this myself, and join you directly."

If they couldn't manage a more civil relationship than this, then their visit to the villa was going to be a trying one indeed, and with a grumbled oath directed entirely at himself, Edward turned to pay the driver of the carriage. As he'd expected, the man wished to haggle in the garbled English that Francesca had predicted, all Sicilians regarding this as the best of boom-times and license to overcharge for everything. By the time Edward was finally able to return to Francesca, she'd seemingly vanished.

More concerned than he wished to admit, Edward's gaze swept around the crowded courtyard until, at last, he spotted the green of her cloak bright against last summer's vines on a stone wall. To his surprise, she was speaking, or rather listening, to a Neapolitan man with an ill-fitting wig, dressed completely in black to his gloves and his stockings, and though Edward couldn't see Francesca's face, he could tell from the rigid set of her back and the way her hands were clasped before her, almost as if she were pleading with the man, that this conversation was not a pleasant one.

Which was, as far as Edward was concerned, reason enough for him to interrupt.

But for Francesca, he'd already waited too long.

She still didn't know how Signor Albani had crossed from Naples to Palermo, whether he'd purposefully followed her or if their paths had crossed here now by accident alone. Yet when the constable had suddenly appeared before her from a shadowy arch on the edge of the courtyard, bowing low over his spindly leg in its black stocking, her shock and dismay had made her gasp loud enough that others had turned to look.

"Good day, my lady," he said with another flourish of his black-gloved hand. He wore the same black horsehair wig she remembered, the same dark suit, as unadorned as a cleric's except for the small white linen ruffle at his throat and wrists. Yet clearly he was among the Neapolitan refugees crowded into squalid lodgings, for those black clothes were rumpled from being slept in, and the white linen was filmed with a grimy line around his neck. "May I congratulate you, my lady, on your recent marriage to His Lordship?"

"Thank you, signor," she said, concentrating on not letting her true feelings toward him show. She must remember that she'd done nothing wrong, certainly nothing that would merit him following her to Sicily. Hadn't she been the one who'd been robbed, her studio vandalized?

Yet meeting Signor Albani here, just as she'd stepped away from Edward, seemed beyond coincidence. She hadn't forgotten the way the constable had somehow twisted her loss into treason, her fear into guilt, and even now her heart was pounding while he wished her well.

"And to wed an English lord, a captain, a gentleman of such power and influence!" continued the constable, his hands raised in wonder. "Who would have guessed you would rise so far, so fast? And to think, my lady, how only a fortnight ago you were sitting in your old kitchen, your eyes bright with excitement while you listened so avidly to that villain Carlo Brigatti, planning for the new day of Neapolitan liberty and freedom!"

Francesca shook her head in vehement denial. "That is not true, Signor Albani, not one treasonous word of it!" she cried. "Carlo is a weak-minded anarchist, a meaningless fool. When I found him in my house, I ordered him to leave at once!"

"My lady!" The constable winced, turning his head slightly to one side. "I would never call my lady a liar, but I would venture that she has misremembered the facts. Carlo Briggati may be mad, but he is also dangerous, a villain to the crown but a hero to the people in the streets. He was among the leaders who stormed the palazzos of those noblemen who chose not to flee. He slit their throats himself, my lady, too impatient for the guillotine to arrive, and washed his hands in their blood after he had raped and murdered their ladies. He is a demon, the worst and most evil enemy of us who remain loyal to the crown."

Francesca was trembling, her stomach lurching at the bloodletting Albani described. She didn't doubt it was true. Palermo was bubbling with rumors of what was happening in Naples since the king and his followers had fled. Murderous retribution, torture, and rape, and looting and burning palazzos and churches were all being credited to a resentful, terrified mob who felt they'd been abandoned by their leaders. In the middle of such chaos, Carlo and his friends could do this and more in the name of their twisted liberty, and be richly rewarded as soon as the French swept down the peninsula.

"But perhaps my lady has her reasons for forgetting Carlo's place in your own household," continued the constable. "The nephew of your housekeeper, welcomed to your hearth whenever he pleased, who even now is making good use of your house and studio with his friends now that you have left it to him."

"But I haven't! I left with his lordship suddenly, without planning or warning, without seeing or speaking to anyone!" She hated the idea of Carlo and his wicked friends living in her house, carelessly using what they pleased and destroying the rest for amusement, eating her food and drinking her wine and even lolling with their slatterns in her rose-painted bed. "I would never have left my house in the keeping of such a man!"

"That is not what your Nanetta told me," said the constable with a smile that hinted that the housekeeper had told him this and a great deal more besides. "But what can this matter to you now? His Lordship understands your weakness for this evil young man, my lady, doesn't he? There are no secrets between newlyweds. Surely you have made your confessions to him, and he has forgiven his sweet little bride, who is worth the trouble and the scandals her past companions could make for his glorious career."

But Francesca hadn't told Edward any of this, not only because it wasn't true, but because she hadn't thought it mattered. Who would have guessed the world would turn so upside down that a madman like Carlo would become a hero? But for her to go to Edward now that they were wed would seem as if she'd purposefully neglected doing so earlier, as if she'd truly been hiding Carlo in her past. Any denials would only make it seem worse—especially now after that awful, confusing conversation in the carriage.

Her desperation growing, she turned back quickly to look toward Edward, who was still trying to settle the fare with the carriage driver. He was frowning as he listened, his mouth set in a grimly perplexed line as he labored to decipher the man's argument in Italian. His hands were clasped behind his waist and his legs spread slightly apart, the way he stood on his own quarterdeck. His cloak fluttered gently from his broad shoulders against the back of his legs and the ends of his blond queue curled below the black ribbon with an orneriness that he hated but she'd always found boyishly endearing.

"Of course, my lady, few people would make the connection between you and Carlo Brigatti," continued Albani with a delicate cough into his black-gloved hand, "and the risk that the gallant Admiral Lord Nelson might hear of it is very slight, yes? Especially since you have already confided in His Lordship. Ah, my lady, how very fortunate you are to have such a good and loving husband!"

The lies could spread in days, far faster than the truth. Albani would see to that, especially if they all remained here in Palermo for the three months or more that Edward had predicted. Albani was still a constable in service to the crown, even exiled here in the other half of the kingdom. While his powers would be reduced, his word would still be trusted as reliable, particularly among the royalists, and it wouldn't matter that Edward was a duke's son, or a hero of the Battle of the Nile, or even the most honorable man she'd ever known.

All that anyone would remember would be that Captain Lord Edward Ramsden had married the bastard daughter of a third-rate painter and his Neapolitan model, a woman who'd let her home be used for meetings of anarchists and republicans plotting the death of the very king he'd helped to escape. Edward would be vilified and mocked, and worst of all, he would be disgraced in the navy that was the center of his life.

Because he'd been kind and noble, and because of her.

And oh, saints in heaven, she would not hurt Edward like this for all the world!

Quickly she turned back to Albani, knowing she hadn't much time before Edward joined them. She couldn't depend on the English fleet sailing before Albani spread his lies. She'd have to do whatever he wished. She had no gold of her own nor jewels to sell, but there would be the cream of her father's collection waiting in London, and for Edward's sake, she'd sell it all in an instant. Until then, she'd have to swallow what little pride she had left and ask Lady Hamilton for a loan. "What do you want, signor? What is the price of your silence?"

Beneath the squared brim of his hat, Albani's smile was studiously bland. "My price, my lady?"

"Perdition, yes!" she said hurriedly. "It's too late to be coy, signor. I understand your meaning, and I will do what is necessary to protect my husband's good name and honor. I know you must be in need of money. Everyone who fled Naples is. Now tell me, what is your price?"

"The diamond plume," he said instantly. "Marie Antoinette's brooch, the one her sister-queen gave to Lady Hamilton, and then to you. That, my lady, is my price."

"The diamond plume?" Vaguely Francesca remembered the brooch pinned to Lady Hamilton's lapel when she'd visited the studio, an extravagant bauble sparkling with a ransom of diamonds. As generous as Lady Hamilton was, Francesca couldn't imagine the ambassador's wife giving her a piece of jewelry like that, not only because of the value, but because Lady Hamilton loved royalty too well to sacrifice a brooch that had passed through the jewel boxes of two queens. "Why would you think she gave it to me?"

Albani's face hardened. "Now I must ask you not to be coy, my lady. Lady Hamilton wore the plume when she went to your studio, and it was gone from her person when she returned. Her maid swears her ladyship left it with you as a token."

"But why believe her maid instead of me?" cried Francesca, panicking in spite of her best intentions. "How can I give you what I don't have, signor? Ask Lady Hamilton herself! She'll tell you! She never made such a gift to me!"

But Signor Albani only sighed. "Lady Hamilton's maid swears otherwise, my lady, and I am inclined to believe her. She had nothing to gain by a lie or to lose with the truth, and you, my lady—you must be a lady who likes to gamble, yes?"

"Francesca, my dear," said Edward, suddenly at her side to take her hand, at once making his connection to her unmistakably clear. "Is this man being troublesome to you?"

"Oh, Edward, no, no!" she exclaimed, switching back to English with a strained little laugh. How much of her conversation with Albani had he overheard, she wondered frantically, and how much of the constable's rapid Italian would Edward have been able to understand?

For one fleeting instant, she considered confessing everything to Edward herself and robbing Albani of his poison. Surely it wouldn't sound quite as bad from her own mouth. Besides, the truth had always served Edward well. Why couldn't it work this time for her, too?

And then Edward smiled down at her, the warmth of that smile outshining the sun, and she knew she couldn't do it. He already thought her former life had been based on deceit, and he'd made his disapproval of it clear enough. But no matter how carefully she phrased the telling, the story of Carlo Brigatti in her kitchen would be infinitely worse than a forged painting or dubious antique sculpture.

Edward would be furious with her, so furious that he might decide to leave her behind here on Sicily when he sailed. No, he'd *have* to do it, to separate himself from her and save his career. She'd be cast off as she deserved, penniless on this extravagantly expensive island, abandoned by the new English friends that she'd made since her wedding. She might even be arrested as a traitor and an enemy of the crown, with Albani himself swearing against her. But worst of all, she'd lose the trust, respect, and friendship of the best man she'd ever known.

So there was her choice. She could let herself be blackmailed by Albani, find some way to meet his demands, and continue as Edward's wife, or she could tell the truth, and risk never seeing him again.

And that, she knew, was the one risk her heart refused to take.

She curled her fingers into Edward's, her heart pounding as she smiled up at him as winningly as she could. "My lord, might I present Signor Albani of Naples. Signor, my husband, Captain Lord Edward Ramsden. Edward, Signor Albani is the constable investigating the theft and vandalism of my studio."

Edward nodded, as much of a bow as was proper. "Honored, sir," he said in brisk English. "I'm delighted to hear you're looking after my wife's property in Naples, though God only knows what will be left of it by now."

"I am your eternal servant, my lord captain," said the constable in staccato Italian, bowing so low his forehead nearly touched his black-stockinged knee. "You are most right in your surmise, my lord. The weather here is most unseasonably cold this year. In Naples they are blaming the snow upon the ash from the volcano, our Vesuvius."

"Aye, sir, no mercy for thieves," agreed Edward in English. "I have never believed in that, especially not for ones low enough to rob ladies."

Francesca glanced sharply from one man to the other, somehow keeping her surprise from her face. Clearly neither man could understand the language of the other, just as neither man would admit his ignorance—a boon to her, if she were cautious.

"We should not keep the admiral waiting, Edward," she said, slipping her hand into the crook of his arm to draw him away. "I'm sure Signor Albani will know how to find me if he has any more information."

"Very well, lass." He patted her hand fondly, and smiled at the constable. "I thank you for all you are doing for my wife, signor. Good day to you, sir."

Albani smiled broadly in return, again lifting his hat with a flourish. "Good day to you, my lady, my lord captain," he said in Italian, understanding their farewell from their posture instead of their words, "and much joy upon your marriage."

"Thank you, Signor Albani," said Francesca, then switched to Italian herself. "We shall speak again soon, I am sure, and until then I appreciate your reticence."

"Soon, yes, my lady, as soon as possible," he said, his smile fading. "You see, I am not always a patient man, especially in a matter as important as this one."

He began to bow again, but Francesca was already turning away with Edward and up the villa's sweeping front steps and under the makeshift embassy's British flag.

"An odd little crow of a man, don't you think?" said Edward as they passed between the two marines standing guard in the hallway. "More like a country parson than a constable. Yet he must be praised for his dedication to his duty and to your affairs."

"Oh, yes," said Francesca wistfully. "Signor Albani is most concerned with me."

"I cannot fault him for that," said Edward gallantly, his earlier unhappiness with her forgotten—so gallantly that Francesca couldn't bear it. She pulled him to a stop on the landing, ignoring the curious glances of others passing on the stairs, but unwilling to wait another minute to speak.

"Please, *càro mio,* please listen to me," she begged, her fingers clinging anxiously to his as she tried not to think of how much simply holding his hand had come to mean to her. "Whatever you hear of me from others, however wrong or foolish or—or villainous it may seem to you, know that I care about you and never, ever wished to bring you harm or hurt. Please always remember that, Edward, won't you?"

He shook his head, not understanding, and who could blame him? "If this is about what I said in the carriage, Francesca, about children and such—"

"No, no, it's not that, not at all," she said miserably, wishing she dared tell him the entire truth, even if she risked losing him. "It's only—"

"Ah, there you two are!" cried Lady Hamilton at the top of the stairs. She was wrapped in three woolen shawls, red, green, and blue, against the damp chill inside the villa, and her nose was rosy from the cold as well. "I spied the pair of you arriving from the window, oh, simply ages ago, so long that I'd feared the French had gotten you and carried you off. Come, come, no more dawdling."

But though her ladyship was trying to be her usual exuberant self, Francesca immediately sensed that something wasn't right. Her blue eyes seemed clouded with sadness, her smile forced, even somber.

Saints in heaven, had Albani already begun whispering tales about her?

"My lord captain, don't you look handsome!" her ladyship exclaimed as she held her hand out to Edward. "I have always thought that there is nothing quite like a splendid uniform to display a well-favored gentleman to perfection. Go ahead now, through those doors, where Admiral Nelson is waiting for you at his desk. My dear little Robin shall stay with me, here in my own bower, for another moment or two."

She took Francesca by the arm, leading her into the small sitting room adjacent to the larger chamber that served as the admiral's headquarters. Because the villa had been built for the summer heat, there were no fireplaces, and the small brazier of coals in the center of the room gave off little warmth into the high-ceilinged room with the floor of marble tiles. After Lady Hamilton sent the footman for hot tea, she motioned for Francesca to sit, but Francesca was far too agitated to take the offered chair.

"My lady, I must speak to you," she began in a rush as soon as the footman had left them alone. "Do you recall the brooch you were wearing when last you came to my studio, an extraordinary French piece fashioned in the shape of a diamond-covered feather?"

Lady Hamilton looked up toward the heavens, waving the tasseled end of one of her shawls to show her indifference. "Oh, little Robin, do you truly believe I can recall what I wore *this* morning, let alone which jewels I chose for a visit weeks ago?"

"But this piece you would remember, my lady," insisted Francesca, not believing her. "It was special, my lady, for you told me it had been first a gift from Queen Marie Antoinette to her sister Queen Maria Carolina, and then to you—"

"My dear, this is most fascinating," interrupted her ladyship, reaching for Francesca's hand, "and I am most sorry to stop you, but you see I must speak to you upon another matter before the admiral summons you to join him and your bonny lord captain."

"Summons me?" asked Francesca, her suspicions and fear growing. "Whatever could he have to say to me?"

"A powerfully great deal, if I am not mistaken," said her ladyship ruefully. "Now mind what I say, little Robin. When you see your husband next, he will not be a happy man, and it will be your place to cheer and support him as best you can."

Francesca shook her head impatiently, not needing this advice from Lady Hamilton. Wouldn't she already do this and more for Edward? And what could make him so desperately unhappy, anyway? "But I don't see that—"

"Hush," ordered her ladyship gently, "and mind

me. This very moment Captain Lord Ramsden is receiving news he will not wish to hear, the worst possible news to him."

"What news, my lady?" asked Francesca uneasily, forgetting her own worries and the diamond brooch, too, in her concern for Edward. "Whatever has happened?"

"He must tell you himself," said the older woman with a sigh. "You *are* his wife, Francesca, and though you came to that position in a peculiar fashion, your captain will need you now more than you ever needed him, to share his sorrow and bring him what comfort you can. And if fortune smiles upon you both as it should, then in the future you may share his joy as well."

"What kind of sorrow, my lady?" demanded Francesca, her uneasiness turning to panic. Though she swiftly considered the disasters that could devastate a man—financial ruin, the death of a parent, a wife, or children, dishonor or scandal—none seemed to apply to him. "Whatever could hurt Edward as badly as you say?"

The older woman smiled, and squeezed Francesca's hand. "So you do feel love for him, don't you? Ah, I'd thought as much!"

But she didn't love Edward Ramsden, did she? At least not the love that Lady Hamilton would mean, the kind she must feel for Lord Nelson, wild, passionate, heedless, headstrong love that could only lead to ruin.

The door between the two rooms opened, and a footman in the Hamilton livery appeared, bowing low. Behind him, Francesca caught a sudden glimpse of Edward's back, his head bowed and a white paper clutched so tightly in his hand that the sheet had crumpled.

"If you please, my lady," said the footman. "Admiral Lord Nelson requests that you and Lady Edward wait upon him at your leisure."

"Which means, of course, we must join the gentlemen at once." Lady Hamilton sighed, and gathered her shawls around her. "You must be brave now, little Robin. Be brave for the sake of the man you love."

But Francesca was already racing through the doorway to join him.

9

*E*dward believed that by this point in his career, nothing could surprise him. He'd weathered hurricanes and typhoons, and survived attacks by pirates, privateers, and whichever other enemy had declared war upon England. He knew how much every sailor depended on weather, fate, and good fortune, particularly a sailor who served his king, and he'd long ago accepted that risk as part of his life. With enough luck on his side, he would finally retire with an admiral's pennant, and without it, he'd drown, be killed, or simply expire from apoplexy or quinsy or any of the other perils that claimed land-bound men. But even in the darkest moments on a lonely watch, the times when he considered how his life at sea would end, he'd never envisioned *this*.

Once again he stared down at the single sheet in his hand, the neat clerk's handwriting on the familiar cream-colored stock favored by the admiralty. These were the first orders he'd ever received directly from the first Lord of the Admiralty himself, but Edward found no joy or honor in the elegantly worded statement, only an emptiness that tasted like ashes in his mouth.

He was to give up the command of the *Centaur* effective immediately. He was to make every effort and haste to London and report to the First Lord as soon as possible. He was to come as a passenger, not a captain, and he must not anticipate receiving any further commands in the future because there would be none. While His Majesty and the board and the entire rest of Britain appreciated his many years of devotion to his duty, such devotion was no longer required.

And that, without question, was that.

No explanations, because the navy didn't believe in them. No apologies, either, for the same reason. Yet he'd been stripped of his command, relieved of his ship, and called back to England with his tail dragging in shame between his legs. How the devil would this be reported in the Naval Review? Would his friends—and enemies—read the notice and shake their heads in pity or disgust or private relief that it wasn't them? At least if he'd been court-martialed, he'd have been given a chance to defend himself. This way he was as good as done, finished, ruined, broken, and he hadn't one single damned clue *why.*

"I am sorry it has come to this, Ramsden," the admiral was saying. The great hero of the Nile was hunched over his borrowed desk, swathed like a baby in coverlets with a pot of tea beside him. "It has been an honor and a privilege to have you serve with me, sir. You shall be most sorely missed, sir, and not soon forgotten."

"Then why in blazes am I being dismissed?" demanded Edward hoarsely, his fury and agony making him forget everything else. Since boyhood, the navy had been his salvation and his home, his family and the source of his closest friendships, and now, for no reason, he was being cut off from all of it. "If I have behaved ill, if I have shamed myself or my country, why, then I ask that—"

"No shame, sir," said the admiral, frowning down at the piles of papers on his desk to avoid meeting Edward's gaze. "And I would not say you are being dismissed—no, no, it is not at all in that fashion."

Edward held his orders out before him. "Then why this, my lord?"

"No shame, no," repeated the admiral, pointedly not answering Edward's question. "Your bravery and loyalty have never been questioned. You were one of the best with me at the Nile, one of my band of brother–captains, and you still are. How could I speak otherwise of you now?"

"Because, sir, you know more than you're saying, sir, don't you?" asked Edward, despair clear in his voice as he forgot all protocol and leaned his hands on the edge of the desk. "The reasons why I am being treated like this?"

The admiral looked up at him sharply with his remaining good eye. "I say what the Admiralty wishes me to say, Ramsden, and I know what they wish me to know. You would be wise to do the same."

With enormous effort, Edward drew himself up straight and squared his shoulders. The admiral was right. He was still a captain, and if nothing else, so far he still had his honor as an officer. The navy might be hell-bent on casting him off, but he still could—and would—live by the hard lessons he'd learned in its service.

For what else, really, did he have in its place?

"Ah, here are the ladies," said the admiral, shrugging off the coverlets and rising stiffly to his feet. "I have asked your wife to join us, Ramsden, since this will obviously affect her as well. Good morning, Lady Edward. I trust you are well this day?"

Aghast, Edward didn't turn. He'd been so wrapped up in his own misery that he'd forgotten these orders wouldn't affect only him. He now had a wife and her future to consider as well.

And what in blazes would Francesca's reaction be? True, they'd married for reasons different than most couples, but he'd been able to offer her certain guarantees about himself and his situation. Now he had none: No home, no future, not even a respectable means for supporting her.

He wasn't entirely without resources, of course. He'd been careful to put aside most of his prize money, and he did have a small income left from his mother. Even in disgrace, he could surely find a place as captain on board a merchant vessel or, with his fighting experience, a privateersman. But it wouldn't be the same, not by half, and he could not blame Francesca if she felt that, after this morning, he was far less of a gentleman than she'd married, and far, far less of a man.

How fortunate now that she'd kept from his bed after they'd wed, for the sake of each other as well as

*for those children they hadn't conceived. Had she
somehow guessed this would happen, and now would
expect her freedom? He'd give it to her, if she asked it,
but dear God, how he'd hate to lose her as well!*

He heard the gentle *shush* of her skirts as she entered the room and the murmur of her reply to the
admiral's question. Without looking he knew the
exact moment she came to stand beside him, smelling the familiar blossom-sweetness of her scent. They
couldn't have been apart more than a quarter hour,
and still he'd missed her.

And yet now he couldn't make himself turn
toward her or greet her. What the devil was he supposed to say, anyway? How could he explain what
had happened when he wasn't sure himself?

The admiral cleared his throat impatiently, obviously expecting Edward to have spoken first. "I've
asked you to join us, my lady, because your husband
has received his sailing orders. Unless he chooses to
leave you here with us in Palermo, we shall be losing
your company as well as his."

Edward heard the slight gasp from her, swiftly
smothered. Was it the news that they were sailing
that had caused that, or the suggestion that he might
leave her behind?

"But that is most excellent news, My Lord Admiral—*bellissimo!*" she exclaimed, though Edward
could hear the tremor of brave uneasiness in her
voice. "My husband has been eager to sail once more
against the French, and now you've granted his wish.
Isn't that so, *càro mio?*"

"It's not my blasted wish, Francesca," he said,

more bitterly than he realized, or would have wanted. "They've taken the *Centaur* away from me, and now I must sail clear to London like so much baggage, to wait upon the pleasure of the lords of the admiralty so I might learn their reasons."

"Oh, Edward," she whispered, too stunned to speak more loudly. "Oh, Edward, *mi dispiace, tesoro mio, mi dispiace!*"

I am sorry, my darling, I am sorry: He'd learned enough Italian from her to know her meaning, and even if he hadn't, he would have understood from her voice alone, such genuine sadness and empathy that he could have wept with her.

Heedless of the admiral and Lady Hamilton, he reached blindly for her hand. When had he come to need the touch of those little fingers so much? "I am sorry, too, Francesca," he said to her, as if the others weren't there. "Sorry for everything."

"Well, aye, aye, Ramsden, that's how life falls, doesn't it?" said the admiral briskly, drumming his own fingers on the edge of the desk as Lady Hamilton came to stand beside him, ostensibly to pour his tea. "We poor mortals do what we can, while our Maker and the Lord of the Admiralty settles the rest around us."

"Aye, sir." No sympathy from the admiral's quarter, then, not that Edward truly expected any. From this day onward, he must expect less than nothing, and be grateful for that.

"Very well, sir, very well," continued the admiral with too-obvious relief. "Unless you have any grave objections, Lieutenant Pye shall become the *Cen-*

taur's acting captain until other arrangements can be made. I have already written the orders to that effect, but I thought it best that you spoke to him first."

"He will welcome both the challenge and the honor, sir," said Edward, somehow managing to make the expected response. Of course the ship needed a captain; not even he could deny that. And what a lucky bastard Pye was, to be handed a plum like the *Centaur*—his *Centaur*. "Of course I shall speak to him, if that is what you wish."

"I do, for the ease of the *Centaur*'s people," said the admiral, eager to move beyond Edward's own feelings. "Sudden changes can disturb the men if not handled well, what? But I am sure everything stands in excellent order with the *Centaur*, Ramsden, and since I have your latest reports, there will be nothing left to hang upon your conscience."

Nothing, that is, except this hideous disgrace that no one seemed capable of naming. . . .

"When must we leave, my lord?" asked Francesca beside him, the question Edward hadn't had the heart to ask himself. Her voice was scarce above a whisper, and more weighted with her Neapolitan accent than usual when she spoke among Englishmen, another sure sign of her own uncertainty. "There will be preparations to make for such a voyage."

The admiral blew his nose loudly, using a handkerchief conveniently offered by Lady Hamilton. "You will be joining your husband, then, Lady Edward?"

"Of course, my lord," she said with a gratifying mixture of surprise and indignation. Gratifying, even though Edward guessed it must be London that was the attraction, and not himself. Hell, at this point his battered esteem would take whatever it could salvage.

But the admiral was looking to him now, his rheumy eyes full of unspoken questions over his handkerchief. Clearly he believed Edward meant to leave Francesca behind like any other officer's mistress in a foreign point, an unfortunate encumbrance quickly shed, the way the admiral would undoubtedly part with Lady Hamilton.

But not Edward, and not Francesca.

"Lady Edward wishes to know when we must sail," said Edward firmly, placing extra emphasis on that *we*. If she was willing to throw her lot in with his after this, then by God, he would take her with him. "Sir."

And most gratifying of all to feel the way her fingers squeezed his, a tiny shared rush of gratitude, empathy, anticipation . . .

"Oh, aye, Ramsden, you inquire only for Lady Edward's sake, I am sure." Irritably the admiral blew his nose again, then pushed through the papers on his desk until he found the one he sought. "I am sending the sloop *Antelope* with reports and dispatches to London, and I shall ask Captain Pettigrew to find you space on board her—you and your lady both. He is, I believe, planning to sail with the morning tide. That should be time enough for your preparations, shouldn't it?"

Edward nodded, again not daring to look at Francesca, and swallowed hard. So this would be it:

the morning tide, tomorrow, a hasty beginning to an inevitable, unenviable end.

There was more said after that, more instructions given and questions dutifully answered before he was at last standing at the bottom of the villa's steps in the cold morning air. The wind swirled dry leaves rattling against the toes of his shoes while Lady Hamilton embraced Francesca, one last, tearful farewell of the sort that so delighted ladies, before she stepped into the carriage.

"And you—you, my lord captain," said Lady Hamilton, thoughtfully running her forefinger along the gold lace on the revere of his coat when his turn came. "I wish you well, too, of course, a safe voyage and happy future and all the rest of it. But you must promise that you will always remember me whenever we may meet again, and not grow too haughty and proud to greet me like a friend."

Dutifully Edward raised her hand to kiss the air over her fingers. "It is very hard for a man to grow haughty and proud, my lady, when he has as little left to his name as I do."

"Oh, but that isn't true, my lord captain, is it?" she asked, and he almost could have sworn the tears in her famous blue eyes were genuine. "You have far, far more than most men ever will, as you know perfectly well."

"Tell that to the Admiralty, my lady," he said, his bitterness and disappointment spilling over once again. "Tell it to whichever black rogue decided I wasn't fit to be the *Centaur*'s master."

"No, no, you great goose, not that," she said, her

hand thumping his chest over his heart, where by rights a medal for the Nile should go. "You have something worth far more than any foolish honors from the Admiralty, my lord captain. You have Francesca."

"Oh, aye," said Edward grimly, "just as she has me, eh?"

"Yes," answered Lady Hamilton with perfect seriousness. "You have her, and she has you, and in short you have the world, because you have each other."

You have each other. How logical and balanced she made it sound, as fine a pairing as any Cupid could wish.

"I'd no notion the ambassador's wife had turned matchmaker as well, my lady," he said with a weary smile as he bowed over Lady Hamilton's hand. "And here I'd been thinking marrying Miss Robin was my idea alone."

"That is precisely what I wished you to believe, Captain." She smiled mischievously, taking back her hand with a twirl of her fingers. "Not such a bad job of it, eh?"

Not for him, no, he thought miserably, but for Francesca—poor dear lass, what had she ever done to deserve *him?*

The next morning, Francesca sat close to Edward in the sternsheets of the *Centaur*'s boat along with their belongings, watching the watery winter sun struggle to rise over the bay. Edward had barely spoken to her, said nothing beyond what he'd had to, even considering how they'd not been left alone together since that grim carriage ride yesterday from the ambassador's villa. But then Francesca would have been more surprised if Edward had confided in her, given how much he prided himself on keeping his feelings locked so tightly inside himself, the way his blessed navy had taught him.

Yesterday, and last night, and this morning: If everything had passed in a rapid blur to her, she couldn't imagine how it must have seemed to him. She'd sat at his side through the final supper in his quarters for his officers, permitted this once to be the lone lady among the gentlemen as the toasts grew longer and more sentimental, brave, strong men moved to tears by Edward's abrupt leaving.

She'd watched as Peart had efficiently packed away every personal item in Edward's cabin, stowed his uniforms and pictures and books, even his bed linens and the gold-rimmed dinnerware reserved for special entertainments, until the cabin echoed, as empty and hollow as Edward's own hopes, and no trace of his captaincy remained.

By lantern light this morning, she'd stood beside Edward as he'd given up the *Centaur*'s command and heard Lieutenant Pye read in as his replacement, and listened to Edward's agonizingly brief farewell from the quarterdeck to his crew, there in the cold hour before dawn, and when they'd cheered him, his face had been as wooden as the ship itself.

When other captains left one command for another, they were entitled to take their favorite crewmen with them to their new ship, an honored privilege for both the captain and the men who joined him. But because Edward had no other ship waiting, he could take no sailors with him beyond his servant Peart; the entire crew to a man felt the slight, and made their cheers all the warmer to show they shared his outrageous misfortune.

She'd seen how Edward's jaw had twitched, the only emotion that betrayed him as he'd left the ship for the last time to the shrill bo'sn's pipes and the marines' salute. Lieutenant Pye, now acting captain, had offered them the *Centaur's* captain's gig to ferry them to the *Antelope,* and Francesca wondered if anyone other than herself had noticed how Edward had paused before he'd sat on that familiar bench, or how he'd given the side of the ship an affectionate little pat, a last farewell for the *Centaur* as well. But like a heartbroken lover determined to make a clean break, he'd kept his head high and his shoulders squared, and not once had he turned back to look at the *Centaur* as they'd rowed across the bay.

Which was why, now, Francesca kept her hip pressed close against him and her hand resting lightly over his, letting him believe that he was comforting her rather than the other way around. She hadn't been nearly so brave when she'd left Naples, watching through her tears until the twinkling lights of the city had been lost in the gloom of the storm. Because leaving the *Centaur* was leaving home for him, she understood his misery, and because she cared for him, she shared it.

But oh, saints in heaven, what she didn't share, that raw shock of guilt she'd felt when the admiral had told them they were bound for London! She'd longed for London, not only for the sake of her painting and her freedom, but because in London she'd be safely distant from Albani's demands and threats.

Yes, yes, she'd wanted London, even selfishly, wickedly prayed for it, but never at this horrible price to Edward. Rationally, she knew none of this could be her fault—what influence could her prayers have had with the British Admiralty?—but in the darkest corners of her conscience she was convinced his misfortune was all her fault.

He had saved her life, and she had brought him nothing but this in return. For Edward Ramsden, she'd become the most unlucky creature alive, and as she bowed her head now beside him, it was not against the salt spray, but from shame and sorrow and guilt for bringing him so much unhappiness.

When she'd agreed to marry Edward, she'd truly believed she could put herself and her own wishes first, the way she always had before. She thought she could slip from his life as readily as she'd slipped into it, with a glib smile, a modicum of truth, and a leavening of teasing charm, the recipe that had always served her so perfectly in the past. But now that escape would bring her more pain than she'd ever dreamed, for somehow she'd come to care for Edward Ramsden more than any other person she'd ever known.

No, more than that: She loved him, just as Lady Hamilton had said.

She loved him.

Plain and simple, three short words that meant

both endless joy and boundless sorrow. For the more she loved Edward, the more she cared for his happiness and his future, the more convinced she became that she must leave him, the day—the minute!—they reached London.

"There lies the *Antelope,* Francesca," he said, startling her from her thoughts. "A sorry change for you from the *Centaur,* I'm afraid."

More likely a sorry change for him, she thought, as she followed his pointing arm. By comparison to the *Centaur,* even she could see that the *Antelope* was tiny, a mere thimble bobbing on the bay.

"With that great flapping mainsail, she's built for speed, lass, not for fighting," he continued mournfully. "Leastways we must hope she was. She only carries six small guns, and scarce men to fire 'em. Why, there's likely more gunpowder in a single Chinese firecracker than on board that sloop. May the good Lord deliver us from the French, because that wretch Pettigrew couldn't to save his own worthless soul."

"Hush, Edward, hush!" she scolded in a shocked whisper. Didn't he realize that every morose word he spoke would be carried back to the *Centaur* by the men at the oars? "You told me yourself you'd never met Captain Pettigrew to judge him a good sailor or bad. And yes, yes, the *Antelope* is a sorry small vessel compared to the *Centaur,* but what ship isn't? All she must do is carry us to England, not fight another battle of the Nile."

"And a damned good thing, too," said Edward gloomily. "If Nelson had had an ounce of mercy in his carcass, he would have simply had me heaved over the side to drown instead of suffering this slow torture."

"What a cheerful thought to begin our voyage, *mio càro,*" she whispered sharply, taking back her hand. "If Admiral Lord Nelson didn't toss you into the water, then perhaps I shall instead, and spare us all."

He scowled down at his now-lonely hand, still resting on his knee. "I am sorry to be such a trial, Francesca."

"And so am I," she answered promptly, "just as I am sorry for your misfortunes and those of the rest of the entire world since the beginning of Creation. But let this be an end of all apologies between us, Edward. You are still a captain, a master, a hero in the greatest navy in the world, and you need not apologize before anyone."

"Except to you, lass," he said heavily. "You never asked to be part of any of this. Once we reach London and I've been officially tossed out on my ear—"

"No!" she cried, so vehemently that the men at the oars forgot to pretend not to eavesdrop, and looked up. "I won't listen to any more of this, Edward, not a word! I refuse to worry and fuss over what might happen in the future. All I care for is this day, this moment, for that is all that's in my power to change!"

He sighed mightily, reaching for her hand again. "You'd sooner change the tide, lass," he said. "Or me. Sailors must always look to the future, reading the sky for portents and the waves for coming storms. We must, or perish. But for your sake, I shall try to think only of today and no farther."

"Grazie," she said stiffly. The way he'd explained it made her sound as flighty as a will-o'-the-wisp, when all she really wished was to be able to cherish what she had with him now instead of the inevitable time when she must leave. But she couldn't have it both ways, and so with a sigh of her own she leaned her head against his shoulder and concentrated on studying the sloop that would carry them to England.

The *Antelope* seemed smaller still as they drew alongside her, her rail not a dozen feet above the water, and though the bo'sn's chair obligingly dangled down for Francesca to use, her ride upward in it to the deck was so short she wondered why they'd bothered.

While the *Centaur*'s main deck had seemed as vast and sweeping as a ballroom floor, the *Antelope*'s deck was fifty feet long at best, and that without a quarterdeck. She carried four small carriage guns on each side, and several smaller guns mounted on swivels at her stern, all the defense she could muster, and uneasily Francesca remembered how Edward had dismissed the sloop's defenses as mere firecrackers.

But most distressing to her was the feel of the *Antelope* beneath her feet. Even during that first storm the night they'd fled Naples, there had been a reassuring solidity to the *Centaur*, while the *Antelope* was already agreeing with her skittish namesake, bobbing and rolling in answer to every swell and ripple in a fashion that Francesca found unsettling both to her well-being and her stomach.

The sloop's entire crew of ten men and two boys presented itself in Edward's honor, and, suspected

Francesca, to satisfy their curiosity as well. Much-decorated, titled captains of ships-of-the-line would be rare passengers on a sloop more accustomed to carrying dispatches and letters. Certainly Edward's arrival had been enough to fluster the *Antelope*'s master, for Edward and Francesca had been on board a good five minutes before Pettigrew finally appeared, red-faced and out of breath and still fumbling with the buttons on his best dress uniform coat.

"Good morning, sir," he said, huffing and puffing as he touched his hat to salute Edward. "Lieutenant Barnabas Pettigrew, sir, master of the His Majesty's sloop *Antelope,* sir, your servant, sir. And welcome."

As a lieutenant without influence or distinction, Pettigrew was only a captain by courtesy, not rank, and from the gray that streaked his hair and the rumfed belly that the rumpled, salt-stained dress coat refused to cover, the tiny *Antelope* was likely to be the only command he'd ever have. To Francesca, his disappointment and envy were clear as his gaze flicked over the gold stripes of braid on Edward's sleeves and the epaulets glittering on the shoulders of his exquisitely tailored coat of dark blue superfine, lined with white silk.

"Thank you, Lieutenant," said Edward with a slight nod and a smile. "You've a pretty little vessel here, and I'm eager to see how you run her out in the open water. I'll wager she fair flies in the right hands, eh?"

"Aye, aye, sir," answered Pettigrew automatically, but instead of preening at the compliment, he'd focussed on Francesca, his eyes narrowing with righteous contempt.

"Forgive me speaking bold, sir," he began, "but the little brown doxie must go back in the boat to shore. I run a God-fearing ship as His Majesty wishes, not a brothel, and I don't ship Italian concubines, not even for the high-born captains of first-rates."

For an interminable moment, Edward didn't speak, and to Francesca it seemed as if the entire crew was holding its breath until he did. She wanted to wither and drop through the deck from shame—not for herself, but for him.

"Lieutenant," he said at last, his voice deceptively calm, though loud enough for everyone to hear. "I believe I misheard you just now. I trust you have read your orders from Admiral Lord Nelson?"

Pettigrew nodded doggedly. "Orders said I was to carry you home to England, sir, fast as ever I could. Orders didn't say I had to carry your harlot, too."

Oh, Edward, my dearest, I know I said no more apologies, but this—for this I must say how sorry I am to be different, to be unworthy, to not be the porcelain-perfect English lady you deserve!

"Your orders said you were to carry me and my party, Lieutenant," said Edward. "And that includes my wife, Lady Edward Ramsden."

"Your *wife*," said Pettigrew with withering disbelief. "She's a dago, isn't she? Look at her, sir! What English gentleman-captain would marry himself to a woman like that?"

"I would, and I did, and was honored that she accepted me." Deliberately Edward took her hand, raising it as he linked their fingers to show the heavy gold band on her hand. "Because we must be shipmates, Lieutenant Pettigrew, I shall choose to overlook the seriousness of this insult you have paid me and my wife, and attribute it to your own ignorance and bigotry. But if I hear one more instance of your disrespect, sir, you shall answer directly to me, sir."

Pettigrew's throat worked visibly up and down, his eyes filling with both fear and resentment. "You would report me to the admiral, my lord captain?"

"No, Lieutenant, I would not," answered Edward with icy precision. "This would be between us. Pistols, sir, or swords. It would make no difference to me. Now my wife is weary, and would like to repair to our cabin."

Pointedly Edward turned toward the companionway to the lower deck, drawing Francesca with him.

"You must never duel on my account, Edward!" she said in a horrified rush. "*Per favore, per favore,* promise me you never will risk your life for such foolishness!"

"I will make no such promise, lass," he said with a lopsided smile that, to her, seemed hideously inappropriate. "My honor and my regard for you make it impossible."

"Your regard, and your stubbornness, to risk your life over something as meaningless as what that man says!"

"Nothing is meaningless where you are concerned, Francesca," he said firmly. "But I wouldn't fret on that sorry bastard's account. Likely he's already fouled his own breeches at the mere possibility of facing me."

"My lord captain, a word, please!" called Pettigrew, belatedly hurrying after them, hat in hand. "My cabin—that is, the captain's cabin—it's not ready for you, not the way you'd expect. Seeing as I thought it was only you, sir, I'd put you in the first mate's quarters. But I'll clear my things out directly, and give it over to—"

"That isn't necessary, Lieutenant," interrupted Francesca with what she hoped was a brilliant smile. Though Edward felt otherwise, she knew from experience there was nothing to be gained by making idle enemies, or keeping them, either. "I've no wish to displace you from your quarters. I'll make do with the usual accommodations, *per favore*. No pretty frills for me."

"Francesca, my dear," said Edward swiftly. "I do not believe such a sacrifice is necessary."

"Oh, but I insist, *mio càro,*" she said blithely. "I do not require fancy quarters for myself."

But she should have guessed as much from Pettigrew's smirk as from Edward's warning that the space between the *Antelope*'s decks would be a far cry from those of the *Centaur*. The companionway was narrow and dank, and lit only by a single, smoky lantern. There were no polished brasses or neat paintwork, no marine guards at attention at the louvered door where Edward stopped. He fiddled with the latch until it gave way, then pushed it open. As Francesca's eyes grew accustomed to the gloom, she saw a low, windowless space that was more a closet than a cabin, scarcely large enough for her and Edward to stand together within. The only furnishings were a ledge-like dressing table tucked in between the beams with a looking glass above, and another, broader shelf with an unpromising mattress and coverlet that she realized was the bunk.

The lone bunk that, as husband and wife, they'd be expected to share.

" 'No pretty frills for me,' " repeated Edward balefully. "Frills, hell. I'll go tell that bastard Pettigrew to give us his cabin, though I doubt it will be much better."

"Don't," said Francesca quickly, resting her hand on his arm to stop him. "I said I'd make do, and I will, and not give Pettigrew the satisfaction of believing otherwise. Besides, *càro mio,* it won't be for so very long."

"Long enough," said Edward, staring grimly at the bunk. "The better part of a month or more, if we run afoul of winds and weather. Peart will find me someplace to hang a hammock."

"I'd rather have you here than let him say you sleep apart from your wife, which you know he will," she countered. There'd be no secrets like that on a ship as small as the *Antelope.* "We can sleep together in this bunk, can't we?"

Now he stared at her, his expression incredulous. "We can?"

"I mean if we remain dressed, of course," she said quickly, her cheeks burning. Her imagination was jumbling all sorts of wicked thoughts and memories together, how his mouth had tasted when they'd kissed, and how her body had responded with a will of its own the minute he'd touched her, and how standing this close to him in this tiny cabin was making her long to do it again. "With our clothes on. And only to sleep. *Sleep*. We could bear that, couldn't we?"

He made a rumbling growl of doubt deep in his throat.

"Well, *I* could," she said with as much conviction as she could muster, which wasn't really very much, considering. "I can."

"And I'd rather take my chances in a duel than lying with you like that," he said. "You're a temptation, Francesca, a powerful great temptation to my weak old soul. How much longer are we going to go on like this, eh?"

"Until—until London," she said, for that was true.

But Edward, of course, couldn't know the truth. "Oh, aye, London," he said, his expression darkening. "You wish to wait until I've word from the Admiralty, don't you? Wouldn't want to be shackled for life to some poor disgraced bastard. I'll sleep elsewhere, my lady, thank you."

"No, you won't, you great fool!" she cried unhappily, shoving at his chest with both her hands. "You belong here, with me, because—because you *are* my husband, and I won't have anyone say anything ill about you, and—and because I would be frightened to stay in this place alone at night, without you with me!"

He caught her wrists, holding her hands against his chest. "You, frightened, Francesca? I don't believe you're frightened of anything."

"Then I'm a far better actress than I ever

dreamed, Edward, because right now I'm frightened nigh to death." She smiled unsteadily, knowing that if she'd any sense left she'd lift her hands from his chest and move away from him as fast as she could. "And so, I think, are you."

"Am I indeed." He slid his hands down her arms, pulling her closer until her face—and her mouth— was directly below his. A perilous place to be, she told herself sternly, yet she didn't move away.

"Oh, yes," she said softly, swaying closer into him, her cloak falling open to include him inside. "We're much alike, you know. We've both lost our moorings, and now we're adrift, aren't we?"

He frowned down at her, more bemused than antagonistic now. "Adrift? Moorings? Where'd you learn to speak sailor-talk like that?"

"From you, *mio marinàro,*" she said, and when he bent down that last inch to kiss her, she welcomed him gladly, closing her eyes to let the desire build and simmer between them. She loved the way he kissed her, almost as much as she loved kissing him in return. Yet there was a bittersweet melancholy to this kiss as well that would be impossible to explain to anyone else, a sense that they shared more than longing alone.

"My charming Francesca," he whispered gruffly, running his thumb along her cheek. "What in blazes does *marinàro mio* mean, anyway?"

"My sailor," she answered with a little squeak in her words as he trailed another few kisses along her jaw. "Which you are. And I didn't misspeak, did I? About the moorings and such?"

"The moorings?"

Saints in heaven, how had he forgotten so soon? "About us both being adrift, Edward," she prompted, refusing to be as distractible. "You have lost your *Centaur,* and I have lost my Napoli, and I cannot imagine a better description of cut moorings and being adrift than that."

He fell silent, his mouth becoming a hard, harsh line of grief, and she knew he was dwelling on all that had befallen him these last twenty-four hours.

"Ah, sweetheart," he said finally. "At least we've been set adrift with each other, haven't we?"

"With each other, *càro mio,*" she echoed sadly. "With each other."

But only, alas, until London.

10

*I*t was beginning once again, the same way it always did, and with the same dread certainty Edward knew he'd be as helpless to challenge and change fate as he had every other time before.

Seventeen French ships, Napoleon's great fleet, attacked by twelve English under Admiral Nelson, yet the English were winning. Even through the disorienting smoke and fire that filled the night sky over Aboukir Bay, Edward had been able to learn that much from the messages read by his lookouts as, one by one, the French ships of the line began to strike their colors and surrender, their masts shattered, their sails and rigging in rags, their crews slaughtered by the merciless English guns.

With victory seemingly so near, it took all of Edward's will and training not to succumb to the same euphoria of blood lust that was already sweeping through the *Centaur*'s crew. Though he should try to keep them under control, he decided instead to use their frenzy to his own purpose, and with a roar calculated to match their own, he shouted at the gun-captains to prepare for another raking broadside as soon as the next hapless Frenchman——the *Heureux,* he thought it was—— drifted into range. If he could make her surrender to him next, then there'd be even more honors, more glory, more praise.

"Steady, Edward, my lad, steady," he muttered to himself, his hands gripping tight to the quarterdeck's rail as he concentrated on the battle around him. His wool uniform was soaked with sweat, prickling his neck and back in the hot Egyptian night, and his white breeches and the reveres of his coat were black with gunpowder. Though he'd lost his hat and his arm had been gashed by a flying splinter, he felt nothing beyond pure exhilaration. If he survived this night and this battle, then he'd be a hero honored by his king and country, and not even his brothers would be able to deny it.

"My God, sir, look!" shouted Lieutenant Pye, his eyes round with horror as he stared past Edward to the starboard. "It's the *L'Orient,* sir, bearing down hard upon us with her stern afire!"

Instantly Edward turned, and saw the French flagship coming toward them, flames shooting from her hull high into her rigging and aft toward her powder magazine, any second she'd explode and God save them all, she was going to take the *Centaur* with her in a fireball of agonizing death and disgrace bound straight to Hell and it was going to be all, *all,* Edward's fault and——

"Oh, *càro mio,* don't, don't!" a woman's voice was crying, and then it wasn't a woman, it was Francesca, his Francesca, here with him where she would die so horribly, too, if he couldn't steer the *Centaur* clear from the *L'Orient*'s path. Disfigured corpses already bobbed in the sea, the water turned red with blood, red as the flames that licked at the French flagship's masts.

"I must order them to cut the anchor chain, lass," he said, struggling to fight through the tangle of fallen rigging to reach his men. "Damnation, Francesca, don't stand in my way, else we'll all die when the fire reaches the powder!"

Yet still her hands were holding him back, just like the jumbled wreckage that was keeping his legs from carrying him below to where he must go.

"Wake, Edward, oh, please, please, wake!" she pleaded, clinging to the place on his upper arm where he'd been wounded, where his blood must surely be staining her fingers. "It's only a dream, Edward, a nightmare—*l'incubo!*—and you must wake to end it!"

But the only way for Edward to end it and save them all was to get the *Centaur* clear of the burning French flagship, and desperately he wrenched free, striking his elbow so hard against something wood—a broken timber, a shattered mast or spar?—that he howled and swore with pain. Yet as he did, the churning bloodred sea turned pale and faded from his sight, taking the ships and the fire and the great guns and even his beloved *Centaur* with it. All vanished, and in their place he was staring at a rough-plank bulkhead and wrought-iron lantern lit with a tallow candle.

"There you are, my darling, there," murmured Francesca as she gently pushed his sweat-soaked hair back from his forehead. "I told you it was no more than a bad dream."

His heart was pounding with excitement and fear, his shirt plastered to his body, and his breath still came in short, rasping gulps. His elbow throbbed with pain, yes, but from where he'd struck it against the edge of the bunk, not from the splinter-wound that had long ago healed, and his feet had been tangled in the coverlet instead of fallen rigging. He wasn't on the *Centaur*'s quarterdeck, but in the mate's cabin on board the *Antelope*, and it wasn't Lieutenant Pye at his side, but Francesca, her face shadowed with more concern and tenderness than a score of nightmares would deserve.

And Jesus, but he felt like the greatest ass in all Creation.

"Go back to sleep, Francesca," he said, his voice thick as he shook off her touch. He swung his legs over the edge of the bunk and leaned forward, cradling his head in his hands as he strove to shake off the last of the nightmare. "I'd no wish to wake you. It was just as you said, a bad dream and nothing more."

"It most certainly wasn't 'nothing,' Edward," she said quickly, her voice low and coaxing, "and I won't be put off as if I were some blindly trusting noddy. You were dreaming of the Nile, weren't you? Of the battle at Aboukir?"

"Francesca, please," he said wearily. The dream always exhausted him, draining him almost as much as if he'd survived the battle once again. "It's done for now, over, and it won't return this night. Now let that be an end to it for us as well, and go back to sleep."

"So you've had the dream before?" she asked curiously, coming to swing her legs in their yellow clocked stockings over the edge of the bunk beside him, pulling the coverlet over both their shoulders like a cozy private tent. He took it thankfully, though without comment, for the sweat was turning to chill in the unheated cabin.

"Truly, I shouldn't wonder if you did," she continued. "I don't know how you fighting gentlemen can sleep at all, given the sights you must have seen in this horrible war."

He shrugged, no real answer. Sometimes he wondered the same himself, though nightmares were so common that men didn't comment on them. On any given night on board every ship he'd ever served in, there'd be at least a half-dozen sailors among the crew asleep in their hammocks who'd wake swearing or screaming or thrashing wildly, just as he'd done now.

But the difference was that he was a captain, and a high-ranking one at that. He was supposed to be beyond such weaknesses and fears, and he wasn't about to begin confessing them now to Francesca.

She wriggled closer for warmth, her feet dangling beside his. She'd braided her hair into heavy braids that hung over her shoulders and her gold hoops with the pearls swung from her ears. She'd slept in her clothes, too, as they'd agreed, and they'd both self-consciously kept their bodies from touching in the bunk. But sitting with her now under the coverlet like this was oddly both more intimate and more unsettling, made all the worse from realizing how much she could have heard when he'd been raving in his sleep.

"Tell me, *mio coraggioso inglése leone,*" she coaxed softly. "Was the Nile that much worse than other battles you'd fought?"

Her brave English lion: ha, so brave that he had nightmares like a child who'd eaten too much treacly candy.

"The Nile was a great victory for Nelson, for England, for all of us," he said carefully. "That is what you need to know about the Nile."

"And you were one of the grandest heroes, la, la, la," she said. "That much I know from Lady Hamilton, who is wicked proud of you. How the *Centaur* and the *Swiftsure* were the two English ships that brought down the *L'Orient,* how courageously ruthless you were to attack a vessel so much larger, yet how you lowered your own boats to help pluck the wounded Frenchmen from the water, showing mercy even in your victory."

"Aye," he said grudgingly, though at last his racing heart was beginning to slow. These were facts, the barest, purest truth, and borne out in the logs of every captain who'd been there. "Aye, that is so."

"Compassion and bravery—ah, *che miracolo!*" continued Francesca. "Everyone in Naples and Palermo knows that of you, My Lord Captain Edward Ramsden, and soon everyone in England will cheer you for it as well. But that is not what I wish to know from you, my darling husband, not if you are to have any peace."

"You mean to torture me that much until I spill my secrets?" he asked, trying miserably to make a jest of it. But this was the first time she'd called him her husband—her darling husband at that—and how could he make a jest of something as significant as that?

"No peace from me, Edward, no," she said gently, linking her hand into the crook of his arm, "for I do not intend to stop looking after you. But if you wish peace for yourself, asleep and awake, then you must speak of this fearful dream."

Still looking down at the deck, he shook his head. "No, lass. Confession's not my way."

"You wouldn't be confessing anything," she said, leaning closer to him so that the end of one long braid tickled his knee. "You'd be telling a story to your wife, no more, and I vow by all that is holy that I shall never repeat your words to another."

He'd thought her a temptation before, and did still, yet what she was offering now was more alluring than any apple from Eve. Confessing might not be his way, but confiding wasn't, either, and hadn't been since he'd been a friendless boy, unable to trust others with his secrets. The chance to unburden himself now would be an almost unimaginable luxury, especially to his wife.

His *wife*. As a husband, he'd believed he must be the one to offer solace and protection, to comfort her, and now it seemed she was doing the same for him. That was what a husband did, wasn't it? He'd no experience of his own with marriage, and having been so long in the navy, he hadn't even had any examples to observe. Were such confidences commonplace for other husbands? Could his bond with Francesca weigh more in this case than his honor and courage as an officer?

Had the admiral himself made such confidences to Lady Hamilton, a lovely and willing replacement for his own wife so far away in England? Had he whispered to her his disappointments after they'd returned from Egypt, his fears, the concerns he couldn't share with his officers without seeming weak or incompetent? Was that the real reason why he'd chosen to linger so long in Naples, for the sake of a gentle female ear to balance the male horrors of war?

"If you can give this dream of yours words, Edward," she said softly, "if you can share your fear with me, then you'll rob this nightmare of its power over you."

He groaned with frustration. He longed to tell her, to be able to part with enough of his past to do as she said. Yet as much as he ached to begin, he'd no real notion of how to give enough shape and words to the nightmare to be able to tell it to her.

And somehow she knew this of him, too, his wise and logical wife in her yellow stockings and golden hoops.

"Was the *Centaur* ever in danger from the *L'Orient*'s fire?" she asked. "Is that why you were trying so hard to save her and your crew?"

"Yes," he gasped, relief mingling with the shameful horror of the dream itself. *"No!* We were close, aye, closer than any other ship save Hallowell's *Swiftsure,* but we swung round with our bows to the *L'Orient* to bear the explosion that way, and we'd closed our ports to keep the heat from our powder, too. There was not one flaw to what was done, none."

"But not in your dream?"

He groaned again. "Then I do nothing right, Francesca, not one damned thing. I am careless and selfish, the worst kind of captain looking only to add to my own glory. I let my crew become ravening, undisciplined beasts, worse than any Frenchmen, and when the *L'Orient* comes straight for us, all I think of is cowardly ways to save only myself from the death I deserve."

"I see no shame in that, Edward," she said softly. "What greater fear could there be than death?"

"But a captain must not think that way! He must be willing to make whatever sacrifice is necessary for the good of the ship and his crew! He must always think first of his duty, Francesca, never of himself!"

"And I say, *càro mio,* that beneath his fine English uniform, your captain is but a man," she said firmly, "with every right to fear for his own pain and destruction. If a man truly has no fear of death, then where is the glory, the courage, in facing it? How can even an English navy captain cherish the rare blessings he has in life without fearing their loss?"

"Why should I deserve any blessings at all if I must behave with so little honor?" he demanded, his anguish genuine. "Over and over I make the same wrongful choices, and over and over I must—I *must*—suffer the consequences!"

"But only in this nightmare, my husband," she insisted. "You do not trust the success the world wishes to lavish upon you, or feel worthy of what you have achieved, and so you punish yourself again and again in this nightmare. But why, Edward—why, why?"

Why, she asked, when the answer was so blindingly obvious he could either have laughed, or wept. As long as he could remember, from his father to his brothers to every other member of his wretched family, he'd never been judged deserving of anything of real merit. Even now, when the rest of the world praised him as a hero, in his nightmare he was again that small, terrified, worthless boy cut off by his family and sent to sea, the one destined always to make the wrong choice and bring dishonor to his name.

"You are no coward, Edward," she said fervently, her fingers tight around his arm as she *willed* him to believe it. "And I will never let anyone say otherwise of you. Not my brave English lion! No, no, my darling Edward: you are the best, the bravest, and the most honorable gentleman I have ever known, awake *or* asleep."

"Not to the Lord of the Admiralty, I am not."

And never was to my father, never could be, from the day I was born.

"And I say you are!" she cried, her conviction vibrating between them. "This First Lord will *not* turn you out in disgrace, the way you dread. Instead he'll heap honors upon you, and medals and ribbons and promotions and a new ship and oh, everything, everything good and fine that you deserve, else—else he shall answer to me, Edward, to me!"

He bowed his head, resting his hand over hers. He wanted desperately to believe her, as desperately as she seemed to be to defend him. He'd never had a champion, nor ever expected to, particularly one in petticoats, and most particularly one that was also his wife. Was this, then, one more thing he'd have to learn about marriage?

He had a sudden, irresistible image of her challenging his three older brothers, George, Frederick, and St. John at once, in a taunting wave of Italian, her little chin high and her hands defiantly akimbo on her hips as she sauntered in a circle around them.

And another image, less dramatic but more possible, of her at his side as he entered the inhospitable doors of the Admiralty Offices in Whitehall, and faced whatever there would be to face. She would be there, ready to share his fate, and even silent she would give him the strength he'd need.

She would do that for him. He didn't doubt it for a moment. So how could he possibly do any less for her now?

"I shall try my best, Francesca," he said, lifting her hand to his lips. "For you, I always will."

"What more could any woman ask, eh?" She smiled crookedly, a glisten that might have been tears in her eyes. "Now come, to sleep. Morning will come soon enough."

But though she tried to pull free, he wasn't yet ready for sleep. "What of you, lass? What are your fears?"

"Mine?" she asked with surprise, then shrugged, trying to dismiss his question. "Oh, mine are little fears, not nearly so noble as yours. I do not like caves or other places under the earth, and I don't like serpents or spiders. Don't you recall yesterday how you said nothing could frighten me?"

He wasn't going to be put off by that, not now. "I've been honest with you, Francesca. Be honest with me."

By the smoky little lantern, her eyes seemed enormous and dark, and in them he could see how she was wrestling with herself even now. From the deck above came the sound of the bell that marked the end of the watch, footsteps and sleepy voices, amazing proof that life continued regardless of what happened here in this cabin. Nervously she smiled again, ducking her chin in the way that always betrayed her anxiety, and with both hands tucked her braids back behind her ears.

"Honesty, honesty," she mused uneasily, hugging herself. "Very well, *càro mio*. You deserve as much, even from a miserable, dissembling creature like me. I fear that I shall die, too, the same as you and every other mortal. But it is not the pain or suffering that scares me so much as fearing I will die before I've done everything I wished. What if I die too soon, and squander the talent I've been given? What if I die before I paint the most perfect painting I can, the one I was born to paint?"

She gulped, and shrugged again. "Papa recognized the gift I have from the beginning, and it grieved him so that he'd died before I'd seen my best work. *Proméssa maestósa mia*—my master-gift, he called it. He made me swear that I'd never stop painting, for it was his dream as much as my own. Oh, I know how shallow and selfish that must sound to you, who have done so much more worthy things, but to me—"

"Nay, lass, not foolish," he said gently, "not foolish at all.

She looked down at her knees. "That is my oldest fear, but there is another, newer one that torments me even more."

"The French?" he guessed. "Napoleon's troops in Naples?"

"Oh, no," she said wistfully, and finally looked at him. "It's you, Edward. After every wonderful thing you have done for me, *càro mio*, I am so very, very afraid that I will hurt you, that against all my wishes I will bring you pain or suffering that you do not deserve."

"You fear that?" he asked in disbelief. "For me? Oh, Francesca, don't."

He slipped his arm around her waist and pulled her closer inside their little coverlet-tent. He took her hand and pressed it against his side, over his ribs.

"Do you feel how sizable I am, lass?" he said. He could feel the warmth of her fingers through his shirt, and he forced himself not to remember how those same fingers felt on his skin. "Though I've had my share of scrapes and scars, I'm still a large man, not easily wounded, and it will take much more than you to leave any lasting damage."

Warily she angled her gaze up at him, unconvinced. "This is not what I meant, Edward."

"Then it must do, whether it's what you intended or not." He turned her chin toward him and kissed her possessively, wanting to mark her as his own.

"Oh, Edward," she murmured warily when he finally released her. Her lips were full and red and wet from his, her dark eyes heavy-lidded and languid. "If we begin this—"

"Not until London," he said, "though it may kill me to keep to such a fool's promise. But because it's you, lass, and I mean to have you with me for the rest of my life, I can wait. I *can* wait."

He pulled her hand into the light, tipping it to show the engraved design of dolphins and anchors on her ring. "Here it is, marked on my ring so you will not forget. If you are adrift, then let me be your anchor. Your anchor, and your husband."

And your love. . . .

But that would keep until London, too. In London, he would tell her he loved her, and show her, and make sure that both were in ways she would never forget.

Francesca sat on the deck with the drawing board in her lap, singing haphazardly to herself as she sketched. She was sheltered from the worst of the spray and bright sun by the canvas windbreak that Edward had had rigged for her, and bundled in the extra shawls and woolen petticoats that Lady Hamilton had wisely recommended, the *Antelope*'s deck was an altogether pleasant place to be.

In the two weeks since they'd sailed from Palermo, the weather had grown milder, the sun warmer, and while Edward warned her once they passed from the Mediterranean and into the Atlantic that winter would return, for now she was content to spend as much of her day as she could here on deck. She prided herself on becoming quite a model female sailor, or at least a model sailor's wife, and she'd learned to share Edward's delight in the ever-changing sky and sea around her.

Now she frowned critically at her drawing, tapping her fingers on the tacks that kept the paper from blowing away. She was sketching three sailors as they trimmed the *Antelope's* mainsail, and she wanted to capture not only the details of their task, but how hard their labor was, how their backs and arms strained beneath the weight of the heavy, damp canvas. Such a subject was a new challenge for her, since before this she'd concentrated on women and children, not the harsher details of men's lives. It was a challenge she enjoyed as well, and she could imagine being quite content to spend all her days sailing about the world, drawing whatever new sight caught her eye.

But while she dreamed, she was also giving a great deal of thought to her more realistic plans for her life once they reached London. First of all, she must find her uncle, the only relative or friend she had in the city. She knew his name and address, and what her father had told her: that his brother John was a gruff old bachelor with a merchant's golden soul and no eye or sympathy for true art, but still with enough of a sense of family duty that he'd welcome his niece if she ever appeared on his doorstep. She hoped Papa had been right, even though she planned to stay with her uncle only until she'd found suitable lodgings for herself and a place to display the *Oculus* and the rest of Papa's collection.

She'd have to be careful with every penny, for the only money she had with her was the fee that Lady Hamilton had paid for her last portrait in Naples. It wouldn't be nearly enough. She'd have to sell something fast, whether it was one of Papa's pieces or a painting of her own.

She would need to decorate her new studio and picture gallery, and hire servants. She must advertise, of course, and send letters of invitation to all the English ladies and gentlemen who'd visited her studio in Naples, to inform them she'd relocated to London and would welcome their custom.

She'd have to have new clothing made, too, for all her favorite gowns and turbans had been left behind, and it was important for her to look the part of an artist. She needed that mystique, that distance that a costume could grant, or she would seem like only one more rootless foreign ballet dancer or opera singer looking for a gentleman to set her up in keeping—the very last thing she wished, for her sake and for Edward's.

But then all her careful plans always came back to Edward, didn't they? When she'd first agreed to marry him, that long-ago night in the Palazzo Sessa, it had seemed easy enough to consider staying with him only until she'd found her feet again. The courts would be sure to grant an annulment as long as she remained a virgin, and especially if she made no claims to his estate.

Even when they'd sailed from Palermo, she'd convinced herself that she and Edward would part once they'd reached London, amicably, with a certain sadness, yes, but as worldly adults, for he'd no more use for a wife like her than she had for a husband like him. She'd be a dreadful handicap for him wherever he went, a foreign-born embarrassment, especially now that her complexion had grown even darker and less English-pale from these days in the sun.

But this voyage had immeasurably complicated that easygoing scenario. Each night that she and Edward lay side by side in that uncomfortable wooden bunk, together but barely touching as the tension simmered between them, they would talk until they were too exhausted to do anything other than sleep. They talked of childhood pets and favorite desserts, of politics and books and plays, of shipbuilding and sculpture, of Saint Paul's in London versus Saint Peter's in Rome, of the very best way to varnish a painting to make it look antique, and the most direct course for sailing across the Bay of Biscay. By the wavering light of the tallow candle, they confessed and listened and laughed and argued and teased and complained and flirted and, once or twice, even wept.

But most of all, they'd fallen in love.

When the sun rose each morning over the blue-green Mediterranean, that care-free parting that Francesca had envisioned in London became more unlikely, if not outright impossible. Now she would no more be able to ask Edward Ramsden for her freedom than he would be to grant it.

Somehow she had reached the point where she could scarcely imagine life without Edward in it, but she couldn't imagine the life she'd planned for herself in London including him, either. As understand-

ing as he was—and for a high-bred English gentleman, that was very understanding indeed—he still
believed his career with the navy must come first for
them both, and worse, he believed that she should be
content as his wife and the mother of his children,
with her painting as a distant, hazy, ladylike pastime.
Each time he spoke so thoughtlessly of her "little
garret," she wanted to weep with frustration.

With a sigh she added a final bit of shading to one
of the figures in her drawing before she unpinned the
paper from her board and slipped it into the portfolio at her feet, replacing it with a fresh sheet. This
time she idly let her chalk wander for own amusement. Today was the seventeenth of January, the day
of the Festa d'o'Cippo di Sant'Antonio, and she wondered sadly if the revolutionaries like Carlo who'd
taken over Naples were allowing the annual proces-
sion through the streets to the cathedral, or whether
poor old Sant'Antonio had been derided and dis-
carded as one more oppressor of the people.

"Good morning, my dear," said Edward, joining
her at last. He'd brought with him Peart's usual
morning brew, a pewter tankard of coffee made so
ominously black that Francesca swore it would hold
a spoon upright, and when Edward kissed her now
she could taste its bitterness on his lips.

"*Buon giorno, mio càro,*" she said fondly. She
loved seeing him like this, dressed in an old and comfortably weather-beaten coat and long canvas
trousers that somehow seemed much more dashing
and romantic than the gold-covered dress uniform
and breeches. Though he'd pulled his hat down low

to keep it from blowing away, his eyes seemed all the more blue beneath the brim, as if they'd stolen their color from the cloudless sky above. This was how she wanted to remember him, relaxed and happy with the sea around him, and so full of unself-conscious masculine grace and power that she longed to paint him, too.

"So once again Peart has worked his morning miracle," she teased, "and found a handsome gentleman inside the hairy beast."

He laughed, rubbing his hand along his new-shaven jaw, even though she made the same silly jest each morning when he joined her. But her teasing was only another part of the ritual they'd evolved for their days, another thread woven into the bond tying them together.

"I need every last second of Peart's assistance in the morning, thank you," he said. "After all, I wasn't blessed with beauty the way you were, with the Graces smiling down upon my cradle."

She grinned and blushed with pleasure, even though he, too, used the same overwrought compliment each morning. How hard it would be now to begin the day alone, without such silly gallantry to make her smile!

"But what manner of drawing is this, Francesca?" he asked, leaning over her shoulder. "You've made that poor midshipman into a bear, haven't you?"

"I think he makes a rather splendid bear, don't you?" She chuckled wickedly, adding an extra flourish to the drawing of a bear with a disagreeable snarl that did indeed resemble the midshipman of the watch, coarse fur poking out of the sleeves and collar of his uniform. "It's only because today in Naples is the Festival of Saint Anthony. He watched over all animals, small and great, and people bring every manner of creature to the cathedral to be blessed. So I suppose by turning the midshipman into a bear, I've offered him up for Saint Anthony's blessings as well."

"Thus as a Ramsden, you'd have no choice but to give me a great blunt nose and curling horns, eh?"

"*Sànto cièlo,* no!" she declared, beginning to draw again. "Rams are stupid, ignoble beasts, concerned only with butting heads with their rivals and covering ewes to beget more offspring in their own stupid likenesses. Please, please, not a ram, I beg you!"

He chuckled with her, even though she suspected she'd shocked him with the bawdy remark about the ewes. Not that she regretted it; she thought it a fine idea to unsettle him like that, to remind him that she wasn't a proper English miss. Besides, it was fun.

"No, I should rather draw you as my brave English lion," she continued, rapidly sketching his face with a properly regal expression surrounded by a flowing lion's mane. "There, Edward, that is more fitting."

"Then what is this?" he asked with amusement, pointing to another, smaller sketch in one corner. "Are those to be jewels for my lioness?"

To her shock she realized she'd drawn the French queen's diamond plume, that one that Lady Hamilton had worn and that Signor Albani had wanted in return for her silence. What, she wondered uneasily, had made her do *that?* By now Albani must have found some other lady to blackmail, but seeing what her unconscious thoughts had remembered rattled her, and swiftly she began another sketch to distract Edward from inquiring further.

"La, what use would a lioness have for jewels?" she asked skittishly, her chalk sweeping quickly over the page. "But here, I'll make you into another beast."

This time she'd drawn him as a man, a stern-faced captain, albeit one without a shirt, his arms folded over his bare chest. But below the waist she'd added a stallion's prancing body, complete with a stallion's impressive endowments.

"Ha, Francesca, you've made me the centaur himself!" exclaimed Edward, roaring with amusement. "Can you imagine what Nelson and the others would say if they saw this?"

"They'd give you back your ship directly, as you deserve," she said promptly as she continued to draw. A handful of quick strokes, and she'd added a sly, long-legged nymph, clothed only in her long, curling hair, lounging wantonly across the centaur's broad back, a nymph that looked suspiciously like herself. "And they'd let you bring your charming wife along, too, for company upon long voyages."

"Captain Ramsden, sir," said Lieutenant Pettigrew, suddenly standing before them. "Lady Edward, ma'am. A word with you both, if you please."

Francesca gulped and blushed, her gaze falling with immediate guilt to the scandalous drawing she'd made, and, of course, drawing instant attention to it. Pettigrew had only to follow her gaze, his response being a gratifying cross between a throttled wheeze and a horrified bray, his eyes bulging so wide she wondered that they remained attached to their sockets.

"Lady Edward is a most accomplished artist, Lieutenant," said Edward, his own voice none too steady. "She especially favors subjects drawn from the classical texts of the ancients. Isn't that so, my dear?"

"Yes," croaked Francesca, who was perilously close to nervous giggles of the most debilitating variety. "Yes, *càro mio,* I do."

"Yes." Edward cleared his throat and bent to pull the tacks from the drawing, briskly rolling it and tucking it into the front of his coat. "And such a handsome job you've done with this one, my dear, that I shall put it away for safekeeping."

"Aye, aye, sir," Pettigrew managed to croak. "Don't want such pictures to fall into the hands of the men, sir. Pictures like that—I told you, sir, I run a proper, God-fearing ship."

"And so you do," agreed Edward, placating the lieutenant while he pointedly avoiding Francesca's eye. "Now, Lieutenant. You wished a word with Lady Edward and myself?"

"Aye, aye, captain." Pettigrew's coloring, and his eyes, had nearly returned to normal, which meant he was once again looking at Francesca with barely-disguised contempt. "We'll be at Gibraltar by nightfall, and I was wondering, sir, if you and, ah, Lady Edward might be wanting us to put into the harbor.

There's a powerful lot of officers' ladies there, sir, and they'll be waiting to, ah, to welcome Lady Edward into their fold."

Instantly Edward's expression turned rigid, and Francesca's heart plummeted. She wasn't a fool; she could read the signs well enough for herself. Those proper English wives of proper English officers wouldn't welcome anyone as *different* as she into their fold. More likely they'd close their ranks against her, and slash her to tiny pieces with tongues sharper than their husbands' swords.

Which was precisely what Pettigrew expected, and hoped for, too. This was his heavy-handed attempt to see her humiliated and shamed, without him having to risk facing Edward in a duel. She didn't care what the other officer's wives said of her, but Edward would, and she'd never do that to him, or give him such an excuse to go challenging half the station on her account.

"I thank you for your concern on my behalf, Lieutenant Pettigrew," she said evenly, somehow keeping the pain from her voice. "But my own humble wishes account for nothing beside the welfare of dear England. The dispatches you carry must be delivered to the Admiralty in London as swiftly as possible, yes?"

"Aye, aye, my lady," said Pettigrew, his disappointment palpable. "But with a fair wind, we're no more than a fortnight from Dover, my lady, and then 'tis only a day and a night to London and Whitehall."

"On to London, then, if you please, Lieutenant," she said softly. A fortnight, a day and a night, and they would be in London. No more than two weeks left of the wondrous fantasy-world of being Lady Edward Ramsden, fourteen days before she was once again hard-working, independent Signora Francesca Robin.

She stared down at Edward's ring on her hand, the golden dolphins and anchors in an endless circle around her finger. She'd return it to him, of course. The ring had meant much to him before he'd given it to her, and she'd no right to keep it.

A fortnight, then, and a night and a day. All that was left before she would give back the ring and lose her anchor, regain her freedom and break her heart.

11

*B*racing his back against the mainmast, Edward stared up into a sky that was as dull and gray as old pewter, and bitterly cursed the fate that had settled such a sky over his head this morning. Oh, he'd sailed long enough to know that the only certainty at sea was uncertainty, but it still sat very hard with him that the *Antelope* would have come this far under the fairest of skies and with the sweetest of winds to fill her sails, only to fall into foul weather so close to England.

He couldn't recall a time he'd been more eager to reach his destination. True, in London he must face whatever waited for him at the Admiralty, with enough grim possibilities to fill any sane officer's head with foreboding and dread.

But in London he also meant to take the best suite of rooms at the one of the fashionable new hotels that were replacing taverns and inns, and disappear into those rooms with Francesca for at least a month. He'd already spent a good deal of time dreaming and planning the details, how he would offer her everything she could possibly desire to make up for the discomforts of these last weeks: the most delicious meals and wines, the softest, most luxurious featherbed with the finest linens, a bath beside the fire filled decadently with steaming water brought up from the kitchen.

And, most of all, he'd offer her himself and his love, freely and openly, a husband to his wife, without any restraints or restrictions or a single stitch of clothing between them, Francesca naked in his bed, exactly like the plump, willing nymph she'd sketched for him. No wonder the paper was growing worn, he'd looked at it so many times, and no wonder, too, he'd felt like he'd been hard in his breeches since Palermo.

"Looks like we'll be in for a nasty blow, sir," said the beardless midshipman beside him with unwonted cheerfulness. "Lieutenant Pettigrew, sir, he says it's coming from the North Sea straight down the Channel for our throats. Lieutenant says, sir, that we could be bottled up here for days."

Edward regarded the boy with the icy reserve of a senior captain, barely containing the impulse to throttle him on the spot. The puppy's only excuse was his callow youth. Otherwise he'd have more sympathy for a man near cross-eyed from lust for his wife, and more sense than to tell the poor bastard they'd be days longer in the Channel before he could be frolicking on a featherbed.

But as unsympathetic as the midshipman had been, his prophecy was right. The first rain began to fall from that pewter sky before noon. By evening, the rain was driving down upon them in sheets, the waves whipped to a frothy chop. By what should have been dawn if the sun could have peeked through the clouds, the wind was howling and shrieking like a banshee through the rigging, flailing and shredding the few sheets of canvas Pettigrew had tried to leave in place. The waves toyed with the *Antelope* like a cat with a mouse, tossing the sloop up high in the air one minutes, only to slap her down with sickening force the next.

Like every other able-bodied man on board, Edward and Peart took their turns at the pumps; with so much water driving into the hold, there was no standing on ceremony, not even for senior captains or their manservants. The muscles in Edward's arms and shoulders ached from the unaccustomed labor, made worse by the chilly, sodden weight of constantly wet clothes.

"A nasty blow, that is all," he told Francesca, borrowing both the midshipman's phrase and his cheerfulness. "In January, they're all too common here south of the Channel."

"Not to me, they're not, Edward." Wide-eyed with fear, she'd braced herself against the pitching waves in the corner of their bunk, wrapped in shawls and the coverlet with her feet tucked up under her petticoats. By staying on the bunk she'd kept clear of the seawater that had flooded down past the hatches and through the companionway, and now sloshed back and forth across the deck as if in the bottom of a basin instead of their cabin. The timbers creaked and groaned with the stress of the waves, and the lantern swung back and forth wildly, casting exaggerated shadows that were even more disorienting.

"The storm when we sailed from Naples was worse," he said. "You weren't frightened then."

"I'm not frightened now," she countered crossly. "I'm terrified, and with every good reason, too."

He grinned. "If you are still feeling clever enough to make jests like that, then you are not terrified."

"And if you show so little sympathy toward me, Captain Ramsden, then you are most barbarously cruel and unfeeling." She stuck her tongue out at him, pulling the shawls higher around her shoulders. "The *Antelope* seems no more than a walnut shell, the way she's being tossed about. *Sànto cièlo,* just like that! The *Centaur* was so much larger and safer that I didn't feel the waves, not in the least."

"You didn't feel them because you were so busy tending to all those bedraggled Neapolitan counts and countesses," he countered. "Here you've nothing to do but listen to the timbers creak and imagine the worst."

She sighed despondently. *"Mi dispiace e mi scusi, e non me ne importànte."*

He looked at her, questioning. She didn't use nearly as much Italian as she once had, and his had grown even more rusty as a result.

She sighed again. "I am sorry and I beg your forgiveness," she repeated in English, "and—and I don't give a damn if you grant it to me or not."

"Oh, lass." He leaned across the bunk to reach her, not caring how much he dripped on the sheets.

She was very dear to him, his Francesca, even so bundled and huddled in wool that it was hard to tell her elbow from her knee. Her face was woefully forlorn, her nose red from the cold and, he suspected, more than a few lonely tears. "I'm sorry I've had to leave you here so much by yourself."

She sniffed. "You're not supposed to say you're sorry anymore, Edward. Besides, you have to help the crew. They'll need you. I'd much rather have you as captain than that wretched, ugly, old Mr. Pettigrew."

"I'll be sure to give him your fondest regards," teased Edward, but at once he turned more solemn when he saw her eyes growing red around the edges. "Don't be frightened, Francesca. I know that's easier for me to say than for you to believe, but I can guarantee that once we're in London, you'll forget every bit of this."

"You promise, do you?" Her wobbly attempt at a smile showed how unconvinced she was, and when she abruptly shoved aside her wooly cocoon and threw herself into his arms, he had all the proof he needed. "Oh, Edward, I do not want to drown!"

"No one ever does, sweetheart," he said, holding her close and stroking her hair to comfort her. "You be brave, and remember how much I care for you, and we'll weather this storm together, just like everything else."

But by the end of the day he wasn't nearly as sure. With an ominous crack that shuddered down to the bottom of the hold, the top of the mainmast broke off late in the afternoon, smashing the ship's boat and dragging the starboard rail with it in a tangle of snarled lines and splintered spars. Worse still happened that evening, when the pins holding the rudder gave way, snapped like twigs by a wave that caught them broadside.

Now they truly were at the storm's mercy, left to wallow without even a pretense of steering themselves. They were shipping more water by the hour, no matter how the exhausted men labored at the pump, and the sloop was sitting visibly lower in the waves. Their only boat had been dashed to sticks, and no one survived more than a few minutes in the icy grasp of a winter sea. Unless the waves miraculously calmed, they would be swamped by dawn, and sink. It was as brutally simple as that.

Unable to take any bearings in the storm and dark, they had no way of guessing whether they were nearer to breaking up on the rocks of the Spanish coast or running aground in English shallows, or even tumbled out into the endless, inhospitable reaches of the Atlantic.

But for Edward, the worst part was knowing he must tell Francesca.

He felt his way down the pitching companionway, the bulkheads on either side as cold and wet as if they were walls to a cave. The door to their cabin was swollen shut with the damp, the latch useless.

"Francesca?" he shouted over the roar of the wind, shoving his shoulder into the door to force it open. "Francesca, lass, it's Edward."

The door gave way with a rush of seawater, abruptly enough that he staggered off-balance and pitched forward into the cabin, barely catching himself on the edge of the bunk. The gust of wind snuffed the candle as he stumbled inside, and as the ship lurched to starboard, the door behind him swung shut, and plunged him into the thickest, blackest darkness.

"Francesca?" he called frantically. "Damnation, lass, where are you?"

No answer, no answer. Could she have gone searching for him in the ship? He should have come back sooner. He shouldn't have teased her about being frightened. He should never have left her alone so long. What if she'd wandered to the deck, desperate to find him? She would have been swept over the side in an instant without anyone noticing, and she would already be lost to him forever.

"Francesca!" he shouted again, his voice growing louder with panic as he groped blindly for any trace of her. *"Francesca!"*

"Edward," she whimpered, and then she was there, finding him in the dark, wrapping her arms tightly around him, drawing him close. "Oh, *mio càro,* I—I thought you were gone, I—I thought you'd forgotten me!"

"I'd never do that, lass," he said fiercely. "Never, mind?"

As much to reassure himself as her, he touched her face, her cheeks wet with tears, her fragrance of orange blossoms and jasmine still magically clinging to her hair in the midst of so much destruction. Everything in the dark seemed exaggerated, as if his other senses had swelled to make up for the darkness. She was shaking against him, her breathing little more than broken sobs against his chest as the ship continued to roll and pitch with the force of the waves.

"You—you said I must be brave, Edward, and I have tried," she said in a tearful rush. "I have tried, *mio càro,* but I know, I know that this—this is not right, is it?"

He would have given all the riches of the world to be able to tell her anything other than the truth. From the first time he'd put to sea, he'd had to prepare himself for an end like this, and he'd always thought he'd be ready if it came. To have it happen now, when he'd been on the verge of discovering the first genuine happiness and joy in his life, seemed in itself a grotesque joke. But for Francesca to die with him—that was damnably, cruelly unfair.

"No," he admitted bleakly. "It's not right. It's wrong as hell. Everything that could save us has been done, but now we're in the hands of fate alone, and I can offer you nothing more."

"But we're together, Edward, aren't we?" she pleaded, her hands moving along his back, along his shoulders, sliding along the front of his coat, then tugging the buttons free to slip inside. "No matter what else happens, we are together, Edward, together, together, and—and—oh, my darling husband, I never wanted it to end like this!"

And then, to his shock, her mouth had found his and she was kissing him, scalding him with desire and with the raw urgency of the life she didn't want to end. At once his body responded, his weariness forgotten, and he tipped her head back over his arm, hungrily deepening the kiss that she'd begun. There'd be no time to stop now, no time even to think, only respond. He knew that, and so did she, and neither wanted it otherwise. Edward had looked at death in the black water churning around them, and he'd felt it trickle down his neck with the icy rain. But Francesca was giving him a chance to cheat death one last time, to be gloriously alive as only a man and woman together could be.

He plunged deeper into her mouth, unable to hold back as he poured a lifetime of wanting her into a single kiss, crushing her lips as he ground his body against hers. She was still shaking, but now from excitement and need instead of fear. The complete darkness and rocking motion that had been so disorienting before now seemed charged with the sensual heat between them, making the tiny cabin a special place of their own making.

She shoved the heavy, wet coat back from his shoulders as he tore first one arm, then the other free from the sleeves and let the coat drop behind him. He reached for her, found the narrowness of her waist, slid his open hands lower along the voluptuous curve of her hips. She'd shed the layers of shawls, and wore only the insubstantial linen of her shift, the warmth of her skin glowing through the thin fabric. His hands slid lower, and he realized she was kneeling on the bunk, the thin shift sliding high over her thighs.

His imagination gave pictures to all he could touch but couldn't see in the darkness. No, she'd even helped his imagination, because what he envisioned was the sly little nymph she'd drawn on the centaur's back, and with a groan he had to kiss her again. She pressed herself against him, her breasts soft and full against his chest, or maybe it was the ship that was rocking them together. He didn't know and he didn't care, not when he reached up to caress her breasts, taking her intoxicating moan of pleasure into his mouth as she stretched upward to offer him more.

For a moment she lifted her arms, a quick gesture he couldn't visualize until he realized she'd unpinned her hair, her fingers swiftly combing out her braids until the silky, scented hair was fanning over her bare shoulders and breasts and falling around them both like a fragrant, sensuous curtain.

But though he could feel her nipples, already ripe as little berries through the thin linen, it wasn't enough, not at all, and he hooked his thumbs into the tiny sleeves of her shift and pulled them down, over her shoulders and the tops of her arms until the fabric tore. She gave a little purr of satisfaction and shrugged, and then her breasts were beautifully bare, filling his hands with their sweet, heavy weight.

She wasn't shy, his Francesca, no missish reluctance, and she wasn't afraid to let him know he pleased her. She wriggled closer to the side of the bunk, swinging her legs over the edge and on either side of his hips, drawing him closer. She dropped her head over his shoulder, her breathing ragged and punctuated with sharp little animal cries of longing and mindless scraps of Italian that seemed all the more erotic because he didn't know their meaning.

Her nipples were so taut, distended, as he pulled and rubbed at them with his fingers and so aching for more that he could have spent the whole night just teasing them, just teasing her.

But there wasn't time, not for them, and like an ominous reminder came the cracking and splintering of wood as another part of the sloop—another piece of the mast, another railing?—gave way and washed over the side. There wasn't any damned time left at all, and already she was reaching between them, shoving aside the tails of his shirt, tugging open the buttons on the fall of his trousers, freeing him, touching him—Jesus, yes!—as if he needed any more encouragement at all, he was so hot and hard and thick, then her whispering more Italian, praise, desire, and hurry, hurry, *hurry*.

Unerringly he found her entrance, even in the dark. She was as ready as he, wet and swollen and so ready that she whimpered and writhed and clung to him when all he did was touch her with his fingers.

Not even the end of the world would stop him from taking her now. He jerked her to the very edge of the bunk and eased the tip of his member inside her, parting her, groaning at this other kind of wet, hot kiss as she panted and tried to wriggle and take more of him. He looped her thighs over his arms, opening her even further, and then with a long, single stroke, buried himself in her as deeply as he could.

She cried out, twisting around him so sinuously that he half wondered if she'd found her release already. Lord, she was tight, in the velvety way that could drive a man mad. He drew back and she trembled, and when he plunged back into her she was rising up to welcome him as he ground himself into her, against her, around her lush body.

Over and over he drove into her, over and over she met him, matching his rhythm and adding her own rocking and twisting and shimmying that drove him harder, hotter, almost mad with wanting her. She clung to his sweat-sheened shoulders, lavishing kisses on his skin that quickly turned to fierce little nips to echo his thrusts.

Higher and higher he pushed her, higher and faster as if they were each riding the howling storm around them as much as each other's passion. Higher and hotter and he thought it would never end and he never wanted it to and then he was exploding into her, more of himself than he'd ever given any woman because it was Francesca, his one love, his wife, his *life,* and all he had left. He heard her peaking cry, a gulping version of his own name as she convulsed around him, and with one last thrust he collapsed with her onto the bunk.

He couldn't say how long they lay like that, their arms and legs still tangled together, the ship still tossing and the wind still howling and the sea still pummeling at the sides of the ship, knocking at their little world inside the bunk. He could tell by how the sloops' timbers were groaning and creaking that the *Antelope* had settled deeper into the water, wallowing in the troughs of the waves rather than riding their crests.

He pulled the coverlet over them and with a sigh she curled her body into his, and as he settled his arm around her waist, he tried to think only of how warm and soft she was to hold and how impossibly dear she was to him, and not how soon it all would be dashed apart.

"My dearest Francesca," he said, gently pushing aside a damp lock of her hair to kiss her. "My own sweet wife."

She shifted over him, lying across his chest, and he wished he could see her face now, to see her smile down at him as he knew she must be. *"Non ce nessuno come te, mio càro."*

"You'll have to translate, lass," he ordered, though he really didn't care if she did or not. From her the words rolled over him like a caress, filled with affection and joy, no matter what they meant.

" 'There's no one like you, my dearest,' " she repeated in English. "Though it sounded much better in Italian."

"Agreed," he said. "Everything sounds more romantic in Italian."

"Then I shall have to teach you to speak it to me, eh?" She traced a fingertip lightly around his lips, both of them pretending that they'd have a future where such lessons could happen. *"Senza di te non ce sole nel cièlo."*

Was it the words themselves, or the bittersweet way she said it? *"Cielo* is heaven, isn't it?" he asked. "You say it often. As in *sànto cièlo,* meaning 'Edward, you provoking clod, how I'd like to take a belaying-pin to your head directly'."

She laughed softly, but when he reached up to cradle her cheek he felt the tears she didn't try to stop.

"*Sànto cièlo* means 'saints in heaven,' to whom I should be praying now instead of lying here with you."

"Then tell me what you said before, sweetheart."

" 'Without you there's no sun in the heavens,' " she whispered, and now her tears were spilling so freely that he felt them begin to drop onto his chest, warm and wet. "*Moriro senza di te, carissimo mio sposo.* 'I'd die without you, my dearest husband.' "

"Oh, lass," he groaned, pulling her closer. How could he possibly answer that, in English or Italian?

"*Moriro senza di te, carissimo mio sposo,*" she said, her voice breaking. "*E moriro con te.* 'I'd die without you, my dearest husband, and—and I would die with you.' "

"Don't say it," he said, his voice thick with cmotion. "Better that I tell you how much I love you, Francesca. Aye, I do. I love you."

"*E ti amo,* Edward," she whispered. "I love you, and always will, however long that always may be. Now hold me, if you please. Just—just hold me, my dearest, and don't let me go."

Silence.

It was the silence that woke Edward, jarring him awake with the same force as a gunshot. The incessant roar of the wind, the creaking and groaning of the sloop's timbers, the rushing and crashing of the storm-waves were so completely gone that their absence left a muted ringing in his head, as if his ears refused to accept such an unfamiliar void.

Instantly awake in the habit of sailors, he sat up in

the bunk, taking care not to disturb Francesca, still sleeping beside him. He wouldn't wake her until he was sure, until he had only good news to tell her, but already his heart was racing with possibilities and fresh hope. Not only were the sounds of the storm gone, but for the first time in days a faint edge of light outlined the closed door to their cabin. Could it truly be daylight, sweetest, most miraculous daylight, a beam he believed he'd never live to see again?

Swiftly he slipped from the bunk, muttering an oath as he stepped into the icy seawater still puddled there. He'd search for his boots and coat later. Hastily he stuffed his shirt into his trousers and buttoned the fall before he carefully opened the door just widely enough to ease through. Sure enough, an anemic daylight was filtering down the steps of the companionway, the hatches removed now, and he allowed his hopes to rise another notch. An end to the storm wouldn't solve all their problems, of course, for the *Antelope* was still riding dangerously low in the water, her mainmast shattered and her boat useless. But at least they'd have a chance now, a reprieve from the end that had seemed so hideously unavoidable last night.

He glanced back into the cabin, where a slice of that glorious pale light fell across Francesca's face. She was sleeping as soundly as a child, turned on her side with one arm flung back and her unbraided hair like a wild dark cloud of curls around her face and tumbling over her shoulders.

No, not a child, he decided, smiling, but that wicked little nymph with the centaur, now sated and blissfully content thanks to her equally sated husband. Her lips were parted, her features relaxed with sleep, and he flattered himself that last night he'd been able to give her that peace along with his love. God knows she'd given it to him. Who would have guessed they'd both fall asleep with near-certain death howling across the deck overhead?

Carefully he closed the door again, climbing up to the deck two steps at a time. If they did indeed have a fresh chance at salvation, he'd wake her, and together they could celebrate in the best way possible. That noisome little cabin was hardly the elegant suite of rooms in London that he'd envisioned for their honeymoon, but he couldn't imagine a more enthusiastic way to become husband and wife. He'd never experienced anything like it, and he felt himself growing hard again at the memory. Who would have guessed he'd find so much passion combined with so much love, and in his own wife at that?

He hated to agree with the rakish officers who'd bragged about their conquests among the local women in Naples, especially regarding his wife, but Francesca *was* different from the English women he'd bedded, uninhibited and ardent, so much so that he marveled that she'd been able to wait as long as she had, night after night on the voyage from Palermo. Perhaps there had been a benefit to those brothel-paintings by her old satyr of a father after all, though as her husband, he intended to be the only gentleman who knew it.

"Captain Ramsden, sir!" called Pettigrew excitedly as he hurried across the deck to Edward. "Have you seen anything like it, sir? In all your born days, sir, have you ever seen the like?"

Edward followed the lieutenant's pointing hand over the starboard rail, or where the rail used to be. The sloop's small crew stood gathered there—a bedraggled assortment, as bruised and battered as the *Antelope* herself, and with three days' beards on their jaws as well—grinning and slapping themselves on the back as they, too, stared out across the water. The sky was still overcast, the weak winter sun working hard to force any light through the low, gray clouds, but it was still bright and clear enough to see the narrow dark band of land on the horizon, rooftops, a church spire, the sails and masts of small boats or ships in a harbor.

"That be Folkestone, sir," said Pettigrew, nearly cackling with delight. "I know it well, my mam being born in Dymchurch parish. We've been blowed clear into the Straits o' Dover, sir, as neat as if we'd asked it. Can you fancy that, sir? The very Straits themselves!"

Edward could fancy it quite easily. They'd not only survived; they'd triumphed. They were within a mile of a friendly port, which was likely already putting out boats to come to their assistance. They'd been blown not off their course, but exactly upon it, the winds of the storm carrying them faster than they could ever expect in fair weather. He and Francesca could well be in London the day after tomorrow.

"*Che miracolo,*" he murmured, hardly believing what he saw.

"Beg pardon, Captain Ramsden, sir?" asked Pettigrew, perplexed. "Ah, but sir, here's Lady Edward, come to see for herself!"

Eagerly Edward turned, taking her hand and slipping his arm around her waist to hold her steady. She'd barely dressed—he could feel that she was naked beneath the long cloak she clutched tightly together, a fact he hoped none of the other men would realize—and her long hair remained untied and uncombed, blowing around her face. She still looked half asleep, her face without its usual rosy glow, her expression bewildered.

"You left me, *càro mio,*" she said plaintively. "I woke, and you were gone."

"But not far, lass, not far." He bent to kiss her quickly by way of apology before he gently turned her to the starboard. "And for the best of reasons! Look, Francesca. That's England, there, not a mile away. Folkestone, to be precise."

Dutifully she looked, holding her hair back from her face with one hand. "Folkestone," she repeated slowly. "England. We are safe then, Edward? The storm is finished? We will not die?"

He chuckled happily. "We've been saved to sail another day, sweetheart." He could wish she'd show a bit more emotion, but then the shock of all that happened to them would likely take its toll on any woman. "We could well be in London the day after tomorrow."

"Oh, Edward," she said softly, with a sadness he couldn't comprehend. "*Che miracolo, eh? Che miracolo.*"

*   *   *

So this was London, the grandest city in England.

Francesca stood alone, apart from the other passengers crowding at the rail of the Folkestone packet. The packet moved slowly along the crowded river, the pilot picking his way among the skiffs and barges and boats and ferries, navy ships and merchant brigs. If London was in truth the grandest city—home to a million citizens was the proud claim—then the Thames was her most traveled road, a constant parade of people and cargo, troops and market goods.

Yet to Francesca there seemed precious little grandeur to be found in London this morning. The river was dirty and murky, as full of rotting garbage and dead dogs as it was boats, no comparison at all for the clear blue waters of the Bay of Naples. The city that streamed endlessly along the river's banks was scarcely more appealing, the buildings crowded together and blackened with the soot and smoke of countless chimneys, either brick or gray stone so somber it made her ache for the joyful candy-pink of her old house, bright as a flower in the warm Neapolitan sun.

There'd be no warmth here, not from this sorry excuse for a sun, and though Francesca pulled her cloak more tightly around her shoulders, she still felt the chill deep in her bones. She'd been cold since the *Antelope* had been blown into English waters, and she feared she'd never be warm again. No wonder her father had fled this grim, gray city. She couldn't imagine his gleeful spirit trapped among these bleak walls and streets, any more than she could imagine her own finding real happiness here, either.

With a shiver that had little to do with the cold, she closed her eyes and tried to imagine herself in Naples instead, her old Naples, where the air was scented with flowers and the salty clean air of the bay, where every street was filled with music and laughter and neighbors calling merrily from one open window to the next, a carefree place where the sun had always shined in the day and the stars were bright as diamonds in the night sky.

A place now lost to her forever, a place where she'd been so certain of herself and her dreams, before she'd let Edward Ramsden into her heart ...

"Here you are, sweetheart," said Edward heartily as he joined her. Because of the size of the packet, there had been no private cabin for them, with Francesca sharing a space with several other women and Edward with the men. This was the first time since they'd left the *Antelope* the day before yesterday that she and Edward had been able to speak with any privacy, out of the hearing of others.

"I thought you were still below," he continued. "But I can't blame you coming on deck, not with a view like this. The glories of London are hard to resist, aren't they?"

She could not say much in favor of London, but certainly the glories of Edward were on full display. Pcart had labored long and hard in the cramped quarters of the packet to make his master ready to face an entire fleet of admirals. Every brass button had been polished like a tiny mirror, every inch of gold wire and enamel-work on the hilt and scabbard of his dress-sword glittering, the perfect broad-shouldered ideal of an English hero. No wonder the other passengers hung back from so great a personage, staring at Edward with wonder and awe.

But Francesca could see beyond the gold lace and epaulets to how the little muscle in Edward's jaw twitched and how often he was clearing his throat. She knew the signs, because she knew him. He was nervous, frightened in a way grand heroes were not supposed to be, and who could fault him? This morning in the Admiralty Office in Whitehall he would be facing a battle every bit as hazardous as any he'd fought at sea, and the stakes—his career and his honor—were exactly the same, even if his enemy would be sitting in a leather-covered armchair.

And now, wretched coward that she was, she would not be there with him.

"You look splendid, Edward," she said softly. "Truly a victorious hero, la! I am most proud of you, *càro mio*. The admirals will be awed and overwhelmed, and able to do nothing but heap more honors on your head."

He smiled almost shyly, so clearly grateful for her faith in him that she hated herself all the more. "It's entirely Peart's doing, you know. I can claim no more credit than any shopwindow display. Was he able to do as much with the wrinkles in your gown?"

She nodded, braving the cold to part her cloak and show how elegantly she'd also dressed this morning. Thanks to Peart, there wasn't a single wrinkle or crease in the cream-colored wool of her gown, a gift from Lady Hamilton in Palermo: a stylish high-waisted robe lined and trimmed with striped cream satin that accentuated her own dramatic coloring. The bodice was cut snug and low to display the lushness of her breasts, though for modesty and against the cold, she'd filled in the neckline with a fine linen scarf, and threaded an ivory ribbon through her dark hair.

Yet as flattering as the gown was, it was far more to Lady Hamilton's English taste than her own, as simple and elegant and blandly monochrome as London itself. But if Francesca were playing the part of Lady Edward Ramsden, then surely this was the precise costume for the role, as the expression on Edward's face instantly told her.

"You look lovely, Francesca," he said with such adoring admiration that she nearly cringed. "Oh, lass, you cannot know how much it will mean to me to have you there by my side when we go to Whitehall, especially looking as fine as this."

"About Whitehall," she said swiftly, wrapping her cloak closed again. "Edward, I—I do not believe I can go there with you this morning."

"You are ill," he said instantly, his face filled with concern as he took her hands. "I thought you'd looked pale yesterday, lass, and after all you've suffered these last days. I understand, I understand entirely."

"You must not worry over me, Edward, not when you've so much else before you this—"

"Hush, and mind me," he said. "Better you remain here, where you can rest, until Peart and I can make arrangements for more suitable lodgings ashore."

"Perhaps that *is* best," she said weakly, seizing at the excuse he'd so innocently provided. Coward,

coward, her conscience cried, but there was no way she could make herself tell him the truth when he looked at her like this, his blue eyes full of kindness and love and concern that she didn't deserve.

"Of course it is." He cleared his throat self-consciously, frowning down at their joined hands. "I've half-expected this anyway, Francesca, though there hasn't been time for us to speak alone before this. I was too rough with you. That is, I was, ah, inconsiderate, a damned inconsiderate, selfish boor, and I'm sorry for it. But the way you acted, how you responded—how could I know?"

"Edward," she said slowly. "Whatever are you saying?"

He cleared his throat again. "I'm saying that it wasn't until later, until I saw, ah, certain signs on my, ah, on the front of my shirt that I realized you'd been a virgin."

If he'd struck her outright, he couldn't have shocked her more.

"Because I was not as cold as your English ladies, because I *loved* you, you needed to study your linen for *proof* of my maidenhead?" she cried forlornly. "Why didn't you believe me when I told you my heart was my own, that I'd never taken a lover? Oh, *càro mio,* wasn't my word good enough for you?"

"Because of those pictures of your father's, and how freely you talked, and flirted—well, what else was I to think?" he said defensively. "Not that any of that matters. I married you regardless, and you're mine now, my wife in every way. I love you, lass, and you love me, and that's all that's truly important, isn't it?"

He smiled again, and kissed her as if everything were as pleasantly well-ordered as he wanted it to be, as if love really were more about possession than giving.

"Oh, blast, there's the boatman to carry Peart and me to shore," he said, looking past her to the water. "I must go, sweetheart. I'll go slay my dragons while you rest here, and then together we shall celebrate, yes?"

She tried to smile, wanting him to have that for a memory of her. "You will take care of yourself, *càro mio?*" she said softly. "Whatever else happens this morning, Edward, you will remember that you are the only one I ever loved, won't you?"

"I will," he said, "and you remember the same of me, mind?"

He kissed her one last time before he hurried over the side and into the boat. She watched as the boatmen rowed to the stone steps that led from the water to the street, and when he paused at the top, lifting his hat to her in salute, she waved, keeping her hand raised for a long moment after he'd turned away and disappeared into the city from her view.

"Mr. Bowden," she called to the packet's bos'n. "Would you please call for a boat to shore for me?"

The man bowed, tugging on the front of his knitted cap. "Very well, my lady. You'll be joining th' lord captain after all?"

"He would like that, wouldn't he?" she said sadly, truthfully. "And please, Mr. Bowden, have my trunk brought up from the ladies' cabin. For when I go ashore, I shall not return."

12

*E*dward sensed the exclusion as soon as he walked past the colonnade and through the archway that marked the entrance to the Admiralty Office in Whitehall.

He didn't belong here, and though no one greeted him with anything other than respect, even warmth and congratulations on the Battle of Nile, it was clear that every male he passed—admirals, fellow captains and lesser officers, seamen, clerks, and porters, even the pair of carved stone sea horses prancing overhead on either side of the archway—knew something he didn't, a very grim, unhappy something that he simultaneously dreaded yet anticipated. He'd waited long enough; it was time, past time, to learn the truth.

Yet as he walked through the courtyard, his heels echoing across the cobblestones, his head high, and an easy, confident smile on his face, his palms were damp inside his gloves and his heart was racing so fast he might as well be marching to Tyburn to meet Jack Ketch instead of the Admiralty Board. He forced himself to climb the stairs one at a time instead of the two or three his feet longed to jump, and when he gave his name and his reports from the *Centaur* to the clerk and took his place on the bench, he managed the perfect measure of officer's impatience and gentleman's boredom, tapping on the side of his leg while the clerk scurried off to arrange his fate.

God, he wished Francesca were here with him. Even though he understood perfectly well why she wasn't, even though it was entirely his fault, even though he hadn't apologized nearly enough to make it right and likely never could. How could he? She'd given him the greatest gift a woman had to give a man, and he'd been such an ignorant, damnable bastard that he hadn't even noticed. He didn't deserve ever to be forgiven after that.

But to have her on this bench beside him now in that elegant new gown, her little hand upon his knee, teasing and praising him and telling him how everything was going to be fine—*naturalmente!*—would be a comfort indeed. All she'd have to do was smile, and he'd feel her love glow and sparkle around him.

He missed her. Pure and simple, that was it, and he'd never said that about anyone else in his life. Before Francesca, he'd always been content to be alone. He'd preferred it, in fact. But now because he loved her, he felt her absence sorely, and missed her more than he'd ever thought possible.

He sighed dejectedly, trying not to look down the hall where the clerk had vanished. He knew that when she'd become his wife, Francesca had sworn to be with him through good times and bad, but so far all she'd had to share was his misfortunes, and he'd no guarantee his luck wasn't going to worsen further, either. No wonder she'd looked so sad this morning on the packet. If he'd been bound to see anyone other than the First Lord of the Admiralty, he would have stayed with her instead.

But he *would* make it up to her, regardless of what happened this morning. He'd already sent Peart to make the arrangements at Clarendon's for rooms and a special dinner. Tomorrow he'd take Francesca to a mantua-maker for new gowns, an evening at the theater or opera, a tour through the Royal Academy Exhibition at Somerset House, whatever she pleased. Perhaps he'd even surprise her with some sort of bauble from a jeweler's as a wedding present. On the same paper as the nymph and centaur she'd sketched a curling plume, a brooch of cut stones that he could have a goldsmith copy.

That would surprise her, especially if he gave it to her one evening in bed. He could imagine her pinning it into her hair at once, wearing not a blessed stitch beyond the pearls in her ears and diamonds in her hair, lolling back against the bolster like some pagan houri with her arms folded behind her head so that—

"Captain Lord Edward Ramsden, sir?" asked the clerk, breaking his customary clerkly aloofness to bow low before Edward. "If you please, Captain, Lord Spencer will see you. This way, my lord."

Edward let himself be ushered down the hallway, his head spinning with questions. Earl Spencer was the current First Lord of the Admiralty, and not one that generally bothered with mere captains. Hadn't Edward's orders told him to report to the board as a whole? For Lord Spencer to see him now, especially without an appointment, made no more sense than the rest of this infernal mess.

The clerk knocked and pushed open the double doors with another bow as he announced Edward. Lord Spencer's chamber was far grander than most of the other offices in Whitehall, with a high coffered ceiling, a marble mantelpiece above a fire that must be consuming at least half a forest, and a red Turkish carpet on the floor. He had the best view, too, with tall windows that looked directly across the horse guards' parade to the Mall and St. James's Park.

But despite its luxury, the office would never be mistaken for a private drawing room or parlor. There were too many maps and charts and reports scattered on every surface, with an enormous globe in one corner and an elaborate wind indicator beside the window. Special hanging cords could be pulled to summon individual clerks and messengers, and the shelves along one wall held not only books and bound maps, but curiosities brought by captains who'd returned from distant voyages: a branch of coral, an enormous butterfly in a crystal presentation box, a many-tiered temple carved from ivory.

"Good day to you, my lord captain," said Lord Spencer, rising and coming from behind his desk to shake Edward's hand. He was a tall, slender man, grown round-shouldered in the service of his country, his close-cropped ginger hair peppered with gray, but his smile was genuine and warm as he motioned toward two armchairs before the fire. "You take me by surprise, my lord. Your passage must have been exceedingly swift."

"The winds obliged your call for haste, my lord," said Edward, waiting for Lord Spencer to sit before he, too, took his chair. Cordiality, no matter how warm, seldom overruled hierarchy, at least not in this building, and not with an earl. But still Edward could cautiously interpret Lord Spencer's genteel interest as a favorable sign. Surely he wouldn't be as hospitable if Edward's next step were to be a court-martial, would he?

"You didn't run afoul of the recent storm, did you?" asked Lord Spencer as he nodded to a servant who had appeared carrying a tray with tumblers and a bottle of claret. "We've had nothing but cold rain and sleet here for days. This is the first morning we've seen the sun, and a welcome sight it was."

"We did run into a bit of a blow in the Channel, aye," said Edward cautiously, knowing better than to burden an admiralty lord with the weather. He shook his head as the servant bowed before him with the tray. "No, none for me, my lord, thank you."

"Come, Ramsden, don't hold back on my account," said Lord Spencer. "Besides, you may well have need of a drop of consolation in your belly before I've said what I must. This is a most fine claret, too. The revenue men have had an excellent season among the smugglers."

This time Edward accepted the claret, though the costly wine could have been rainwater for all the taste it had in his mouth now. "You have questions regarding my report, my lord?"

"The secretary shall read it for me," said the earl with a dismissive wave of his hand. "However, knowing your record, I doubt I shall have any queries or quandaries that require elaboration."

"Then if there have been other occurrences, my lord, that have made me judged unfit to retain my command of His Majesty's ship *Centaur*—"

"None whatsoever," answered the Lord Spencer with maddening evenness. "Your record with the navy has been exemplary. I believe, in fact, you are in line for a decoration in honor of your conduct at Aboukir Bay."

A medal for the Nile: at least Francesca would be proud. But Edward frowned down at the claret in his tumbler, his frustration almost unbearable. "Then forgive me, my lord, if I do not understand why I have been relieved of my command and summoned here to you."

"Because I could conceive of no more proper way to do this," said the earl with a sigh. "I cannot recall ever having to perform such a task, and I am heartily sorry for your sake that I must do so now. You are already aware, of course, of the death of your brother Major Lord St. John in Spain, sometime in the summer, I believe."

Edward sucked in his breath. Letters often went astray due to the war, and even official dispatches had been slow to reach them in Naples. But St. John dead, gone so long without him knowing—he felt the shock of it even though he hadn't been close to his brother.

"No, my lord," he said softly. "I had not received the news of his death."

"Ah, ah, Ramsden, I didn't realize." The earl grunted, and shook his head. "Hellacious circumstances, too, being shot by one of his own men. A great loss, of course. To your family, and to the country. My condolences."

Edward nodded, silent. He had not seen St. John in at least five years, nor had he wished to. Perhaps because he'd been the brother closest to Edward in age, as boys he'd always taken pains to ally himself with George and Frederick against Edward, and the tendency for bullying had lingered into his adulthood. Edward suspected St. John must have made a miserable officer, but he'd never guessed his brother's life would end because of it.

"That is not all, Ramsden," warned the earl ominously, rubbing on his cheek. "There is, I fear, considerably more. At least Major Lord St. John died in the service of his king. The same cannot, I fear, be said of your other two brothers."

"My other two brothers?" repeated Edward faintly, though his thoughts were already racing toward the inevitable, ironic conclusion of this whole unspeakable farce. "What has become of them?"

"An 'accident' of the most grievous, most ludicrous sort." The earl grimaced, as if even to speak of such events was distasteful. "While you were risking your life for your country in the company of Admiral Lord Nelson, your two brothers were risking theirs for the purest folly imaginable. They had hired a French balloonist to take them high aloft in the company of two harlots they had likewise hired for their lascivious diversion. You can, I am sure, guess the rest, and the shameful scene when the wreckage was discovered. The scandal was enormous—the print-makers and wags have never had such sordid grist—and the only good that shall come from such a mess is that you, Your Grace, are a gentleman capable of removing the stain upon your family's ancient name."

Your Grace? Edward shook his head, grasping at the arm of his chair as the only way to keep his bearings. All three of his brothers lost, and him the only one left. All three of his brothers gone, dying the same wretched ways that they'd lived. All of them dead, and him the only one left, and not a single chance remaining for reconciliation or apologies or answers or whatever else he'd always hoped for from his brothers but now would never have, not in this life.

Your Grace? He had never remotely considered himself an heir to the title, nor did he want to possess it now. Instead he wanted to be the *Centaur*'s captain again, with an honorable purpose in life. Hell, they could make him master of a tiny sloop like the *Antelope*, and he'd prefer it to this. He did not want to wear a cloak trimmed with ermine, or attend the king at court, or sit in the House of Lords, or oversee at least four separate households, or accept the responsibility for the lives of countless servants and tenants, and most of all, he did not want to become his brother or his father, either.

Your blasted, bloody, double-damned *Grace*. Edward, seventh Duke of Harborough, Earl of Heythrop, Baron Tyne. He'd have to learn to answer to that now whether he wished to or not. If his three brothers and father had together wished to contrive one final, vindictive cruelty to inflict upon him, they had succeeded beyond measure.

"Perhaps you should have been told earlier, Your Grace, but a letter seemed most heartlessly impersonal. His Majesty himself suggested that this would be the better way to ease the shock you must be feeling." The earl rose slowly to his feet, bowing stiffly before Edward. "I am honored to be the first to wish you well, Your Grace, and many long years of happiness and contentment."

Damnation, he now outranked the First Lord of the Admiralty. He was supposed to *sit* here and be grand while the Earl of Spencer bowed to *him*.

He rose abruptly to his feet, thumping his tumbler on the table beside him and splattering claret across the carpet. "I do not want this, my lord, and I never have. Why can't I remain a captain? What the devil will a medal for the Nile mean to me now? Why can't I continue to serve His Majesty in the way I can be of the greatest use?"

"You know the reason yourself, Your Grace," said the earl patiently, "else you would not be asking now. As much as I hate to refuse the talents and experience of an officer such as yourself, you know as well as I that the navy cannot have a peer of the realm rushing about in battle."

"But damnation, I was—I *am*—a captain in the king's navy first!"

"This is as much about what you represent as who you *are*, Your Grace," said the earl severely, his eyes turning hard as a flint. "If a duke, a peer, were captured, can you imagine what Napoleon would make of it? No, I am sorry, but it will not do. It *cannot* do. His Majesty himself was most adamant about that fact. When you gave up your commission to the *Centaur,* you were removed from the list of able and active captains."

To be removed from the list was as good as being dead. Somewhere another captain had moved up the list, into his place, another captain who could rejoice in knowing he was one step closer to becoming an admiral.

Another captain who hadn't been cursed and ruined by being made a damned *duke* instead.

"There are other ways to serve, Your Grace," continued the earl. "I should be honored and grateful to have your expertise here in the Admiralty, and the Navy is always in need of advocates in the House of Lords."

He didn't want to spend his life rotting behind a desk. He could give up the fighting if he had to, but not the sea, landlocked forever the way the navy wished for him. Hell, the sea was where he *belonged.*

But all anyone else could see was astounding good fortune. Clearly Admiral Lord Nelson had thought that——he'd known the truth in Palermo, of course, he and the Hamiltons both, though all of them refused to admit it—and even Lady Hamilton had believed the same. What was it she'd said to her outside the villa? Something about whatever happened in life, he'd always have Francesca, just as she would have him.

Francesca.

"I must go tell my wife," he muttered, as much to himself as to Lord Spencer. "I have to tell her now."

"Your wife?" asked the earl with obvious delight. "I'd no idea you'd wed, Your Grace! What splendid news! Who is this fortunate new duchess?"

"A lady who has lived her entire life in Naples," said Edward. He couldn't guess what Francesca's reaction would be. Most ladies would be thrilled to learn they'd become an English duchess, but Francesca was so unlike other women that she could just as easily see the title as a grand, glorious trap—exactly as he did himself. "I doubt you would know her, my lord. She accepted my offer at Sir William Hamilton's palazzo, and we were wed just before Christmas."

"With Vesuvius shooting fire and the Isle of Capri in the background?" marveled the earl. "Lud, she'll have every lady in London—Lady Spencer most of all—desperate to know how she coaxed you into such an idyllic wedding!"

"Excuse me, My Lord, but I must go to my wife now," he said, already on his way to the door. *"Now."*

He took his hat from the clerk and hurried down the hall, down the stairs, past every grinning jackass who wanted to wish him well, all of them knowing what he'd only just learned. He kept his gaze straight ahead, mercilessly intent on not letting them say one blasted word. He could do that, couldn't he? Wasn't that one of the ridiculous prerogatives of being the damned Duke of Harborough?

What if one of them reached Francesca before he

could? What if she learned of this from someone else, or worse, thought that he'd known and kept it a secret and hadn't told her himself?

"Aha, good day, Your Grace!" called a braying voice he unfortunately recognized at once. "A new-minted duke, a hero of the Nile, and the luckiest bastard this side of heaven! Come, let me stand beside you, and see if some of that gilt will rub off upon me!"

"Good day, McCray," said Edward grudgingly as the other captain fell into step beside him. It somehow fit with the rest of this wretched day that he'd meet Stephen McCray here in the Whitehall courtyard. Edward had always found McCray irritating, given to too much forced familiarity, heavy drinking, and whoring, and known for a ready willingness to ignore regulations when his superiors wouldn't notice.

But the irony was bitterly unmistakable: Here was McCray grinning up at him like a mongrel dog in his shabby uniform with the tarnished braid and dandruff on his epaulets, one of the most unworthy examples of an officer in the entire service. Yet McCray still held his place on the captain's list, while Edward in his spotless superfine uniform, with all his honors and flawless record in battle, did not.

" 'Good day', aye, I'd say it was if I were you, with so much good luck plopped like a plum into your pocket," continued McCray with a broad wink. "But then you always were one to play your cards close to your chest, weren't you, Ramsden? Oh, pardon, pardon, I meant *Your Grace*. Tell me, Your Grace, have you grown too grand to come drink a pot or two with an old shipmate?"

The last way Edward wished to spend this afternoon was drinking with Stephen McCray, and being too grand was the least of his reasons.

"Forgive me, McCray, but I have another engagement," he said, lengthening his stride to try to rid himself of the other captain. "Another time, perhaps."

But McCray refused to be shrugged off quite so easily, trotting along to keep pace. "Off to see your lady-bird, then? Now that's an appointment any man would wish to keep, dawdling between the sheets with a pretty little hussy, and before the sun's down, too!"

Now the man was talking pure rubbish, and at the archway to the street quickly Edward nodded to the porter to summon him a hackney, the only sure way to escape a bore like McCray. "You are mistaken, McCray. Now if you'll excuse me—"

"Nay, not mistaken, not hardly," insisted McCray. "Oh, don't be shy about it, Your Grace. I know how you high-bred officers live. Cards at White's, a box at the opera, and a fancy mistress primed and paid to spread her legs whenever you wish it. I saw an old lieutenant of mine just this morning, and he told me all about how he'd carried you and your trollop clear from Palermo. Pettigrew said she was a hot little Italian piece, ready for—"

That was when Edward's fist found McCray's jaw. Instantly, efficiently he caught the other man beneath the chin, feeling the fleshiness beneath McCray's jaw as he knocked him backward and off his feet and hard to the paving stones. One blow, that was all it took to silence him, and without a single look backward Edward climbed into the hackney and ordered the driver onward. He had a muddled impression of gaping, startled faces as the hackney pulled away, of some men laughing and others pointing and jeering, and the horrified porter rushing to help McCray, for no officer, however shabby or disreputable, should be found on his threadbare ass before Whitehall.

With a groan, Edward sank back against the squabs and closed his eyes. His heart was pounding with unthinking fury, his blood boiling with anger at what that bastard Pettigrew had said about Francesca. But he also realized how dangerously close he'd come to pounding McCray to lifeless pulp and bone, using him to lash out at all the frustrations of this morning. What the devil was happening to him, anyway? Even a duke could be tried for murder.

Che miracolo, indeed. Wearily he gazed from the hackney's window, and tried to think of how he'd explain his—no, their—newly upside-down world to Francesca.

To his wife.

To Her Grace, his duchess.

As the hackney jostled its way through the crowded London streets, Francesca once again took the well-creased scrap of paper from her reticule, smoothed it over her knee, and read the address. *John Peacock, 12 Barlow Street, Westminster, London.*

She didn't know why she needed to read it again, for it was certainly a simple enough address to remember. Perhaps it was the words themselves that offered reassurance more than information. Written long ago in her father's familiar slapdash penmanship, the ink fading away now just as he'd done himself, the note was the one connection she had between her and her father, and now her and her uncle.

How like Papa to change his surname when he'd moved from London to Naples, and how like him, too, to trade the gaudy, proud Peacock for the sprightly Robin! He'd laughed merrily when he'd explained it to her, though as a girl she'd never quite understood the jest. Now it simply worried her. What would this proud Uncle Peacock of hers make of a magpie Robin like her, suddenly appearing to beg a place in his nest?

She wondered if her father had even written his brother of her existence, and if her uncle had accepted the artwork and antiques she'd shipped to his address from Naples. There was always the chance that her uncle could have died like her father, or simply moved to a different house, or the ship with her treasures could have foundered or been captured by the French, and never arrived in London at all.

The hackney slowed to a stop before a neat brick house with glossy black shutters and three well-scrubbed white steps to the front door. The neighborhood was quietly prosperous and genteel, an appropriate residence for a retired merchant like Uncle Peacock was supposed to be. As the driver hauled her single traveling chest to the door for her, she hesitated, considering asking him to wait until she was sure she'd be welcome. But it was too late for doubts now, and shoving back her hood, she paid the driver and knocked upon the door, head high and her smile as blithely confident as she could make it.

Besides, where else would she go? She'd left Edward, and she couldn't go back. She had no money, no friends, no family in London beyond this single old gentleman.

Oh, Edward, I am sorry!

With a creak the door opened quickly, so quickly that Francesca suspected the housekeeper who'd answered had been watching her arrival.

"Good day," she said. "Is Master Peacock at home?"

"Might I ask who is calling, ma'am?" The housekeeper's expression remained properly impassive, her hand remaining on the doorknob as a precaution. She was an older woman with a round, ruddy face, her plumpness accentuated by an old-fashioned starched pinner-apron and an extravagantly ruffled cap tied beneath her chin.

Without thinking Francesca took an extra little breath. "Miss Francesca Robin of the city of Naples, in the Kingdom of Two Sicilies," she said, "and I believe Master Peacock is expecting me."

"Oh, indeed, miss, he is, he is!" cried the woman with a joyous shriek, her hand fluttering to her breasts as she flung the door wide for Francesca. "Oh, Master Peacock, it *is* her, saved from the French! She has come, sir, just as you wished and prayed! Your niece is come at last!"

"Has she, Mrs. Monk?" A short, heavy-set man in an old-fashioned wig bustled into the hallway as fast as the cane he used for his gout would let him. "So you are my niece, young woman? You are my brother's fair Francesca? Come, come, stand here in the light so I might look at you properly!"

Promptly Francesca did as she was told, standing in the center square of the black and white marble checkerboard floor of the hallway, lifting her face to the sun washing in through the fanlight over the door. As the man studied her, she in turn studied him: a stern face, softened with age, a thin-lipped mouth that would brook no nonsense. But to her shock the eyes in that stern face were exactly the same as her father's, dark and full of mischief, with wildly bristling brows that curved and swooped across his forehead and now rose with dramatic disbelief.

"You are Thomas's daughter, no doubt," he proclaimed with wondering satisfaction. "You have his spirit, his eyes, though thank the lord your mother gave you her beauty instead of his. Doubtless you have Thomas's willfulness, too, if you found your way to my doorstep clear from Italy."

"You are . . . *kind,*" whispered Francesca, overwhelmed with relief and his generosity. His eyes were so much like poor Papa's, it was as if he were here with her again.

"But you are my only kin, missy," countered her uncle, "and I will not turn you away. Scarcely, ha! You must consider my house as your own, and you must stay as long as it pleases you. Welcome home, Miss Francesca, welcome home."

Home, home: and Francesca burst into tears.

*   *   *

Edward sat sprawled in an overstuffed armchair before the fire in the most lavish and most costly suite of rooms in the Clarendon, the same rooms, claimed Peart in uncharacteristic awe, that were always requested by a certain Russian archduchess whenever she came to London. But damnation, now they were *his*, thought Edward gloomily, the exclusive quarters of the seventh Duke of Harborough.

He took another long pull from the bottle of claret beside him, not bothering with the glasses— *two* damned glasses, as if he'd expected company— that the footman had provided on then same silver tray. He didn't even particularly like claret, expensive or otherwise, but that was what dukes were supposed to drink, and tonight he intended to get as righteously drunk as any mortal duke could.

For what seemed like the thousandth time that evening, he looked up at the drawing of the centaur and the nymph that he'd tucked into the frame over the mantelpiece, covering the genteel still life. He held the bottle up, haphazardly toasting the nymph, then swore and drank again.

She'd been gone when he returned to the *Antelope*. No note, no message, nothing to prove she'd ever been there, not even his old gold anchor ring that he'd been so proud to give her at their wedding. She'd barely waited until he'd been out of sight, then as cool as you please, she'd asked for a boat to shore, and vanished.

The boatman was sought, and produced, and could say no more than that. No one around the steps or wharf had seen her afterward, no driver that was questioned could swear they'd taken her as a fare. He had promised rewards to a score of men who sought her, but he already knew they'd find nothing.

He'd always admired his wife's cleverness, her resourcefulness, and if she didn't wish to be found, she wouldn't be. She had disappeared into London, and she had left him.

In her way, she'd been honest with him. She'd said from the beginning that they would part if they didn't suit—her words, as if she'd been referring to a bespoke waistcoat instead of a marriage—that she wouldn't burden him or make demands upon him afterward. She'd even said good-bye after a fashion, there on the dock of the *Antelope* when he'd been so all-fired eager to be off to Whitehall. She'd told him everything, and though he'd listened, he hadn't heard a blessed word.

She'd been honest, aye. And if he were being honest now himself, he'd admit that nothing in his life hurt as much as having her decide he did not suit as a husband.

"Forgive me, Your Grace," said Peart, gently shaking his shoulder as if he were some old sot snoring in his favorite chair at White's. "But you've a visitor, Your Grace."

"The hell I do," grumbled Edward crossly, slurring his consonants only the slightest bit. "And I heard you knock, Peart, so don't smirk and pretend I didn't. Now send this bloody meddlesome pest on his way, go, go! Haven't I told you I'll see no one?"

"But you'll see me, Ned," said the tall gentleman as he dropped easily into the armchair across from

Edward's. "Though damn me if I wish to be called a 'bloody meddlesome pest.' Hardly civil, especially from my oldest friend."

"A bloody meddlesome friend, then," said Edward, unable to keep a delighted smile from spreading slowly across his face despite all his most melancholy intentions. "I should have expected you'd appear, Will, like black soot on white linen."

"Ah, Ned, you were ever the gracious host," said William, Earl of Bonnington, taking the second tumbler of claret that Peart had so thoughtfully filled for him. "But with all London chattering of little else but the prodigal return of the heroic new Duke of Harborough, I couldn't bear to keep away."

"To the devil with them all," said Edward, but his heart wasn't in it. Because of the war, he hadn't seen William for nearly three years, yet the months fell away in an instant as soon as his friend had grinned, almost as if they were boys again, building another fortress in the elm tree. Not only was William now a full-fledged peer himself, but he'd improved considerably from his gawky, gap-toothed youth, growing into the sort of rakishly handsome gentleman that made the ladies sigh, with broad shoulders, black curling hair, and a smile of staggering charm. But to Edward he was still the same old Will, fifty-six days his junior and the best friend he'd ever had, and the only one he'd welcome here now to share his misery.

"So," began William, crossing one leg comfortably over the other. "I have heard that you have taken a wife, Ned. Truth, or lie?"

"Truth," admitted Edward with a groan. "The

warmest, most intelligent, most charming, clever, and beautiful lady you will ever meet. There's not a woman in London who can hold a candle to her, Will."

Pointedly his friend glanced around the room. "Then where are you hiding her? Where is this paragon, this ideal, this goddess of feminine perfection?"

"Gone," said Edward bleakly, covering his eyes with his arm. "As soon as we reached London, she disappeared, and I haven't seen her since."

"She wasn't carried off? No foul play?"

Edward shook his head. "I would have heard if there were. She left me, Will, plain and simple, turned her back and walked away."

William whistled low. "Did the wretched little harlot know she'd become a duchess?"

"Francesca's not a harlot, Will," said Edward sharply. "You might be my oldest friend, but I'll still insist on satisfaction if you call her that again."

"Because you love her, don't you?" William smiled sadly. "You poor old bugger. You finally find a lady to your liking, and she doesn't return the favor."

"But she does love me, Will, I'm sure of it!" Edward pounded his fist on the arm of the chair from frustration. "That's what makes this all such a damned puzzle. I love her, and I'd wager my life she loves me the same. So where in blazes is she hiding?"

"That's what we must discover, isn't it?" William poured himself more claret, then refilled Edward's glass as well. "My two greatest talents are hunting and women, so combining the two should make for divine sport. Your little vixen won't keep herself hidden forever, you know. Have you a likeness of her?"

"Only that," said Edward morosely, pointing at the sketch of the nymph and the centaur. "It's not exactly her, but close enough. Mind you look only at the face, Will or I'll have to strike out your eyes."

William whistled again, this time in unabashed admiration. "You did enjoy yourself in merry old Italy, didn't you? No wonder you want her back, and on her back, too, from the—"

"Will," warned Edward ominously. "Recall that Francesca is my wife, and that I have always bettered you at swords and pistols both."

"You will never let me forget it, will you?" His grin softened again. "But we shall find her, Ned. Wherever she is, we'll find her."

But Edward was still gazing up at the sketch.

"Oh, my sweet Francesca," he said, his voice a rough whisper of longing. "I do love you, you know. Still do, and always will, even though you played me for the world's greatest fool. *Grazie, grazie,* and devil take the rest, eh?"

With the neck of the bottle dangling between two fingers, he stared down into the dying fire, watching the sparks explode and scatter upward when the last log finally burned through and collapsed in two. All he wanted was to find her, and talk to her, and say whatever he had to make her come back.

And later, after William had left, much later, and for the first time since Edward had left Palermo, the familiar nightmare of the *Centaur* and the *L'Orient* returned like a forgotten old lover to steal his sleep.

13

$\mathcal{F}$or two weeks of hard work, Francesca had anticipated this moment, and with a chisel and mallet she carefully began to pry away the nails that had sealed the first of the wooden crates.

"Shouldn't we ask one of the footmen to do that, miss?" asked Uncle Peacock anxiously as he watched Francesca wrestle with the crate. "That's heavy work for a lady, miss."

But Francesca only grinned as she pulled off the top planks and plunged her hand deep into the wood shavings that filled the crate. She'd been hearing that anxious cry from her uncle and Mrs. Monk repeatedly since she'd begun transforming these two ground floor parlors into her new London gallery.

Once her uncle had assured her that he never used the rooms—that he in fact seldom came below stairs at all on account of his gout—she had thrown herself into every detail of planning, striving to make the long, dark room feel as much like her airy Neapolitan studio as possible. She'd had the carpets taken up and the floors left bare, chosen shades of pink (a choice that clearly horrified her uncle) for the painted walls, and replaced the elderly dark furnishings with wide garden benches and striped cushions.

Secretly what she yearned for was much more complicated: a home like the one she'd had to flee in Naples, a place to make her own. It wouldn't have to be grand. She didn't want that, even if she could afford it. What she craved was the warmth and security, and in a strange way, the coziest little nest she'd ever called home had been the tiny cabin she'd shared with Edward on board the *Antelope*.

She'd done as much of the work as possible herself, an apron around her waist and her hair tied up in a kerchief. She'd toiled not only because she wished to keep her expenses low, but also because she hoped that, if she kept her hands busy, then her head and her heart would be more at peace.

Yet even so, not a minute passed that she didn't think of Edward, of how he'd laugh at this or tease her about that, or how the lines etched by the sun around his eyes would crinkle and fan when he smiled at her. She'd worried so much about what had happened to him that day at Whitehall, and though she was convinced it must have been only good—he was simply too fine a man and an officer for it to be otherwise—she still cared too much about him *not* to worry.

But the sorriest truth was that she worried because she cared, and she cared because she loved him, loved him more each day they were apart rather than less, loved him so much that each night she lay alone in her bed with her hands clenched at her side in the dark and stared at the canopy overhead, unable to sleep, unable to cry.

Most likely he'd already left London, and gone back to sea with new orders, where he'd always be happiest, and happier still without the inconvenience of an unsuitable wife. Most likely, being a man, he'd already begun to forget their wonderfully foolish marriage. For both their sakes, she believed she'd done the right thing—she *knew* she had—yet all the believing in the world didn't seem to ease the pain and the longing she felt.

But this morning she must concentrate on unpacking, and carefully she grasped the heavy frame with both hands and pulled the first picture from the crate. She pulled off the linen wrap, scanned the surface of the canvas quickly to make sure it hadn't suffered during the long voyage from Naples, and then turned to display it to Uncle Peacock, sitting on one of the benches with his gouty leg propped high and eager for his private showing.

"Ah!" he exclaimed with genuine pleasure. "A view of the Forum in Rome! Very handsome, very handsome! Canaletto or Pannini?"

"Giovanni Paolo Pannini," replied Francesca, setting the first painting down against the wall as she reached for the next. She'd been agreeably surprised by her uncle's knowledge of art; he might not have had her father's talent for painting, but he certainly shared his eye for others' work. It was much of the reason he had given over these rooms to her, to gain a private gallery of his own, too.

One by one she unpacked the paintings and vases, sculptures and etchings from the crates, dividing them into those she would sell, and those that were her father's best treasures and not for sale, until only two boxes remained.

One held the last Madonna she'd painted before she'd left Naples, and as she pulled it from the crate, she remembered the afternoon when she'd taken Edward upstairs to her little studio up under the eaves. That had been the first time she'd seen more to him than the proper English officer. He'd been concerned for her even then, warning her to take care, and she knew if she let herself remember any more, she would cry, here in front of her uncle. But Edward had liked this painting so especially that it was difficult for her to look at it now and not think of him, sentimental fool that she was.

"Ah, now, that one is perhaps the finest of the lot," said Uncle Peacock, nodding with approval. "The expression in the faces, the empathy and love between the mother and babe is exquisite."

"I'm glad you see so much in it," she said softly, bringing the painting closer for him to see. "It is one of my favorites, too."

"As it should be." He peered at the surface through his spectacles, his smile one of pure happiness. "So who is this rare artist, eh?"

"Francesca Robin," she said shyly with a disingenuous little laugh. "And how flattered I am, Uncle, that you'd find such merit in my humble brush!"

He looked over his spectacles at her, his eyes carrying exactly the same gleeful glint that her father's had. "I may be as old as Father Time, my dear, but I am not a fool. False modesty has no place with a gift such as yours. You must be confident in your talent, and take pride in such a rare blessing. Certainly your father did, you know. He claimed you'd surpassed him, and if this truly is your work, as I suspect, then he was right."

Francesca flushed. "I do take pride in my work, Uncle," she ventured. "But no one in Naples wished to show it on account of my being female."

"Then it was high time you left, my dear," he declared. "This is a most marvelous painting, worth ten times the rubbish the Academy showed last year. You are to be congratulated, not scorned."

"But will the dealers and the critics agree?" she asked anxiously.

"If they but use their eyes, they will," he reasoned." The love captured here could only be understood so completely by another woman, and that is what makes this painting so special. Even an old bachelor like I can see it, Francesca. It's your gift, but it's also what will set you apart from the men, no matter what they might say. And if my eyes can see it, then every expert in town will as well."

"But I will not be selling to experts," she said. "I intend to invite only my oldest and most loyal English patrons who visited me in Naples, and pray that they will be interested in my work as well as the, ah, the Raphaels and Guidos that Papa and I sold."

"The forgeries, you mean." He clicked his tongue, scolding. "An English gentleman touring through Italy is willing to toss his money away without a thought. He is on holiday in a foreign land, free of guilt and common sense, and because the spending is a pleasure unto itself, he doesn't care if he must later hang the so-called Raphael in the back parlor at home to avoid his friends' mockery. But here in London, he will consider his purchases much more closely, and before they buy a Raphael, he will insist on an expert appraisal, and you, miss, would be exposed."

"Exposed?" she repeated faintly, not liking the tone of this lecture at all.

"Exposed," he said again, more firmly, "and if those experts determine that you willfully intended to defraud your customers, which indubitably you have, then you will be hauled before the magistrates for fraud and deception, and thence to prison. London is not Naples, my dear. We take such matters vastly more seriously."

"Perdition," she murmured, and sank forlornly onto the bench beside her uncle. "It's always been the Raphaels that have drawn the most custom. I do not know if anyone will come for my own work alone."

"And I say they will," he maintained. "Mrs. Cosway, Mrs. Kauffman—they've prospered at painting in spite of being female."

"But I do not wish to be trapped painting fashionable flattery!" she cried miserably. "How can I achieve anything of merit if I must worry whether I've made the subject look too fat or cross-eyed, even if she is!"

"Then you do not belong in London, Francesca," said her uncle severely. "If you wish your painting to become a favorite of fashion, you must flatter. There is no other way."

"But what if I wish to paint what *I* see, what *I* feel?"

Her uncle sighed, and shook his head, the powder from his wig drifting lightly to his shoulders. "What you feel, what you feel! You are so much your father's daughter that it stuns me. Poor Tom had too much passion in his soul to survive in London, and I never wondered that he fled south."

Too much passion: Oh, yes, she could understand that, and unconsciously she felt for Edward's ring under her gown. She'd taken it from her finger, but she hadn't been noble enough to leave it behind, and instead she wore it always on a chain around her neck, where the gold circle hung beneath her shift and intimately between her breasts.

"It was a woman, of course," her uncle continued. "A pretty little creature, the middle daughter of a knight's family. He was her handsome young drawing master, they were unwisely left much alone together, and the row when their 'great love' was found out was quite exceptional. He'd no choice but to flee the country, while she married someone more suitably of her class. And, obviously, since you are here, Tom found at least one more love to console his broken heart, didn't he?"

Francesca listened, stunned that Papa had never confessed any of this to her. And yet the story made sense of much else in her father's life: why he'd taken so many women into his bed, but none to his heart, why he'd wanted Francesca to promise never to fall in love. Passion and desire, but no love, not after that one English girl he'd had to leave behind, not for the rest of his life.

What if she were like that, too? What if there were only one true love in her life, and what if she'd already let him slip away?

"And what of you, Francesca?" asked Uncle Peacock. "If you will forgive your old uncle's inquisition, what became of the boy you left behind in Naples?"

Francesca gulped. Had her thoughts really been so transparent on her face? She hadn't shared any of the details about her brief past with Edward because it was over and done, and of interest only to the two of them.

"Oh, don't dissemble," said her uncle, impatiently tapping his cane on the floor. "It wasn't entirely Bonaparte that brought you to my doorstep. You are too much like your father for it to have been otherwise, and too comely, too, even if you are given to forgery and fraud. How wrong was this rascal for you, eh? Did he tell you pretty tales and cast you off? Or was he an older rogue with a wife?"

"There was no rascal, Uncle," she said defensively, and truthfully, for no one would ever call Edward a rascal. "And no rogue, either. I promised Papa that my art must come first in my life, and so it has been."

Her uncle frowned, and sighed. "You are generally a better liar than that, Francesca. Protect the scoundrel if you must. All I need know is if he will someday come after you. I want no surprises, my dear, no worthless, swarthy young men appearing to make claims upon my fortune."

She smiled sadly. "No worthless young men will come calling, Uncle. I promise you that."

"I suppose I am thankful for that blessing." With a grunt, he rose to his feet, waving aside her assistance. "You finish here, my dear. I hear my tea and my library calling me. Mrs. Monk will help me up the stairs. Oh, and I have left the copies of the *Morning Post, Herald and Daily Advertiser,* and *London Chronicle* with your advertisements. I trust you shall consider what I said about your, ah, collection of offerings before you throw open my doors, yes? I should like to keep my house a respectable one, my dear, if at all possible."

Francesca smiled, but her conscience was heavy indeed as she turned to the last crate. She'd purposefully saved it for last, knowing that inside were the *Oculus Amorandi* paintings, and knowing, too, that the sight of them would likely give her poor uncle apoplexy. So much for his respectable house if she tried to exhibit them to the public!

With care she pried open the crate. As she lifted each panel free, she automatically began reciting to herself the little speech that accompanied the particular scene, just as she'd recited it countless times for each visitor since her father grew too ill to do it himself. The writhing bacchante with grapes in their hair, the wayward gods and goddesses half-clothed in animal skins, the satyrs with their stubby horns and goatish nether-parts, all were cavorting madly away exactly as she remembered.

Except that this time, she was the one who was different. She frowned, slow to realize the change.

But now when she looked at the bacchante and the nymphs and all the other women tossing about so wantonly, she understood, and worse, she blushed. Thanks to Edward, she'd learned about passion and desire, too, and the rare, shuddering joy a man could give to a woman. She had, quite simply and in every way, lost her innocence.

Her father had wanted to keep her clear of men to protect her and her art. He'd always said that love would steal away her talent, and perhaps with him it had. But what if love didn't stunt her talent, but freed it? What if love echoed from her heart to her canvas, and made everything she painted warmer, brighter, richer?

Because of Edward, she now knew of more than those little painted figures, and perhaps more than her father had as well. Not more in the sense of acrobatic variety, or positions better left to satyrs than human men, but in the knowledge that came from love. With Edward, she'd learned the magic of love-making that focused on *love*, not just coupling for fleeting pleasure.

Lightly she traced one of the small, smiling figures, the bright colors blurring with her tears. Oh, yes, she knew the difference, and because of it she doubted she'd ever be able to show the *Oculus* to visitors again, or tell the oddly impersonal stories with it. And after making love—making *love*—with Edward, she'd never be satisfied with anything less, or any other man.

The one man she'd left, and lost, forever.

Saints in heaven, she must not let herself think this

way! She'd made her decision, and now must abide by it, and briskly she slid the panels of the *Oculus* back into their case. She would decide what to do with them later. Now she must see to her announcements in the papers, and pray that patrons would see them as well.

With a resolute sniff for her tears, she sat on the bench and spread the first newspaper before her. Londoners were mad for gossip about royalty and other fashionable gentlemen and ladies of the first rank, and she was astonished by the number of scandal sheets that were produced in the city each day. Of course these were the ones that were read, while the more serious papers with news of the war went begging, and it had been obvious to Francesca in which she should place her own notices. Purposefully she flipped through the pages, hunting for the little box with her announcement in it.

Then she stopped reading, unable to continue, and cried out with shock, and pressed her hand over her mouth to keep from crying out again.

> *His Grace the Duke of Harborough continues to be the most elusive target for ladies of fashion who seek him for drawing rooms. How can they resist such a quarry, His Grace being well-favored in face and form, mild and charming in manner? All know by now that before his providential if sudden ascendancy from Captain Lord Ramsden to Duke of Harborough, he was also one of the sterling heroes of the Battle of the Nile.*

How could this be true? Edward was a navy captain, not a duke. What could have happened to his three older brothers? Was this why he had been called home, to become a great lord? Is this what Lady Hamilton had predicted as the good fortune following the bad? Her heart pounding, she tore through the rest of the paper, desperate to learn more beyond that single paragraph.

There was no other mention of Edward in the first paper, but she soon found more in the second.

> *One surmises that the new Duke of H**b****gh must needs grow accustomed to the great change in his life & fortune, & is to be granted that allowance. Yet already the fair young Dianas of the* ton *are readying their bows and arrows for His Grace, surely the most prized bachelor to venture into their forest this season.*

But Edward wasn't a bachelor. He was her husband, the single great love of her life. With trembling fingers she pulled the chain with his ring from the front of her shift, holding it tightly in her hand. He'd sworn he'd always be her anchor, and now instead he was a "most prized bachelor"?

But an English duke would need a true English lady for his duchess, a beautiful young woman of breeding and refinement to take his name and bear his heir. He would not wish a wife who was dark and foreign and nearly twenty-six years old, or one whose unmarried mother had been an artist's model of dubious repute.

She bowed her head in misery, clutching the ring. If she and Edward had been unsuited to one another before, they were doubly, trebly unsuited now, and the best thing for them both would be to continue on the separate paths they'd already taken. She had been the one to insist that they would be together only for convenience, hadn't she? So why, now, when their marriage was no longer convenient to either of them, did its dissolution hurt so very much?

But still she could not resist searching through the last paper for his name, and soon enough she found it.

> *Whilst in mourning for his brothers, His Grace the Duke of Harborough has lately removed from his suite of rooms at the Clarendon to Harborough House, his residence on Green Park, where he is as yet receiving no callers.*

That single sentence told her much. His brothers had somehow died, making him a duke. He had traded the packet's cabin for a hotel, then for his own house—of course he'd have one in London, and doubtless others in the country as well—on Green Park. Oh, how miserable he must be, so landlocked and apart from his beloved sea! And if he wasn't receiving callers, he wasn't yet courting any of those fashionable huntresses of the *ton,* either.

She looked across the room to the painting that her uncle had so admired. The model she'd used had been a fisherman's young wife and her first-born son, and the love between the mother and son had not only bloomed on Francesca's canvas, but had filled her with longing for a child of her own.

Had the painting made Edward feel that way, too? He'd spoken so warmly of having children that day in Palermo, in the carriage, yet as a man he'd never suffer the same emptiness that a woman would. Last week, when she'd first discovered the blotch of blood on her shift that meant her courses had come, she had waited for the relief, even happiness, that she'd felt sure she'd feel knowing that no child had been conceived during that last night on board the *Antelope*.

But instead she'd wept, deep, wracking sobs of grief for what she'd lost and what now she'd never have. No babe with golden curls and bright blue eyes like Edward's, no nursery full of sunshine and baby-laughter, no chance to become the family that neither she nor Edward had ever had. She couldn't give him that, not now, but she could give him something special to remind him of everything else they'd shared.

Quickly, before she lost her nerve, she took the pen and wrote what she'd told him the night of the storm. *Senza di te non ce sole nel cièlo:* Without you there is no sun in the sky. Nothing more, for she didn't wish him to think she'd contacted him only because of his new good fortune. She folded the paper once, wrote Edward's name upon the front, and tucked it into the frame of the painting before she repacked it in the crate, and rang the bell for the footman.

"Have this crate taken to Harborough House, on

Green Park," she said. "Leave no address, and do not wait for an answer.

Edward stood at the tall window in the front parlor of Harborough House, his hand clasped behind him and his legs slightly spread from long quarterdeck habit. The window was hardly the same as a quarterdeck, of course, being stable, dry, and not nearly as drafty, but for now it would have to do. If there were no sails to survey or crew to oversee, at least standing here between the silk damask curtains did offer one of the more elegant views in London.

To the left of his house stood Devonshire House, belonging to the Duke of Devonshire, the Earl of Spencer's home was diagonally across the park, and in the distance lay the Queen's Gardens. Despite the swirl of snowflakes on this chilly afternoon, a few hardy riders were parading up and down the park's drive, displaying their horses and themselves to the ladies in their carriages, snug behind the glass windows, hands tucked into fur muffs and feet propped upon tin warmers full of coals.

This was supposed to be his world now. Since that first shock of the news in Lord Spencer's chamber, he'd tried to accustom himself to his new position. If he didn't want to be his father or brother, the surest way would be to accept the responsibilities of the title, and not just the benefits. He had been the captain of a ship of the line, and he doubted that running an estate could be any more difficult than that. He was equally sure he could do much good in the House of Lords, once he set his mind to learn the ropes, and with grim

determination he had spent most of the day again clos-
eted with the family's solicitors and managers.

It was hard work, challenging work, and by the
time they'd left Edward had a raging headache and a
foul temper to match. But despite the solicitors' interminable explanations and the sheaves of papers
covered with closely written numbers, one inescapable fact had trumpeted through: he was rich,
richer than he'd ever imagined, one of the richest
men in England and therefore in the world. Though
his brothers had tried their hardest to gamble and
spend themselves into oblivious ruin, not even they
had made much of a dent in the Harborough fortunes.

And he hadn't a genuine interest in any of it.

Perhaps if Francesca had stayed with him, then
he'd take pleasure in showing her the houses and the
lands that bore his family's name. With her at his
side, he might have enjoyed discovering a life that
had, as a boy, been largely denied to him. He would
have delighted in the changes she'd make to this
grim old house, the sunshine and bright colors that
she'd use to banish the dust and ghosts, and he would
have laughed long and wickedly as they'd made
themselves the most original duke and duchess that
fashionable London had ever seen.

And if they'd had a child, boy or girl, he would
have an heir to inspire him as well as to love. That
much at least was still possible, after that single night
at sea; it would be early days for Francesca to know
for sure, and he clung to the possibility with ridiculous hope. For if there were a babe, he would make

sure that dear small person had all the love and kind-ness showered upon him or her that he'd never known himself, everything that his vast holdings could never buy.

But for now there was no Francesca and no child, and he was living like a lonely gypsy in a handful of rooms in his cavernous town house. Mourning for his brothers was an ironic mockery, but it did serve as a useful excuse for keeping to himself.

Already he was planning his escape. Yesterday, while those same solicitors had pulled long faces of dis-approval, he had bought the sweetest, fastest schooner he'd ever sailed, an American smuggler taken as a prize in French waters. As soon as he'd settled his af-fairs here, he meant to fit her out, sign on a crew, and shove off for a voyage of, oh, at least two years' length. He would set his sails for all the ports around the great world he'd yet to see, and try not to imagine Francesca cozy in the teakwood bunk beside him.

Even in her absence, she had managed to make those solicitors' long faces longer still. When Edward had told them he had a wife, they'd smiled with hap-piness, for a wife was the first step toward securing the line. But when Edward had answered a few par-ticulars regarding their wedding and Francesca's family, and admitted that she was at present missing, the solicitors' happiness had vanished, and at once they'd begun plotting ways for him to escape such a dubious marriage. But Edward wouldn't hear of it. No matter where she was hiding herself, Francesca remained his wife, and the only woman he'd ever love.

But blast and damnation, why hadn't she loved him enough in turn to stay?

He heard a crash from the hall below, followed by raised, disgruntled voices, an unusual sound for this tomb of a house. Curious, he sauntered to the top of the stairs and leaned over the marble railing. Two footmen—*his* footmen, he supposed, since they were wearing Harborough livery—were wrestling with and swearing at a flat wooden crate while Peart tried to order them about as if they were seamen and not footmen, with predictably disastrous results.

"And what, pray, is that, Peart?" called Edward down. "More tribute for My Grace?"

He liked the shocked, upturned faces of the footmen, though he couldn't tell if he'd shocked them by speaking of himself so, or simply by catching them swearing at one another.

"Aye, aye, Captain Your Grace," answered Peart contritely. He was the only one who bothered to include the *captain* into his title, and for that Edward would be forever grateful. " 'Tis another gift for you."

"Then take it the hell out of here, if you please, Peart," said Edward. Because he'd refused to receive visitors, it seemed that all of London had decided to send him gifts of congratulation instead, Trojan horses designed to breech his walls and win his favor. Most had been mundane, trinkets, books, wine, and sweetmeats, but there had been one involving perfumed garters and a lewdly suggestive poem from his brother's last mistress that he'd found astoundingly distasteful. "I've rubbish enough, thank you."

"But this one is different, Captain Your Grace," said Peart. "I took the liberty, Captain Your Grace, of guessing you'd rather see it than not."

"Did you now, Peart." This could be interesting, for Peart knew him well.

"Aye, aye, Captain Your Grace, I did," said Peart with growing confidence. "because this here crate has come direct from Naples, and inside is a painting by an artist you favor most particular. *Most* particular, Captain."

"Then open the damned box, Peart," Edward roared, racing down the stairs. "Handsomely, now, handsomely!"

As soon as the top plank was pulled off, he was digging through the packing himself to pull the painting out. Before he'd unwrapped it, he knew what it was, and he knew who had sent it, yet still he caught his breath when he saw the finished picture. It was even more wonderful than he remembered, more luminous, more magical, and more full of Francesca, too. He was so enchanted with the painting that at first he didn't see the note tucked into the frame. When he did, when he read it, he swore, long and low and straight from his poor wounded heart.

"Senza di te non ce sole nel cièlo": then why the devil didn't she come back to him? He'd hang that sun back in the sky soon enough once she did, and the stars and moon with it.

"Where'd this come from, Peart?" he demanded. "What house? What address?"

The footmen stared guiltily down at the floor.

"They didn't ask, Captain Your Grace," said Peart

righteously. "They didn't know why's they should be asking."

"Hell." Disconsolate, Edward sat on the marble steps, the painting in his hands. Why the devil had Francesca sent this to him, anyway? Did she mean to remind him of that afternoon when she'd shown him her little garret room, or to torment him with the possibility of a child of their own like the one in the painting, or had she simply sent him a gift that she knew would please him, with no secret significance at all?

"Shove off with that crate now, you blighters," ordered Peart, and with a final significant glare, the two footmen cleaned away the crate and its packing.

The knock at the front door echoed like a cannon in the hall, and without bothering to wait for the footman to return, Peart himself opened the door, only enough to peer outside and preserve Edward's privacy there on the stairs.

"Tell me your mooncalf master's within, Peart," said William, pushing the door open to look over the servant's head. "Ah, there you are, Captain! I do believe I've caught the scent of your vixen."

He pulled a folded newspaper from his coat pocket as he entered, and handed it to Edward. "I came across a maid reading this in a tavern last night, and though I know it's low trash—the paper, not the dear little chit that was reading it—I thought you'd want to see this particular notice regardless."

Quickly Edward looked down at the paper, to the corner that William had thoughtfully folded to accentuate a small boxed advertisement announcing the opening of a new business in Westminster, of all places.

SIGNORA ROBIN
Newly arrived from Naples & Palermo,
Wishes to Advise all Ladies & Gentlemen of
Quality, Rank, & Discernment,
& those of her Especial Acquaintance
that she welcomes Such Visitors to her
Collection,
viz., Only the Finest Examples of
Antiquities & Paintings
of the Greatest Masters of Rome & Florence,
well-known to Connoisseurs &
other Gentlemen of Taste in the Arts
At her *studio d'artista,* in Barlow Street, Westminster

So she was still in London, still Francesca, even prospering, it seemed. At least now he knew she'd stayed away by choice, and not because she'd been, oh, captured by gypsies and sold to the Turks, which would certainly have been the more flattering eventuality from his perspective. But for her to have abandoned him for the sake of opening a common shop in Westminster was not flattering in the least. Did his love really mean so little to her, then?

He remembered how she flirted with her customers, how she wooed them and practically seduced them into buying her mostly worthless stock, how she so bedazzled the poor males into emptying their purses then and there. Is that what she wished to do here in London as well? Was that world so much more enticing than what he could offer her? And though there was no mention of those infernal brothel pictures, she'd made such a pretty penny showing them in Naples that he couldn't believe she wouldn't display them here, too.

He glanced back at the smiling mother in the painting, that wondrous testimony to Francesca's true, rare talent, and then back to the advertisement for her mountebank collection of forgeries. Damnation, she should be painting for herself, not pandering to the vanities of would-be connoisseurs!

"She seems to be calling herself Signora Robin," said William, "but I'd wager it's the same lady, don't you?"

"Aye, it is," said Edward, his expression stony. How long would it be before some wag realized the signora was also the new Duchess of Harborough? He'd end up challenging every blade in London, defending her honor.

"Shall I go ready your dress uniform, Captain Your Grace?" asked Peart with an undeniable gleam in his eye, the same as he'd shown when the *Centaur* would prepare for battle. "There's no lady alive that can refuse a uniform as grand as that one."

"Aye, aye, Peart, clear for action," said Edward, setting the painting on the floor with a determined thump. He was done with sentiment, with rattling around in this huge tomb of a house and pining after Francesca. He'd never hung back from a battle before, and by God, he wasn't going to do it now.

"We're off to the signora's gallery, are we?" said

William with a gleam of anticipation in his eye. "I do so enjoy a good showing."

"Not today, you won't," said Edward firmly. "I thank you for your help this far, but this must be between Francesca and myself. The lady's fired first, and it's time to take her challenge. And mind me, Will: I'm not hauling back until she surrenders."

14

❦

"*O*ooh, this vase is monstrously fine, signora," said Lady Hingham, lifting the vase to the light in the window. "And very ancient?"

"I believe it so, my lady," hedged Francesca, remembering her promise to her uncle to tell only the truth regarding the pieces for sale. "Though I cannot say with any precision exactly how old."

"Ha, you shopkeepers are so coy, striving to drive your prices higher!" said her ladyship archly. "My eye is most excellent in these matters, and it tells me this black-figured vase is from the days of the Caesars and not one minute older. What say you, Chetwynd? Would this do for Lord Hingham's birthday?"

More accurately the vase was from the days of last June and not one minute older, but Francesca knew better than to correct a customer. Instead she dutifully stood to one side in silence, ready to catch the vase if the lady's grip wavered.

Lady Hingham was a leader of style and fashion, her approval important to Francesca's success. She'd already spent the better part of the afternoon considering nearly every piece in the room, raising each one in turn to display her bosom and her profile to the Honorable Henry Chetwynd. Francesca was quite sure the two were lovers, although Lady Hingham was a good ten years older than she painted herself to be, and far older than Chetwynd. Chetwynd *was* handsome, but, in Francesca's opinion, he was also so woefully simpleminded that her ladyship practically needed a leash and dog collar to keep him from wandering off.

No matter: Francesca had seen worse arrangements in her time, and as long as Lord Hingham's purse was deep enough to indulge his wife's fancies, then Francesca resolved to be happy. Or she would be, anyway, if she didn't have to keep dodging Chetwynd's constant attempts to squeeze her bottom each time the older lady's back was turned.

"It's vastly fine, Sophronia, dearest," drawled Chetwynd. "by all means, buy it for his lordship. That is, if he can find any use for an empty vessel."

Her ladyship gasped, then giggled, and jagged at Chetwynd with her elbow. "Oh, you are *too* wicked! An *empty* vessel, indeed!"

"Much better to have 'em filled, eh?" he leered, leaning forward to kiss her neck. "Beautiful and stuffed to bursting, I say."

Deftly Francesca rescued the vase, and carried it to a table well away from danger. "Shall I have the vase sent to you in the morning, my lady?"

"Yes, yes, of course," said Lady Hingham breathlessly, disentangling herself from Chetwynd, "with the reckoning to Lord Hingham's attention. Ah, signora, you have so many lovely things!"

Francesca nodded, already watching to see what next would be in peril. She'd been busy like this since she'd opened for trade, and though she'd shown her paintings to a great many more people than she'd expected, she'd forgotten the effort of always being charming, always agreeable.

It had been over a year since she'd had so many customers in a single day, and nearly three months had passed since she'd left Naples entirely. In that time she'd grown accustomed to the luxury of painting and drawing without having to sell as well, and forgotten how hard it was to be always entertaining and charming.

Even the effort of dressing the part—today she wore a high-waisted gown of Indian muslin, a rich emerald green with gold tasseled fringe along the hem and edging the sleeves and neckline, red ribbons stitched with golden discs like coins threaded through her dark hair, all faintly inspired by the ancient woman painted on the vases—seemed more taxing than she'd remembered. But as long as she must earn her living, what other choice did she have?

Only three other customers remained besides Lady Hingham and Chetwynd, and when they could be guided through the door and into their carriages, she would close. She caught the eye of Mrs. Monk, who was using the lighting of the evening candles as an excuse to gawk at the gentry in what used to be her master's parlor.

"Tell the footman not to admit anyone else

tonight, *per favore,*" she whispered to the house-keeper. "I fear my mouth will crack if I must smile at yet one more new face."

Mrs. Monk nodded and bustled away, just as Chetwynd lunged for another attempt to fondle her. Saints in heaven, this day could not end soon enough!

"Ah, my lady, isn't that a lovely small angel?" she said, sweeping to Lady Hingham's side even as she swatted Chetwynd's hands away. *"Bellissima,* yes?"

But Lady Hingham wasn't listening, at least not to her.

"Pray, signora, what was that racketing?" she asked coyly, always eager for a new scandal to share. "It sounds rather like some rogue is attempting to *force* his way into your gallery!"

Uneasily Francesca glanced over her shoulder toward the door that led to the hallway. There was in fact some sort of commotion taking place beyond the closed door, with Mrs. Monk's voice distinctly, and unhappily, raised above the others.

"Excuse me, if you please, my lady," she said, dropping a rushed curtsey before she turned toward the door to investigate. The last thing she needed was a scandal so soon after opening, especially with Lady Hingham such an eager witness.

But Francesca was already too late. The double doors to the room swung inward, and there was Edward.

"Good day, Francesca," he said, smiling as he came toward her with his hand out to take hers, as if they'd parted only this morning, as if they hadn't parted at all. "You cannot know how pleased I was to receive your invitation."

He was almost blindingly handsome in his dress uniform, the candlelight glancing and glinting on all the gold and gilt and polished brass, even his sleekly brushed blond hair. He'd been dressed like that when she'd seen him last on the deck of the packet, except that now there was none of the restless uncertainty she'd sensed then. Now, here, holding her hand, poised to crash into the careful new world she'd created for herself, he seemed so confident as to be almost ruthless. Yet it wasn't his new title that made him this way—she knew him better than that— yet still it horrified her to realize how much she'd hurt him.

"Invitation?" she repeated faintly. Somehow she'd managed not to shriek, or faint, or fall into fits, or any other reaction that would, under the circumstances, seem entirely appropriate. Instead she simply stood there before him, not moving until he gently took her hand in his own, kissing her wrist in a way that made her shiver. At least that much of her was capable of moving, just enough to send the pearls on the hoops in her ears trembling against her cheeks. "Invitation, Captain My Lord?"

He smiled at her over her hand, reminding her of the first time he'd kissed her wrist on board the *Centaur.* "Aye, *càra mia,* the invitation. The painting. That *was* my invitation, wasn't it?"

He'd never called her that before, the Italian unsettlingly seductive coming from him. But then, everything about having him here was like that, both unsettling *and* seductive, and she felt as off-balance as if she were standing on one leg.

"But that painting was a gift, not an invitation," she protested, all too aware of Lady Hingham now quivering with excitement beside her. "Because you'd admired it so much, and offered once to buy it, Captain My Lord, I—"

"It's 'Captain Your Grace' now, lass," he said softly, his smile widening to a grin that was anything but reassuring. "Or haven't you heard? Thanks to the unfortunate deaths of my dear brothers, I've become the seventh Duke of Harborough."

"Your Grace!" gasped Lady Hingham, sinking to a sweeping curtsey at Edward's feet. "Oh, Your Grace, I had no *idea* it was you! I am Lady Hingham, Your Grace—your servant! To discover you here, in this company! Henry, Henry, come, *this* exceedingly handsome military gentleman is the Duke of Harborough! Oh, Your Grace, Your Grace, I am so honored I cannot express myself!"

"Then you are doing a remarkably fine approximation of it, my lady," said Edward, his gaze still fixed completely upon Francesca, "which makes me honored as well. Wouldn't you agree, Francesca?"

"Oh, miss, I tried to keep him out!" whispered Mrs. Monk frantically, her round face wreathed with anxiety at Francesca's side. "You'd given orders for no more today, miss, and I did try to turn him away, me and the footman both, but he insisted, saying he was an old acquaintance of yours and a duke as well, and I couldn't—"

"You did nothing wrong, Mrs. Monk," said

Francesca, trying to relax enough to smile. If she concentrated, she'd get through this; if she forced herself to think of something other than how much she'd missed Edward, then she might manage to survive with a tatter of her dignity left. "Edward—that is, His Grace is in fact an old acquaintance of mine from Naples. He wasn't trying to mislead you. *Veraménte,* a dear and old friend."

"Oh, yes, signora, I can *see* that," said Mrs. Hingham with greedy interest, her gaze darting from Francesca to Edward and back again. "The connection between you and Your Grace is so obvious I can practically *feel* it myself, like a veritable *current* flowing through the room!"

"Then you will understand, Lady Hingham, when I say that I should like to speak with the lady alone," said Edward easily. He glanced around at the other customers, his smile including them watching and listening with unabashed fascination. "You will all excuse us, won't you?"

"Edward, don't!" said Francesca, shocked by his effrontery. "You cannot simply dismiss them! These good ladies and gentlemen are my customers, my patrons, and if you send them away, they most likely will never return, and I shall be ruined before I've truly begun!"

"Oh, *I* shall return, signora," said Lady Hingham, smiling suggestively up at Edward even as she looped her fingers into the crook of Chetwynd's arm. "For not only are your wares most enticing, but I find the company you've attracted to your studio is, um, *trés beauissimo.*"

"You are very kind, my lady." Francesca smiled and dipped a slight curtsey, the more flattering response than pointing out to Her Ladyship that there was no such garbled expression in either English, French, or Italian. Besides, it was meant as a compliment for Edward, not for her. Let him be the one to correct her if he wished. He was doing everything else exactly as he pleased, wasn't he?

Nor was he done yet. He smiled at Lady Hingham, with the exact degree of warmth and favor to reduce the woman to a simpering, blushing jelly-head. *Che miracolo,* thought Francesca unhappily, where and when had Edward learned such a trick? He should be the one selling counterfeit crockery, not her.

"I can tell you are a lady of rare sympathies, Lady Hingham," he said. "You understand my need for privacy, yes?"

"Of course, Your Grace," trilled Lady Hingham, preening as she basked in his attention and completely ignoring poor Chetwynd. "I understand *all* the needs that a great lord and hero such as yourself might have."

Great or small, that was too much for Francesca.

"Then you will oblige His Grace by bidding him farewell, my lady, as he requested," she said with far less patience than was perhaps wise. But she didn't care for the way Lady Hingham was behaving with Edward, enough that if the woman never returned to her studio she wouldn't care about that, either.

"I shall see that your purchase is delivered to your home tomorrow morning, my lady, as you requested," she continued, gesturing toward the door to usher them along, "and I thank you and Lord Henry for your custom."

"And I thank you as well, Lady Hingham," said Edward, slipping his arm around Francesca's waist with a proprietary ease, "for granting me the privacy to speak to my dear wife alone."

"Your *wife!*" Lady Hingham's stunned gasp was echoed by every other person in the room, including Francesca herself. "Your Grace! Surely you do not mean Signora Robin!"

Edward's easy smile vanished, while his arm tightened around Francesca's waist.

"I mean it, my lady, because it is true," he said, and the tone of his voice allowed no discussion or doubt. "Miss Robin and I were wed by my chaplain on board my ship the *Centaur,* at Naples on the day before Christmas."

"But—but such a *foreign* lady, Your Grace!" exclaimed Lady Hingham with both horror and fascination. "As your wife, as your duchess!"

"She is both my wife and my duchess, Lady Hingham," answered Edward curtly, "and my love besides. But I must ask you to save your congratulations for another day. Her Grace and I are still newly wed, chary of our time with others."

After that there was nothing left for Lady Hingham or the others than to say their good-byes, adding a few perfunctory wishes for happiness and health as they left. There was even less for Francesca to do, either, except to smile in tight-lipped silence, and grimly wonder how much of this fiasco would appear in the next day's scandal sheets.

Last to leave was Mrs. Monk, hesitating at the door. "Will you be needing anything more, Your Grace?"

"Thank you, Mrs. Monk, that will be all," said Francesca stiffly. "Good evening, Mrs. Monk."

She waited until the housekeeper closed the door, watching the knob turn and latch shut, before she flew apart from Edward.

"How *dare* you, Edward?" she cried furiously as she spun to face him, the gold fringe on her gown trembling in sympathy. "Do you know what you have done to me and my chances this afternoon? *Sànto cièlo,* I have worried and worked for weeks to make this right, and in ten minutes you sail in here, grand as any admiral, and make a mockery of it all! It isn't fair, Edward, it isn't fair at all!"

"Then was it fair for you to leave me like you did, Francesca?" he demanded, his anger instantly a match for her own. "Damnation, was it *fair* that you disappeared into London without leaving me even a note of farewell or explanation?"

"I did it for you, Edward!"

"Oh, aye, for me," he said with withering scorn. "Entirely for me, and how grateful I am, too."

"But I only did what we'd agreed, Edward!" she pleaded. "If we couldn't please one another, we agreed we would separate, and I knew from the beginning I could never be a proper wife for you. You heard Lady Hingham. I'm so *foreign.* I would have been a dreadful handicap to you in the navy, but now—now with you raised to a duke, I would be worse than a bucket of stones around your neck!"

"So I was to be the only one who suffered?" he demanded. "You would have been blamelessly cheerful otherwise?"

She shook her head, hugging her arms around her body. "I would have been a wretched wife to you, Edward, and a miserable one as well. I need to paint and draw and *see,* and not be left behind to make a mess of managing a great house and staff while you went about doing grand, lordly things!"

"But pandering to the ignorance of Lady Hingham," he said, sweeping his hand through the air as if to sweep aside her objections with it, "cajoling a foolish woman like that into paying ten times what a fake pot is worth—that is better, more noble?"

"I must earn my living!" she cried unhappily. "I do that only so I can paint for myself! I know this sounds very selfish of me, but I cannot squander the talent that God gave me, and try to be something I'm not."

"Yet you decided it was better to vanish from my life than discuss it with me first, didn't you?" He shook his head with furious disbelief. "Hell, Francesca! Couldn't you comprehend that I might be willing to make compromises for your sake? Or are you the one so determined not to change?"

"I didn't say that!" But saints in heaven, he was right. She'd been telling herself she'd been bravely protecting his happiness, when instead she'd been too cowardly to risk changing for the sake of love.

He was right.

"You didn't have to tell me anything, did you?" He glanced around the room, taking in the fresh paint and other improvements she'd made. "Though I must say you've certainly landed on your feet fast enough, Francesca. Or was it upon your back with your legs apart, to earn a place such as this?"

"Don't be hateful, Edward, *per favore.*" Francesca flushed with shame. "I am living here through the kindness of my uncle, my father's only brother."

"But with a different name," he said. "Which is why you'd managed to hide yourself away so completely from me."

"It was a conceit of my father's to change his name from Peacock to Robin when he left England for Naples," she explained, wishing now her father had been content to leave his name alone. "You will find my Uncle Peacock is an eminently respectable older gentleman."

"Oh, they always are, aren't they?" he said, his sarcasm cutting and bitter. "Older and respectable gentlemen are the ones with the most kindness and the deepest pockets. Did your good friend Lady Hamilton advise you about that as well?"

"Stop it, Edward, stop *now.*" She raised her chin defiantly, though inside she was crumbling to pieces. Her first anger had been protective, defensive, but its fire had quickly burned itself out, leaving nothing but ashes. How could she stay angry when he was the one making more sense? "You don't have to believe me. I never said you did."

"No, I don't," he said. "The real challenge with you, Francesca, is deciding how much of what you say is true, let alone worth believing."

"You knew how I was when you married me," she

said, her voice wobbling. What would he say if she told him she still loved him? Would he believe her, or doubt that as well? "But I have always tried to be truthful with you, *càro mio.* Truly."

His expression didn't change. "It would seem that you've tried harder some days than others."

"I never stopped trying, Edward," she said, more wistfully than she realized. "Only some days I do better at it than others. On the *Antelope,* we promised to be honest, didn't we?"

"I have always been honest with you," he countered. "I still am, even now that our circumstances have changed."

"Oh, yes." She barely stopped herself from feeling for the chain around her neck and his ring tucked inside her shift. "You have become a grand gentleman, a duke, far above the rest of us, while I am what I always was."

"That's not what I meant," he said, so sharply that she realized that this time she'd wounded him. He turned away, restlessly running his finger around the rim of the vase that Lady Hingham had bought. "If I have gotten you with child——"

"No child." Her voice was brittle, unable to disguise her longing and regret. "No heir to your precious dukedom."

He wheeled around to face her, and the almost desperate hope she saw in his eyes stunned her. "It's very soon to be so sure, isn't it?"

"I am sure. I was last week." She gulped, and looked down. She would *not* cry. "If that was all you came here to learn——"

"Not by half," he said, and took a deep breath. "I came to see if you were happy."

She turned half away from him, not sure what he wished to hear. "Are you?"

"No," he said instantly, and the burden of that single word rang with the truth. "Not for a moment since you left, Francesca."

"Oh, *càro,*" she murmured, overwhelmed. "I am sorry."

He shrugged, and shook his head, trying to prove that none of it mattered when of course it did. "And you? Are you happy, lass?"

Now was the time for her to be as honest as she wanted to be: to apologize for everything she'd done, to admit that she'd been wrong and a coward as well, to tell him how much she'd missed him, how much she'd longed to be with him, how she loved him more, not less, than when she'd left.

Now. And of course, perversely, when so very much was at stake, she couldn't do it.

"I have been very busy," she said instead, her words—the wrong words—tumbling over one another. "There has been so much to do, to make this space my own! Unpacking and arranging and displaying everything, writing letters and announcements, ah, you cannot know, you cannot know!"

But now he was the one who looked down, the candlelight glinting on the top of his golden head.

"Once you said I was your anchor, lass," he said, his voice as heavy as lead, as heavy as her heart. "But no more, eh?"

"Oh, Edward, my darling husband," she whispered, reaching out to him. *"Il mondo e vuoto senza di—"*

"Don't," he ordered so harshly that her hand jerked back as if it had come too close to a flame. "Show me your pictures."

"But Edward, that doesn't—"

"Show me your blasted pictures," he said again, and when he now lifted his gaze, she found his eyes shuttered against her, closing her out. "That's what you chose to do, isn't it? If these paintings and this gallery mean so bloody much to you now, then show them to me."

She hesitated, torn, before she finally nodded. If this was the game he wished her to play now, she would.

"Then first you must make yourself at ease, *per favore,* Your Grace," she said, and he sat on the cushioned bench, his gaze intent upon her. She tried to smile, wishing desperately that he would smile in return, and with a graceful arch of her wrist she turned toward the nearest painting.

"This pretty little Saint Catherine comes from the studio of Guido Reni," she began, "and with its rosy palette of colors and gentle subject, it is—"

"Show me your father's brothel paintings, Francesca," he interrupted. "That's what I want to see. The pictures that made your studio so damned popular in Naples."

"This isn't Naples, Edward," she said swiftly, his request taking her by surprise, "and I'm not showing the *Oculus Amorandi* here in London. Those pictures do not seem to have a place here."

She didn't want to explain that, because of loving him, she now found the pictures too unsettling to show to others, but somehow he seemed to guess that anyway.

"You can show them to me, Francesca, can't you?" he said, challenging her. "I'm your husband. We've no secrets between us, do we?"

Why was seeing the *Oculus* suddenly so important to him? His expression was studiously blank, revealing nothing, but if this were some sort of dare, she'd take it. Without a word she went to the far corner of the room, behind a screen where she'd stored the crates containing the *Oculus*. She pulled a panel free from its wrappings, relieved to see that it was one of the less explicit, a scene from the ancient myth of Danaë receiving Zeus as a beam of golden light.

Even Francesca's imaginative father had had trouble depicting such an abstract coupling as that, and so he'd chosen simply to concentrate on showing Danaë as the kind of plump, alluring, and mostly naked young woman, lounging on her bed, that both gods and mortal men apparently found irresistible. Lightly Francesca touched little Danaë's winsome face, her shining dark eyes and her tousled hair curling over her bare shoulders. Perhaps if she were lucky, some of Danaë's charm might rub off on her in return. Saints in heaven, she'd need all the help she could muster if she was to redeem herself with Edward.

With the picture tucked under her arm, she returned to him. But instead of standing before him to display it, she sat on the bench next to him, bracing the small painting on her knees, where he'd have to lean closer to her to see it.

"This is called *Danaë Receiving the God Zeus as Her Lover,*" she explained, aware of how he'd shifted nearer to her. "I'm sure you recall the legend, *càro mio,* how her father had imprisoned her in a tower to keep away all lovers. But Zeus is too ardent a lover, too wily, and manifests himself to the willing Danaë as a shower of golden light through the window, raining down upon her ripe and eager body."

She'd explained the picture and the myth more times than she could recall, but she'd never felt as nervous and unsure as she did now. Most gentlemen would make some flippant comment while they ogled Danaë's bare breasts, about how that old rogue Zeus had all the luck and the pretty women, too.

But Edward said nothing, and Francesca's uneasiness grew.

"Certainly Danaë looks quite pleased with her lover, doesn't she?" she said, striving to fill the silence. "But then Zeus would—"

"She reminds me of a certain nymph in a drawing, a nymph with a centaur," said Edward, his voice rough and raw. "Not that she's the same model, but her sly smile, her eagerness, how her hair falls over her shoulders—aye, that's there in my nymph, too."

"You kept that drawing?" she asked, turning toward him with surprise.

"Of course I did, lass," he said. "It's all I had left of you."

She was terribly conscious of how closely he was sitting beside her on the bench, of how his arm and his thigh were touching hers, of the simmering heat between them that had nothing to do with Danaë and Zeus.

"I could show you other paintings in the *Oculus*," she said breathlessly, trying not to stare at him. She'd forgotten the contrasts of his mouth, how this close she could see the little gold whiskers that framed his lips, and how when he'd kissed her, those lips could be both soft and demanding and so ready with pleasure that she wondered what he'd do if she leaned forward and kissed him now, right now. "I could show you Zeus with Leda, and Zeus with Io, and Zeus—"

"To hell with them," he said, slanting his face toward hers. "All I care about now is Edward and Francesca."

When his mouth found hers she could have laughed with all the joy and relief and pleasure, too, that was rising up inside her. Instead she closed her eyes and parted her lips, welcoming him deep into her mouth. He wasn't lost, and even better, he was forgiving her, and wordlessly she rejoiced, slipping her arm around Edward's shoulders to draw him closer. She let the painting slide from her fingers to drop to the floor with a *thump* that she ignored, and Edward likely didn't even hear.

But surely Danaë would understand, and approve.

Blindly Francesca unhooked the clasp on the front of Edward's coat, then began the long row of buttons down the front of his waistcoat. Women were always being faulted for their dress, but ah, how vastly more complicated was a gentleman's uniform.

He broke away and began feathering breath-stealing kisses along her temple, down her cheek to her jaw, to make her turn her face up at him with a little gasp of delight.

"Mi coraggioso inglése leone," she whispered fiercely. *"Ti amo,* and I love you in English, too!"

"And I love you, my wicked little nymph, in English and Italian and whatever other language you please," he said, tugging at the tiny ball buttons on the back of her bodice so he could slip it forward from her shoulders. "I cannot promise you it will always be smooth sailing between us, because it won't."

She kissed him again, her happiness welling up inside her. "You are too honest, Your Grace. I must do my best to corrupt you."

"I am serious, lass," he said, though he couldn't keep from dropping another kiss across the bridge of her nose. "We've both lost our pasts, and our only hope to be happy in the future is to build one together."

"There will still be people like Lady Hingham who'll judge me unworthy of you, Edward," she said, her joy flagging. "They will talk."

"Let them talk all they want," he said, smoothing her hair back from her face. "Just don't listen."

He made it sound so simple, as if he hadn't become so frighteningly angry with Lieutenant Pettigrew. And there remained one more question to be settled, too.

"There will be time for me to paint, Edward?" she asked anxiously. "Not just as a lady would, dabbing willows and roses upon tea trays, but in a studio of my own, where I might hide myself away and paint as I wish? As I must?"

"Your, ah, *proméssa maestósa mia?*" His mouth twisted wryly as he mangled the Italian. "You see, I did pay heed. Your promise to your father, wasn't it? For the sake of your art? How could I stand in the path of that?"

"You remembered?" she asked, incredulous. How could she not love a husband like this? "You would do that for me?"

He nodded. "On the condition that you must sign only your name, and paint only what *you* wish. No more forgeries, understand?"

"Yes, yes, of course!" she agreed eagerly, until he held his hand up between them for her to stop.

"One other condition, too, pet," he cautioned. "I can no more give up the sea than you can your painting. While I could ask you to let me go alone, I'd much prefer to have you sail with me, and make pictures there."

"Aye, aye, my captain, as long as you promise I shall always be your first mate." She leaned forward to kiss the place to the front of Edward's ear, there where Peart so carefully shaved away his beard. "Two hearts, two souls, one love. I did not understand when Lady Hamilton first said it to me, but oh, have you made me believe it as truth now!"

"She told you that?" he asked with surprise. "I would never have thought it of her. Ah, so this is what you've done with my ring!"

Slowly he drew it from her shift, teasing the chain across her skin until she shivered as he lifted it over her head.

"I couldn't give up wearing your ring," she confessed. "You were still my anchor, even when I wouldn't claim you as my husband."

"But you will now." He pulled the ring from the chain and slipped it back onto her hand, folding her fingers closed over it for good measure. "I won't have my wife forgetting her husband."

"Then love me, *sposa càro mio,*" she ordered in a husky whisper as she pulled him back with her onto the bench. "Love me, and remind me, and never let me forget."

15

They made love slowly, taking the time to discover what pleased one another and to let their passion glow and smolder before the flame rose white-hot between them. Last time they'd been driven by the urgency and despair and the dreadful certainty that that single moment would be all they'd have to share before death claimed them. But this time, on a pillowed bench with the tiny painted Danaë as a witness, the promise of a long, shared life before them gave a richness and a freedom to their lovemaking that Francesca had never dreamed she'd find with anyone.

"Come back to Harborough House with me now," he asked as, at last, he began to dress. "The duke's bed is at least the size of Hanover Square, and I promise we'll test every inch of it before dawn."

"I can't, *càro mio,*" she said, stretching indolently against a cushion. "I must tell Uncle Peacock about you first, and that must wait until breakfast."

"I could persuade you, Your Grace," he said, coming back to rest his palms on either side of her waist as he leaned over her and took one rosy nipple into his mouth, teasing her flesh with his tongue. She gasped as sensation rushed through her blood again, and she marveled that her body could still be so responsive after all they'd already done. "And there would be the carriage ride to consider as well, Francesca. The cushions are wide, the springs accommodating, and the coachman discreet. Consider it, lass, consider it well."

"No, Edward, don't!" she cried, giggling as she rolled from the bench and beyond his reach. Swiftly, if haphazardly, she began to dress herself, not bothering to repin her hair and counting on the swath of her shawl to cover any deficiencies. "When you return tomorrow and meet my uncle, then I'll leave with you, but not now. Come, I'll see you to the door myself, so we won't shock the servants."

But despite the hour, she'd underestimated Mrs. Monk's loyalty, curiosity, and her desire to wait upon a duchess.

"Your Grace," said the housekeeper, bustling forward importantly as soon as Francesca stepped into the hallway. "Shall I fetch supper for you, Your Grace?"

"No, thank you, Mrs. Monk," she said, grateful that the hanging night-light in the hall would hide both her blushes and the telltale creases in her muslin gown; she and Edward had been too caught up in each other to be particularly reserved, and she didn't want to consider everything that Mrs. Monk likely had overheard here in the hall. "His Grace is just leaving now."

She wanted to kiss Edward again, but not in front of her uncle's housekeeper. Without a thought for the chilly night, Francesca opened the front door herself and stepped outside, pulling Edward by the hand after her. His carriage was waiting in the street, and though the footman hopped down at once from the box to open the door, he discreetly turned back toward the horses when he saw Francesca. She didn't want to cause a scandal on her uncle's doorstep, but a minute wouldn't hurt. Only a minute, she told herself, a quick farewell to send Edward home thinking of her.

"Whatever are you doing, Your Grace?" teased Edward as she slid her hands beneath his cloak and inside his coat, both to keep warm and to touch him one more time. "We cannot have this sort of low behavior in a respectable neighborhood like Barlow Street!"

Beneath the lantern, her laugh showed like a puff of white in the cold air, and when he pressed her back against the wall she could feel the chill in the bricks through her thin gown. But inside his wool coat it was warm indeed, the slippery silk lining holding not only the heat of his body, but the male, animal scent of it as well, and she burrowed against him with sensual delight.

"Then kiss me quick, husband," she whispered, turning her face up toward his, "before the watch comes and catches us!"

He kissed her as she'd asked, his mouth doubly warm in the cool night air, and when she felt his hand cover her breast, she pressed against his hand with a little groan of pleasure.

"Who needs to go inside to see th' pictures if we can have a show for free in th' street?" called a man's raucous voice, loose with drink. "You didn't lie, Mc-Cray, when you promised us a rare bawdy sight at th' Italian doxie's house!"

Francesca gasped and jerked her shawl over her rumpled gown, frantically trying to look around Edward to whoever was in the street. But though she moved fast, Edward was faster, turning instantly not only to face the men but to shield her with his own body.

"McCray!" he roared, at a volume more suited for the quarterdeck than for a quiet street in Westminster. "What the devil are you doing here?"

Finally Francesca wriggled free, and over Edward's shoulder she saw three men, all of them in uniforms and boat cloaks like Edward's, the high curved silhouettes of their hats marking them as other navy captains. No wonder he was so angry, to be treated so by his peers!

"Ah, Ramsden, don't be so blasted righteous," called back the captain who stood in the middle, a stocky bulldog of a man with straggly dark hair. "You can't blame us for coming to see your little foreign missus' wares. She's the one that put the announcement out, wasn't she?"

"I'll thank you not to speak of my wife like that, McCray," said Edward, his voice as ominous as his warning. "Don't you recall our last conversation?"

"Oh, aye, I recall it, Ramsden," said McCray, stepping forward. "You turning so high and mighty that you'd not share a dram with a fellow officer and gentleman who'd wished you well. Your *Grace*. So bloody high and mighty that you knocked me down upon the cobbles and walked away before I could demand my satisfaction."

"Edward, *càro*, don't do this," begged Francesca, clinging to his arm. Already shadows and candles had appeared at the windows of the surrounding houses, and here and there the sashes had squeaked upward, drawn by the angry raised voices. "Someone truly will summon the watch if you do not end this."

But it was almost as if Edward hadn't heard her, he was so focused on the man in the street.

"I'll treat you like a gentleman when you deserve it, McCray," he said with disgust, "and not before you retract what you said of my wife before the gates at Whitehall."

"Oh, Edward, please, please, do not do this for my sake!" she pleaded. She knew where this was headed, and knew where it would end: He'd once made a jest about fighting duels, but there was nothing amusing about this at all. "Please, love, please, you cannot challenge every man who'll speak ill of me!"

"Aye, so that's your dear *wife* looking after you, isn't it?" jeered McCray. "The one that paints the sinful pictures to show what postures and positions she knows? I should've guessed from how she was rubbing up against you in rut."

One of the other captains grabbed McCray's arm, trying to pull him back. "He's been drinking all night, Captain Your Grace," he explained nervously. "He doesn't know what he's saying."

"Hell, I know exactly what I'm saying, and to

whom," insisted McCray, shaking off his friend to take another step toward Edward. "A tawdry dago bitch with filthy habits is what you picked for your duchess, Your Grace!"

"Damn your impertinence, McCray," said Edward. "You leave me no choice. Who shall be your second, sir?"

"No, *càro mio,* don't!" cried Francesca with anguish torn straight from her heart. *"Sànto cièlo,* don't! This—this *madness* and pride is not worth your life, Edward, nor our happiness!"

But he didn't even turn to look at her.

"It's not madness, my love," he said, his initial anger now replaced by an odd sort of calm that frightened her more. "It's a question of honor. I cannot let this bastard cast my wife's good name and virtue upon the dunghill. You do not deserve such treatment, nor do I. McCray, your second?"

"Robinson here will oblige me," declared McCray, ignoring how the man who'd tried to stop him now twitched with startled misery. "And yours?"

"The Earl of Bonnington," said Edward curtly. "rest assured that he shall be calling upon Captain Robinson this night to arrange the details of our meeting."

"Pistols," said McCray with far too much anticipation to please Francesca. "You're challenging me, and I say pistols."

The man hadn't hesitated to accept Edward's challenge; in fact, he'd seemed to relish it. Was he that skilled with a pistol, to be so confident? Was Edward in even greater danger than she realized?

"Pistols, then," said Edward grimly. "And let us say eight o'clock tomorrow morning, in the west corner of St. James's Park."

"As good a time as any for me to send you directly to the devil, Ramsden," said McCray with a mocking bow before he turned to leave. "Send your second to me and Robinson at the Red Dolphin. And kiss the duchess good night for me, won't you?"

Francesca seized Edward's coat, the thick wool bunched in her fingers. "Don't listen to him, *càro mio,*" she said frantically. "You told me you would not care what people say. So why must you challenge a man like that? Why risk your life over a handful of words?"

He sighed, and shook his head, lightly running his fingers over her cheek. "Because those words impeached my honor, lass, that's why. He's a vile bastard, but I shall deal with him handily enough."

"You don't know that, not for certain!" she cried softly, searching his face for any doubt, any chance that he might change his mind. "Look at me, Edward! You wish for a child, a son or daughter to carry your name. What if we conceived one here tonight? What if you die tomorrow never knowing your own son?"

That made him pause, his face by the lantern's light growing inexpressibly sad, but it wasn't enough to change his mind.

"I should much prefer to spend the night with you, Francesca," he said, "but I have a thousand things to do before morning."

"Before you put yourself before another man's

gun," she said bitterly. "Before your stubborn male pride begs him to kill you."

He sighed again, and smiled wearily. "I'll be back for breakfast, love. Kiss me for luck, won't you?"

She did, though there were tears on her eyes and cheeks, a quick kiss of farewell that seemed over before it had begun. Then he was gone, too, into the carriage and down the street and around the corner, while she stood there in the doorway as the sound of the horses' hooves on the cobblestones faded away. Still she stood there, feeling the warmth, *his* warmth, fade from her body and the chill of the night steal the heat of his last kiss from her lips.

"If you please, Your Grace," said Mrs. Monk as soon as Francesca stepped back inside the house. "A moment, if you please."

One look at the trepidation on the housekeeper's face proved that she'd heard and seen everything that had just happened on the doorstep. For a household that was usually so quiet, it had been a most eventful day.

"Edw—His Grace will be fine, Mrs. Monk," she said, forcing herself to reassure the older woman when she'd no real confidence herself. "He has survived so many battles that a duel will be next to nothing to him."

"As you say, Your Grace," the housekeeper answered dutifully. "I shall keep him in my prayers tonight. But it is the other gentleman I meant, Your Grace, the one that's been waiting so long."

"What gentleman?" asked Francesca. She already knew she must climb the stairs to her uncle's rooms and answer what would inevitably be a great many questions, and she'd no time to squander on anyone else. "I told you before that I would receive no more customers today."

"He's not a customer, Your Grace," said Mrs. Monk indignantly, "else I wouldn't have let him wait. But with him being from Naples and all, I thought sure you'd wish him to wait."

"From Naples," repeated Francesca, shaking her head. "But I am not expecting any gentleman from Naples, Mrs. Monk, especially not at this hour."

From the corner of her eye she saw the motion first, the shift of black darker than any shadow. Then the shadow glided into the hall and became a man, a man dressed all in black with a jackal's smile of yellow teeth, bowing low before her.

Signor Albani had come to London.

Edward held the long-barreled pistol in his hand, testing the weight and the balance.

"Whatever your father paid for these guns was worth it, Will," he said as he lined the sight even with a Chinese porcelain monkey on the mantelpiece. "I've never held a pistol that sat so neatly in the hand. So exactly how many men have this one and its twin killed?"

"That's not the point, Edward," said William patiently. "What's important is that *you* survive. Why else would a gentleman keep his own pistols?"

"We'll learn that in the morning, won't we?" Carefully Edward placed the pistol back into its fitted box. Of course William had agreed at once to be Edward's second, the one request among gentlemen that must never be refused, but the one that friends could try to undo.

"We don't have to wait until then, you know," said William carefully as he snapped the catches on the box closed. "You can still retract your challenge, Edward. When I met with Robinson, he gave me the impression that McCray might agree if you acted first. No one will think ill of you if you do."

"The hell they won't." Edward snorted derisively, flopping back into his armchair with his legs sprawled before him. It must be close to three in the morning by now. He was exhausted and he was disgusted with himself, and to make it all worse he was more than a little drunk. "I'll be the laughingstock of the fleet if I run a white flag for a little mongrel like McCray, and you know it as well as I do."

"What I know is that you'll run afoul of both the Admiralty and His Majesty himself if you see this through," insisted William. "You know the laws against duels. Spencer will be furious. If you kill McCray—"

"Which I've every intention of doing."

William glared at him, for once completely in earnest. "If you kill McCray," he repeated, "you might have to leave England, or be charged with his murder. The navy could stand to lose two captains in the morning, losses that the service can ill afford, and the French won't have to lift a finger to do it."

"What, haven't you heard?" Idly Edward lifted his glass, swirling the golden liquid so the light from the fire glittered through the crystal. "I'm not wanted.

I'm retired, cast off like an old boot. Peers can't fight, you know. Our tender hides are too damned precious."

"Then what of your wife?" demanded William. "If she means enough to you to defend her in this manner, then isn't she reason enough for you to live?"

Edward stared into the glass, picturing Francesca. He'd yet to wash since he'd come home, and he'd purposefully let her scent cling to him, haunting him with her presence.

"My wife," he said softly, "means everything to me."

"Then how the devil can you risk leaving her a widow so soon after you've married her?"

And for that Edward had no answer. He'd always believed his honor and good name came above everything else, and because he loved Francesca so much, he would not tolerate any insult to her. He'd been raised to defend himself that way, and the navy, founded as it was on honor and bravery, had encouraged that in him as well. It was even much of the reason he'd wed Francesca in the first place, to save her from the French, of course, but also to keep her reputation safe as she'd traveled with the English navy. He'd fought three other duels—two with swords, one with pistols—and won them all, to great acclaim and vindication. Yet Francesca had managed to shake a lifetime of conviction with one small question.

What if you die tomorrow never knowing your own son?

He thought of Francesca smiling up beneath him after they'd made love this evening, her face flushed and her hair tangled and her nose red and her eyes swimming with untidy tears of joy. He thought of the children he longed to have with her, and of the painting she'd given him. Just as she had during the storm, this night she'd offered him life with her love, rich, glowing, and full of sparkling promise.

And all he'd offered her in return had been the possibility of his own death, bleak, swift, and final.

"If you will not call off this meeting with McCray," William was saying, "then for God's sake, give me your word that this will be the last time you'll be tempted into this kind of murderous misadventure."

He wanted children, and happiness, and love. He'd had enough of fighting and war and death.

And after tomorrow, if he won, if he survived, that was how it *would* be.

"I'll give my word to you, Will, aye," he said softly. "But I'll do better than that. I'll give it to my wife."

"Do not look so surprised, Your Grace," said Signor Albani as Francesca swiftly closed the door of the gallery behind them. "At first I did despair of finding you in so vast a place as London, but once you so obligingly placed your announcement in the paper, my task was an easy one."

It was the first time in months that she'd conversed in Italian. "But to follow me clear from Palermo—"

"And why not, Your Grace?" he said with an artfully careless shrug. "Because of the wars, I have no home, little money, and my fortunes do not prosper. You, my lady, offer my best hope of a reversal."

He smiled, but there was no denying that his

claims to poverty and misfortune were accurate. He was thinner, his face haggard and drawn, and his black clothes were frayed and worn at the seams, hanging stiffly about his diminished form like a bat from a rafter. She could not imagine the circumstances he must have survived to have journeyed here, through the war and with no money or connections to ease his way.

Yet while King Ferdinando's flight from Naples had robbed Albani of his official power as a magistrate, suffering had honed a fresh edge to him. There was a new desperation in his eyes, a sense that he had so little left to lose that he would risk it willingly, and when he smiled with his yellow dog-teeth, Francesca felt dread race up her spine.

She clasped her hands and drew herself up as imperiously as she could. "I am sorry to hear of your trials, Signor, but I assure you that you are quite wrong to place your hopes in me."

"Do not be so modest, Your Grace," he said, chuckling with amusement. "You have raised yourself even higher since last we met. You are an English duchess, second in this land only to a royal princess. I have stood outside Harborough House, and marveled at such grandeur for a single family, and marveled more to learn it is but one such house now owned by your husband."

"But I've very little money of my own," she said as firmly as she could. "And I will not go to my husband for more."

"Ah, ah, could you really have forgotten, Your Grace?" he asked plaintively, placing his palms together as if in prayer. "I have not come so far to you for money. I have come for something more dear, more precious than mere gold. I have come for Her Majesty Marie Antoinette's diamond plume."

She shook her head emphatically. "And I shall tell you again, signor, that I don't have it, and never did."

"Ah, ah." He bowed his head, his once-proud magistrate's wig now drooping and sadly out of curl. "You say you do not have the jewel. I am distraught, Your Grace, distraught."

He stood still, head bent, for so long that Francesca wondered if he'd been taken ill. "Signor," she said, more gently, "I can understand your disappointment, but that does not change the truth."

"Shall I tell you how I pass my days in London, Your Grace?" he asked, answering her question with one of his own. "In their coffeehouses, these English will leave their newspapers common for all to read upon the tables, free to whoever pleases. Such a rare generosity to an impoverished foreigner to improve his English, Your Grace, and what I have learned! How these Londoners live, what they eat and buy and what crimes they are hung for. It is a wonder to me, a wonder."

"Yes, signor," said Francesca uneasily. "But if we have no more to discuss, then I must say good evening."

"And the nobility, Your Grace!" he continued as if she hadn't spoken. "Such interest in their doings! Can you imagine what the papers would make of your own past, Your Grace? What they would write of your republican sympathies, your friends among the rebels, even those famous lewd paintings you showed?"

"But I do not have the plume!" she cried. "Why will you not believe me?"

He shrugged again, disdainfully, such a Neapolitan gesture. "Because, Your Grace, I am certain you are lying," he said, the yellow jackal's teeth smiling. "What will your passionate husband say when he reads the stories of you, I wonder? How many more duels must he fight in your name? Ah, how you must fear for him, Your Grace!"

"There must be no public scandal," she said, her voice shaking, all the awful possibilities that she understood far better than anyone else. "I have sold much these last days, signor. I will give you all—*all*— I have earned if you will keep your lies to yourself."

"The queen's diamonds, and nothing less." He plucked his hat from the table and, tucking it beneath his arm, turned to leave. "Your servant, Your Grace. And pray be sure to tell the duke I shall be eager to congratulate him upon his victory tomorrow morning."

"You would attend the duel?" she asked, appalled. "You would watch?"

"I would not miss it, Your Grace." He bowed, and without waiting for a footman to show him out, he left.

She would not cry. This evening she had blissfully rested in Edward's arms as his lover and his wife, and tomorrow she might be no more than his widow, their life together done before it had really started. And even if Edward wasn't killed or grievously wounded, Albani would be there, ready to tell him lies calculated to cause the most heartbreaking damage imaginable, ready to ruin her for the sake of a brooch she didn't have. Her world was falling inward like a child's house of cards, and she was helpless to stop it.

But she would not cry. Better to put things to order here in her gallery, now, for there'd be no time tomorrow, and with a shuddering gulp she began to pack Lady Hingham's purchases for delivery. But as she reached over the table, her shawl caught on the handle of the black-figured vase. It wobbled on the edge of the table, tangled in the shawl's fringe for an endless instant, then toppled off and smashed on the floor.

Horrified, Francesca crouched down to gather the shards that had been the vase. The biggest unbroken piece was the base, and as she reached for it, she saw a lumpy white package still stuffed inside. With care she pulled the package free, a lady's fine linen handkerchief knotted with a note scribbled on a scrap of Francesca's own drawing paper.

> *Given to you Little Robin to ease your*
> *way in London*
> > *Yr. Friend Emma Ldy H.*

A gift from Lady Hamilton, hastily tucked inside the vase when Francesca had been packing her belongings, a gift impulsive and innocent but also as generous as the giver, a gift of value enough to help stave off a refugee's poverty. With fingers made clumsy by excitement, Francesca unknotted the handkerchief and pulled the makeshift bundle apart.

And into her lap tumbled the dead queen's diamond plume, all glitter and folly.

"Francesca, my girl," rumbled her uncle crossly from the doorway behind her, his cane tapping with impatience as he leaned on the footman's arm. "I am tired of waiting for you to come to me, and we have too much to say for us to wait any longer. Come, come, and tell me the truth. What mischief have you fallen into? Are you in fact wed to the Duke of Harborough?"

Swiftly Francesca tucked the diamond brooch into her pocket before she turned toward him, knowing that even with her uncle there must be degrees of truth.

"Yes, Uncle Peacock, I am married to the Duke of Harborough," she confessed. "But oh, *sànto cièlo*, that is only the beginning. . . ."

16

$\mathcal{I}$t was a corner of St. James's Park much favored by navy officers for settling affairs of honor. A small hill combined with a copse of trees offered some measure of privacy, yet the tall brick chimneys of Whitehall with the Admiralty's telegraph tower were just visible in the distance, oddly comforting in times like these. Snow had fallen in the night, just enough to dust over the winter grass and ice the bare branches of the trees and make a bleak landscape even more stark in the gray morning light.

"Cheerful sort of morning you've picked, Ned," grumbled William, blowing into his cupped hands to warm them. "Colder than a witch's tit."

Edward's smile was obligatory as he leaned back against the leather squabs of the chaise. The chill of the morning suited him, as did the colorless landscape. Duels often began with heated tempers, but like the battles he'd fought at sea, they were won with cold reason and an icy composure. He must focus his anger, narrow it to build his concentration instead of scattering it. He'd only have one shot from that beautifully crafted pistol. He needed to make it count. There'd be time enough later to sit before the fire with his boots off to warm his feet and Francesca on his lap to warm the rest.

If, of course, there was a later. And damnation, he couldn't let himself think of Francesca, or he'd never get through this.

"Remember what I've told you about McCray," said William hurriedly as the chaise began its final lurching path down the hillside. "I've heard he's fought a score of duels in the West Indies, dishonorable scuffles in tavern-yards, but enough to make him a cocky bastard now. Because he's near blind in his right eye, he'll use his left to aim, and cross his right arm over his chest. You won't have much of his shirt to shoot for. And odds are he'll have found his courage in a bottle, too, so as soon as you take your pistols, be wary of a jumped start or misfire. He'll cheat any way he can. He's like that, scarce what you'd call a gentleman, and for the life of me I still can't say why he's meeting you like this."

"Because he believes I've had too much good luck in my life, while he has had none," said Edward dryly. "I daresay he feels the imbalance should be corrected, beginning with insulting my wife."

But this will be the last time, Francesca my love, the last time, I swear. . . .

"If he kills you," said William grimly, "he'll learn about true bad luck. Spencer himself will make sure he'll spend the rest of his days on land on half-pay."

Edward smiled. "That makes me almost wish to be killed, just from spite."

"For God's sake, don't even make jests like that," ordered Will with a grimace. "No use in tempting fate. Blast, look at all the gawkers!"

As the chaise drew to a stop, Edward could see the small crowd that had gathered to watch. Word had traveled fast overnight. They were mostly men in dark boat-cloaks and captain's hats, the ribbon cockades standing out like bristling little birds against he snow, though Edward couldn't guess whether they'd come in support or simply for entertainment. There was also a smattering of other gentlemen in the group, stomping their feet in the snow like horses trying to keep warm, and a handful of boys darting among the men. Horses had been tethered at a respectful distance, where they wouldn't bolt at the gunshots, and footmen and drivers sat on the roofs of their parked chaises and coaches to get a better view.

"It's like a damned circus," said Edward. The other duels he'd fought had been small, private affairs on foreign beaches, without any scandal or fashion attached, nothing like this. "What a pity McCray didn't choose swords, so we could give them all a better show."

"If it had been swords, McCray would have backed down," said William with a sniff of contempt. "No skill or talent to pointing a pistol and blasting a man's fool head away."

"Ah, words of true comfort," said Edward wryly as the footman hopped down to unlatch the door. "Now come, time to give them all the blood and thunder they're hoping for."

But William paused, holding his fist out to Edward. "Mates forever," he said softly. "Good luck, Ned."

Edward smiled, and tapped his fist to his friend's, their old boyhood signal. "Mates forever. And I don't intend to rely upon luck."

He climbed down with his head high and the slightest of smiles on his lips, terribly conscious of how every head turned to watch him and how the murmur of excited conversation seemed to wash around him like a lapping wave. He felt like a Drury Lane player who'd just made his entrance, and he understood now why William had insisted they come in the chaise, instead of walking across the park from Harborough House as Edward had suggested.

A king's officer cannot simply stroll to his affair of honor, William had argued, not like some rustic farmer off to his fields, and besides, there was the surgeon to consider. *Considering the surgeon* had been William's discreet way of not mentioning a body, much to Edward's macabre amusement. But he did have to admit that the chaise would be far more convenient for hauling away a mangled corpse, especially with such a bloodthirsty crowd eager to see exactly that.

McCray was already waiting, standing off to one side with Robinson and the surgeon. He'd already removed his coat and waistcoat, standing in his shirtsleeves and swinging his arms, yet his face gleamed with an anxious sweat. When Robinson offered him a pewter flask, McCray grasped it eagerly, drinking long before he handed it back with a shuddering whoop and a teeth-baring grimace.

"Wouldn't you hate to rely on that face beside you in battle?" muttered William beside him. "No wonder he's banished to the Indies. Can you fathom what the men must make of a grinning ape like that for their captain?"

"Haul it aback now, Will," said Edward softly, "else you'll find yourself facing him next."

William snorted with disgust as he stepped forward to meet Robinson. Edward watched, tugging off his gloves finger by finger, while Peart took his cloak and then his coat, folding them neatly over his arm, and Edward began unfastening the long row of brass buttons on his waistcoat. It really was like a drama, with roles to play and lines to be spoken, even marks on which to stand. Perhaps that was why Edward felt so calm, almost resigned. The reality of the danger he would shortly face was still missing; ritual like this always disguised the threat of death.

"My Lord Bonnington, sir," called Robinson with a wobbly bow and bloodshot eyes that showed he, too, had applied himself to the pewter flask. "I've, ah, come to see if the duke wishes to, ah, withdraw his challenge."

William bowed back. "Only if Captain McCray is willing to make a complete and abject apology to Captain His Grace the Duke of Harborough, and to retract in writing his slanderous calumny in regard to Her Grace the Duchess of Harborough."

Nervously Robinson swallowed, glancing over his shoulder for reinforcement from McCray, who shook his head. "Captain McCray regrets that, ah, he is unable to accept such terms," he said from carefully rehearsed memory, "when they would, ah, require him to deny what is known and accepted truth about the, ah, lady and her past."

The thread holding the last waistcoat button snapped beneath the jerk of Edward's thumb, the brass disk arcing high before it plopped and vanished into the snow.

For every foul word that McCray had said of Francesca, he must suffer; for every lie, he must pay.

His Francesca, laughing, teasing, dancing away from him with her hair loose around her shoulders ...

"Forgive me for interrupting, Your Grace," said an older gentleman in an old-fashioned wig, leaning heavily upon his cane for support. "My name is John Peacock, Your Grace, and I come bearing a final plea for peace in this matter."

"Your servant, sir," said Edward uncertainly, struggling to place the man's name and face, the brightness to his eyes that seemed uncannily familiar. "But as you can see, there is no hope of any peaceable resolution as long as Captain McCray insists on insulting my wife."

The gentleman nodded. "My niece would be willing to forgive every insult, Your Grace, and urges you to do the same."

He started, the man's name now where it belonged. "Forgive me, sir, for not realizing you were Francesca's uncle."

"Given your distractions, Your Grace, you are absolved," said Peacock with a grunt. "But you are the one who must find forgiveness for your enemy in your soul. Come, captain, come! Your wife waits."

"Francesca is here?" Aghast, Edward looked to where Peacock pointed with the tip of his cane.

She stood alone on the hillside, not far from the carriages, at the end of a path of snow flurried by her skirts. Above the sea of somber dark uniforms and cloaks, she wore a red gown and a cloak over it to match, her dark hair loose beneath the hood and her hands inside an oversized black fur muff, and even at this distance he could see her face was pale despite the cold.

Red for passion, red for fire, red for love, red as the blood that would soon spread across the white snow . . .

"She insisted on coming, Your Grace," said Peacock. "You know how strong her will can be. She thought perhaps her presence would alter your mind."

"Then she was mistaken," said Edward sharply. Damnation, she did not *belong* here! No ladies attended duels, especially not when they were the cause of them. Already she'd been noticed, pointed out, remarked on, and assessed. He was proud of her beauty, and that other men would admire his wife, but he didn't want her linked in any way to McCray's slanders, which her presence here would irrevocably do. "Please, Mr. Peacock, take her back to your house directly."

But Peacock only sighed, and solemnly shook his head. "She will not go, Your Grace. She says she will stay until you change your mind, and if you don't, she will watch."

She was watching him now. He glanced up at her

again, furious at himself for doing it, and saw her draw her black-gloved hand from the muff to raise it in silent salute. Her red skirts fluttered in the breeze, the hood ruffling around her face.

She was stealing his focus being here, weakening him, robbing the power from his anger. Instead she was making him think of how infinitely much more he'd prefer to be with her beneath the velvet coverlets in his enormous bed in his house, *their* house, across the park with that red gown on the floor, how her skin would be warm and fragrant with her womanly scent, how she'd sink into the featherbed beneath him, how tightly she'd hold him with her thighs curled around his waist, sleek and wet and willing and *he must not think of this now.*

Or he would die.

He turned away from her and back toward Peacock. "Tell her, sir, if she stays, she may see sights that she won't easily forget."

Peacock bowed, genteelly agreeable. "She knew you'd say that, Your Grace, and told me to tell you that she is prepared for that possibility."

"Prepared, hell." She'd never seen what a lead ball could do to flesh and bone at close range, or realized how much blood could drain from a man's body in only a minute, and he'd rather she didn't learn now, especially not at his expense. "She hasn't the faintest damned notion of what could happen here."

"Your Grace?" William's expression was uncertain. "Are you ready to proceed?"

"Aye, aye, I am." He yanked off his waistcoat and tossed it to Peart, and followed William to where the others stood. The spectators backed away to a more respectful distance, and a safer one, too, leaving the snow where they'd stood trampled and muddied. But here where Edward and McCray would stand, the new snow was still untouched, waiting for the stain of blood.

And a red hooded cloak fluttering in the breeze upon the hillside....

Edward nodded at the surgeon, a thin-faced man brought up from the hospital at Greenwich by William this morning. Then, for the first time that morning, he looked McCray squarely in the eye. The man didn't flinch—Edward would grant him that—but he was sweating so profusely that the hair was plastered to his temples, and his worn shirt clung limply to the softness of his belly. The collar of that shirt had been turned to mask the edge frayed by his beard, and beneath McCray's chin was a forlorn little darned patch in the linen, a sadly human detail that Edward desperately wished he hadn't noticed.

"Pistols, gentlemen." William presented the mahogany box with his father's guns, already loaded, and like a child faced with a choice of chocolates, McCray let his fingers hover greedily over first one pistol, then the second, before he finally pounced and grabbed one, pulling it away as if he feared Edward would try to take it.

Edward, of course, didn't. He'd tested both pistols last night, and knew they were equal. He held his lightly, warming the polished butt in his hand. Like all the most modern dueling pistols, these were fitted with hair-triggers, extra springs in the lock that would make the pistol fire at the slightest pull, and without disturbing the aim. As William had noted before, it no longer took much talent or even nerve to blast a man's fool head off.

Solemnly William handed the empty box to Peart. "For the final time, gentlemen, and in the name of the king you have sworn to serve, I ask if you can be reconciled?"

"He's still married to a wretched foreign trollop," said McCray doggedly, "and I'm not about—"

"Enough, McCray," ordered Edward sharply. "Lord Bonnington, I believe you have your answer."

"Very well, Your Grace." William cleared his throat, the sound echoing so that Edward realized all the others had ceased to talk. "I shall ask you to take your positions, gentlemen."

Edward turned so his back was against McCray's. He held the barrel of the pistol with the muzzle toward the gray morning sky, the barrel resting lightly against his collarbone.

"Five paces apart, gentlemen, then turn inward."

Silently Edward counted his steps, his footfalls muffled by the snow, then turned. McCray was already facing him, his eyes blank. Edward remembered what William had told him, how McCray would twist his arm before him to compensate for his weak eye, how he'd present a smaller square of white shirt. Better to aim a fraction lower, toward his belly.

Oh, Francesca, càra mia, are you still watching from the hill?

"I will count to five, gentlemen," continued William. "One, two, three, four, five. Upon the final

word, you may fire at will. Are you ready, gentlemen?"

"One, two . . ."

I love you, lass. Even if I die, that will never change.

"Three, four . . ."

*This is the last time, Francesca, I swear it. I want the
life, the love that you give me, not this. Damnation, I
must be sure to watch McCray's arm. . . .*

The flash came first, brilliant yellow-white, the
way only gunpowder can be, a half-second before
William called five, and well before Edward's finger
could squeeze the trigger.

*And too late now to remember what else William
had said. Be wary of a jumped start or misfire, for Mc-
Cray will cheat any way he can. . . .*

He felt the sharp stab in his upper arm, the pain that
began small and swiftly grew, streaking down his arm
and up to his shoulder with the slower spread of blood,
his blood, warming his own chilly skin inside his sleeve.
Around him rumbled the shock and outrage from the
other men, matched by his own furious oath at being
gulled by the oldest trick in the coward's book.

But his fingers still held the pistol, no bones broken or tendons severed. He'd been winged, that was
all, and ten paces away was McCray's ashen face, his
mouth slack, hanging open with shock and terror.
The wisp of gunsmoke drifted from the muzzle of his
spent pistol, and his darned shirt was as broad a tar-
get as any man could wish.

"Take the bastard now, Harborough!" bellowed a
man from the crowd. "Send McCray to hell, the
double-damned coward!"

Everything seemed squeezed into this single moment, as if it were being compressed through the narrow neck of a bottle: William's stunned face, the gaunt-cheeked surgeon kneeling to open his bag, Peart standing open-mouthed with his coat and cloak so neatly folded, the gray sky and the red blotches on the white snow there at his feet. But what remained clearest was McCray, dropping to his knees with a keening wail for mercy, his face turned loose with horrified anticipation, hovering there just above the sight on Edward's pistol.

"Kill him, Your Grace! Give McCray what he deserves!"

Was Francesca watching? Waiting, weeping for him though his wound was slight? He hated seeing her cry, especially when it was his fault. But he'd promised her this would be the last time, hadn't he? No more killing, not like this. He loved her too much for it to be otherwise.

I love you, lass.

With McCray kneeling in the snow before him, Edward raised his arm high, the pain slicing down its length and back again through the torn flesh, and pointed the muzzle upward. With a little grunt of pain, he squeezed the trigger, and fired into the sky.

"There is my satisfaction," he said. He let the pistol slip from his fingers and turned toward the hill, toward salvation, toward Francesca.

The hill was empty. She was gone.

She could not make herself look away.

Even though Francesca knew Edward could die as

he'd lived, killed as surely by his precious honor as by the other captain, she watched. Even though she might see things that would haunt her as long as she lived, she watched. How could she not? This was Edward, her husband and her love, and her fate was too entwined with his for her to do otherwise now.

The morning was cold as death, the snow wet ice beneath her slippers, clinging in pellets to the hem of her skirts and cloak. Though Uncle Peacock had told her to stay in the carriage, she'd come to stand here as soon as he'd left her, watching, watching. She'd seen her uncle make his way slowly through the other men, reaching Edward at the last possible moment. Though she couldn't hear the words, she'd known what her uncle said, because she'd given him the words. She'd held her breath, her hands twisting restlessly inside her muff.

Then Edward had sought her out, his gaze like a caress across the distance, linking them together. Hope, sweet and pure, rose up in her heart as she dared to believe he'd choose her and her love instead of this awful fate.

But how could love ever triumph over honor? She watched him shake his head, refuse her plea, turn away from her and toward the other men. He chose his pistol, marked his paces, faced McCray, listened as Lord Bonnington counted.

One, two . . .

She whispered heartfelt prayers in Italian, anguished pleas and beseechings and bargainings for Edward's life.

Three . . .

Saints in heaven, but she loved him, her darling, dearest husband with the golden hair. She always *would* love him, no matter what happened next.

Four . . .

An eternity seemed to stretch between each number, yet time was racing past too fast for her to stop.

Five . . .

God help her, she could not watch any longer, and whipped around with a sob just as the shot echoed across the park. One shot, only one shot, and a disjointed garble of voices.

Not Edward, oh, dear God, not Edward!

"Your Grace, Your Grace?" said Albani, out of breath from running up the hill to her. "You have come!"

"My husband," she gasped. "My Edward—"

"He is the victor, Your Grace," said Albani, "and he lives."

She felt her knees buckle with relief beneath her, and Albani caught her arm, keeping her upright. She twisted enough to look back down the hill, where Edward stood, still tall and proud, clearly the victor as Albani said.

"You have brought the brooch?" he demanded. "Come, do not torment me another minute, and tell me instead! Do you have the brooch as you promised?"

"Yes," she said unsteadily, "but I must go to Edward, I must—"

"You must come with me for now, Your Grace," ordered Albani curtly, dragging her with him through the snow, back among the carriages and chaises. "Your husband has survived one threat yes, but he is still in a different danger if you do not come with me."

He didn't need to explain further. She knew what he wanted, and what he would do if she didn't obey. She let him hurry her into a waiting hackney, the driver starting almost before she climbed inside.

"Where are we going?" she asked, then gasped as she heard the second shot, twisting to try to see from the hackney's window. "Oh, Edward!"

"The Duke is unharmed, Your Grace," said Albani. "I saw the duel. That shot is meaningless, no more than a misfire, perhaps. Now where is the French queen's diamond plume?"

Francesca sat back, bracing herself in the rocking hackney. They'd left the snow-covered grass of the park, and were on cobbles now, passing by a rambling building that her uncle had pointed out as Whitehall. They must be coming close to the river, near to where she'd landed from the packet that first day.

"The brooch is in a most safe place," she said. Her fingers brushed across the diamonds now, tucked deep inside her muff, though she'd no intention of telling that to Albani yet. "But before I can give it to you, I must have your assurance that you will never spread lies about me or my husband again."

Albani scowled, and sniffed derisively. "A most brave demand, Your Grace. Until your message this morning, you have denied ever even having the jewel in your possession, and yet you expect *assurances* from me now!"

The hackney lurched to a stop, snarled among the

wagons and carts around the docks, but Albani didn't seem to notice. "If you want to be certain of me, Your Grace, you must first give me the plume."

Francesca swallowed, belatedly wishing she'd asked her uncle for his advice about this as well. Last night, when she'd discovered the brooch, she'd been sure she could deal with Albani herself, but now, facing him here alone, she wasn't nearly as confident. She didn't want to live with the threat of Edward fighting another duel; she wanted this settled now, which was why she'd brought the diamond plume with her. But the jewel was all she had for bargaining, and she had to be sure before she gave it away.

"You do not even know the value of what you have," he sneered. "A piece like that! worn by a martyred queen, I can sell it as a relic, a memento, to an émigré who mourns Her Majesty. Or I can offer it to another who will use it as a rallying cry, a symbol against Napoleon and for the Bourbon cause. Or best of all, I can restore it to our own dear Queen Maria Carolina when His Majesty King Ferdinando is placed back on his throne, and receive the most lavish of rewards in return for my loyalty. Ah, Your Grace, you cannot guess how valuable such a piece can be to me!"

But as Francesca's fingers traced the brooch's curling outlines, she thought not of the politics these diamonds represented, but of the unhappy women who'd owned it, women caught in wars that were not their doing: of Marie Antoinette, sending the plume as her last gift to her sister in Naples, of Maria Carolina who had kept her head but lost her home and

throne and her little son when she'd fled Naples; of
Lady Hamilton, desperately in love with one man
and married to another; and now herself, the one
with the chance to be the happiest of all, if only she
could save her husband this way.

"You must write a statement for me, swearing I
am the same virtuous and honest woman I was
known to be in Naples," she said urgently. "You must
sign it, too, before I give you the brooch."

"And pray, Your Grace," he asked scornfully,
"what would I use for writing this document here in
a hackney?"

"We can stop at an inn or tavern," she suggested
eagerly, glancing out the window. "Surely they would
have pen and paper."

Then he smiled, the yellow teeth as ruthless as a
jackal's. "You have it with you, don't you? On your
person, pinned to your shift, perhaps hidden somewhere else, ah?"

His gaze flicked lower, to the muff, and in an instant he'd grabbed the fur and jerked it from her
arm. But when he'd pulled the muff free, the brooch
had remained clutched tight in her fingers. Before he
could realize his mistake, she lunged for the latch on
the hackney's door and shoved it open, and jumped
out into the street.

"Watch yerself, miss!" shouted a carter as she
ducked beneath his horse's nose and bolted across
the street, her skirts and cloak flying behind her. Another horse reared at the sight of so much flapping
red cloth, a woman screamed and more men swore at
her, yet she didn't stop and she didn't look back, de-

termined to escape from Albani. Ahead lay the bridge to Westminster and her uncle's house, one of the few places she recognized in London, and she raced toward it as fast as she could, her heart thumping in her breast and the diamond plume clutched tight in her fingers.

But the cobbles on the bridge's walkway still carried the glaze of snow that had frosted the grass in the park, and as she darted across her feet slipped. With a cry she tried to catch herself, but her heels tangled in her skirts and she pitched forward to the cobbles, her breath driven from her lungs but the brooch still in her hand.

"Mi scusi, mi scusi," said Albani, pushing past two marketwomen who'd bent to help Francesca. "Excuse me, please, my ladies, and let me tend to my sister."

Unable to catch her breath to speak, Francesca tried to pull free as he raised her, gasping, to her feet, but Albani only shook his head, and smiled sadly at the two women.

"She isn't well, my sister," he explained in halting English. "Some days she will claim to be an English duchess! We have come here from Naples, for her to see your English doctors."

The women nodded, at once accepting the story of these two foreign-looking folks.

"Poor lamb," said one of the women, patting Francesca's arm before they moved away. "Let you brother look after you now, that's a good girl."

Albani's grip tightened on her forearm. "If you fight me," he said in Italian, "I shall knock you over the rail and into the river, and say you did it in your madness, yes?"

But still Francesca tried to pull herself free. "If you do," she gasped, "then you shall never have the plume, will you?"

"Don't be ridiculous," he snapped, grabbing her hand and beginning to pry her fingers apart. "If you believe that I—"

"Let her go, you bastard," ordered Edward. "Let my wife go free *now*."

She looked up, startled, not sure whether to believe her ears. Yet there her husband stood, with Lord Bonnington and Peart jumping from the chaise behind him. Edward, her Edward, a bit disheveled with his coat tossed over his shirtsleeves, but alive, gloriously alive, and furiously alive now, too.

"I said let her go," he repeated ominously, and now Albani did.

She ran the three steps to Edward and threw her arms around his waist. Instead of hugging her back, he grunted with pain, and only then did she notice the makeshift bandage around his arm and the blood soaking through his shirtsleeve.

"Oh, Edward, you *were* hurt!" she cried miserably. "Oh, love, I cannot—"

"Not now, Francesca," he said, his gaze—and his pistol—still directed toward Albani. "Instead I should like to know what in blazes is happening here with you and this, ah, constable? Signor Albani, isn't it?"

"Your servant, Your Grace," said Albani quickly, bowing low. "I can explain, yes, though it sorrows me.

I have been following this woman since she left Naples, to charge her with the theft of a rare jewel from Her Majesty Queen Maria Carolina herself, and—"

"Oh, you lie, signor, how you lie!" she cried, and unfolded her fingers to show the plume to Edward. "This was given to me by Lady Hamilton, Edward, a gift before we sailed, though she'd hidden it in one of the vases for me to find later, and I just did, but Signor Albani wished to blackmail me and you, too, and slander us in the newspapers if I did not give it to him and—and—it is all *lies,* Edward!"

But Edward's expression didn't change as he studied the plume, the diamonds winking in the sun. "You would tell this tale to the scandal sheets, signor?"

Albani bowed again. "A great theft such as this is of interest to the people, Your Grace," he said. "Unless, of course, you would wish to avoid such scandal. I could be persuaded to return the brooch to Her Majesty myself, Your Grace, for a consideration, and—"

"To hell with your consideration," thundered Edward. "My wife is no thief, and no liar, either. If she says Lady Hamilton gave this to her, then by God, that is what happened."

"Oh, *per favore,* Edward, don't," begged Francesca frantically. "No more challenges, no more duels, my love!"

For a long moment he looked down at her, then suddenly smiled. "No," he said. "No more duels, my love."

She stared at him uncertainly. "No?"

"No," he said firmly. "I have realized something, lass. *You* have made me realize it. What I have with you is more important than any glory, any honor, and as long as I have you to love, then nothing that anyone else does will matter."

"You would do that for me?" she asked in wonder.

"All that," he said firmly. "Loving you is a great deal more agreeable than staring down the muzzle of a pistol, Francesca."

"I am sure there are writers who will be most interested in your wife's past," persisted Albani sourly. "There is much that I can tell them about her, and you, and Lady Hamilton and Lord Nelson during your stay in Naples."

"Then tell away, signor," said Edward, his smile widening to a full grin. "They'll write whatever they want, anyway. My wife and I will always be a damned uncommon duke and duchess, but as long as we have one another, then we will be happy, and to Hades with the rest of the world."

"But Your Grace," protested Albani, still looking longingly at the diamond plume, even now unable to accept that he'd failed. "If your wife—"

"No more, signor," said Edward firmly. "No more. Now you'll excuse us, signor, but I'd prefer being with my wife alone. Isn't that so, my love?"

"*Veraménte,*" she said softly as they turned away. "Do you know that is what Lady Hamilton told me? Not the part about Hades, but the rest. That once I'd find my true love, I'd be willing to risk everything else to be with him. And I will, Edward. That is, I *do.*"

"And so do I, my brave little nymph." He took the

diamond plume and pinned it to the front of her gown. "I believe that Lady Hamilton is the wisest of women and a deuced fine matchmaker, too, to realize how exceptionally well we'd suit."

She grinned shyly, aware that here in the middle of the Westminster Bridge, her husband was regarding her with the same wicked intent as the centaur had the nymph in her drawing. "But we *will* be a most uncommon duke and duchess, *càro mio.* I don't believe we could be any other kind."

"Ah, Francesca," he said as he bent to kiss her. "I wouldn't want it any other way."

SONNET BOOKS
PROUDLY PRESENTS

The Very Comely Countess

MIRANDA JARRETT

Available November 2001
from
Sonnet Books

Turn the page for a preview of
The Very Comely Countess. . . .

𝒯he Duke of Harborough's carriage lurched to a rumbling start, or at least as much of a start as any vehicle could make for itself so close to Whitehall in the middle of the day. The iron-bound wheels scraped over the cobblestones and the springs sawed back and forth with a queasy rhythm as the driver tried to make his way through the carts and chaises and wagons, porters and sailors and apprentices and idlers, that always crowded the streets near the Thames. The sun was too bright and the river too rank, and, with a groan, William, the present Earl of Bonnington, sank back against the leather squabs and pulled his hat lower over his eyes, trying to keep out every last ray of the infernal sunshine that was making his head ache even more.

"Will you tell me now what ails you, Bonnington?" asked Edward, the seventh Duke of Harborough, Earl of Heythrop, Baron Tyne, and a gentleman who, unlike William, never shied from the midday sun. "Aside from your usual depravities, that is."

"I would not dream of keeping anything a secret from you, you insufferably cheerful bastard," said William, without raising his hat from his eyes. "What ails me is simple, and not in the least depraved. I am in great need of a new woman."

Edward chuckled, more amused than a true friend

had any right to be. "Having finally wearied of Emily, you are in the market for her replacement?"

"I did not 'weary' of Emily," said William. Emily had been his last mistress, a luscious little dancer he'd set up in keeping for nearly two years, until her avarice had finally counterbalanced her uninhibited imagination and abilities, and with a parting gift of rubies, William sent her on to an older marquis. "One was wearied *by* Emily, but never *of* her. It is Jenny I must replace."

"Ah." Instantly Edward sobered. "Jenny."

"Yes, Jenny." William pushed his hat back from his face; there'd be no hiding in any discussion of Jenny Colton. "Have you any notion of how close she came to getting us both captured?"

Uneasily Edward nodded. Jenny had been his idea, and now she'd be his fault as well. "I'd some idea of the problems, aye. Your report made it clear enough that the arrangements had not gone, ah, exactly as planned."

" 'Exactly,' hell," said William with disgust. He hadn't wanted to mention this in the Admiralty Office, not knowing who might be listening even there, but here now in Edward's carriage he had no such qualms. "She decided she was far too *intelligent* to follow orders, and began plotting and playing games she'd no notion how to finish. If we hadn't been able to clear the French coast three nights ago, then Robitaille and his men would have swept us up for certain."

There wasn't much cheerfulness to be found in Edward's face now. "Where is she at present?"

"Back in the theater at Bristol," said William, "where I fervently hope she remains for the rest of her mortal days, or at least for mine. I've no great desire to explore French republicanism through the wonders of the guillotine on account of some third-rate actress."

He could make light of it now, but the *Fancy* had

barely slipped beneath the French guns and into the safety of a dense fog. It had been close, damned close. No wonder his head ached.

Edward frowned, restlessly tapping his fingers on his knee. When he'd given up active duty to assume his title, he'd also given up wearing his gold-laced captain's uniform except for dress, but the years he'd spent in the navy still showed as much in the formal, straight-backed way he carried himself as it did in his sun-browned, weather-beaten face. He didn't look like any of his fellow peers in the House of Lords, and his experience was beyond theirs, too, having served with honor at the Battle of the Nile with Admiral Lord Nelson.

"I am sorry, William," said his friend now. "I thought you'd find Jenny amusing. I thought she'd be to your, ah, taste."

William allowed himself a small, exasperated grumble. It was bad enough that the scandal sheets breathlessly painted him as a sinfully charming rakehell, a carefree despoiler of maidens and defiler of wives. It simply wasn't true. Not entirely, anyway. He was very fond of women, and women in turn were very fond of him, and he'd never seen the wickedness in obliging their fondness, or letting them oblige his. But to have Edward believing these exaggerations and treating him as if he were no better than a stallion in perpetual rut—well, enough *was* enough.

"I am not insatiable, Edward," he said testily. "And I do not regard these runs across the Channel as pleasure-jaunts filled with drinking and whoring. I know that is precisely what we wish the French to believe, but if I begin to believe it, too, then I'm as good as dead. Hell, if you chose Jenny only to warm my—"

"She came highly recommended," said Edward defensively. "For her reticence, that is. Not her other, ah, talents."

"Oh, no, of course not," said William with a certain resignation as he settled back against the cushions, arms folded over his chest. "Spoken like the old married man you are. You're so blessed content with your new little wife that you can't bear to think of us wicked old bachelors behaving decently at all."

"My contentment has nothing to do with this." Irritably Edward tugged at one white linen cuff. "You know damned well I'd never willingly put you at risk, not after you've already done so much for the Admiralty and the country as well."

"I know, Ned. But do recall that you're the great hero, not I." William sighed. No one who knew them both would ever make such a mistake, which was exactly why he had been so successful with his missions. Who would believe anything so patriotic, so *selfless*, of the Earl of Bonnington? "I am simply tired and cross, and I want nothing more than a drink to settle my temper. But I do believe I shall choose the next hussy myself."

"I wouldn't wish it otherwise," said Edward, grumbling but still clearly relieved that William wasn't going to raise more of a row about Jenny than he had. Not that William would. He and Edward had known one another since they were boys running wild together through the Sussex countryside, nearly thirty years ago now. While their lives since then had taken very different turns, that bond would always be there between them, and was certainly not worth straining for the sake of a self-centered chit like Jenny Colton.

"And no more actresses, Ned," warned William. "They're too damned caught up in preening over their own beauty to be trusted. You cannot imagine the strain of being penned up in the *Fancy*'s cabin with Jenny Colton for a fortnight of dirty weather."

Edward nodded. "But a woman won't be much use to you as a distraction if she's not beautiful."

"A different kind of beauty, then. More subtle. More like a true lady." William sighed again, rubbing the back of his neck. He'd shaved and washed and changed his clothes before he'd called upon Edward, but he still felt gritty and edgy from lack of sleep. "A lady who'll understand that there are perhaps times when she would do well to be quiet and listen."

Edward snorted. "The woman will be posing as your mistress, Will, not your wife. Though to hear you, perhaps that's what you're finally searching for, eh? A lovely demise to your overrated bachelorhood?"

"Oh, hardly." William grimaced, for ever since Edward had fallen in love and married last year, he'd become the most earnest of matchmakers. It wasn't that William had any real argument against marrying—his own parents had been happy enough models for him—but he simply couldn't see any reason *for* it, either, not just yet. Eventually, when the time was right to sire an heir, he'd have to find himself some well-bred young lady to carry the family name, but not in the immediate future.

"All I wish for now is a replacement for Jenny," he declared, "a sweet-tempered little hussy with a strong enough stomach for the sea, one who will take orders like a soldier and be willing to risk her pretty neck for the sake of her king and country. I'll know the woman when I find her, Ned. Perhaps she'll even find me first."

Edward groaned, reaching for his hat from the seat behind him. "Oh, aye, most likely she will. They always do with you, don't they? But at least she'll have two months or so to chase you down."

"Two months?" repeated William with surprise. "I thought I'd head out again Monday, to finish—"

"Two months," said Edward firmly. "Maybe longer. After this last adventure, I think it best to let the

French forget about you for a bit. Ah, here we are, home at last."

Harborough House had been built by Edward's grandfather, in a time when all the grandest houses were made to rival, and sometimes outdo, the royal palaces themselves. Outwardly it was also one of the most grim, built of grey stone made gloomier still by the city's constant rain of soot.

But while the exterior of the house remained stark and severe, the inside had blossomed under the fresh touch of Edward's wife, a lady famous for her great artistic gifts. Francesca had transformed the house into a place that fashionable London loved to visit, and William was no exception. The hall was cool and inviting after the noisy, dusty streets, and while Edward quickly sifted through the small pile of letters and cards presented by a footman, William's gaze rose to the painting hung in a place of honor and attention between the twin staircases.

It was, of course, painted by the duchess herself, for she always placed her newest work there for her guests' amusement, admiration, and criticism. The paintings changed often, for Her Grace was prolific as well as talented, but in all his visits to Harborough House, William had never been struck so instantly, or so intensely, by a picture as he was by this one.

The subject was simple enough, a beautiful young woman painted as a pagan goddess Venus, seated on a bench with her hands resting loosely in her lap. Her round cheeks were deliciously rosy, almost flushed, and wisps of her auburn hair had escaped from the ribbon around her head to curl around her face and neck. Her gaze wasn't directed at the viewer, but at something beyond, the unguarded expression in her wide, gray-blue eyes so rapt and joyful that William nearly turned to look behind him.

"So you like my new picture, Bonnington?" asked the duchess, suddenly there at his side. "It pleases you?"

If Edward was an unusual duke, then his wife was a thoroughly unusual duchess, not the least because she'd hurried to greet her husband here in the hall instead of waiting to receive him in her own rooms. She'd obviously come directly from her painting studio, for she wore a paint-stained striped half-gown over a full-sleeved chemise, her dark hair tied back and gold hoops swinging from her ears, more like a gypsy than a peeress.

"This new picture does please me, Francesca," said William, his gaze already wandering back to the painting, "so much so that I'm neglecting you entirely."

"William is feeling churlish, my dear," said Edward, looping his arm fondly around his wife's waist as he bent to kiss her. "He even admits it. He is tired, and ill-tempered, and thirsty, and therefore cannot be responsible for his behavior."

But William was too engrossed in the picture to rise to Edward's challenge, too lost in the image of the rosy-cheeked young woman.

"She's the one, Edward," he said softly. "Mind how I told you before I'd know the next girl when I saw her. This is the one, in this painting. This is the girl."

"What girl?" asked Francesca, her dark eyes lighting with curiosity. "Whatever are you saying? Ah, my dear friend! You sound at last like a gentleman ready to fall in love and marry!"

"Perhaps I am, if I could only find this fair goddess of yours," said William, trying to make a jest from his inadvertent confession. The duke and duchess were closer than most married couples, but there was still a good deal about his activities in the Admiralty that Edward would rather his wife didn't know, and William's trips across the Channel were among them.

"A perfect English Venus like this one—how could I not fall in love outright?"

"Fah, what do you know of beauty?" Francesca wrinkled her nose with contempt. "When you look at this picture, you're seeing the girl as I painted her, not as you'd see her for yourself."

"You're saying I'm no judge of a pretty face?" asked William, bemused. Certainly all his worldly experience among the fair sex should account for something. "That I've no eye for telling a sow's ear from a silk purse?"

But the duchess was serious. "No, Bonnington, listen to me. Real beauty is more than a pretty face, and deeper, too. Women see more in our sisters than men ever will, and discover the beauty that comes from grace, or intelligence, or cleverness, beauty that you men so willfully overlook. You could come within three paces of this girl as she really is, and not recognize her."

"I would know this lady anywhere," said William confidently. She was so fresh and different from any other woman of his acquaintance that perhaps she truly *was* the girl—no, the goddess—he was meant to marry, and for perhaps an entire two seconds, he amused himself with the notion. "How could I miss such elegance, such breeding?"

"And how perfectly you prove my point, Bonnington!" said Francesca with a merry laugh. "Granting her all blessings, simply because I dressed her as a goddess!"

"You can't claim all the credit, Francesca," insisted William. "Not for that face. To have her gaze at me like that, all sweet devotion—what man could want for more?"

" 'Devotion,' hah," said Francesa, raising her gaze toward the ceiling with dismay. "When I drew this girl, Bonnington, she wasn't gazing at you. She was watching the antics of the ducks on the pond in St. James's

Park. She didn't even realize I was sketching her. I never spoke to her, nor will I likely ever see her again. A great pity, that, for I'd love to draw her again."

"But surely the lady's sweetness, her gentility—"

"She was *not* a lady, Bonnington," said Francesca, the hoops in her ears swinging emphatically against her cheeks, "at least not how you mean it. She was an orange-seller in the park with her empty basket on the bench beside her, and her look of happiness likely came from having sold all her wares so early in the afternoon. *That* was what made her as beautiful as any goddess to me, and that was what I wished to capture: her satisfaction and joy in the afternoon."

An orange-seller. William smiled wryly as his sentimental ideal disintegrated. The girl would never be his countess, then, nor anyone else's. All the beauty in the world wouldn't compensate for her parading through the park selling fruit and likely herself as well. A pity, a royal pity, and William sighed with genuine regret as he looked at the painting again.

Not that he was ready to forget her completely. She still might do as his companion on board the *Fancy.* An orange-seller wouldn't be shy, but she'd know her place, and wouldn't cause mischief by putting on airs above her station the way Jenny had. No one of any consequence would miss her if things went wrong and she disappeared, either, for London swallowed up common girls like this each day. She'd be malleable, agreeable, and obedient, and she'd still be beautiful, no matter how Francesca had tried to deny it. The girl would do, then; she'd do.

And once he found her, perhaps he could steal a bit of that glowing, enchanting joy of hers for himself.

"Thank'ee, lad, thank'ee," said Harriet Treene, smiling as she handed the little boy his orange. He took the fruit solemnly, staring at it in his hand like a golden prize as he trotted back with it to his hovering nurse-maid. The poor overbred little gentleman was so trussed up in white linen and leather slippers, his blond hair long and curled like a girl's, that it was a wonder to Harriet how the sorry mite could manage to move. If he were *her* son, he'd be running barefoot and free like a regular boy, getting into dirt and mischief. But then if he were hers, he'd be selling oranges, too, instead of buying them from her, and with a wry shake of her head, she shifted the remaining fruit to the front of her basket, and smoothed the checkered cloth around them.

"Sweet Indian oranges, oh, so sweet!" she called, her voice lilting up and down. Every girl had her own cry, as distinct as a bird's call, and in the four years since Harriet had begun she'd never stopped perfecting hers. It had to be loud enough to be heard over a summer crowd, yet clear and never shrill, as sweet upon a buyer's ears as the orange would be upon his tongue, and as easy to call with a tired voice at sunset as it was early on a fresh new morning.

But Harriet's workdays rarely lasted so long. To her considerable pride, she nearly always sold every last one of her share of the oranges from Shelby's wagon before the Westminster bells chimed three. Not only would her penny-laden pocket swing against her leg with a comforting heft, but she'd earn a precious hour for herself in the park.

She'd only eight more oranges left for today. On an afternoon this fair, she could sell them all to a single buyer, if luck were with her. Resolutely she lifted her head and smiled sweetly, eagerly, as if her shoulders didn't ache from her basket's straps and the sweat wasn't prickling her forehead beneath her wide straw hat or trickling down her back. No, instead she must look as if selling these eight oranges were her greatest single pleasure in the world, and sound as if she meant it.

"Sweet Indian oranges, oh, so sweet! Buy me sweet Indian oranges, oh, *so* sweet!"

"Here, darling, here," called a man's voice behind her. "I'll try your sweet oranges."

"Ah, good day, sir, good day!" Harriet turned gracefully with the basket before her, on her toes the way she'd seen the fine ladies do so their skirts would twirl around their ankles. Gentlemen liked such niceties; she'd learned that here in the park, too. "Fine Indian oranges, sir, direct from the ship what brought them! How many shall you try, sir? How many shall you take?"

The gentleman was astride his horse, a tall bay with black-stockinged legs that seemed to echo the man's own dark polished boots and buff-colored pantaloons. With her view shaded by the broad straw brim of her hat, those well-muscled legs were all Harriet could see of the man, but they were enough to judge that he rode often and in more challenging places than this park.

He was wealthy, too. Only rich men could afford to wear breeches that were so perfectly tailored and so flawlessly spotless. Faith, even the *soles* of his boots were blacked and polished! A fine gentleman like this could afford the rest of her basket without thinking twice, and before Harriet lifted her gaze she lightly bit her lower lip to make it redder, then smiled.

And gasped.

He was, quite simply, the most beautiful gentleman she'd ever seen. She couldn't describe him any better than that. He had black hair cropped fashionably short, a straight nose and a firm jaw and chin with a disarming cleft, and beneath the black slash of his brows his blue eyes seemed to glint and dance with some wicked secret, just between the two of them. He was tall and lean, with broad shoulders, his clothes tailored to display his natural elegance without being foppish or overdone.

And when he returned her smile, she felt herself turn soft and melt inside like butter left in the sun.

"Here you are at last," he said, easily swinging himself down from the horse to stand before her. "I knew I'd find you, sweetheart, though it's taken me nigh on a week of searching through this infernal park."

Instantly Harriet's smile took on a wary edge. Was she such an addlepated ninny as that, to forget everything she'd learned here on these paths? She was eighteen, no green lass; she knew something of the world. She'd seen what became of girls who disappeared into the bushes with gentlemen, eager to lift their petticoats for an extra shilling or two. Men were men, no matter how fine they dressed or how blue their eyes. "Searching for her," hah: Did he truly judge her simple enough to believe such trumpery as that?

She plucked one of her oranges from the basket, not only holding it out for him to admire, but also to remind him exactly what was for sale, and what wasn't.

"Mine be the sweetest oranges in the park, sir," she said, tossing the orange lightly in her palm. "You'll find none better, sir, not for all the silver and gold in a great Pharisee's purse."

"Pharisees? Here?" he asked, bemused, as he gently stroked his horse's nose. "In St. James's Park?"

"Aye, sir," she answered promptly, though no one else had ever questioned her about Pharisees and their habits before. "And I ask you, sir, where else would a Pharisee o' fashion go a-walking in London, eh?"

"You amaze me, lass," he said, leaning forward and lowering his voice as if to share a fresh confidence with her. "Here I'd thought they'd be carried about in a sedan-chair like any other gray-bearded worthy!"

"Oh, no, sir, they be walking for their constitutions, and in this very park." She grinned; she couldn't help it. Who'd have guessed such a handsome gentleman could banter like this? "Where else would you have them Pharisees go, sir? Tripping through Covent Garden to pick through yesterday's turnips?"

"To the Tower?" he asked, sweeping his arm through the air with a dramatic flourish. "To London Bridge? To White's to parse the rules of the faro table?"

She laughed, delighted both by the foolishness of the images and with the playful wittiness of his words. "Nay, sir, they must stay here in the park, to buy me sweet oranges!"

He chuckled in return, a warm, rich, conspiratorial sound. "Then I must be sure to look for these worthies, to pay my respects. Considering this park is home to a true goddess like you, why not Pharisees, and pharaohs, and even a sibyl or two?"

"No goddess, sir," said Harriet. "Only an honest lass what wishes to make an honest bit of coin."

"Ah, but you are a goddess, and I've the proof." He reached into the front of his dark blue frock coat, and drew out a sheet of cream-colored paper. Carefully he unfolded it, and held it up for her to see. "There you are, proof enough. Can you deny now that you're Venus herself?"

Once again Harriet gasped, but this time not with admiration. The page was covered with red-chalk drawings of *her,* sitting beside the duck pond. The likenesses were unmistakable, her face and form as expertly captured as the portrait-prints of the queen and king pinned over the bar in every tavern in the country.

But that was exactly what unsettled Harriet, and

angered her, too. Her face was, well, *hers,* one of the few things that truly belonged to her alone, and to see it set down there for every passerby to criticize—the too-round cheeks and the wide-set eyes, even the way her hair was curling into untidy wisps around her forehead—how could she not feel as if something had been stolen from her?

"Here now, sir, how did you come by those?" she demanded, her cheeks flushed. "I never gave no artist leave to do such a thing, and it—it be wrong, it do, like stealing!"

"Hardly," said the gentleman, surpised by her reaction. "Consider it an honor, my dear, and a flattering one at that. What woman wouldn't want her beauty captured so splendidly?"

"*I* wouldn't," declared Harriet, dropping the orange back into the basket and reaching for the sheet of drawings. "Those be mine, sir, mine! That thieving artist robbed me of me face, sir, sure as if he'd clipped me pocket, and I've a mind to call the watchman on him, if you don't give them pictures to me."

But the man held the sheet up in the air, out of her reach. "Ah, ah, sweetheart, pray contain your fervor! These pictures aren't mine to give away, nor would the artist who drew them be pleased to hear you call her thieving and conniving."

Harriet lowered her hand. "A woman drew them pictures?"

"A lady, you ungrateful creature," he said lightly, somehow making that sound like an endearment instead of an insult. "Her Grace the Duchess of Harborough. And despite how you're threatening her, she would gladly draw you again if you'd but present yourself at Harborough House. Likely she'd even pay you for your time, more than you'd make in a week selling oranges."

"She would not!" scoffed Harriet with a disdainful sniff. "A duchess drawing pictures, paying to make pictures of *me*—that's stuff and nonsense, sir, nonsense and stuff!"

"Perhaps it is," he agreed, his smile curving wryly to one side, "and perhaps, sweetheart, it isn't at all. You've spirit and beauty for ten goddesses, but even the most clever deity must learn to discern true opportunity from empty promises."

"But you've made me no offers, nor promises, neither!"

He shrugged with disarming carelessness. "So I haven't, have I? You *are* clever, lass. I'd say I've judged you right."

She sniffed again, keeping her chin high. "Then mayhap *you* be the Pharisee, trying to judge me this way or t'other."

This time he laughed outright, his eyes crinkling with pleasure. Slowly he lowered his arm, refolded the sheet with the drawings, and tucked it into her basket behind the oranges.

"There," he said. "The pictures are yours, to do with what you will, even burn them, if that's what pleases you most."

Swiftly Harriet covered the folded paper with her hand, half-expecting him to change his mind and try to take it back. Surely pictures like these must be worth a pretty sum, even to a rich man like him. But instead of taking the paper, he reached for her hand, bowing forward slightly as he raised her fingers to his lips, his *lips,* oh, dear God in Heaven, and now he was kissing the back of her hand the way she'd seen gentlemen do with fine ladies, his mouth brushing lightly over her skin, grazing it, teasing it, warming it, making her flush and stammer like a worthless, befuddled idiot.

And he felt it, too. She could tell from the way he

looked at her when he freed her hand, the odd half-smile that could—should—have been smug but wasn't. Instead he seemed almost thoughtful, as if considering her in an entirely new way.

"If you ever change your mind, sweetheart," he said softly, "bring that paper to Harborough House, and you'll be welcomed like the goddess you are, with nectar and ambrosia. Now good day to you, my Venus, and sweet dreams for your night."

Still she stood there like a dumbstruck ninny, watching while he lifted his hat to her—to *her!*—before he climbed back upon his horse and gathered its reins to head down the path and forever, forever from her life.

And at once Harriet came back to life.

"Wait, sir, wait!" she called breathlessly, hurrying after him. "Your orange, sir! You forgot your orange!"

He turned in the saddle, and she held the orange up to him.

"Ah, so I did," he said, winking as he leaned down to take the orange from her. "I'd leave behind my head, too, if my hat weren't there to keep it in place upon my neck. I've forgotten my orange, and to pay you as well."

"You *are* a clever gentleman, aren't you?" she said, tipping her head to one side to wink back as she echoed his own words back to him. Oh, what she was doing was a dangerous game, bold as new-polished brass. She'd never behaved so forward with any other man she'd met in the park.

But this gentleman wasn't like any of the others, and he certainly wasn't like any man she'd met among the costard-mongers and butchers who lived in her street. He was young and rich and wickedly handsome, but what made him different was something that hovered in the air between them like a conjurer's trick, something she couldn't find the words to explain. Most likely she would never see him again, for London was a grand, sprawling place, and his station was far, far above hers. But for this moment she could fancy, she could dream. That much in life came for free, even for girls from Threadneedle Court.

"You owe me nothing, sir," she said now, squinting a bit as she looked up at him and the sun behind him. The shadow of his hat's brim shielded his eyes from her, his expression unfathomable, and she gave a nervous little laugh at her own daring. "You gave me the pictures, sir, and now I'm giving you the orange. For remembering me by."

"But I won't forget you, lass," he said, his voice low and so unexpectedly earnest that she almost could believe him. "Indeed, I doubt I ever shall."

"Oh, nay, sir, of course you won't," she said. "Leastwise you won't until after you eat the orange."

Harriet turned away quickly then, so he would not see the regret in her face, and turned back to her life as it was, as it must be, and the ripe, golden fruit in the basket before her.

Sweet, oh, so sweet. . . .

Look for
The Very Comely Countess
by Miranda Jarrett
Coming in November 2001
from Sonnet Books